BLACKBEARD'S JUSTICE
BOOK 3 OF:
THE VOYAGES OF
QUEEN ANNE'S REVENGE

JEREMY MCLEAN

POINTS OF SAIL
PUBLISHING

Points of Sail Publishing
P.O. Box 30083 Prospect Plaza
FREDERICTON, New Brunswick
E3B 0H8, Canada

Edited by Ethan James Clarke
http://silverjay-editing.com/

Cover Design by Kit Foster

This is a work of fiction. Any similarity to persons, living or dead, is purely coincidental... Or is it?

ACKNOWLEDGEMENTS

Thanks to my family and spouse who support me throughout my journey, and who give me feedback and encouragement when I need it most. Thanks to my editor, Ethan James Clarke, who keeps me on my toes and forces me to learn from my mistakes, even when I don't want to.

If you're in need of editing, check out his services at: http://silverjaymedia.com

Ethan also has a novel of his own:
www.amazon.com/dp/B00NP4U6KW
Spoiler: It's amazing.

TABLE OF CONTENTS

1. I'M COMING FOR HIM

William's forehead was slick with sweat. The sun was approaching high noon above the clear skies of Bodden Town, and the heat had been rising steadily all day. It didn't help that he had been digging up dirt all morning.

He held a sharp spade in his hands, his exposed muscles taut from work. He slammed the spade into the ground and ran his fingers through his wet hair away from his eyes. The men he was working with were slowing down, and even he was tiring.

"What say we break for noon, men?" William asked.

The men let out sighs and some even dropped their spades and bodies to the ground, taking great heaves of air to regain their strength. Keeping at William's pace since early morning had taken its toll on them.

William turned to one of the Boddens' attendants. "Fetch us some food and drink, would you?"

The young man nodded and then ran off towards the Boddens' home not far from where they were.

William sat down on a pile of wood which was standing by for use after they'd laid the foundation. His eyes gravitated towards the harbour where ships of all sizes were entering and leaving. He couldn't see the bustle created by the ships, but he could imagine the multitude of characters arriving and leaving as the locals did business with them. He imagined the smell of the glistening fruit, the rich vegetables, and the various cured and cooked meats on display in the market. Though William was not one for fine dining—food was for sustenance, not pleasure—he could not help but enjoy the scents dancing from his nose to his palate, and often enjoyed walking the market for that reason alone.

"When's the captain due to return?" one of the men asked.

William turned his attention back to the men with him. They were breathing heavily and wiping the sweat from their brows as they talked. Some of them looked at William, anticipating his answer.

"Our captain is set to dock in a few days' time, should their prospects hold true," William replied.

"I wonder what the captain'll bring back this time," the same crewman said.

"I pray for some spices. Old Liz from the Boar's Hat says spices have been too expensive for them to buy, and the food's bad enough as it is without something to mask the taste," another of the *Queen Anne's Revenge* men commented.

"It's yer own fault if ye keep eatin' there when ye hate the food."

"Boys, it's simple: he ain't there for the food and drink. He wants to wet his other whistle." A ripple of chuckles went around.

"Hey now, Elizabeth is warming up to me. Only a matter of time a'fore I bed her."

"Not if the owner has anything ta say about it!"

William let the voices of the men fade from his consciousness as he began meditating. He tried to clear his mind, but his thoughts lingered on his captain, Edward Thatch, and his charge, Anne Bonney, whom he'd promised to protect. William had volunteered to stay and help build new houses for Bodden Town while the majority of the crew left to secure a cargo ship, but he couldn't help but think he'd made the wrong decision. As the days turned to weeks of them out to sea, William couldn't shake the feeling of foreboding, as if there was a lasting gooseflesh in his mind.

The captain will protect her. There is nothing to worry about.

The sound of footsteps approaching forced William's eyes open. The Boddens' attendant rounded the bend with a tray of food—light sandwiches, dried meat, and cheese—and a pitcher of water in his hands.

William allowed the other men to dine first, then approached the young man and took the tray and pitcher from him. "Thank you. That will be all for now, so you may rest." The young man thanked William, then ran off back to the Boddens'.

William set the tray down on some timber nearby, and, despite their protests, proceeded to fill everyone's cups. With the other men looked after, William took some of the food for himself and sat back down to eat.

The men continued to talk about various affairs: when they would sail again, how long they would be working for, what tavern they would attend in the eve, and which women they would court from the local brothel and elsewhere. The steadfast William was not the type to engage in such talk, so he stayed to the side as he ate, not paying them any heed until one topic caught his attention.

"What do you think that ship is doin' out there?" one of the men commented.

William peered to the harbour as he chewed on a tough piece of spiced meat and soft cheese. He spotted the ship the other crewman was talking about. The vessel seemed to be circling the edge of the harbour, and, if William's memory served, he recalled seeing it earlier.

The ship piqued William's curiosity. "Perchance is anyone carrying a spyglass?" he asked.

"Here you are, William," one man said, removing the tool from his belt and handing it to his mate.

William took the instrument and studied the harbour through magnified gaze. He could see the ship was a lighter class with no gun deck, but a complement of thirteen cannons on its main deck. Perhaps it was the foreboding feeling William had been having, or boredom, but he could not take his eyes off the ship despite seeing nothing out of the ordinary. He continued to watch the ship and the men manning it as he chewed his leathery meat, until his men were ready to return to work.

William tore the spyglass away from his eye and rose to his feet. As he turned to present the glass back to its owner, he had to do a double take.

He'd noticed two other ships join with the first out of the corner of his eye. William turned back around to review the harbour again, and it was unmistakable that the three ships were approaching Bodden Town.

He put the spyglass up to his eye once more, and he could see the crews of each of the ships hailing the other as they prepared their cannons. At the same time, each ship raised another sail—or rather, a flag: black with a red trim, and in the middle there was a large skull with crossed cutlasses beneath it.

"Warn the citizens. Prepare for battle!" William shouted over his shoulder.

The men's jaws dropped and some snorted a nervous laugh before questioning William's statement.

"Pirates are attacking. We must evacuate everyone we can and prepare for a counterattack."

William's words stunned them still, but when their eyes took in the harbour and the ships approaching, they were swift to move.

William began running towards the Boddens' to warn them and rally the militia, but the roar of cannon fire hit his ears. There was just enough time for him to glance down the hill and see the wave of destruction sweeping towards them.

The walls of the houses near him exploded as cannonballs tore through the wood and stone. William jumped and landed on his stomach in a nearby alley with his hands covering the back of his head, as wood and stone rained on him from above. Chunks of cobbled stone hit his arms and legs, and jagged pieces of wood struck his back.

When the hail of wood and stone subsided, William uncurled his body and rose to his feet. He surveyed the area to see his crewmates in varied states of turmoil amidst the wreckage of recently built homes, upturned earth, and billowing dirt.

The Voyages of Queen Anne's Revenge

William closed his eyes and took a breath. "Move, men!" he shouted. "Someone get to the Boddens' and ensure their safety. The rest of you, gather weapons. We won't take this assault lying down."

One of the men headed up towards the Boddens', and some moved in the other direction to the militia's barracks, while a few stayed behind for a brief moment.

"Where are you heading, William?" one of the men asked.

"I'm taking the fight to them," he replied.

William exited the alley and rushed down the dirt street. All around him, the houses had been blown open from the cannon fire, and men and women of all ages were running in the opposite direction. He had to push past them and weave his way through the crowd trying to escape the mayhem.

Wide-eyed and frightened parents carried screaming and crying children, and the elderly tried to keep pace with the young. Some had minor injuries like cuts and scrapes, and many were covered in dirt and debris from the cannonballs' upheaval.

William could hear the faint sound of battle above the din of screams and frightened shouting around him. The smell of gunpowder hit his nose and reminded him of bitter, cruel days of fighting aboard the *Queen Anne's Revenge*. Despite his loathing for bloodshed, his body knew the sensation and reacted by invigorating him, readying him for what was to come.

Another wave of cannon fire swept over the town as the sound of the cannons met William's ears mere seconds before the carnage began. The crowd around him ducked in response to the sound, an automatic response that only the battle-hardened could prevent. William had the sense to stand his ground this time, and he watched as the cannonballs ripped the feeble houses to shreds. Pieces of the former shelters were flung at those it had previously protected.

Dust and dirt and debris forced William to cover his face with his arm as he pushed through the cowering crowds. After passing through the dense throng he could run more freely.

As William ran he could see some stragglers in a slow advance up the town's street. The closer he got to the harbour the more injured the people. He couldn't stop to help them; he would be more use at the coast.

"Help! Help please!" a voice in a nearby home cried.

William's paced slowed, but he didn't stop.

"Please, someone help my baby!" the voice called to any brave soul that would listen.

He glanced in the direction of the voice, then to the harbour where he could see rising smoke and hear the clang of metal clashing. He gritted his teeth in frustration, but headed to the poor woman begging for help.

William followed the screams to a half-demolished home. The building was falling apart before his eyes, as cannonballs had sheared off some of the support beams. Another blast and the whole house could come toppling down.

He entered the house and made haste to the back where a woman was trying to lift pieces of wood from a fallen corner. When she noticed William out of the corner of her eye, she flew to him as though he were a lifeline during a storm. She was on the verge of tears and her eyes filled to the brim with fright. Her hands gripped his arms in a desperate vice, as if she felt he would leave and she had to keep him there.

"Please, please, my son, my boy, he's trapped beneath the rubble. You must save him, sir, I beg of you."

William nodded before moving closer to the collapsed area of the home. He could see the young child, possibly no more than two years of age, crying in the middle of pieces of timber and stone with a few gashes on his forehead and arms. One of the support beams for the side of the house was leaning almost on top of him, holding up parts of the roof just over the boy's head. There was no way to grab the boy from where he was.

"I'll lift the beam, and you must grab your son. You must move quickly, I don't know how long I can hold it."

The woman nodded and thanked William profusely while holding back tears.

William stepped over jagged pieces of wood and rough stones, cautious as he made his way to where he could lift the beam. He positioned his legs as best he could to give himself the support he needed when lifting, then wrapped his arms around the fractured beam. He looked over to the mother, and she nodded to him with a determined yet still anxious look in her eyes.

William lifted up with his legs, and forced his already strained muscles to work. The beam and bits of roof were heavier than he'd expected. He grunted as he pushed with his legs and pulled with his arms. His muscles bulged with the effort. He panted in short breaths as sweat beaded down his face, cheek, and chin. With each breath, the beam inched upwards, and it became both easier and harder to continue lifting—easier because momentum was helping him, harder because the grip he had on the beam became awkward.

William fixed his eyes on the child, and his only thought was on saving the life of the innocent in front of him. The thought gave him strength, and helped him maintain his shaky grip on the beam.

When the beam and bits of roof were high enough off the remaining rubble, the mother crawled her way over to her child and grabbed him in her arms. The sobbing boy wrapped his tiny arms tight around his mother's neck. She crawled back out and back to safety, allowing William to gradually let the beam down.

"Thank you, thank you so much, sir." The woman repeated her thanks over and over, the tears she'd been holding back now streaming down her powdered cheeks.

"We must take our leave of this place before it comes down upon us," William warned. "Once free, run inland and do not look back until you can no longer hear the sound of the cannons."

The woman nodded with a renewed look of urgency on her face, and the two headed outside.

The sounds of battle rang on all sides, closer inland than it had been before. William glanced down both ends of the side street, and could see more people running from the harbour, but this time there were people with weapons chasing after them.

"You must move, quickly," William urged. He guided her away from the centre of town.

Before they could make it to another street leading inland, one of the pirates attacking the city turned around one of the bends. The man stopped on his heels when he noticed William and the woman and her child.

"Well, whut do we have 'ere? A precious family too slow on their feet, eh?" the pirate mocked.

"Get behind me," William commanded.

The woman shielded her son as she cowered behind William's back.

"Aww, ain't that sweet. Too bad it'll do ye no good, missa. First, I'll have my way with ye, then I'll have my way with yer missus." The pirate brandished his cutlass and licked his foul lips in sick anticipation.

William, though he held no weapon, raised his fists and steeled himself for the fight.

The pirate howled a ghoulish laugh as he rushed towards William. He slashed with his cutlass, aiming for William's shoulder. William punched the pirate's wrist, and the cutlass fell to the stone street with a clang that echoed around them. William punched at the rogue's throat, but he deftly dodged and darted out of the way before jumping back.

"Hoo, yer better than I thought," the pirate said with a toothy smirk.

William's thoughts echoed the pirate. He tensed as he got a glimpse of the man's skill. He was no normal pirate.

"All right, les' have a friendly fist fight then." The pirate raised his hands in the air and balled them into fists.

William hunched down and readied himself for the next assault. Just as he was about to go on the offensive, he felt something hard touch his hip. He instinctively glanced down, leaving himself open.

The pirate didn't miss his opportunity and barreled towards William, throwing a punch his way. Before the fist made contact, the pirate stopped in his tracks. The meaty thunk of a cutlass hitting flesh sounded in William's ears.

"Sorry, I've no time for a fist fight," William said.

The pirate looked down to see his own cutlass embedded in his stomach. He lurched back a few steps with his hands on the blade, looked at William and chuckled as blood gushed out of his mouth, then fell to the ground with a thud.

William turned around to ensure the woman was well. "Thank you for passing me that sword. It made that fight easier."

"I should be thanking you, you save us once again."

"It's not over yet. You must get to safety. Will you be able to make it on your own now?"

"I hope so, sir," The woman said as she tip-toed her way past the dead pirate. "Thank you again, sir." She took a brief moment to wave back to William with a smile.

For the third time, the sound of cannons firing washed over the island. The sound was quicker than the doom it ushered, but not by much.

William's eyes went wide. He shouted "Run!" just as another wave of cannonballs peppered the houses.

The woman didn't have William's reflexes, and she could only pull her son in tighter and squeeze her eyes closed as the speeding iron cracked the corner beam of a house at the foundation. The house gave way, and the roof fell to the side towards the woman and her child. She opened her eyes just as the roof collapsed on top of her.

"No!" William screamed.

He ran over to the wreckage, but it was no use. There was no doubt that the woman and child were dead. Blood pooled around her rubble-covered body, trickling towards the harbour like dark red treacle.

William's hot, heavy breaths made his cheeks flush as he

watched the pool make its way through the cracks of the stone. His fist tightened and his shaking fingers dug into his palm near to the point of drawing blood. He pulled the cutlass from the pirate's dead body and turned around in one swift motion. He stalked towards the main street where most of the pirates were invading.

On the main street, William could see men and women still running from the continued onslaught, and no organized militia as there should have been to drive the devils out. Farther down the street he thought he could see pirates carrying women slung over their shoulders to shore, or attacking those not quick enough to run.

The town was in shambles. The new town square was torn to bits, the fresh cobblestone ripped apart by the rolling cannonballs, and the square's shops and architecture destroyed. Homes and businesses along the main street were halfway demolished, and throughout the town smoke and dirt wafted and swirled in the wake of the pirates' attacks.

William was able to see one man fighting against the horde, and he rushed to join his comrade-in-arms. He ran over to a group of pirates set upon his friend, slicing one in the back, and another in the gut. After another second, his mate dispatched the others with two mighty thrusts of his spear.

Pukuh, the Mayan warrior, turned around to face William, ready to strike, but when he saw the face of his friend and crewmate he smiled. "You join the hunt, brother?"

"Yes, and by the looks of it we're on our own for now," William said, glancing down the main street with pirates running towards them.

Pukuh grinned. "Too bad for them," he said as he spun his spear between his fingers.

William couldn't help but smirk before he readied himself for the next wave of enemies.

Five pirates stormed at them with various sharp blades in hand, their one-time-use gunpowder weapons evidently spent closer to the harbour. Three charged the one-armed Mayan, while the remaining two went after William.

The two after William attacked at the same time in coordinated strikes. One man swung his blade horizontally, while the other thrust forward in case William decided to jump backwards. William kicked the second man's hand, knocking his blade away and at the first man mid-swing. The blade spun and nicked the first man in the leg, forcing him to stop and take a step back. William stabbed the pirate with no weapon in the chest as the other swung at him again. He clashed blades before grabbing the pirate's arm and pulling him forward to slice his neck open. The pirates were no amateurs, but William was the superior fighter.

Just as William was about to head to help Pukuh finish off his remaining two enemies, the glint of another sword caught his eye. He pulled his head back just in time to see the blade flash in front of his face. He jumped away and slapped the blade with his own before he took sight of his opponent.

The man in front of him had two inches on his five foot eleven, and easily twice William's bulk. He wore cotton-print clothing, and his face was clean-shaven. There was a scar that went from his right eye down to his mouth.

Calico Jack! William thought as he took in the giant before him.

"Where is Blackbeard?" the pirate asked in a calm yet forceful voice.

William's answer was to slash at the pirate captain in front of him. Jack Rackham, better known as Calico Jack, swung his blade to counter William's. There was a brief clash where the sound of metal ringing echoed off the buildings before William felt no resistance on his end.

William looked down to see his cheap blade split in two. It was then that he noticed Rackham had a blade made of a golden metal. It reminded him of Edward, his captain, and the golden cutlass he owned, which was made of a mysterious and unbelievably sharp alloy.

Before William could recover from his shock, a large hand

gripped his throat. Rackham picked William up off the ground, and slammed him onto the cobblestone on his back. There was a loud snap as several of his ribs broke, and the blow knocked the wind out of his lungs. It felt like a hand was gripping him on the inside, not allowing him to breathe. As he struggled on the ground, Rackham rose up to his full height.

William could hear Pukuh running towards them, but he stopped short. William looked over, and Pukuh's eyes were wide with what he thought was fear. It looked like Pukuh had seen a ghost.

Calico Jack scowled, looking down on the two in front of him with unmatched contempt. "Tell Blackbeard I'm coming for him."

2. (IN)JUSTICE

Edward waited on the quarterdeck with Herbert, the quarter-master, as the crew of the *Queen Anne's Revenge* secured their vessel to a merchant ship. He stroked his long beard as he watched the crew of the *Fortune* do the same on the other side of the merchant ship.

After a month of travel, bribes, and biding their time, the dual pirate crews had found the ship they had been searching for.

Armed to the teeth, the two ships were ready to take on the merchantman and secure its cargo by force, but it was unnec-essary. There was no great battle, no bravado, no clash of swords with a mast at one's back as the wind whipped the sails. No, mere moments after dropping the black, their mark had raised the white and furled their sails.

Now, after half an hour of suspense as the ships slowed to match speed with each other, the cowards were aboard the main deck. The men threw the pirates curious and fearful glances as they assisted their transgressors in their task.

The noonday sun shining above them was blistering. Invis-ible steam rose up from the sea water sprayed on deck during sailing, and it created small mirages when looked at from cer-tain angles. The smell of brine and seaweed and fish was strong in the air due in no small part to the steam. Edward didn't mind the heat, nor the smell. He was used to all the features and forms of the sea from years of experience working on a ship. He might even go as far as to say that he loved the smell if only his companions would not use it as ammunition for some form of jesting. Although, anything served that purpose for Bartholomew Roberts, the captain of the *Fortune*.

After the crew secured the ships, one of the mates approached and informed Edward. "Ensure the crew holds no weapons, and keep them in line. Move the captain to the stern. I will be over presently." The crewmate nodded and issued orders to other men aboard the *Revenge*.

"How's the weather looking, Quartermaster?" Edward asked, looking at Herbert. "Are the waves going to give us any trouble?"

Herbert leaned over in his wheelchair to look off the bow at the sky. "Should be clear, Captain."

"How are you adjusting to your new position?"

Herbert smirked. "Well, I was already working the helm, so now it's essentially just more responsibility on my hands."

Edward patted Herbert on the back. "I'm sure John would be proud of you. You've been doing a fine job."

"God rest his soul," Herbert said, and Edward copied the chant.

Anne Thatch, a fiery redhead and Edward's wife, approached him on the quarterdeck. She held one hand firm on the hilt of a cutlass, ready for anything. "They're acting rather cooperative, wouldn't you say?" she said with a smirk.

"Aye, I would say. Very cooperative," Edward replied. "Do you believe it to be a ruse?" he said with a sarcastic tone.

Anne frowned in thought, then looked over her shoulder at the merchant ship. The crew was searching the men's belongings and rounding them up, being more than a touch rough with them as they did so.

"Hard to say, truly. They did fly the white rather quickly."

Edward eyed the ship and the two pirate crews as he leaned on the quarterdeck's railing. He fiddled with the gold ring on his finger for a moment before he rose. He sauntered down the quarterdeck ladder and over to a gangplank connecting the ships, with Anne following behind him. He crossed to the merchant ship and Bartholomew Roberts approached him.

"You'll handle the search below?" Edward asked.

"Aye, and, God willing, I and my men will find what we've

been looking for," Roberts replied.

"You sound confident."

"So far, your first mate hasn't steered us wrong," Roberts said, patting Anne on the side of her arm with a grin.

Anne smiled and bowed her head to the Pirate Priest. Roberts returned to the bow, and then he and a few of his mates descended into the belly of the merchant ship to search for their treasure.

Edward and Anne walked to the stern of the ship to where the merchant's captain was. "He's right, you know. You're the best person for the job, and you can't keep ignoring the crew's vote like you have been."

Anne's mouth became a line. "I know, it's just..." She trailed off with a pensive look on her face.

Edward stopped walking. "What is it? If you have some misgivings, I'd like to know. I am your partner in more ways than one," he coaxed.

Anne nodded. "It's big shoes to fill. Henry was an age-old friend and confidant long before I came into your life."

Edward nodded, thinking back on his friend and the terrible night when he'd left. Henry couldn't handle life as a pirate, and had decided to leave the crew. Edward had run after him alone, and pointed a gun at him in desperation, trying to convince him to return. He hadn't meant to hurt Henry—would *never* have harmed a hair on his head!—but when the local authorities had intervened, things had gotten out of hand quickly, and Edward had shot his friend in the back, killing him. He still hadn't told anyone of the incident.

Edward shook his head to shake off the memory of that night, and didn't touch on what Anne had said. "The crew trusts you with their welfare, and I know they would have no one else in charge of their battle training. You've proven yourself time and time again."

Anne smiled. "I suppose that's true. I've already been training many of them since day one. Especially you, husband."

"Yes, and I recall that you led them into battle against three enemy ships that time I was kidnapped."

Anne frowned. "Well, the actual number was two. Roberts and his crew took care of the third."

"Still, that's not something I could have done, nor many others aboard this ship."

Anne smiled again, but changed the subject. "Come, we've work to do."

"Right," Edward replied.

Edward walked over to where the captain of the merchant ship waited. One of Roberts' men had a pistol trained on the captain, and another was lazily holding a cutlass in his hand, pointed in the merchant's general direction.

"How do you do, Captain? What may I call you by?"

The older gentleman scoffed. "What does it matter? Just take what ye came for and be gone. I do not wish to prolong this injustice."

Edward chuckled. "Injustice?"

"You believe what you are doing is just? I never knew pirates to think so highly of their own integrity."

Edward rubbed his chin as he glanced at the ship's deck, and then he moved to the merchant ship's stern railing. He leaned his back against the railing and folded his arms.

"You know, my father used to tell me these stories of a man named Robin Hood. I don't remember all the details, as I'm sure any can say of stories from childhood, but his actions always stuck with me," Edward said while gesturing with his finger. "Robin Hood stole from the corrupt rich to give to the poor, and he was the hero."

The merchant settled his thumbs between his belt, and looked annoyed. "What does this have to do with anything?" he spat.

"You are rich, we are poor."

The merchant gritted his teeth. "You believe yourself to be the hero, boy? I may be the owner of this ship, but these men are the ones who will pay for your theft," he said, pointing to his crew. "Though your attack stings, I have savings. Most of the men here are not so lucky. In a month's time they'll have to return to their wives and tell them how a *hero* stole their cargo, so I couldn't pay them. Then, their children who are sick with fever will die because they couldn't afford the medicine, or they'll starve because food is too expensive." The merchant's voice grew louder and louder as he spoke until his entire crew could hear him. "Why do you think I flew the white so fast? Did you think me a coward? I did it because men like you would kill men like us. At least this way these men keep their lives and have another chance to right your wrong. Steal what you want, take it all, but don't you dare hide behind some twisted morality that affords you sleep at night."

Edward was quiet during the captain's speech, but within a moment of it ending, he burst out laughing. His unrestrained and lengthy howl was boisterous to the point that many in the merchant crew thought him mad by the time he ceased.

"You're good. I'll give you that." Edward got to his feet and raised his voice to ensure the whole crew could hear him. "There's just one thing though: Who said that we're here to steal your cargo?"

The captain eyed Edward suspiciously, but before he could question him Roberts returned from below deck with a notebook in his hands. Edward walked over to Roberts.

"Does it have what we were looking for?"

Roberts nodded. "Just as expected."

Edward smiled. "Good." He took the notebook in hand.

"Who are you?" The captain had a confused look on his face as he eyed Edward up and down.

Edward grinned. "I'm Blackbeard." He began thumbing through the notebook.

"Stop! Stop, I say," the merchant commanded, reaching for Edward.

Roberts' crew stepped forward, but it was Edward's massive hand on the merchant captain's throat that stopped him. "No," he stated simply.

Edward, at his height of six feet four inches, lifted the merchant captain up in the air by the throat with ease. He walked over to the crew amidships and tossed the captain unceremoniously to the deck.

"Crew of the *Tabernacle*, you may see me as nothing more than a common rogue, but I am here to right a wrong that was going to be committed on you. I am here to avenge those that had this wrong committed on them in the past."

"Don't listen to him, men! He's nothing but a liar and a thief," the captain shouted.

Edward called to some of his men to bind the captain and gag him, which they carried out with no amount of gentleness. Once complete, and sure that the captain could no longer interrupt, Edward continued.

"Your captain was so fervent to denounce us as thieves, as you no doubt overheard earlier, and while that may be true we are not the only ones. As is often true, the most vocal detractors of a sin are those most guilty of it." Edward pulled up the notebook and showed the pages to the crew. "Your captain recently purchased rather large insurance precisely two weeks before your journey. Should pirates attack this ship and steal the cargo, he would stand to make a small fortune. But you wouldn't know anything about that, would you, Captain?"

The merchant captain tried to yell through the gag in his mouth, but only muffled expletives filtered through.

The crew, understandably confused, called Edward a liar at best and variations of what the captain was saying at worst. One thing stood out from the rest: apathy. An insurance policy wasn't proof of guilt.

"I hear what you are saying, but I can assure you that your captain was going to let this happen. In fact, he hired another pirate crew to attack the vessel and steal the cargo. We intercepted them on our way here to stop them."

The merchant crew were less enthusiastic with their objections, but still not entirely convinced from what he could tell.

Edward shook his head. "Of course, you don't have to trust in my word. After all, I am a dirty pirate," he said while shrugging his shoulders. "James!"

A man, not of Edward's crew, came from the *Queen Anne's Revenge* over to the *Tabernacle*. He was plain, and every bit the normal-looking sailor. As he came into view, the captain's eyes widened further, and his muffled screams ceased, to the notice of the other crewmates.

Edward backed up a few paces to allow James some room, and he sat down on top of a barrel near the mast.

James pointed to the merchant captain. "This man was once my captain."

At the declaration, the current crew of the *Tabernacle* glanced from James to their captain and back.

"I was hired as a gunner a month before departure on a shipping contract going from Jamaica up north. One thing the captain told me was odd, but it wasn't what he said, it was the way he said it. He told me that if everything went according to plan then there shouldn't be any need to use the cannons, but he was smiling like a man ready for a payday."

James looked at the captain with contempt as the other crewmates continued glancing at the two as he told his story.

"After we departed, it wasn't long until we were beset by pirates. It was a small sloop with fewer guns than we had, so I thought it was a given that we would attack and I readied the cannon I was in charge of, but we were told to surrender. Our entire cargo shipment was stolen, and we were never paid because the captain said he couldn't afford it. We went back to Jamaica, but he didn't hire us again. I later found that the captain had purchased a new, larger ship. It never sat well with me what happened, and so I followed the captain around to find him hiring the pirate crew to attack his new ship. Unfortunately, or fortunately, the pirates found me out and attacked me, but Edward Thatch saved my life," James said, pointing at Edward. "I told him my story, and he promised me and my former crew revenge."

Edward stood up from the barrel and went over to stand next to James. "If you won't believe my word, then believe this man's." Edward pulled out a pistol from his belt, and pointed it at the merchant captain. Despite all the evidence presented, and the testimony from a former crewmate, the crew still protested to the violence. He ignored them, and a few nudges from Roberts' crew silenced them. "I would ask what kind of twisted morality allows you to sleep at night, but what does it matter? I do not wish to prolong this injustice." Edward flashed a devilish grin, cocked the pistol, and fired it at the captain's chest.

The bullet hit the captain in his heart, and he slumped over, hitting the deck with a thump.

Another smell emanated from the pistol and overtook the aroma of the sea. Edward also loved this scent, though for a different reason, and he would never admit it even to himself.

As blood drained from the slumped-over captain, his crew watched on in a mix of horror, indifference, and praise over justice being done. Quite a number were nodding as they looked at the body and whispered various versions of "serves him right."

"Now," Edward said, the pistol in his hand still trailing smoke, "there is the matter of your cargo. Who is first mate aboard this ship?"

After a moment, a man raised his hand and stepped forward to answer Edward's call. "I am, sir. Y-you're not going to kill me, are ye? I tell you true, I had no part in this plot," he said while wringing a cap in his hands.

Edward chuckled. "No, no, the captain was our only target today. What I wish now is to buy your stock, and seeing as the position of captain is left wanting, you will have to fill that role. You have many spices, which will fetch a good price where I hail from. Of course, I will not pay anywhere close to the market price, but if you divide it amongst the crew it will be more than your standard wages. Does this appeal to you?"

The man glanced from Edward to the dead captain, then over his shoulder to all the armed pirates surrounding them. After a moment he nodded, accepting the deal.

The Voyages of Queen Anne's Revenge

Anne came over and pulled the first mate aside. "Let us discuss the particulars in private, Captain," she said sweetly as she took him to the captain's cabin.

"Men, let's get this cargo moved!" Edward commanded.

Over the course of an hour, the crews of the *Queen Anne's Revenge* and *Fortune* moved several tonnes of various spices to their respective holds. The merchant crew stood around, watching the pirates with wary glances. They never seemed comfortable with the idea of pirates taking their precious cargo, even if it was technically paid for.

James, the former sailor on the merchant ship, thanked Edward for his service, and decided to stay with the merchant ship to return to fairer shores, as he was not a Bodden Town native.

After they'd secured the cargo, and Anne had issued payment, Edward met with the new captain for the last time. "Good day to you, Captain," he said, holding out his hand.

The man glanced from Edward's eyes to his hand, and then gave it a shake with an expressionless face. "I hope you do not take offence to my saying this, but I hope we never meet again."

Edward grinned, and without a word he returned to his ship, then addressed his crew. "Let's return home. Our business here is done!"

3. SCARS

Edward watched the horizon as Bodden Town came into view. It would still be some time before they would land, but he could already see the small edge of the Caymans as it grew larger.

The sun was close to setting, but it would still be light out when they arrived. Edward could see the sun, resolute in its arc, off to his left when he stood at the bow. It was bright, but not harsh as it was during the day. Its soft glow shimmered on the water as the sea danced endlessly to the east and west.

The light heat helped the sea's stench subside, taking on an overall pleasant tone, and helped productivity and morale.

The men seemed excited to see their home close, and they worked all the harder to coax more wind into the sails. Sweat glistened off many of their faces as they pulled rigging lines, but they wore small smiles as they did so.

To Edward's right, off the starboard bow, the *Fortune* was well ahead of them. Being the smaller ship, the *Fortune* had the advantage in speed, and Bartholomew Roberts enjoyed rubbing it in whenever he beat Edward to port.

Edward chuckled to himself, remembering the last time Roberts had made a glib comment, and Edward had threatened to sabotage Roberts' sails if he kept it up. The serious look on Roberts' face after Edward's comment still made him laugh.

Tala, a wolf with reddish-grey fur, jumped up beside Edward and placed its front paws on top of the bow railing. The suddenness of Tala's arrival startled him, but he quickly recovered and patted the wolf's back. Tala was panting and glanced from him to the approaching island before barking.

Edward grinned. "That's right, you'll have solid ground under your feet soon enough."

"There you are, Tala! Don't run off like that," Christina, Tala's owner—if a wolf could be said to have an owner—came running up after the animal. "Hello, Captain," she said with a wave.

"Sometimes I wonder just who the real owner is between you two. She has you running around more often than not some days."

Christina grinned as she brushed some of her strawberry-blond hair out of her face. "Some days I'm not so sure myself." Christina patted Tala, and the three watched the island as the ship bobbed up and down on the waves. "She seems to know when we're approaching land."

Edward glanced at the wolf. "Perhaps it can hear when the crow's nest calls down that they see land."

"She."

"Pardon?" Edward questioned with a raised brow.

"Perhaps *she* can hear," Christina corrected.

Edward stroked his beard. "Yes, my apologies. She."

"Perhaps you are right. She is a smart one. Yes you are, aren't you Tala?"

Tala answered with a loud bark, then moved down from the railing and lay down at Christina's feet.

"So, my eyes and ears, how are the crewmen faring?" Edward asked affectionately.

"They're doing well. They groan about the usual matters: taste of the food, seasickness, when they'll next be on land and at the brothel. Morale is high, though. They've been through much on this voyage, and so it will take much more than tedium to break their spirits."

"Good, good." Edward nodded.

"There is one thing, the same thing actually." Christina leaned her side against the railing and folded her arms. "The men are wondering, what with all this revenge business, when we're going to go and rescue Sam and kill Kenneth Locke for what he did."

Edward gripped the railing and cast his eyes to the deep abyss of the sea. "And I suppose you wish to know this as well?"

Christina gave a short, derisive laugh. "Of course I do," she answered in a harsh whisper. "We have had this conversation three times already, and you never give me an answer. I know for a fact I'm not the only one either."

Edward let out a sigh; even now the name Kenneth Locke caused his hands to tremble inexplicably. The only thing he could do to mask the tremors was to grip the ship's railing. He wasn't afraid of Locke, but the thought of him brought back painful memories. Memories of John's death flashed in Edward's head, and after them the remembered wounds of torture ached all over his body.

"We're just concerned, Ed, that's all," Christina said as she touched his arm. "And the sooner we settle things with Locke, the sooner we can move on to Herbert's revenge and mine, like you promised."

Edward peered at Christina suspiciously. "Yours and Herbert's?"

Christina removed her hand. "Yes. I want the same as my brother, and why should I not? Calico Jack deserves to die for crippling him. He deserves much more than that, actually."

"Well, you'll have to have some patience. The Boddens are looking into Locke's whereabouts. Sam will be able to take care of himself until then."

"Yes, but it's been four months. Perhaps the Bodden Brothers aren't qualified to handle the task if they still haven't found anything."

Edward held the railing so tight his knuckles turned white. "Drop it," he said.

Tala opened her eyes and looked up at Edward, no doubt sensing his anger. Christina was taken aback and blurted out, "Excuse me?"

"I said, drop it," Edward seethed.

Christina stood there for another moment, her mouth a

line. "Fine. I guess that's what I get for trying to help. *Venir*, Tala," Christina called, and the two left, one of them in a huff.

Edward closed his eyes and took a few deep breaths. John's dead eyes kept appearing, and the blood pouring from the poor old man's neck felt like it was filling his lungs and choking him. All over his body he could feel sharp pain in specific spots, each one a reminder he would carry for the rest of his life.

He could feel a cold sweat on his forehead despite the cool breeze. He wiped his forehead and took a few more deep breaths as he stared at the ring on his finger. After another moment, his heartbeat slowed, and his chest no longer felt constricted. He could breathe normally again.

When Edward was sure that the feeling had passed, he turned around to leave the bow. He went down to the main deck, where he noticed Jack Christian, the musician, and boatswain in William's absence.

"Jack," he called. Jack walked over to Edward. "I'm retiring to my chambers. Keep the crew busy and send someone to fetch me when we're closer to land."

Jack nodded, a definite note of concern in his eyes, but he didn't address Edward's obvious pallor. "Aye, Captain."

Edward descended to the gun deck and headed to the stern where the captain's cabin was. He noticed Anne talking to the ship's surgeon, Alexandre, but Edward was in no mood to talk so he tried his best to avoid being seen. He entered the captain's cabin and closed the door behind him.

He went to his bed and flopped down in it, clothes and all still on him. He lay there, staring at the wooden boards of the ceiling as he held his head in an attempt to prevent a headache.

What's wrong with me?

Edward awoke with a start as a crewmate jostled his shoulder. He grabbed the man by the scruff of the neck before he recalled where he was. When his senses came to him he let the man go.

"Sorry, you startled me."

The crewmate adjusted his clothes. "My apologies, Captain. I only meant to wake you as we're approaching land. Jack says there's something you need to see."

Edward raised his brow as he stretched his legs and got up from his bed. "What is it?"

The crewmate shrugged his shoulders. "A group'a the men gathered at the bow, but before I knew what the general commotion was about I was sent to fetch ye."

Edward nodded, but he felt it could mean only one thing: Something bad had happened to Bodden Town. He rushed out of his cabin and up to the weather deck.

The sun was a thumb above the edge of the horizon now, giving off a reddish glow to the darkened sky. There were few clouds in the deep blue above them, and in a few hours it would be a dark night.

Edward could see crewmates hanging onto the rigging while standing on the side railings or leaning on the rope ladders as they looked towards Bodden Town. Some peered through spyglasses with their mouths agape, before a neighbour slapped their shoulder to steal the opportunity to look through its magnified scope. There were also many crowding around the bow doing the same. They stood on their toes, leaning to the left and right as they tried to see over their the heads of others.

Edward approached the crowd and began pushing people aside. "Make way for your captain," he instructed.

He weaved his way forward as he stared ahead to the enthralling scene. At first he didn't notice anything off, but as his eyes focussed and he took note of the state of the homes and ships, it dawned on him.

"Someone hand me a spyglass," he said as soon as he reached the front of the crowd.

"Here, Captain," Jack offered.

The Voyages of Queen Anne's Revenge

Edward took the magnifying device and peered through it to take in the state of Bodden Town, the town he partially owned, in its entirety.

The majority of the homes and businesses nearest the shore were completely destroyed, mere husks of their former selves. The palms and grass and flowers in front of the harbour market were torn, disturbed, or outright obliterated. In the harbour, there were several boats and ships which were also decimated from what looked like cannon-fire. The place was more wreck than town.

When Edward had last seen Bodden Town, it was the polar opposite. The sun had been shining, birds chirping, and people bustling. It used to be a lively, thriving, and growing town that he'd taken pride in helping build up. Now he nearly couldn't bear to look upon it.

Edward handed the spyglass back to Jack, and gripped the bow railing. As the ship closed in on Bodden Town, Edward grew more and more enraged. He gritted his teeth as his thoughts shifted to his crewmates whom he'd had stay behind to assist in building homes, and he wondered whether they were still alive. William, Pukuh, and Nassir, his ship's carpenter, were all among those who'd agreed to stay in town—each one of them an irreplaceable friend to Edward.

"Who or what do you believe is responsible?" Jack asked.

"Pirates," Edward guessed.

"Pirates?"

"If it were the British Navy, or any navy for that matter, they wouldn't have left. We would still see them in the harbour. If pirates attacked, they took what they wanted and left. And there is no chance of a storm causing this type of destruction. I struggle to think of another explanation."

"Why would pirates attack Bodden Town?"

Edward scoffed. "Why indeed. It's not as if we've made any enemies," he said grimly, his tone dripping with sarcasm.

Jack nodded. "Yes, I see your meaning. The question is then: which of our past transgressions comes back to haunt us today?"

Edward caressed his beard. "I can only think of one pirate with the power and the gall to do this," he replied.

Jack raised his brow. "Oh?"

Edward glanced over his shoulder at Herbert sitting in his wheelchair, manning the helm with Christina beside him, and Tala the wolf beside her. Jack followed his gaze to the brother and sister, and nodded when he understood.

Edward leaned close to Jack. "Best to not mention him by name. I could be wrong," he said in a low whisper.

"I see," Jack said, glancing around. "I fear you may be right. I am surprised it took this long. It's been, what, two or three years since we killed one of the captains in his squadron?"

Edward glanced down at his sword, the weapon made of a mysterious alloy that was the last remnant of the captain that Herbert had killed. Given that some called Calico Jack the King of the Caribbean, such an offence would require an equal and opposite response, lest Calico Jack be considered weak.

"Whoever it was, they will pay for what they've done."

The crews of the *Queen Anne's Revenge* and *Fortune* eased into the far end of the harbour and dropped anchor before securing themselves to the dock. The dock was also damaged and in need of repair closer to the main road, but it was not as dire as the rest of town.

Edward didn't wait for a gangplank to be dropped, and instead opted to jump off the side of the ship to the pier.

"Edward!" Anne called before following him.

Edward scanned the wharf until he saw people on a nearby boat cleaning debris and removing the small mainsail. He sprinted over to them, and they turned to look at him when his heavy footsteps met their ears.

"What happened here?" he asked.

Some of the sailors eyed him and Anne and their ship. One of the ones more focussed on his work answered. "What, ye just arrived, did ye?"

"Yes. Did pirates attack?"

"Aye, must have been. Though, don't ask us who they was. We was too busy running to ask them their particulars," the man said with a laugh.

Edward turned to Anne. She had a concerned look on her face, no doubt thinking on William, her friend and protector. "It is as I feared. Tell the crew to stay on alert and remain on the ship." Edward began walking off without another word.

"Wait, where are you going, Edward?"

Edward turned around and walked backwards a few paces. "I need to speak with the Boddens and learn more of this attack. They will know."

"Hold, hold, I wish to join you. I need to know what happened to our crewmates."

"Wait a minute, you're that Blackbeard fellow, ain't ye?" the sailor from the boat asked. Edward and Anne both turned their attention back to the man, but neither answered. "This is all yer fault!" he shouted.

Edward and Anne both looked at each other, confused. "I believe you are mistaken, sir. I have not been here in near abouts a month. I had no part in this, I assure you."

"Yea, ye may not 'ave shot the guns, but you brought them here."

Edward stepped forward, his brows furrowed. "What do you mean?"

The sailor pointed to the harbour street. "I was about when those bastards rained iron down on us, and before I could get me and mine out I saw clear as I see you a man calling for your head. They came here for you, and you weren't here."

The man was becoming agitated, and it was then that Edward noticed that the men in the boat had various bandages and visible injuries. He also saw them picking up tools or thick pieces of wood and holding them menacingly.

"Edward, perhaps it's time we leave," Anne whispered as she placed her hand on his chest and pushed him back, all while keeping her eye on the sailors.

"Yes, I believe you are right." Edward turned around and

the two stepped away at a quick pace.

"Oh no, you can't just walk away from this, you dirty pirate," the man yelled.

The sound of boots hitting wood echoed across the pier, and it soon turned into sprinting. Edward and Anne had no choice but to face their aggressors, or they would be attacked from behind.

"We want no part of this, hear? No part!" Edward said with a swipe of his hand.

"You should'a thought of that before ye brought this to our shores."

The men all stood in front of Edward and Anne, seven in total, ready to strike with their makeshift weapons.

"I don't believe we can reason with them, Edward," Anne said.

Edward glanced at her, knowing she was right but wishing the opposite. These people were rightfully angry, but their anger was misdirected.

Edward slowly placed his hand at the hilt of his cutlass. He glared at the men, looking down on them with all the fury he could muster. "Are you sure you want to do this?"

The men wavered at Edward's look and his stature, glancing at each other. The original man who had started the conflict seemed undeterred, and he lunged forward, aiming a metal tool at Edward's head.

Edward didn't draw his sword, and instead grabbed the sailor's weapon mid-air and punched him in the stomach. The man doubled over, clutching his belly.

With their mate's display of courage, four of the men went to attack as well, while two ran away because of Edward's display of power. The attackers all came after Edward and ignored Anne, possibly thinking she wouldn't fight.

Anne twisted her hip, leapt into the air, and kicked one of the men in the side of the head. The man sprawled the ground, unconscious.

Edward ducked under another man's attack and swept his

leg. He fell to the pier, hitting his head violently on the wood.

Anne punched another man in the back of the head, and when he turned around to face her she kicked him in the stomach and face in rapid succession.

The last sailor rushed at Edward with a wooden beam raised high in the air. Edward slammed his body into the man's chest, grabbed his legs, and used his momentum to flip him onto his back. After he landed, Edward punched him in the face for good measure and rose to his feet.

Edward and Anne were not winded in the least. Their attackers were simple fishermen from what Edward could tell, and no match for trained fighters.

A moment after their battle, Jack, Christina, Roberts, and Roberts' first mate, Hank Abbot, came running up to them. "What happened?" Roberts asked, glancing at the bodies lying on the pier.

Edward noticed that their commotion had caught the attention of others on the pier and around the harbour. Many eyes were on them, interested in what was happening. Edward could hear some people calling for the militia.

"It seems some are under the impression that we are the cause of the attack. The pirates who attacked town were after me," Edward explained. "We need to hurry to the Boddens' before anything else happens. Roberts, would you join Anne and me?" Roberts nodded. "Jack, Christina, keep the crew on the ship for now. I don't want any further trouble in town until we have this situation sorted."

"We're on it," she replied before she and Jack ran back to the *Revenge*.

"Hank, it might be wise if you do the same," Roberts said.

Hank nodded. "I reckon that's wise. I'll inform the men."

After Hank set off to the *Fortune*, Roberts, Anne, and Edward went farther down the pier to the main street. Luckily, those who had seen the scuffle didn't recognise Edward, and none pursued them so they were free to move.

The three of them did their best not to bring attention to

themselves as they walked up the damaged cobblestone. Most of the people in the street were working at cleaning or repairing the broken homes and businesses, too busy to notice them.

Now that Edward had a closer look, the town was even worse off than he had thought. It looked as if some of the buildings had also been burned during the attack, and like the fire had spread throughout the area before it could be stopped. The smell of burnt wood, fresh dirt, and spent gunpowder lingered in the air, but there was another smell Edward couldn't pinpoint until he looked at his feet.

There were spots and pools of dried blood that had yet to be washed away, all along the main street. It wasn't fresh, but the faint smell lingered in the air.

"The attack could not have been more than two days ago," Anne speculated as the three walked along the street.

"We just missed it," Edward said.

"It is good providence that we were so fortunate." At Roberts' comment, Edward and Anne glanced at him with pursed lips. "Had we been here, we would not have been able to help." Roberts pointed to the destruction around them. "This was not done with one ship, unless it was a galleon. If this pirate was after you, there was not much we could have done to stop them."

"I suppose you're right," Edward conceded.

The three of them quickened their pace. They passed by the many different citizens, a multitude of whom had a bevy of wounds all over them. Despite this they continued work to fix their broken town.

They made their way quietly to the Boddens' mansion, and met no resistance along the way. At the Boddens' gate there were more guards than usual, and Edward could tell that they were from his crew.

As Edward approached, his crew recognised him. Before they could do anything to alert passersby, Edward placed his finger over his lips. "Where is William?" he asked.

"He's bedridden in the Boddens' estate. Good to see you,

Captain. It's been pretty bad here the past few days."

Edward glanced over his shoulder "Yes, I've come to see that firsthand. Let us in, would you?"

The crewman nodded and opened the lock on the gate before swinging it open.

"Was there always a lock?" Roberts asked.

Edward shook his head. "Things must be truly bad, and I'm afraid once word spreads of our arrival it will only get worse."

"We must be quick about this then," Anne suggested.

The three walked up to the front door of the mansion, waving to the crewmates keeping watch. Edward went to open the door, but it too was locked. He glanced at his companions with a frown before knocking on the door.

Another crewman holding a musket opened the door, and his eyes opened wide when he noticed his captain standing in front of him. "Captain!" he shouted.

"In the flesh." Edward bowed his head. "Care to allow us entry?"

The man looked flustered and stepped aside. "Sorry, Captain. It's just surprising to see you."

"Yes, well, under the circumstances it almost feels as if we shouldn't have returned."

The man chuckled. "The people are on edge. They'll calm themselves soon enough."

Edward nodded. "Where are William and the Bodden brothers?"

"William is in the balcony room on the left side with the Mayan—"

"Pukuh," Edward interjected.

The crewmate nodded. "And the Boddens are in their study working on construction plans with the negro."

"Nassir," Edward said, giving the crewmate a foul look. Edward looked at Anne. "You'll be seeing William first, I imagine?"

Anne nodded. "You don't think you'll need me with the Boddens?"

"I'll manage. I'm not completely useless without you," Edward said with a grin.

Anne smirked. "Not completely." She gave him a kiss and headed up the wide stairs to the second floor to see William.

Edward and Roberts headed up the stairs just behind Anne and through double doors into the Boddens' study. The Bodden twins, Neil, who was wearing a red jacket, and Malcolm, wearing a blue jacket, were working at a desk near the back. They were looking over what appeared to be plans with Nassir, Edward's dark-complexioned shipwright.

They looked up when Edward entered. "Mr Thatch," Niel said.

"We were expecting you back soon, but not this soon," the other brother, Malcolm added.

"Our business went smoother than expected."

"Welcome back, Captain," Nassir said in his heavy accent, flashing a smile.

"Nassir, I'm glad to see you safe and unharmed."

"I was one of the lucky few."

Edward looked at the brothers. "Can you tell me what has happened here?"

The brothers looked at each other and then sighed. "It is one of our greatest fears realised. The pirate, Calico Jack, attacked us three days ago while you were away."

"There were three ships, and thankfully we and the majority of the houses this far inland were spared the brunt of the attack."

"And how are repairs going?" Edward said, looking at Nassir.

"Everyone in town is helping in rebuilding what was lost. Much of the work we did in the past few months and before was undone. Some have left for better shores, as they lost their homes, but those that remain are committed to the work."

Edward nodded at his friend's assessment, then turned his attention to the Boddens. "You are putting some money towards this, I hope?"

The immaculate and lavishly clothed brothers nodded as they said "Of course!" in unison.

"We sent one of the unharmed ships to hire workers from other towns to assist in our repair efforts."

Edward nodded. "Good, use my funds at your discretion. We can't stay long, as the townspeople seem to be against us. Gather any information you can on Calico Jack and his crew's whereabouts so we can prepare a counterattack. Nassir, would you be opposed to remaining here to continue repairs?" Edward asked.

Nassir shook his head. "I will gladly stay and help for now. But I ask that I join you again before fighting Calico Jack. Christina is like a daughter to me, and I would help her and her brother with their vengeance."

Nassir's eyes were fiery, and Edward recalled that Christina had had a relationship with his son before he passed away. Edward knew that if Nassir wasn't there and something happened to Christina, he would never forgive him.

Edward nodded. "I won't leave for that battle without you," he said before he turned around to leave and visit William.

The brothers' brows raised and they glanced at each other. "You plan to fight the King of the Caribbean? That is madness!" Niel said.

"He attacked our town. If we back down now, what does that tell other pirates? Besides, we planned on going after him someday. There's only one king, and I'll be the one to take that title." Edward started for the doors again, but Malcolm stopped him.

"How will we get you the information?"

"We'll return once this all blows over." Edward paused just shy of the doors leading back to rest of the mansion. "When the citizens have calmed, paint part of your mansion red so we'll know it's safe to land."

The Boddens looked dumbfounded by the quickness of the meeting with their partner. Edward didn't wait around for them to regain their composure.

Outside the Boddens' room, Roberts grabbed Edward's arm. "Edward, you never mentioned to me that you angered Calico Jack."

Edward glanced at Roberts' hand, and he removed it. "I suppose I did not. I'm sorry, it never came up. Is it a problem?"

Roberts chuckled. "No, not in the slightest. I'm simply curious what it was you did to provoke his wrath."

"You're familiar with Herbert, our quartermaster?" Roberts nodded. "When he was a young man, he was working on Calico Jack's ship. There was an accident involving gunpowder, and it left him crippled."

Roberts shook his head. "Powder-monkeys. As I learned more about running a pirate ship, and the ease with which misfortunes such as that occur, I banned the practice. I believe I mentioned that to you already, when we created the Pirate Commandments."

Edward nodded. "I remember. I can assure you, from Rackham's treatment of Herbert he has no qualms about using powder-monkeys. Instead of taking care of Herbert after the accident, and raising him to a different role, he left him in Port Royal with nothing. Herbert and his sister had nothing but hardships after that, and they asked me to help them exact vengeance upon Rackham. As we searched for the keys to my ship, we came across one of his commanders and battled him. The man is no longer of this world, and I have this sword as a reminder," Edward said as motioned to the golden cutlass at his side.

Roberts gave a hearty laugh. "You always know how to pick them, don't you, my boy?"

Edward joined in the laughter, but didn't quite know how to respond. The two of them moved on to find William.

Edward and Roberts went to the left side of the Boddens' mansion to the room in which William was staying. The door was open, and when Edward entered he saw Anne and Pukuh sitting on stools near the bed, and William lying down with dressings wrapped around his entire chest. He looked sick with fever, and there was an odour that could only be from William being bedridden for days, and the application of foul medicines. His eyes were baggy, his lips chapped, and his face as pale as the white sheets under which he lay.

"Dear Father, William, what happened to you?" Edward exclaimed as he rushed over to William's bedside.

William flopped his head over to the side to better see Edward, and gave a listless salute. "Hello, Captain. I apologise for what has happened. I take full responsibility for not mounting an effective defence."

"Nonsense. I will hear no more of this. There was nothing you could have done. I heard from the Boddens that there were three ships. No matter what happened it would have turned out the same with that kind of firepower. You did what you could and that's all that matters," Edward said, folding his arms. "Though I do wish to know how you became so injured. Did you fight against Calico Jack himself?" Edward asked with a chuckle. An awkward silence came over the room, and when Edward eyed William, Anne, and Pukuh, they all looked sheepish.

"Good God, man!" Roberts blurted out.

William turned his head and stared at the ceiling. "He is a fearsome man indeed. He broke my ribs like they were nothing. His men kill, maim, and rape without regard for innocent life. He is every bit the reason common men fear pirates, because he encourages violence. I could see the anger and hate in his eyes, as a storm hurtling waves forty feet tall." There was no fear in William's voice. All Edward could hear was the same anger that he had spoken of, and a desire for vengeance that wasn't typical of him. William looked at Edward. "If you were here, I do not doubt that he would have killed every man, woman, and child in this town."

Edward glanced at Roberts. "Perhaps it is as you said—it was better that we were not here."

"There is more," William said.

"More?"

"Rackham seems to have a sword similar to the one you have. It is made from the same strange metal you recovered from one of his officers, and it was sharp enough to break a cutlass I was using in two."

Edward glanced at the cutlass at his side, curious over how Rackham had come upon such an abundance of the strange metal which made their swords.

William continued his story. "Before Rackham left, he pulled a dull golden hunting horn off his belt and used it to issue their retreat."

Golden Horn? But that's... Edward looked at each person in the room, finally settling on Pukuh, who had been silent throughout William's story. He looked angry and confused.

"Calico Jack is Benjamin Hornigold," Pukuh declared.

4. TRAPPED

"That's impossible," Edward said.

Pukuh's expression was as stone. "It is true. I saw him with my eyes. I am telling you, the man who attacked us was Benjamin Hornigold."

"How can you be sure?"

"I remember him from my childhood. I will never forget his face, and the man I saw had the same face but older. It was him."

Edward was going to object again, but Pukuh's eyes brooked no further argument. He'd seen what he'd seen. Benjamin Hornigold, the man who'd given his ship to Edward one fateful, black-out drunk night, the man whose clues had sent them on deadly quests for the keys to that same ship, and the man who had been friends with the Mayan warrior's father—that man was now called Jack Rackham.

Edward ran his hand through his hair. "Why would he do such a thing as this? Why change his name? Why... why?" was all he could think to add.

"Men change," Anne said. "From what I understand of the timeline, Benjamin Hornigold was only with Pukuh's father for a few years at most, and that was over ten years ago." Pukuh nodded in agreement. "Much can happen in ten years, much to change a man. Think about the past three years or so since *you* started sailing as a pirate."

Edward thought back on his adventures of life and death against Benjamin's game for the keys, his year of imprisonment for his crimes, his torture at the hands of Kenneth Locke, and the many friends he'd lost, and the one he'd killed. He was no longer the whaler he had been three years ago, and no longer the naive boy he once was.

"You have a point," Edward conceded.

"He could have changed his name for any reason. He was famous as Benjamin Hornigold; he could have wanted to turn over the hourglass. A new name, a new identity, and a new personality completely different from the Benjamin Hornigold who loved riddles and playing games." Anne glanced over to Pukuh with her last comment, and he looked down at the floor.

"But why give me the ship and then attack me? Where is the sense in that?"

Roberts spoke up this time. "Perhaps the man knows not who you are." Edward eyed his friend and raised his brow, intrigued. "You call yourself Blackbeard now, as you did with the man in his crew you killed, going by what you told me. He sold that ship to an Edward Thatch, not Blackbeard. Not to mention that the ship used to be called *Freedom*. Now it has a new name, one he wouldn't recognise."

Edward nodded. "That seems possible, though hard to believe." He stroked his beard in thought for a moment, all eyes watching him. After a moment he let out a sigh. "I suppose this doesn't change what we were going to do, unless you have a problem with killing him now, Pukuh."

Pukuh shook his head. "No… He's not the Benjamin my father sailed with. Not anymore."

"Now the question is how we get William and the rest of our men back to the ship without being seen?"

Anne stood up. "What? No, William cannot be moved, he needs to rest."

"The longer we stay here the more dangerous it is for us. As we speak the men who attacked us could be rallying others to find us or go after the ship. There's between six hundred and a thousand people living here, and only a little over two hundred of us."

Anne furrowed her brows in anger. "He'll die."

"I can make it," William croaked as he tried to sit up, but his arms were trembling under his own weight and he eventually collapsed back in a heap as he struggled for air.

Anne pulled Edward aside and whispered to him. "He is safe here with the Boddens. You can leave. I will stay with him and Roberts here until he is healed, and in the meantime I will attempt to bring order back to the town. If we cannot, we shall meet you again at sea."

Edward looked into Anne's sea green eyes filled with concern, and then at William's sweat-drenched face and clothes as he tried to catch his breath. He let out a sigh. "I suppose that is for the best... Roberts," Edward called.

"Yes, my boy?" the giant Roberts said as he came over.

"Anne has elected to stay here with William as he heals and attempt calming the citizens. Would you and your crew stay with her to try to keep the peace, and then meet up with us at Montego Bay?"

"Aye, I'll stay and ensure the princess isn't bored to tears," Roberts said with a grin.

Edward gripped Roberts' shoulder. "Thank you, friend. I know we've been neglecting your desire for vengeance for some time, and I'm sorry for that. Once we find out where Walter Kennedy is, and settled this business, we'll go after him."

Roberts shook his head. "The Lord will deliver Walter Kennedy when it is his time, and no sooner. Do not worry about me. You find the man who did this and bring him justice."

"We will," Edward replied. "Together," he said as he squeezed his friend's shoulder.

Roberts smiled and put out his hand to shake, and the two laughed as each gripped the other's hand as hard as they could as a show of strength. After a moment they released their hands and Roberts pulled Edward in for a bear hug.

After Roberts released him, he gave Anne a goodbye kiss and then looked at Pukuh. "Pukuh, let's get back to the ship so we can find the man who destroyed our town, whatever you want to call him."

Pukuh rose to his feet and grabbed a spear resting against the wall in his one hand. "I am with you, brother. Benjamin has much to answer for, and I wish to question him before I shove my spear through his heart," he said with a menacing look on his face.

Edward grinned. "Well said." He went over next to William's bed. "William, we've decided to let you stay here and be the lazy sod you have been for a bit longer. Use your vacation well, as I'll have you working double-time to make up for it when you're back with us."

William stared at Edward with a stoic expression on his face. "I wouldn't have it any other way," he replied. "Godspeed, Captain. Give him hell for me."

Edward could now see the anger he heard in William's voice reflected in his eyes. "You have my word," Edward said.

Edward and Pukuh gave their final goodbyes to William, Roberts, and Anne, and exited the room. They headed down the stairs and to the front door of the Bodden mansion, quickly telling the crew serving as guards that they were leaving and that Anne was in charge.

Upon exiting the mansion, Edward noticed that it was close to dark out. The red glow from the sun was nearly gone, and he could see long bands of light stretching across the sky. They rushed to the front gate, but as they got a better view of the main street they slowed their pace to a stop.

There was a large crowd of people walking up the street, led by a man that, at least from as far away as he was, looked like one of the men Edward had fought on the pier. Many in the crowd held makeshift weapons like hammers meant for construction, timber, and farming tools.

"This isn't good," Edward said. "Men, get inside," he said to the men guarding the gates.

The crewmates jumped at the sound of his voice, and glanced over their shoulders at him and then back at the advancing crowd. One of them fumbled with a set of keys in his hand to open the lock as he kept peering at the angry mob headed straight for him. He shoved the key in the lock and twisted it open. Edward pushed the gate open and pulled his men in, then slammed it shut again.

"Lock it! Lock it!" he shouted, eyeing the mass of people marching towards them.

The crewmate nervously wrapped the lock around the bars of the gate and closed the clasp just as the crowd reached the mansion.

Men, women, and children from across Bodden Town made up the crowd. Edward had seen many of them before, either in their businesses, walking around town, or today cleaning the main street. They were so different than before, with their anger directed at him. Wrinkled foreheads, furrowed brows, and clenched teeth plastered many faces in front of him. The people were calling for blood. Blackbeard's blood.

The man at the front, the sailor who had attacked Edward before, stepped up to the gate.

"Goin' somewhere, Blackbeard?" he said with a smirk.

Edward gritted his teeth. "End this, sir, before any further blood is shed. I want vengeance as much as you, but you are asking for it from the wrong man. End this and I will bring you Calico Jack's head."

"Oh, you'll bring us his head, will you? Just so his men can come back to attack us for yer murder? What about when another pirate comes because of something ye did? Or what about when the Brits come after you and charge us for treason because we helped ye?" The man shook his head. "The only way this ends is if you never sail again."

Edward backed up a few paces, but kept his eyes on the crowd. They were hitting the gate with their homemade weapons, and the metal clanged with each blow. They attacked the surrounding stone walls as well, and it all mixed with the din of the mob. It wouldn't be long before the throng brought ladders in to scale the barrier.

Edward turned his head towards his men, but kept his eyes on the crowd. "Is there a way out back?" he asked.

"Yes, Captain. There is a door at the back of the mansion leading outside the wall."

"Let's hurry," he replied.

The four of them ran to the side of the mansion and to the back. They could hear the sound of the angry voices behind them, but before long they could hear footsteps on the other side of the wall following them. When they reached the small door near the corner of the mansion's perimeter, it moved. The men on the other side were testing the door, but thankfully it was locked.

"Get something from the house, we must barricade the door," Edward said.

Edward and Pukuh stayed behind as the other men rushed into the Bodden mansion from the back door.

The simple pushes from outside the door quickly turned into full-blown attacks meant to break the door down. Edward and Pukuh bolted to the exit and pressed their bodies against the wood. The door was the weakest link in their defence, and it buckled under the strength of the adversaries behind it. With each hit, the door jolted forward with a crash, and it pushed Edward and Pukuh back with it.

The crewmates came back with chairs, and a few others carried a lavish floral-patterned couch. They put the couch up vertically and after Pukuh moved aside they jammed it against one side of the door. Edward kept his shoulder on the door as the other crewmates wedged one chair up against the knob and the other in some fashion between the first chair and the couch. Edward and Pukuh continued to hold onto the furniture until more, heavier items were added to the collection. When Edward felt that the door was secure, he stood up.

Edward was sweating. "Hopefully that will hold. Keep an eye on it just in case."

"Aye, Captain."

Edward and Pukuh entered the Boddens' mansion and went to the main hall. Anne, Roberts, Nassir, the Boddens, the rest of Edward's men, and some of the Boddens' men were standing in the middle of the hall talking amongst themselves with looks of concern on their faces.

When Anne saw Edward her face lit up. "Edward!" She ran over and hugged him. "When we saw the crowd and no sign of you we thought the worst. What's happening out there?"

"The citizens have revolted, they're after my head, and we're trapped in here."

5. SNARE

"How much food do you have in your storehouses?" Edward asked the Boddens.

"Edward, you cannot be thinking about defending this place, can you?"

"What other choice do we have? We're trapped."

Anne looked at the Boddens. "Is there any other way to escape here?"

"I'm afraid not," Niel Bodden said.

"We only have a defensible basement, which you're familiar with already, with enough food to last a month."

Edward nodded. He pointed his crew and the Boddens' men. "I want you to go on the second floor or to the roof, take all the bullets and gunpowder you can, and shoot at anyone who tries to climb the wall. Don't kill anyone unless you have to, and try to stick to warning shots."

The men nodded and ran off to fulfill their orders.

"Have you tried talking with them?" Roberts asked.

"I tried talking with their supposed leader. It's the same man who attacked us on the pier. He won't listen to reason, and the rest are too riled up."

"What will we do then? Eventually we're going to run out of bullets, and they outnumber us ten to one," Anne said, folding her arms.

"We'll have to take everything as it comes. I can't see them trying to breach the walls this late at night. If we take shifts we can keep watch to make sure no one sneaks over the wall, and in the morning we'll see if they'll be more willing to listen to reason."

Anne sighed. "I see no other way around this, so we'll go

with your plan. Nassir, why don't you and I start boarding up the windows?"

Nassir nodded. "I know where the supplies are. I'll lead the way."

Before Anne and Nassir could get far, they heard loud pops coming from outside and reverberating through the house. Not long afterwards, the shouts from outside became louder.

Edward and the rest of them glanced at each other, and were about to head outside when the glass of the main hall windows shattered open. A large rock had been thrown in from outside and crashed on the floor of the mansion.

Edward looked at the rock, pursed his lips, and ran up to the second floor and to William's room. William was sitting up now, and had a concerned look on his face. On the balcony was one of Edward's crew with a musket in hand. He was aiming at the front gate, preparing to fire.

Edward gave a cursory glance over at William and dashed over to the other crewmate. Outside, someone was already climbing up the front wall with a ladder.

"How many shots have you fired already?" he asked the crewman.

"Only one, but there must be other people trying to breach the wall, because I heard shots on the other side of the house."

"Stop this," Edward shouted at the horde of people pressing against the gates. "There's no need for anyone to lose their lives!"

A cacophony of responses flooded in from the crowd, but Edward caught the general gist of it. He noticed Anne and Roberts come into view on the balcony on the other side of the mansion.

Edward's crewman fired a shot at the stone of the wall, causing the man climbing to duck down and then give them a dirty look, but he didn't stop. He pulled himself up to the top of the wall.

Edward pulled out a pistol from his belt, and fired. The bullet hit the climber in the leg. He clutched his leg and fell forward into the grounds of the mansion.

There was a collective gasp from the crowd. Edward jumped over the balcony and rolled when he hit the ground. He went over to the man he had shot and picked him up by the scruff of his neck. He dragged the man over to the fence, where the crowd watched in relative silence.

"This is what will happen to each of you who tries to breach the wall," he yelled. "We also have cannons. Do not test us. There has been enough bloodshed here over the past days. There is no need for more. Take the night. Be with your family, your brothers, your sisters, your sons and daughters, and come back with clearer heads so that you can think on who the real enemy is, and what the best course of action for this town is."

The crowd murmured amongst themselves as the cold of night took over the town. The orange glow of lanterns shone between several members of the mob. It illuminated the faces, allowing Edward to see their confused and tired eyes clearly.

The leader was also looking at the crowd as they whispered to each other. Eventually, he spoke up. "Some of you go home, and whoever wants to volunteer to stay watch, stay here," he said. "Come back tomorrow and we'll settle this."

After another moment, the majority of the crowd dispersed, their lanterns bobbing in the distance as they moved. Within five minutes only twenty people remained.

"Step back so I can give this man to you," Edward said. "His wound needs to be dressed."

The sailor leading the charge nodded and waved to the others to move away from the gate. Edward called for someone to open the gate, and soon one of the Boddens' men tentatively exited the mansion with keys in hand. He opened the gate and Edward pushed the injured man outside where he fell to the ground, still clutching his leg. Edward locked the gate once again as someone helped the injured man up to take him away.

The twenty men still left stared at Edward as he backed away and into the Bodden mansion. Soon Anne and Roberts returned to the first floor of the main hall to join Edward with Pukuh and Nassir already there.

"Well," Roberts began, "that went well." He gave a hearty laugh.

Edward ignored Roberts' comment; he was in no mood for jesting. "There are still people watching us, so we won't be able to leave, but at least now they're not trying to tear down the gate to get at us."

"That bought us more time, but what are we going to do with it?" Anne asked.

"We'll keep an eye on the people outside the gates, and make sure that they don't try anything. I'm hoping tomorrow the rest of the townsfolk will have clearer heads and stop this."

Anne had one hand on her hip. "And if not?"

"If not," Edward sighed, "perhaps I can convince them of who the true enemy is."

Anne, Roberts, Nassir and Pukuh all looked at Edward with confidence shining through. They believed in him, and the look in their eyes showed it. The Boddens looked less than enthused, but Edward didn't blame them given that their home was under siege.

"We can take shifts for watch. Any volunteers for first watch?"

Anne stepped forward. "I'll take first watch, if there are no objections."

"I will as well," Pukuh said.

"Good… Boddens, could you work with my men and yours to create a rotation so we have all sides of the perimeter covered?"

The Bodden brothers nodded. "It will be done."

"Nassir, you get some rest. You've been working hard enough here all day already."

"Thank you, Captain," Nassir replied.

Anne and Pukuh both went up to the second floor and went to watch from each of the balcony rooms. Edward, Roberts, and Nassir stayed on the first floor and went to sleep in one of the guest rooms.

All three of them lay awake, trying to sleep against the backdrop of the night. Birds, crickets, and the faint rustling of trees filtered in through an open window along with fresh, clean air devoid of gunpowder, saltwater, and, most importantly, blood.

Despite the siege, Edward's mind was clear. He could think of only a few outcomes to this scenario, and he was prepared for any of them.

"So, what happens if you cannot coax the townsfolk back to your side? I'm well aware of your charisma, my boy, but nothing is certain even where the Lord is concerned."

Edward stared at the whitewashed wood of the ceiling for a moment. "Then we'll have to kill them."

"Edward, wake up," Anne's voice called.

Edward's eyes opened a crack, finding the blurry orange glow of a lantern directly in front of him. He turned over and blinked a few times, and the orange glow turned into red curls, sparkling green eyes, and freckled cheeks.

He pulled himself up out of bed, his bare chest exposed to the cold night. He glanced outside and could see the stars but not the moon, so he had no idea what the hour was. He sluggishly placed his feet over the side of the bed and donned his boots and clothes and weapons.

"Any movement?" he asked.

"None," Anne replied. "They are keeping watch and rotating shifts, just as we are."

"Good, let us hope it stays that way."

Edward and Roberts sleepily made their way to the balcony rooms to keep watch from there. They left Nassir alone to sleep, as he needed it more than they. Edward headed to the left with William, and Roberts headed to the right with another crewmate keeping watch.

The Voyages of Queen Anne's Revenge

As Edward entered the room he yawned and stretched, feeling the call of the captain's cabin. The pitching and rolling of the waves was soothing in a way, and he wasn't able to sleep as well without it, despite the ship's bed not being anywhere near as comfortable as the Boddens'.

William was awake, and welcomed Edward. "Captain," he said with a shaky salute.

"William, you should be resting," Edward replied.

Edward went to the balcony and sat down in a chair already stationed outside. Near the chair, on top of a table, he saw a musket which appeared to be fully loaded and ready to fire. He pulled it closer to where he was sitting for ease, and then rested his feet on the balcony railing.

"Sleep comes and goes. I slept the day away, and so the night welcomes me instead."

"I suppose when one is sick day and night are meaningless," Edward said.

"Most times," William replied. "Tell me, how does it look?"

Edward scanned the town and the wall and gate protecting them at the moment. Lanterns moved in the night, carried by men with heavy clothes on. The faint glow cast angry shadows on their faces, faces which didn't need more anger. It was quiet, save for the creak of the swinging lanterns and the *clack clack clack* of hard leather on stone. The night animals had quieted, and the wind lost its howl as it stopped moving.

"It's calm, but the men outside carry tension on their faces. Lost sleep will not help their mood, I'm afraid."

"I didn't mean out there. I meant how does it look for us? Will we make it out of this?"

Edward looked at William, but aside from his sick, tired eyes, he carried no expression. "I never knew you to be afraid, William."

"I don't care what happens to me, only Anne."

Edward chuckled, and then went back to watching the wall. "We've been in worse situations."

There was a short pause before William said, "That wasn't

an answer."

"Go to sleep, William," Edward said with a smile on his face.

Behind Edward, he could hear William shuffle around with his bed sheets, and then he went silent.

Over the next hour, Edward kept a diligent watch, though it was quite boring work. One of the Boddens' housekeepers brought him coffee, which he sipped on, and it helped keep him awake. It would still be several hours before morning, and he needed it.

Edward was looking down the main street when he thought he noticed movement. At first, he thought his eyes were playing tricks on him, but when he saw movement again, this time closer to the Boddens', he decided to investigate. He rose to his feet and pulled out a spyglass from his belt. He scanned the street for what he had seen, and at first he couldn't see anything more, but after another moment he noticed two cloaked figures running towards the mansion.

Edward stopped looking through the glass and knocked on the wooden railing of the balcony to draw Roberts' attention. After a few raps on the hardwood Roberts looked over. Edward motioned with his spyglass and then pointed to the street. Roberts caught the message and pulled out his own spyglass to peer through.

The two of them watched the street and the approaching figures. While they were being cautious, it seemed they were trying to hide from the men standing watch outside the wall, not from Edward and crew.

When they were fifty feet away from the gate, Edward put down the spyglass and picked up his musket. Roberts noticed the noise, and went to do the same, but Edward motioned for him to stop. He wasn't sure who it was, and it could be one of his crew. If someone was going to have the blood of his crew on their hands over a mistake, it was going to be him.

The two cloaked shadows continued their advance, careful to avoid the light of the homes and standing still when the townsfolk made their rounds. Edward wasn't able to tell who they were, or if they carried any weapons, but he could tell that they were skilled in stealth.

Could it be Calico Jack's men here to finish me off?

Edward looked upon the figures in a new light, and he gripped the musket tighter. He leaned his head up against the barrel, and he could smell the gunpowder resting on the weapon's pan. He traced the movement of the figures with the gun barrel until they came up to the last houses before the Bodden mansion. The two paused as a man passed in front of them, his lantern swaying in his hand. Edward pulled back the hammer and lowered the frizzen over the pan, then fully cocked his gun. The hammer snapped as it locked into place.

That distinctive noise was not loud in the least, but in the dead of night it was easy to hear. For those not familiar with the sound, it could be brushed off as an animal or someone dropping something, but for those who recognised it, it was undeniable.

The two cloaked figures knew the sound of the gun cocking, and instantly looked at Edward. He swore to himself, and moved his index finger to fire before it was too late. The front cloaked figure unmasked himself.

Standing there was Alexandre, the surgeon aboard the *Queen Anne's Revenge*, in all his baggy-eyed glory. He waved to Edward with a smile on his face before he motioned to keep quiet.

Edward let out a sigh and released the cocking of the musket. He gave an exasperated look over to Roberts, and Roberts shrugged his shoulders.

The ever-eccentric Frenchman Alexandre and his companion eyed the men keeping watch on the mansion for a few moments as they whispered amongst themselves. After a moment, the one at the back ran—while being inexplicably silent—over to the gate and knelt down while holding a shield above his shoulder. Alexandre followed soon after and jumped on top of the shield, then the other figure vaulted Alexandre up the side of the gate. He placed his hand on the top of the gate, swung his legs over, and landed on the other side with a roll. The other figure then ran to the edge of the gate where it met the stone wall and jumped off the side of the gate to the stone and back where it gave him enough height to vault over the side of the gate.

Edward's jaw dropped at the sight of it all. The event only took a matter of seconds, but the ease with which it happened was almost a thing of beauty. He hadn't thought that Alexandre was that dexterous, and had he not seen it with his own eyes he wouldn't have believed it.

Edward dashed back inside and to the second floor's main hall. "Open the door," he commanded his men.

They obeyed and let Alexandre and the other crewmate in.

Alexandre peered at his surroundings with squinted eyes. "I do not believe I've been in here," he said nonchalantly. His eyes opened wide and he raised his finger. "*Non, non*, that is not true. I have been here... perhaps."

Edward rubbed his eyes with his thumb and forefinger. "Alexandre, what are you doing here?"

"*Le plaisir* to see you as well, Captain. We came for a few reasons. First, we wanted to know if you needed help escaping, or if you wanted us to have the crew come to the rescue."

Edward thought on it for a moment. If they escaped, or attacked, then there was no chance to keep the town as their home base. The townsfolk wouldn't accept him as their leader if they couldn't trust him. Even then, the chances of them escaping were slim with all their numbers. Not all were as agile as Alexandre was.

"We can't take the risk. Our only chance is to convince the townspeople to stand down. The situation's not as dire as it once was, so I'm hoping tomorrow they'll listen to reason. Tell the crew to stand by in the harbour, captain's orders. We may still need to use force, but for now we're safe."

Alexandre bowed his head. "We thought that you might say something like that. We are also here because one of your crewmates has something to tell you," he replied, looking at the crewmate who'd come with him.

The crewmate pushed the cloak back, but it was a woman Edward didn't recognise. His jaw dropped open. *A woman, one of my crewmates? But, only Christina and Anne are…* He stared at the woman's face, and she stared at him. After a few seconds, it finally dawned on him. "Victor!"

The crewmates around them were just as astonished and voiced their amazement with several expletives.

Alexandre smiled, but the woman remained was expressionless. "Her true name is Victoria, but yes, *Capitaine*, you knew this person as Victor, my assistant." Victor punched Alexandre in the arm, eliciting a glare. "My partner," he corrected, although begrudgingly.

The news stunned Edward. Victor had been aboard his ship almost from the beginning, as far back as he could remember, and he had never seen anything out of the ordinary.

"Don't trouble yourself, *Capitaine*. She's good at hiding her identity. It even took me some time to figure it out."

Edward took a moment to review all of his and Victoria's interactions up until that point, and then he shook his head. "Why, why… why now? Couldn't this have waited for a better time?"

"No, Captain, it couldn't," Victoria said, the hint of an unfamiliar accent present in her voice.

Victoria's sober face and serious tone spoke to the gravity of what she needed to discuss. Edward nodded; there was evidently more to this than just revealing her true self.

Edward pointed to one of the guards on the door. "You, take my post. You two," he said, pointing at Alexandre and Victoria, "come with me."

Edward went into the Boddens' study and Alexandre and Victoria followed in behind him soon after. Alexandre closed the door behind him.

"This had better be good. Truly, I couldn't care less that you're a woman aboard my ship, and you should know that already. Why did you hide your identity from the crew?"

Alexandre was leaning against an alcove bookshelf, wearing a smug smile. Victoria, on the other hand, was as stone-faced as William.

"I hid it because of the crew I was with before this. I knew that if anyone found out, especially the young navigator and his sister…"

Edward clenched his fist. "You were on Calico Jack's crew?"

"A long time ago, yes."

"So I assume the crew has found out about who attacked the town?" Victoria nodded. Edward gritted his teeth. "Damn. I was hoping we could have this resolved before Herbert found out."

"Oh, the boy knows," Alexandre said. "Do not worry yourself, he is sleeping right now on the ship."

Edward nodded. "So, what was so urgent about your previous captain that you needed to tell me now?"

"It's regarding the way he operates. I was with him for many years, and I've seen similar occurrences as what happened here. Jack Rackham is a calculating man, and he would not have left, and allowed the townspeople to live, if he didn't expect this to happen," she said, motioning towards the town. "He knew that this was your town, so he sowed the seeds of discontent to ensure the people turned on you. There could even be some people he paid to see that things progressed this way. This is his snare, his trap, but so far you've managed to save yourself from the noose. His goal is to make it so you no longer have your safe haven, and will run in fear."

"What would he have done if I was in town?"

Victoria looked at him as if he were the village idiot and folded her arms. "He would have killed you, of course," she said. "This was his backup plan."

Edward scratched his face sheepishly. "Yes. I should have known that."

"Now, what you do with the information I've provided is

up to you, but you may be able to convince the townspeople of Calico's plot and stop the riot." Victoria pulled her cloak up over her head, and made her way to the door to leave the study.

"Wait, where are you going?" Edward asked.

Victoria turned around, the same look plastered on her face. "I'm going back to the ship. I don't want to be here should you fail," she said before turning around and leaving. She muttered some further things under her breath Edward couldn't make out.

Victoria's candor had caught Edward off-guard, and left him speechless. Before she got too far, he said, "We're going to have to talk more on this later." She waved the back of her hand to him without turning around. Edward glanced from her to Alexandre, who still wore a grin.

"Yes, Captain. She's always like that," Alexandre said before pushing himself off the bookshelf and walking to the door.

"You seemed to enjoy that, didn't you?"

Alexandre turned around and walked backwards, still with the wide smirk on his face. "Of course. She's entertaining, and a bit challenging. I like that in a woman."

"I know the feeling," Edward said, mimicking the grin. Before Alexandre was out the door, Edward grew serious. "Keep an eye on Herbert for me."

"*Oui*, Captain."

Edward went back to his post and relieved the crewmate. He watched as Alexandre and Victoria went back the same way they'd come, jumping over the wall and sneaking off into the shadows.

Victoria's comments about Jack Rackham helped Edward plan what he would say to the townspeople if they were still incensed about the attack. He would have to discuss Victoria's allegiances, and broach the subject with Herbert, but that would be for another time.

As night turned to day, Edward and the others had no more disturbances. The sun gently poked up from the horizon and illuminated the town in a clear light. The birds of the morning sang their songs, and the sound of footsteps and various voices drifted up from outside.

The townspeople, just waking from their slumber, were returning to the mansion in droves. Many yawned and stretched as they walked alone and in groups up the small hill. Despite the many that were gathering, no children were attending, and with good reason. Edward was glad for that at least. If it came down to shedding blood, he didn't want children in the way.

Anne, Pukuh, Nassir, and the rest of the crew also rose from their slumber to join those who had taken second watch. Anne and Pukuh joined Edward, while Nassir and the other crewmates joined Roberts. Edward called Roberts and his crewmates over to his side.

"Did you sleep well?" Edward asked Anne.

"Yes, despite how little of it I managed, it was pleasant to be on solid ground again," she said.

"After all this time you're not used to sleeping on a ship?" Edward said with a smirk.

Anne folded her arms. "It's not that I am not used to sleeping on a ship, it's just that I'm accustomed to certain… luxuries from my former life. I claim no responsibility for the things my mother gave me. I was simply privileged, and it will take me more time to become accustomed to the constant waves, and… and… shut it, you big brute," she finished with a pout.

Edward laughed at the look on Anne's face, and she smiled back.

Roberts, Nassir and Edward's crewmates joined him on their side of the balcony. "Have some of the Boddens' men—" Edward started, but stopped when two of the Boddens' men walked onto the other balcony. "Forget that. Prepare William for transport. I want him ready to leave on a stretcher at a moment's notice."

Two of the crewmates nodded and went to find a stretcher for William.

"Do you think it will be necessary, brother?" Pukuh asked,

glancing at William and then the crowd.

"I don't want to take any chances," he replied. "To that end, perhaps it would be best to arm yourselves."

The group nodded, and everyone save Pukuh and Nassir left to retrieve weapons. Nassir prepared William for transport, and helped clear some of the sweat from his brow as Pukuh, with his spear in his hands, walked over to the balcony edge.

"The gods laugh at you, Edward. They have given you the gift of making everyone hate you."

Edward chuckled. "At least that would give me some peace of mind. Then I would know the reason why we can't seem to have it easy for longer than a month at a time." Pukuh laughed with his friend. "I'm glad to see you in better spirits."

"Sleep is a friend to a weary mind and a troubled heart."

"That it is," Edward concurred.

Pukuh took on a sombre look as the crowds were almost finished gathering. "Something your mate said helped." Edward looked at Pukuh, eager to hear what he had to say. "When we were discussing it, she said that the seas could have changed him from the time with my father... You know, in the Maya, we have no god for the sea?"

Edward grinned. "No?"

"We have a god for rain, lightning, those things, but not the sea. Maybe one of the lesser tribes had one, I do not know. If there was to be a god of the sea, I would imagine him to be a great serpent. A serpent that loves to create and ride the waves, but also enjoys the calm, still waters of sleep. When it strikes its fancy, I would imagine he would jump from the sea to the heavens, perhaps angering his brother, Kukulkna, the god of the wind. When the serpent lands back in the sea, he causes great waves in his wake, and his brother sends winds of anger his way so that together they create the storms."

Edward laughed with a wide smile. "Did you come up with that just now? It sounds like it could be real."

Pukuh shrugged. "Perhaps it is, who knows?" he said. "The sea is like this fickle serpent, and those who ride in its wake are forced to withstand the storms, or be broken by it. I feel that Benjamin was too kind a soul, and those storms broke him. Now, he is Calico Jack, a broken man desperate to withstand the next storm."

Edward stared at the sea, and at the *Queen Anne's Revenge* with his precious family aboard it. "I wonder if we will be able to withstand that storm."

Pukuh chuckled and slapped Edward's back, then looked at him with wide eyes. "Brother, you *are* the storm."

I am the storm? Edward was speechless as he stared at Pukuh, the Mayan warrior prince. *I am the storm.*

Edward turned towards the gathering crowd. It appeared that all that had been present the day before had returned, and brought more with them. They watched him, waiting to see what he would say or do.

"People of Bodden Town," Edward began. "You know me as Blackbeard. Perhaps you may think of me as a pirate, a scoundrel, scum who steals from others so he may gain. What you may not know is that my name is Edward Thatch, and many years ago my dream was to own a whaling boat, as my father did before me."

The crew returned with a stretcher, and Anne and Roberts with weapons. Nassir quickly and gently placed William in the stretcher. Anne and Roberts stayed back, out of view of the townsfolk so they wouldn't see their weapons.

"My dream was stolen from me before I could even sell my first catch, and soon I found myself on the run. As I ran from men trying to steal my freedom from me, I found a new dream with the family I created aboard that ship you see in the harbour." Edward pointed to the *Queen Anne's Revenge*. "I found a new dream here, in this town. A dream where men and women could be free to pursue their passions without oppression and tyranny."

As Edward gazed upon the faces in the crowd, he could tell that many were responding to his message. Men nodded, and women listened with perked ears. Some whispered to their neighbours, and in those whispered to theirs. It appeared that he was winning them over.

"Calico Jack now threatens not just my new dream, but yours as well. He wants to tear down what we've built. He wants us to fight amongst ourselves. He wants us to rip ourselves apart so he doesn't have to. Do. Not. Let. Him."

The crowd seemed to be more riled up now. They were talking along excitedly, shouting words of agreement. Some still had their arms folded, but their heads nodded in agreement.

"You have lost sons, daughters, lovers, parents. For mercy's sake, do not lose yourself to the true pirate who seeks to steal your dream you've built so hard to protect. I vow to be your sword on the sea. I vow to be your veng—"

The sound of gunfire ripped the sound from Edward's voice, and he and the others instinctively ducked down and covered themselves. The men and women of the crowd gasped, and Edward heard the sound of many footsteps running away from the mansion.

Edward checked himself for injury, and when he felt no pain and saw no blood he rose back to his full height. His heart was beating like a drum in his chest. "Is everyone well?" he asked his crew. Everyone responded with various affirmations.

Edward looked over to the balcony, and noticed two smoking muskets lying on the table. *Those were the Boddens' men over there,* he thought.

A scream let out in the gathered crowd again, this time more focussed, more high-pitched, and more terror-filled than the first. Edward turned his attention to the crowd, and he could see two men, dead, pools of blood already forming beneath their bodies.

"Edward, look!" Anne shouted as she pointed to the harbour.

Edward followed Anne's finger, and saw the *Queen Anne's Revenge* in full sail, leaving the harbour.

Edward clenched his teeth and his fists. "Herbert."

6. LURE

Yesterday

A crewmate came running up to the quarterdeck, where Herbert and Christina stood. "Herbert, you'd better look at this," he said, handing him a spyglass and pointing towards town.

Through the magnified gaze, he could see all the way up the main street of Bodden Town. A group of about a hundred people were heading towards the Bodden mansion. They appeared to have weapons on them.

"Oh Father, this isn't good," Herbert said as he peered through the spyglass.

"What is it?" Christina asked.

Herbert wheeled himself over next to Christina and handed her the spyglass. Tala glanced back and forth between the two of them, panting and unsure of what was going on, but riled up by the excitement. "The townspeople are trying to overtake the Boddens."

Christina looked through the spyglass. "First Edward is attacked, now they move on the Boddens? Why? Is it something to do with the attack? We had nothing to do with that."

"The townspeople might not see it like that. Whatever happened, they seem to hold either us or the Boddens responsible."

Christina gasped. "I think Edward is trapped inside."

"What?" Herbert looked at his sister with one brow cocked.

"Edward came to the gate just as the crowd closed in, and they had to lock the gate from the inside." Christina took her eye away from the spyglass and gave her brother a concerned look.

The Voyages of Queen Anne's Revenge

Herbert clenched his teeth and moved his wheelchair around so he could look over the quarterdeck railing. "Someone fetch Jack, and get our men ready for battle. Our captain is in trouble."

Two crewmates nodded and went to task. The others on the weather deck, near abouts twenty out of the crew, retrieved some muskets and proceeded to load them.

Christina started to leave the quarterdeck with Tala following behind her. "Where are you going?" Herbert asked.

"I'm going to load a weapon and grab a cutlass," she replied with a quizzical look.

"I need you to stay with me. We're going to need people to defend the ship in case some of the townsfolk decide to attack us, and I want you by my side."

"But—"

"Please, Christina," Herbert pleaded, "I need you here. I'm not fit to fight in my state, you should know that."

Christina stared at her brother for a few seconds before letting out a sigh. "Well, when you put it *that* way," she said. "Just so we're clear, forcing guilt on your sister isn't fair."

Herbert smirked. "It worked though, didn't it?"

Christina lightly punched Herbert in the arm, but with a smile on her face.

A few minutes later, Jack and almost the entire crew of the *Queen Anne's Revenge*, a little over two hundred of them, came to the weather deck. Some gathered weapons, while others went to the bow or clambered up the rigging ropes to catch a glimpse of the scene unfolding. There was a buzz amongst the men itching for a fight.

"Listen up, men," Herbert shouted. The crew turned their attention to the quartermaster. "It looks like our captain needs us up there, but I don't think I have to tell some of you that the townspeople are not to be harmed. Some of you hail from this town, so you know their feelings. To everyone else, keep your pistols at the ready, but you are to be no more than a threat. These people have been through enough already, and they're only doing this because they're scared. Get the captain, and get out of there without bloodshed. Understood?" The crew agreed loudly. "Move ou—"

"Herbert, look!" Christina called out, pointing to the pier.

Herbert lifted himself up with his hands on the wheelchair to see properly. A group of fifty or so people were coming from all directions to their ship. They were running towards them with crude excuses for weapons and angered looks plastering their faces.

"Bring the gangplank up!" Herbert commanded. The crewmen were watching the approaching townspeople. "The gangplank! The gangplank!" he shouted.

A few crewmates heard the order and pulled up the temporary bridge. Just as they finished, the townsfolk rounded the bend to their dock.

Herbert wheeled himself over to the port side of the ship. His wooden apparatus creaked and groaned as it moved, complaining of its age and closeness to sea water.

Jack was also on the port side, and he leaned his elbows on the railing. "Hello gentlemen, what might we do for you?" he called down to the approaching men.

Herbert looked over the group, and they were all the epitome of normal. He could tell some were sailors, with their rugged hands and weathered faces, and others, with their tanned forearms and hair lightened from the sun, were farmers. None of them were fighters, and they were a far cry from pirates.

They wouldn't last five minutes, the lot of them, even if they had the same weapons as us.

"Would ye mind droppin' yer plank for us? We have something we need to discuss with ye," one of the farmers said.

Jack cast his gaze on the many people gathered, then shrugged his shoulders. "I'm sorry, gentlemen, I simply cannot in good conscience have my men lower our gangplank. You see, I'm not generally a violent man, but these men here?" He motioned to the crew. "These men are quick to violence because they are generally used to life-or-death situations. If I lower that gangplank, and you board, I cannot say what would happen. My captain wouldn't like it if any of you were injured."

The men gathered around the ship seemed to calm down at the threat. They took in how many crewmates there were, and how many carried actual weapons.

The farmer pointed a sharp hoe in Jack's direction. "Your captain is the reason I lost my brother!" The man's words seemed to rile up the crowd and give them renewed courage in the face of overwhelming odds.

Jack scratched his face. "That's strange, because up until today we had been out to sea. If you're referring to what happened to the town, we were not responsible. Trust me, sir, I know your plight. I have lost loved ones in the past, but I would not put the blame for their murder on someone not at all involved in it."

The farmer did not seem convinced, though he paused for a moment to consider his words. "The pirates who attacked us kept shouting to bring them Blackbeard. We don't want any further trouble, so we're going to bring your captain's head to Calico Jack and be done with it."

Herbert's heart stopped, and it felt as if the icy hand of the Devil had gripped hold of it. Calico Jack, the pirate he used to work for, who left him with nothing after he was crippled, was the one who'd attacked Bodden Town. He froze in place, and he could no longer hear the words exchanged between the farmer and Jack.

"Herbert!" Christina called. "Herbert, are you well?" she said as she knelt down and gripped his arm. Tala barked excitedly, mimicking her master's concern.

Herbert shook his head. "I'm here, I'm here," he replied.

"I can't believe it… Calico Jack was the one to attack. Why?"

Herbert was still reeling from the mention of that name. It took him a moment to answer his sister's question. "We killed one of his subordinates. Of course he would want vengeance. The real question is… where is he right now?"

Herbert could feel a great surge of anger welling up inside him. He too desired vengeance. Vengeance for what Jack Rackham put him through. Edward had promised to help him in his quest, but now he was stuck in the Boddens' mansion. The more time they wasted here, the farther Rackham got away from them.

The sound of gunshots rang out from up the hill of the town. Several sharp pops caused all eyes to turn in its direction.

Herbert grabbed the spyglass that Christina still held and looked through it. He could see the crowd at the mansion had placed a ladder in front of the stone wall, and someone was climbing up it. On the balcony of the second floor, one of their crewmates was re-loading a musket as Edward stepped out. He had a concerned look on his face as he questioned the mate, his massive beard moving as he talked.

One of the rioters climbed the ladder, and the mate shot at him, but missed on purpose from what it looked like. The rioter ducked down, but after another moment he resumed his climb. When he reached the peak of the wall and stood atop it, Edward shot a pistol at him, hitting him in the leg. The man fell inside the mansion grounds before the sound even reached the ship.

Edward jumped down and out of sight, but soon reappeared in front of the gate with the injured man held by the scruff of his neck. After some words from Edward, and a long pause, the crowd dispersed. Twenty or so of the townspeople remained, and the worst of it seemed to be over, but the twenty weren't allowing Edward to leave.

Jack and several other crewmates had also been watching the event as it unfolded. Afterwards, he turned back to the townsfolk at their ship. "It seems as though we no longer have an issue. Most of your neighbours have gone home," he said with a smile.

The farmer looked confused. "What?" he said. He looked at those gathered, then towards town, and at Jack. From their position on the dock, they weren't able to see the Boddens' house. After another moment of internal debate, the lead farmer stormed off in a huff with everyone else following soon after.

"Well, it seems as though the captain managed to calm most of the people down," Jack said to the crew.

"So now we storm the rest of 'em, right?" a crewmate asked.

Jack laughed. "No, no, that won't be necessary, unless the captain wants us to. We need to speak with him first and see what he wants us to do. Although I doubt the townsfolk will let us get close. Someone needs to sneak inside the Boddens' to talk with him. Any volunteers?"

Immediately, a lone crewman spoke up. "I will."

Jack nodded. "Victor, thank you for volunteering. Anyone wish to help Victor?"

"That's not—" Victor began before being interrupted.

"I will go," Alexandre said, placing a hand on Victor's shoulder.

Jack raised his brow. "Truly? Well, I suppose you can see if there are any injured. Thank you, Alexandre."

"*Pas de problème*. We will watch how they patrol and sneak in later in the *nuit*."

Jack nodded before fielding a flurry of questions and objections from the crew on what they should do next.

"We should leave," Christina said.

Herbert cocked his brow. "What?"

Christina began whispering. "Think about it, Herbert. These people were just attacked. Wherever Calico Jack went, he can't have gotten far. We can catch up to him if we hurry."

Herbert paused for a moment. It was as if his own thoughts and desires had been spoken aloud. He badly wanted to chase after Calico Jack, but his concern for Edward overpowered it, even if only just.

"We can't, the captain needs us."

Christina glanced at the Boddens' house. "He's going to be fine. Most of the crowd has left. He just needs to convince those left over to stand down. Besides, we'll just be the advance party. Once Edward's out he can ride on the *Fortune* to join us."

Herbert scratched his chin. His sister made a good point. Splitting up might be the better option if they wanted to find Calico Jack quickly.

"The crew would never accept it," Herbert said.

"They would, if we convinced them," Christina replied. "They trust me. I can tell them how it's a good idea, making it seem as if it's what we should be doing, and soon enough everyone will be saying it. Then, by tomorrow, all you have to do is say a few words and they'll follow."

Herbert looked at the sole of the deck. "I don't know."

Christina pulled his neck up. "This is our best course. You want revenge, don't you?" she asked.

"Yes, of course I do."

"If we don't move soon, we won't catch up to Calico Jack, we won't have the upper hand, and you won't have your revenge."

Hebert had no rebuttal. He was caught between an uncontrollable urge to do as his sister suggested, and staying to ensure his captain—his *friend*—was safe. He sat there in silence for a moment as his sister's gaze bore into him.

"Very well, you don't have to decide. The crew can decide."

"What?"

"We'll put it to a vote tomorrow, after Alexandre and Victor return with Edward's orders. If he doesn't order us to attack, then we'll propose a vote on whether to stay or leave."

"But how? The captain is the one who has the final say."

Christina sprouted a devilish grin. "Only in battle, and only if he's here. The quartermaster is next in line—that's you. The crew voted you into the position after John passed, and you gained all the privileges that comes with the rank. You are the authority now."

Herbert peered at his sister with newfound respect and terror. He knew she was intelligent, but he didn't know when she'd become so devious.

"Mr Christian," Christina called in a sweet voice.

The crew seemed to have calmed down, and that allowed Jack to see them. "Yes, what is it, my dear?"

"I was just thinking that it might do us well if we raised the anchor. We may need to depart rather quickly," she said with a smile.

"You may be right. Good thinking," Jack replied. He issued an order to raise the anchor, and several crewmates hopped to complete the hours-long task. Jack glanced at the brother and sister with concern written on his face. "How are you two holding up? Trust me, I know how I would be feeling if…" Jack paused a moment and took a breath. "If the man I wanted revenge on was just here."

"I am well," Herbert replied. "I just want this business concluded so we may move on and catch Rackham before he does any more harm."

Jack nodded as he scrutinized Herbert. He appeared unconvinced. He was about to say something else, but a voice from the pier stopped him.

"Oi, is everything well over here?"

Herbert looked over the railing as Christina and Jack turned around to see who was hailing them. Hank Abbot, Bartholomew Roberts' first mate, was at the pier with a few armed crewmates.

"We are well, thank you Hank. Come, Christina, help me with the gangplank."

"Tala, *rester*," Christina commanded, causing her wolf to sit patiently beside Herbert.

Christina and Jack went to the weather deck, and, with the help of some other crewmates, they restored the wood and rope gangplank so that Hank and the crew of the *Fortune* could board.

As they worked, Herbert watched them and petted the reddish fur of the wolf. "What do you think I should do, girl?" he asked the wolf. Tala looked at him when he spoke, but soon went back to watching her mistress, providing Herbert no insight on his dilemma.

Hank boarded and shook Jack's hand, and then he, Jack, and Christina walked up to the quarterdeck. Hank, a shorter but well-built man, looked distraught despite the brave front he seemed to be trying to maintain.

"It seems that we have a slight problem on our hands," Hank said.

"Indeed," Jack replied.

"At least most of them have backed down," Herbert added.

Hank nodded. "Yes, that is fortunate. It looked as if you were planning on heading up to the mansion with your forces until the townsfolk showed up. What will you be doing now?"

"We thought it best to wait, as the immediate threat is over." Jack motioned to the crewmates pulling on the rope of the anchor. "We've decided to raise anchor in case we need to make a quick getaway. Perhaps you should as well."

"Wouldn't want our trousers stuck around our ankles, now would we?" Hank said with a laugh.

"Most certainly not."

Hank told one of his crewmates to go back to the ship and get the others working on the anchor. "Did the townsfolk let slip anything on our captains or any more information on the attack?"

"All we were able to find out was that it was Calico Jack who attacked the town, and they were here for Edward."

Hank unfolded his arms in shock, and several of his mates' jaws dropped. "Now, you wouldn't be tellin' me you had a run-in with this Calico Jack before, would you?" he asked, his face reddening and on the verge of sweat.

"We killed one of his men…" Jack glanced Herbert's way, and Herbert nodded to the silent question. "Our quartermaster here also has some business with Calico Jack."

Hank eyed Herbert, but then focussed on Jack. "He's a dangerous man. Does Roberts know about your involvement with him?"

"I'm sure he does now," Christina replied with a chuckle.

"This won't sour our relationship, will it?" Jack asked.

"No, we have nothing to do with the man, but everyone's heard the stories of Mad Jack Rackham. I reckon any one of us would steer clear of him if we had the choice."

"We don't have a choice, not with him," Herbert said.

Hank stared at Herbert, and nodded after a moment. Hank was afraid, and he had every right to be. If the stories were true, Calico Jack was the truest of villains, and not someone to be trifled with.

"We need to find out where he went."

All eyes were on Herbert after his statement. Hank had a look of concern, but Jack appeared resolved, and Christina smiled. Even Tala seemed to sense the mood and let out an eager bark.

Hank spoke up. "My men and I can go to the local tavern and discreetly ask around. They don't know us like they do you, so we shouldn't have to worry about getting into fights."

Jack chuckled and looked at the broken town. "You think there's still a tavern left?"

Hank joined in the laugh. "With the state the town is in, there's somewhere selling ale, I guarantee it."

"Stay safe Hank, and get some sleep, yea?"

"You as well, friends. I have a feeling we won't have much over the next while."

Hank and the crewmates of the *Fortune* left the ship and walked towards town to gather information. Through all the excitement, Herbert only just now noticed that the sun had descended fully below the horizon. The town was dark, and the cold of the sea wind came in full force.

In an instant, Herbert's upper body was shivering. He looked down at his legs and placed a hand on the thin, frail thing that was half his body. He could feel through his hand that his legs were freezing. The feeling in his legs had been stolen from him by a pirate who probably didn't care. Though the feeling would never return, he wanted revenge regardless.

Herbert told himself that it wasn't just for him. He told himself that he was going to get revenge for everyone else... but he didn't feel grief, or sadness, or any shred of empathy for those who'd lost something because of Calico Jack. He felt only anger. A single-minded, self-serving anger which consumed him the more he thought on it. If he hadn't have heard that name, he could have gone through another day not even thinking on the fateful day when his ability to walk was stolen from him, but that was all it took. Two words, and a flood of memories gripped him and wouldn't let go.

"Herbert, are you well?" Christina asked.

Herbert looked up at his sister's face. Her sweet, caring face that he knew and loved was now grown, and slightly weathered from hard work aboard the ship. He hoped that she would never feel the cold that he felt deep inside, but he feared that it was already too late. She, too, had lost something that had crippled her, but she had been able to build herself back up again. She still carried the weight. He could see it in her face, and in a memento from the past: a carved wooden rose hanging from her neck. He wondered if she was as fragile as he, and if, like him, two words could take her legs from her as well. Whatever the case, he resolved to protect her from that ever happening.

Herbert smiled. "I am well," he said. "Let's leave, shall we?"

Herbert hoped that his words were not lost on Christina, and from the look on her face it didn't seem like they were. She smiled, and the two of them went to the crew cabin to eat, sleep, and wait for word to get back from Alexandre.

"Herbert, wake up," Christina's voice called.

Herbert opened his eyes, blinking to help him focus. It was pitch black inside the ship, as it usually was, so he had no sense of what time it was. Christina held a lantern at her side, and she was fully dressed.

Herbert pulled himself up and moved his legs so they were dangling off the side of his hammock. "What's the hour?"

"Before dawn. It's time for us to make our move. Hank informed us of the direction Calico Jack went, and I've prepped some of the crew's more influential members. Should we put it to a vote, I'm confident they will vote in our favour."

"What of Edward? What of the townsfolk?"

"They haven't awakened, but they will soon. As for our captain... Alexandre said that he's going to stay behind and try to convince the townsfolk that he's on their side." Christina picked up Herbert's clothes from his pack tied to his hammock and tossed them to him. "And," she added, taking a breath, "he's going to stay and help with the repairs."

Herbert eyed his sister. Something about the way she said it made him question her sincerity. "He is?"

"Yes, so we don't have to worry if we leave anyway. Edward will stay as a sign of goodwill, and we can pursue Calico Jack. Then, once they're ready, the *Fortune* can catch up with us. If need be we can leave letters at each port to inform them of where we've gone."

Herbert nodded. He wanted to believe his sister, and that desire made him convince himself that what she said was true.

He moved from his hammock to his wheelchair with a plop, and after he adjusted himself for comfort he wheeled over to the ladder leading up.

Along the way he noticed Tala sleeping on the sole of the deck. She looked at the two of them as they made their way to the ladder, but went back to sleep a moment later. Their dealings didn't excite her at this hour. Herbert felt the complete opposite. He could feel the blood rushing through him, invigorating him in the moment.

At the foot of the ladder there was a rope specifically for him to climb, and he used it to go to the gun deck while his sister carried his wheelchair up for him. They did the same for the next ladder, and then they were on the weather deck.

It was still dark out, but the fringe rays of the sun peeking from beyond the horizon added some light to their surroundings. Christina placed her lantern on a notch above the main mast's fife rail. The wind swirling around the ship caused the lantern to sway and creak.

"Which way did Calico Jack go?" Herbert asked.

"South, south west. Possibly to Panama."

Herbert scanned the skies, shifting in his seat and looking out to sea as far as he could. "The wind is in our favour, and the sky is clear."

"All the more reason to leave now."

Herbert noticed that there were quite a few crewmates on deck, more than usual at this hour. They glanced at Herbert and Christina as they talked to each other, clearly waiting for something. Herbert could also tell that the sails were prepared and ready to be released and secured at a moment's notice.

"Someone bring Jack here," Herbert commanded.

One of the crewmates said they would, and descended to the crew cabin to wake Jack up. During that time, Herbert and Christina went up to the quarterdeck. Herbert used a platform attached to a pulley created by Nassir to raise himself up to the helms level rather than having to crawl up the steps. Once there, they waited for Jack to come up.

After a few minutes, Jack appeared on the weather deck. When he noticed the multitude of crewmates already there, he looked confused for a moment. He saw Herbert and Christina and went to join them on the quarterdeck.

"Herbert, has something happened at the mansion? Why is the crew gathered?"

"They are gathered because I... they feel we should be pursuing Calico Jack instead of waiting around."

Jack chuckled, believing it to be in jest, but his smile faded as he glanced at Herbert and his sister. "You're being true with me?" Herbert gave a slight nod, but kept his face expressionless to ensure Jack didn't think this driven by emotion. "Our captain is in danger right now, and you want to leave? He gave orders to stand by in case we're needed." Jack looked to be straining to keep his voice low.

"The captain can handle himself, and if anything goes wrong then the *Fortune* can help. We know where Calico Jack went, as does Hank, so the captain can join us when he's ready by travelling with them. In the event that we pick up the trail and have to leave another port, we can leave letters for them so they know where we've gone," Christina's words echoed from Herbert's mouth.

Jack's jaw was open and he was speechless. He uttered a few single laughs, then shook his head and covered his mouth with his hand. "This is madness," he said. "Not that it amounts to much, since no one here has the authority to make such a decision."

"The crew does," Herbert replied. "Article one of the Commandments, which I shall remind you were created by Edward and Roberts, states that each crewman may vote on current affairs. I would wager that this is considered a current affair, would you not, sir?" Herbert, though sitting, did his best to cast his gaze down upon Jack. "Or shall we put that to a vote as well?"

"Those Commandments were meant for outside of battle," Jack retorted.

Herbert glanced around, then raised his brow. "I don't see a battle happening currently… do you?"

Jack simply stared at Herbert for a moment, still speechless, but this time his good humour was spent. He closed his eyes after a moment, let out a sigh, and knelt down. "Herbert, trust me when I say I know how you're feeling, but this isn't going to help things. It is best if we wait for the captain to be done with his business, and then we leave these shores together. Don't let your anger cloud your mind."

"Tell me then, Jack, if you have such intimate knowledge of how I feel, what would you do in this situation?"

Jack paused for a moment, then his gaze hit the deck. "That should have no—"

"As I recall, there was once a time when you pulled a musket on the man on whom you want revenge," Herbert said.

"I was—"

"You were endangering the crew, because at the time we were surrounded by enemies, and you were provoking them. And then, after that incident, you did what?" Herbert said, his words harsh and biting. "You drowned yourself in bottle after bottle for a year, trying to swallow your sorrows in drink." Jack had no more words, and despite the mournful look on him, Herbert pressed on. "I have looked upon this situation from all angles, and weighed the options. This is the best course of action, and it doesn't affect Edward's situation in the least. Perhaps it is your mind that is clouded."

Herbert wheeled himself forward to the quarterdeck railing, leaving Jack there, still knelt down. After a few seconds, he heard Jack pick himself up off the sole and leave to go below deck. If he was not so caught up in the moment, he might have felt remorse for what he had said to Jack, but he was numb to pity right now.

"Men, right now we have an opportunity to catch the bastard that destroyed Bodden Town. This ship was renamed in the spirit of vengeance upon our enemies, and if we wait any longer we risk losing out on vengeance for you, and for the people of this town," Herbert shouted. "All those in favour of setting sail and finding Calico Jack to put him to death, say aye!"

The crew responded with a resounding "Aye" which echoed from the ship out onto the great wide sea behind Herbert. They looked at Herbert with more respect than they ever had in the past.

"Hop to it, then. I want this ship moving immediately," Herbert commanded.

"You heard the man," Christina added. "Clear the mooring lines, shove us off, and jump those halyards!" she shouted.

The crew shouted another "aye" and went to work. The men ran this way and that, removing the ship's ropes from the pier, pushing it away from the dock with spars, and unfurling the sails.

Christina looked over to Herbert and smiled at him. He smiled back to her, excited at the prospect of finally getting his revenge.

As the *Queen Anne's Revenge* turned itself around with the wind, Herbert thought he might have heard the sound of gunshots in Bodden Town. With all the noise of the crew and the wind beating the sails, however, he couldn't be sure, and so he paid it no heed.

7. BODDEN TOWN'S END

Edward's ship diminished in size as it got farther and farther away from Bodden Town's port, heading south-southeast to God-knows-where. The *Fortune*, on the other hand, stayed where it was, moored to the pier.

The sounds of angered screams told Edward to focus on the immediate issue at hand. The townsfolk believed that he was the one who'd shot the muskets and became enraged by the death of more of their people. They had been incensed the other day, but mostly tired and desiring an end to the bloodshed. Now, against an enemy they knew they could defeat, and with fresh wounds, they were rioting outside the gates.

Edward ran out of the room and jumped over the second-floor railing to the main hall. He landed on the hard wooden floor and rolled before jumping to his feet. Just as he expected, he noticed two of the Boddens' men heading towards the secret basement entrance beneath the stairs to the second floor.

Edward drew his cutlass, and the golden blade sang. The two men heard the beautiful tone, and their heads flashed to the side, their eyes wide with fear. Edward took two steps forward, reared back, and threw his blade at the man closest to the basement entrance. The first man was able to jump through the door, but the second man moved into the path. The sword hit him through the chest with such force that it knocked him against the wall and pinned him there.

Edward flew over to the corpse and yanked his sword from it. The other man was running down the winding staircase, his footsteps echoing through the corridor. Edward pursued the man down the steps, jumping down two at a time like the lion that he was. He would have his prey; it was only a matter of time.

He caught up at the bottom of the steps where he leapt at the man with his cutlass poised overhead. He swung it down with both hands at the man's skull, and nearly cleaved him in two with the blow. Blood splattered across Edward's face and clothes, dyeing his hair and beard reddish-black as it dripped from one strand to the next.

The anger of the townspeople was as a child's tantrum compared to Edward's fury. He'd trusted the Boddens, and they had betrayed him. They didn't even have the decency to do the work themselves, and used one of their men to do it for them. Whatever reason they betrayed him for—money, power, or their own version of revenge—they would not live to see it to fruition. Edward would make sure of that.

He went down a hallway into a small square room with man-made cover of stacked wood and sandbags. At the back of the room was an iron vault, the door of which was halfway opened. He peeked around the corner to check for traps, but the vault was empty.

He had first seen the vault when he'd fought the Boddens for control of the town, and when he entered it again he saw a familiar scene. There were lanterns on the walls, loaded cannons on wheels, and stacks of cannonballs and many barrels of gunpowder in the vault, but there was something new: A door leading out the back.

There is an escape route. Those bastards will pay for this!

Edward dashed forward, but stopped after a few steps. The door leading out was open a bit, and he could hear voices from behind it.

"Light it, quickly!"

It was one of the brothers, and they were just on the other side of the door.

An idea struck Edward. He pulled one of the cannons in front of the door, and lit a linstock in one of the lanterns, then opened the door.

Standing there in a long, dark hallway which seemed to go

back for miles, were the Bodden brothers, Neil and Malcolm. One of them was doing something on the floor, but Edward's wasn't able to see what it was.

Edward didn't say a word; he allowed the brothers to realise for themselves their fate. After a few seconds they turned around to see the cannon facing them. Edward waited just long enough to see the fear and shock in their faces before he lowered the linstock into the cannon.

The cannonball exploded from the cannon towards the brothers. The angle wasn't quite as straight as Edward would have wanted, and it caused the cannonball to strike only one of the brothers in the chest. The power of the blow knocked the brother back as it crushed in his ribs and killed him instantly. The ball then missed the other brother and flew off down the corridor.

The second brother had covered his face and ducked down during the blast. He glanced around in his crouched position when it was over. When he noticed the dead body of his brother beside him, he called out to him, tears streaming down his cheeks.

Edward stalked forward, ready to finish the job, until he noticed what the Boddens had been doing before he interrupted. There was a large set of gunpowder kegs with fuses bunched together, and the fuse was lit.

Edward jumped backwards, slammed the door shut, rolled to the side, and covered his head with his hands. A few seconds passed before the gunpowder ignited and exploded. The door blasted off its hinges and into oblivion, and sent chips of wood flying everywhere. The explosion shook the entire home, as far as he could tell, and it didn't end immediately. The shaking and rumbling noise lingered for a few moments past what Edward would have thought was normal.

When the shaking subsided, Edward removed his hands from his head and examined his surroundings. Dirt swirled and flowed into the vault from the Boddens' escape route. He stepped over to the opening, and looked at the hallway. He waved his hand to try to disperse the fragments of earth in the air, and after a few seconds it settled and he was able to see the corridor.

The corridor was no longer a corridor; the earth above and below had been blasted away, causing a cave-in. Mounds of dirt and rock blocked the escape route, and Edward could not see how far the rubble extended. On the ground and the sides of the walls he noticed great splashes of blood, and the remains of unrecognizable body parts. The corridor had become the final resting place of the Bodden brothers, and the end of their era.

Footsteps came from behind Edward and several people entered the vault. He turned around to see Anne, Roberts, Nassir, and Pukuh there. Anne had a sword drawn, and she raced to his side and clutched his arm.

"Edward, are you unharmed? What happened?"

Edward took a few quick breaths. "I'm well. I caught the Boddens as they were making their escape. They had planned to explode this tunnel, and they succeeded, but not before I stalled them enough to have them caught in the explosion as well."

"You are certain they are dead?" Roberts asked.

Edward nodded. "I am certain. Their blood stains the walls of this place now, and this will be their grave."

"Now we have no escape, and the people are soon to breach the walls. Will we fight?" Pukuh asked, holding his spear at his side.

"We will never win if we fight. They have the numbers, while we have an injured man to worry about, and we have no way to signal our..." Edward paused for a second, looking away. He shook his head and looked at Roberts. "Your crew," he finished. "We have no way to signal your crew to help us."

"Then what will we do if we cannot fight?" Nassir asked, concern written on his face.

Edward glanced around the room, thinking on their options. "I only see one way out of this, and it will be dangerous."

"I doubt there is an option that wouldn't be," Anne said.

"Point taken," Edward replied. "Anne, I want you to take some of the men to remove the furniture from the back door. Nassir, you and another mate bring William down to the main floor and be ready to leave." Anne and Nassir nodded and ran out of the vault together. "Roberts, help me remove this cannon from its mount."

Edward and Roberts went on either end of the six-pounder and gripped it as best they could. "One, two, three," Edward said.

He and Roberts lifted the cannon off the mount. The cannon was easily over three hundred pounds, but the two were able to manage. They gently dropped the cannon to the floor, and it rolled off to the side of the room.

"Now we need to take the mount upstairs. While Roberts and I handle this, Pukuh, I need you to take some of these gunpowder barrels upstairs as well. Make sure to bring some of the fuse wire as well."

Roberts laughed deep from his gut. "Edward, you can bring some barrels yourself. This is nothing for me," Roberts said as he slapped Edward on the shoulder.

Roberts, a giant even by Edward's standards, bent down and grabbed hold of the cannon's mount. He then lifted with his legs, and brought the wooden apparatus over his shoulder and above his head in a monstrous feat of strength.

Edward gazed in wonder at the teetering mass of wood which must have weighed over one hundred pounds, possibly even two. "Are you sure you're fit to carry that?"

"It's just a tad awkward, is all, but I will manage. I once had to carry Hank through the jungle for three days as we were chased by—" Roberts paused mid-sentence, his mouth open, but he closed it and waved his hand. "Perhaps this is a story for another time," Roberts said before he slowly moved from the vault to the other part of the basement.

Edward shook his head at the sight, and at Roberts' carefree attitude despite all that had happened. He didn't know how Roberts managed to keep so positive in the face of imminent death. *Perhaps some of it comes from his Welsh accent. It nearly sounds as if he'll start singing with each sentence.*

Edward helped Pukuh place one of the gunpowder barrels over his shoulder, and then took one for himself after storing some fuses in his trouser pocket. They left the vault and walked up to the main floor while staying mindful of their cargo. Once on the main floor, they placed the barrels near the door leading outside.

Edward could hear the townsfolk outside, still rioting and presumably acquiring the tools to scale the wall. They were lucky that it seemed none had the foresight to bring any equipment back in the morning. *If it hadn't been for those fools the Boddens, I could have convinced them to lay down their arms.*

Edward rushed back towards the basement. "Come, we need at least two more," he said.

Edward and Pukuh went back down the spiral staircase. They met with Roberts halfway down, still carrying the cannon mount. They were cautious as they bent down and walked underneath the wood and metal device.

Once it was safe, they rushed to procure another barrel of gunpowder each. By the time they were back upstairs, Roberts was in the main hall, bending down to drop the mount.

Nassir and another crewmate were also there, with William strapped into a stretcher between them. "What do you want us to do, Edward?"

"Stay here, we're going to leave soon. Be ready to move."

Nassir nodded, his strong arms taut and ready for work. He would have no trouble carrying his end of the stretcher.

Edward set his barrel down and helped Roberts drop the mount. Once it stood on solid ground, he glanced from it to the door leading outside. *It looks to be just the right size. Perfect.*

"So, what now?" Roberts asked as he caught his breath and rubbed his arms.

"Now we tie the gunpowder on the cannon mount, and move it to the front gate," he said before picking up one of the barrels again.

"You don't mean to…?" Roberts asked, looking at Edward with a stern expression.

Edward placed his barrel on top of the mount and held it there for a moment. "It's just a distraction. There should be enough time for the townsfolk to run away, and then we'll escape out the back and into the woods."

Roberts nodded at Edward's explanation and helped the other two place the other three barrels onto the cannon mount. They used rope from a nearby storage closet to tie everything down, and Edward placed fuses in each of the barrels. He took the fuses and tied them together beneath the centre of the mount so it was dangling on the ground.

After they finished, Anne and one of Edward's mates returned. They were sweating and breathing heavily.

"The back door is clear, Edward," Anne said. She looked between the three men at what no doubt looked like an odd contraption. "What is that?"

"It's what's going to get us out of here," Edward replied.

"Well, whatever you have planned, it must be done soon. They are about to clear the walls."

Edward walked over to the front door of the Bodden mansion and grabbed two lanterns. He turned one off and emptied the oil all over the mount. "Now, when I open the door, you must push that out as hard as you can. It needs to reach the gates."

Roberts nodded, and positioned himself behind their powder kegs on wheels. Edward placed his hand on the doorknob. Roberts bent his knees and put his shoulder on the mount.

"One, two… three!" Edward shouted as he opened the door.

Roberts pushed the cart forward with all his strength. The hundred-and-some pound bomb stood no match against the seven-foot-tall bear of a man. As he and the cart approached the door opening, he picked up speed. When he reached the opening the cart jumped over the threshold and bounced down to the stone walkway below. At the last second, he gave the cart one last shove with his shoulder. The cart tumbled down the walkway and smashed into the iron gate with a loud clang.

Edward took the burning lantern in one hand, reared back, and threw it as he had his sword not ten minutes ago. The lantern arched through the air, the tiny flame protected by glass. It landed just beneath the cart, and the glass shattered on impact. The oil spilled out from the lantern, and the tiny flame ignited it into a fair-sized blaze. The oiled wood of the cart attracted the fire, and before long it enveloped the mount.

The townsfolk saw the mount and the kegs and the flames and feared what would happen next. They ran away from the gate and the mansion, some trampling over each other to get farther away.

Edward waited until he saw the fuse ignite, and then closed the door. "Run!" he shouted.

His men, and his wife, ran through the Boddens' mansion to the back. Nassir and the other crewman carrying William did their best to keep up.

When they reached the back of the mansion, the thunderous roar of an explosion shook the walls. Screams, louder than before, filtered through from the outside.

Edward and the others left the mansion and continued their mad dash to escape. He kicked the back door open and held it for the rest of his friends. They ran through as quick as their tired legs would carry them. After Nassir and his helper were through with William, he rejoined them in their flight.

In front of them was a long stretch of cleared field, then grass followed by waist-high bushes, and only then did the forest start. Two hundred metres separated them from freedom, and it was the farthest two hundred metres Edward had ever had to travel in his life.

When he reached the grass, his legs were already burning. Halfway through the grass he was breathing heavily and his lungs were calling for more air than he could manage at such a pace. As they approached the waist-high bushes and shrubs, his body was pushing against him, telling him to stop. He couldn't help but slow down and look behind him, and when he did he noticed townspeople pointing in their direction.

"They've spotted us," he yelled between deep breaths.

Edward's group entered the woods and continued advancing as best they could amidst the branches, bushes, and roots. The dew of the morning wasn't helping either, adding slickness over the roots.

Nassir's foot caught on a spindly root, and he stumbled, nearly dropping William, but he held his grip firm. Edward helped Nassir up and they kept pressing onward, every so often glancing backwards. William, though still sleeping, didn't look well, and the travel was not helping.

Sweat beaded on Edward's forehead and cheeks. It slid down into his brows and beard, mixing with the blood and keeping it wet in his hair. He could feel the clingy moisture all over him, making his body heavy and his tongue thirst for water.

Edward could hear the townspeople behind them in the forest, but he couldn't see them when he glanced back, which was good. It meant they were also hidden.

Anne was leading the charge, taking them in a random route to best hide them. Edward could tell she was favouring the west to keep them in the woods yet still not far from Bodden Town. She was thinking ahead to when they would need to return to the *Fortune* once free of their pursuers.

William hindered their escape, and, if their angered shouts were any indication, the townspeople were catching up.

After they had been running for over an hour, there was a small rise of a hill which sloped to the south. Anne took them up it and travelled near the edge to give them a vantage point over their pursuers. When they reached the peak, Anne called a halt.

She motioned for everyone to kneel down, and she creeped over to the edge of the cliff. She went down on her stomach and crawled forward to get as close as she could.

Edward joined her cliffside. "What is it?" he whispered.

Anne pointed down to the forest below them, and Edward noticed some of the townspeople, this time with guns in hand. He recognised them as former militia-men. They were searching the area below. Now that Edward wasn't running, he was able to hear.

One of the men came upon the cliff, and let out a sigh. "Dammit all, we've been at this for hours and they keep getting away from us."

"It hasn't been hours," another replied. "They're around here somewhere, and they're bound to be tired. We'll catch them soon, you'll see."

"That's what you said twenty minutes ago."

The two men bickered for a moment until someone else came running through the trees to them. The two pointed their weapons at the newcomer until they noticed it was another townsperson.

"Need you... back in town..." the man sputtered through ragged breaths.

"We can't leave now, we've almost caught that bastard Blackbeard," the first man said. When his friend gave him a look he shrugged his shoulders.

The third man choked down air. "We need everyone back... some of the houses caught fire after that explosion."

"Fire?" the two men said, and then they started running back with the third.

Anne and Edward rose to their feet. "I suppose that explosion you caused was an even greater boon than we thought," Anne said.

"Yes, I suppose it is. I pray none were injured."

Edward said the words, but even as he said them he could tell he didn't feel it in his heart. He had been betrayed by the Boddens, yes, but he was also betrayed by his people. If they hadn't stormed the mansion the first time, or if they hadn't come back in the morning, this wouldn't have happened. He didn't feel any remorse for any loss of life that he caused; perhaps it was just for their betrayal.

Now that they didn't have to worry about being chased, they were able to rest and take their time heading back to shore. Edward was eager to see whether Roberts' crew knew what happened with the *Queen Anne's Revenge*. At the very least he hoped that they knew where it went.

As they walked, Edward wiped the sweat from his brow and tried to dry his hair. The trees gave them no respite from the heat, and with it came flies. There was no end to the mosquitoes attacking him, despite his furious swatting. The buggers got everywhere, and he knew that soon he would itch all over.

Anne stayed back with William and did her best to feed him water while on the move. She kept his blanket and body secure in the stretcher, and even wiped the cold sweat off him. After happening upon a natural stream, she wet a cloth and placed it on his forehead.

After they had walked for an hour, heading southeast in a roundabout way back to Bodden Town, Edward and Roberts switched with Nassir and the other crewmen in carrying William. Edward was at the back, and Roberts at the front.

"He's gotten worse," Anne said.

"He has to get worse before he'll get better," Edward replied.

Anne stared daggers at him. "Does it not concern you in the slightest when one of your crewmates is on the verge of death?"

Edward scoffed. "Don't be so dramatic, woman," he said. She clenched her fist, and looked about to strike him. "I'm sorry," he said quickly. "All I mean is that William is the strongest among us. He will make it through this. He's been through worse. Trust me, we shared a prison for almost a year."

Anne took a deep breath and unclenched her fist. "I hope you're right."

Everyone was quick to tire of walking. The flies were making a meal out of them all, and there was no end to them. The heat was oppressive, and seemed to be trapped beneath the forest's canopy. It was never this hot aboard the ship, at least not while on the weather deck. Perhaps in one of the lower decks from time to time, but Edward could escape from that. Here, he was stuck, and it was wearing on him.

Mercifully, after another hour, they were able to leave the forest. They were a mile out from Bodden Town on the lower west end, and quite near the harbour. When they reached open air, the sea breeze cooled them and renewed their spirits. Soon they would be on the *Fortune*; all they had to do was sneak into town and down to the harbour.

Edward and Roberts switched William back to Nassir and the other crewmate as they reached the edge of the forest. Upon stepping out from under the canopy, Edward's gaze first went to the harbour. He could see *Fortune* still docked, which lifted his spirits.

"Oh Father," Anne cursed.

Edward glanced at her, then followed her gaze. What he saw knocked him back a few steps as if he had been punched in the gut.

Towering flames reaching twenty or thirty feet high engulfed half of Bodden Town. The red and yellow inferno was taking over the town, and showed no signs of slowing. From Edward's small blaze, the entire town was being burned away.

Edward was stunned into silence. Despite his feelings on their betrayal, this was too much harm for retribution. The townspeople didn't deserve this. Not after they had already lost so much.

He also felt mourning over the work that he and his crew had put into the town. They had made it their own over the years, and it was all being destroyed in front of his eyes.

Roberts placed his hand on Edward's shoulder. "Come, there is nothing we can do to help them now," he said, pushing him forward.

Edward's steps became listless, and his gaze centred on the fire in the middle of town. The buildings soon covered his view, but they could hear the crackling and breaking of wood as the fire consumed the houses. It even felt hotter in town than outside, as if the heat from the blaze was able to reach them where they were.

No one was in the streets, so they were able to reach the pier in no time. In the centre of the pier, people had lined up in a human chain, passing buckets of seawater to each other in a futile effort to douse the flames. Others watched as their homes burned, either wide-eyed in shock or broken down in tears. More still were running around with their belongings in hand, boarding the only undamaged boats and ships to flee the devastation.

At the *Fortune*, a throng of people were pleading with the crew to let them aboard. Men, women, and children all tried to get aboard the ship, but the armed pirates kept them at bay. Hank was on the bow, looking at the people with sorrow clear in his eyes.

Roberts gave a loud whistle a few times to get Hank's attention. When Hank noticed and looked their way, he almost couldn't contain his excitement. He whispered orders to the crew, and twenty of them left the ship with muskets raised. Those twenty forced the begging crowd back. At the same time, men pulled in the mooring lines. Edward noticed the anchor had been raised already, so the lines were the only thing keeping the ship in dock.

As the crew pushed the citizens back, some fell off the pier and into the water. After a few minutes, they had moved back enough to allow Edward and the others to enter the pier and board. As quick as they could, Edward and his friends ran from their spot between the houses and up the pier and onto the ship. The twenty men with muskets followed them onto the ship.

After they were all aboard, the crew pulled the mooring lines in, and the ship floated away. Other crewmates tried to push the *Fortune* back with spars, but the townsfolk grabbed them and pulled on them.

Roberts motioned for Nassir to head below deck to get

William looked at by their surgeon.

Hank walked over. "Glad to have you back, Captain," he said.

"Let's save the pleasantries for later. Right now, let's get this ship moving."

Roberts' crew responded with a loud "Aye, Captain!" and got to work turning the ship around.

Some of the townsfolk jumped into the water and swam over to the ship as it was trying to leave. They clung to the sides, and tried to climb aboard. The crew pointed muskets at them to deter them, but some didn't stop. They had to throw a few families overboard, and kicked some men right off the side as they all screamed for their lives.

It took them twenty-some minutes to get the ship oriented and the sails to the wind, all the while dealing with desperate townspeople trying to board them to seek safer shores.

When it was over, Edward, Roberts, Anne, and Pukuh all flopped down on the deck, exhausted. Behind them, they could see in full the burning town they once knew as home. Somehow, distance made it appear not as bad it was, but Edward knew better. The town was gone forever. On the other hand, it had been gone well before the blaze took it. It was already gone the day Calico Jack attacked, and the day the Boddens betrayed him. They no longer had their safe haven, and now they too had to seek safer shores.

"What now?" Roberts asked.

"Now, we go after Herbert," Edward said. "I've lost my town. I will not lose my ship."

8. INFLUENCE

"All I'm asking is that you set aside some of your men to work during the night," Edward said. "I'll join them as well. I'm not asking them to do something for me that I wouldn't do for them."

"I am sorry, Edward. I will not have my crew run ragged to increase our speed by a whisker or two," Roberts replied.

Edward and Roberts were sitting in his cabin on opposite ends of a table. Roberts was drinking tea, holding the cup in his hands to stop it from spilling with the waves. The ship rocked up and down with the small ocean swells. Edward held his cup as well, but he was not yet interested in partaking of his host's hospitality.

"We lost hours in Bodden Town, and if we do not do this we will lose days. Herbert will be running my crew in shifts to keep the ship at top speed, and you don't know him as I do. His madness will drive him to coax more wind out of the sails than any other."

"I understand your desire, Edward, and I know what will happen, but this is all that we can do. We have a small crew, unlike yours. We can afford a few crewmates to watch the sails and warn of impending storms, but that is all."

"It doesn't have to be many more than that. I can—"

Roberts held up his hand, and Edward stopped his plea. "Let us move on to other business," he said. The look in Roberts' eyes told Edward to not say another word. He was slow to anger, but Edward could tell that he had pushed past what was acceptable. "I am not one to be troubled over such things, but the crew has a right to know what you will do about their lost money. We, too, had invested in the town, and that was lost when you burned it to the ground."

"I will repay you all in full at a later date. There is some money aboard the *Revenge*, and we have yet to sell the plunder from our previous exploit. You may have all the profit from it instead of the half we agreed upon. That should put a dent in what we owe you."

Roberts nodded. "Aye, that it would. What say we call that even? I know the crew would not blame you for what happened, so I'm sure they will accept that as payment."

Edward leaned forward and finally sipped on his tea. "Thank you, Roberts. You are a true friend."

Roberts laughed. "You honour me. Truthfully, you have also done much for us. We are only returning the favour."

Edward shook his head. "No, it is more than that. You honor yourself by your actions. You could have left at any time, heading off to complete your revenge, but you didn't."

"Justice, Edward. Heading off for justice," Roberts said, lifting his cup.

"Yes, justice," Edward replied, lifting his cup as well.

Roberts took another sip of his tea, and then set it on the table with one hand holding the side. "I have to say, you have shit for luck."

Edward chuckled. "Perhaps," he said.

He glanced off to the bright interior of Roberts' quarter-deck cabin. The large windows and lanterns provided much light in the generous space. He could see the sea from the stern, churning and swirling in their wake.

"I cannot fathom what Herbert was thinking, nor how he convinced the crew to join him."

Roberts smirked. "He may have a bit of that Edward Thatch magic in him. A stirring speech and off they went," he said with the wave of his hand. "Something like that, perhaps?"

"Perhaps. I can't help but feel responsible somehow."

Roberts raised his brow. "How so?"

"I built my crew on one thought," he said, lifting his finger. "Freedom. Freedom to choose how we want to live our lives.

Freedom from oppression. As you no doubt recall, as soon as we had our freedom, I called on my men to change that focus to revenge. Herbert's always wanted revenge on Calico Jack and his men, and gone to great lengths to get it. My shift in focus could have emboldened him to do this. He knew that your crew was still ashore, and that if anything happened you could come to our aid, and then follow after them. He's gone to such lengths just to gain a few days' head start on finding Calico Jack. For revenge. And, in a way, I taught him it was a good idea."

For a moment, the two were silent. Edward hunched over in his chair, staring at the tea as it gently rocked in his cup.

" Ezekiel eighteen-twenty: *The son shall not bear the iniquity of the father, neither shall the father bear the iniquity of the son,*" Roberts recited.

Edward looked up from his cup at Roberts, pausing for a moment to consider the words. "So, we're responsible for our own actions?"

Roberts smiled. "Yes, that is the core of it."

"I'll be sure to tell him that when I sock him in the face," Edward said with a smirk.

Roberts grinned with his friend and raised his cup. Edward returned the gesture, and the two took swigs of their drink.

There was a knock at the cabin door. "Enter," Roberts said. Anne opened the door, stepped inside, and closed it behind her. Roberts rose to his feet, and Edward joined him. "Ah, join us, princess. Come, come, we were just having a bit of tea." He put his empty cup down and filled another with some fresh tea, holding it out for Anne.

"Thank you, Mr Roberts. I should quite like the refreshment."

Anne took her cup and sat down next to Edward. The men sat again, and Roberts poured himself some more of the drink.

"How is William?" Edward asked.

"Better now that he's stationary, but he is still in the grips of a fever. He was badly injured in his fight, so it will take some time for him to recover."

"What did my surgeon say? He might not be as skilled as your Frenchman, but he gets the job done."

"He said that there was nothing we could do save making him comfortable. Since then, he's been feeding William rum by wringing a soaked rag over his mouth, to dull the pain," Anne said.

Roberts grinned. "That gets the job done too," he said with a wink.

Anne held back laughter and looked away. "So, what were you gents musing about?"

"Fathers and sons, my dear," Roberts answered. "Fathers and sons."

Anne raised her brow and looked at Edward. He shifted in his seat to better see Anne. "We were discussing whether I am responsible for Hebert absconding with my ship."

"Ah," Anne murmured with a knowing look on her face as she glanced at Roberts. "Ezekiel eighteen-twenty."

"Spot on, my dear," Roberts said, pointing at her.

"Well, as much as I would enjoy having a dissenting opinion, I have to say Herbert is responsible for his own actions. He is an adult."

"That's what I said," Roberts added with a hearty laugh. "You see, Edward? Even your wife agrees with me. You should listen to her, she's a smart woman."

"That she is," Edward said.

"Not to diminish your compliment, Mr Roberts—thank you as well for that— but if I were to play Devil's advocate for a moment I would say that it's not entirely one way or the other. We cannot deny that you have enabled Herbert in many ways. He wouldn't be seeking out revenge if not for your intervention."

Edward gestured towards his wife, but peered at Roberts. "See? She can see what I am thinking."

"Of course, he is responsible for taking the ship, and should be punished for it."

"Of course," Edward repeated.

"But to deny that we are influenced by our surroundings, or the company we keep... well, that isn't right, now is it?"

"Yes, but to be influenced we must allow ourselves to be influenced. Even if that influence goes by unheeded, it is due to our looking the other way or choosing not to be bothered by it."

Anne's mouth was a line. "So, you believe that we are who we are from birth?"

"We are as God shaped us, and from there, we grow into that mould by our decisions."

Anne shook her head vehemently. "No, no. There is simply no truth to that. We certainly make choices, and I do believe that inaction is choosing not to act, but there are many things outside our control which affect our perception of the world."

"Tell me then," Roberts said.

"Tell you what? Tell you of something outside our control?" Roberts nodded. "As babes we are told certain truths by our parents, but who is to say whether they are truths? We are not in control of what our parents tell us is the truth."

"Yes, but when one grows and becomes an adult, there is no longer an excuse to be blind to the real truth of the world. Blindness is a choice as well."

Anne let out an angry sigh. "Sometimes you can be so bull-headed," she said, but her anger was only on the surface. Edward chuckled aloud, and Anne glanced his way. "You've been silent this whole time, Edward. What's on your mind?"

"Nothing," he replied. "I'm simply enjoying this bit of theatre between you two."

Anne grinned and finally took a sip of her tea. Her eyes widened. "Is there rum in this tea?"

Roberts put his finger over his smiling lips. "Shh, it's my secret brew."

Edward grinned and raised his glass to Anne before downing the last of his cup and filling it again.

Anne chuckled and she too drank of the Pirate Priest's special brew. The three of them drank well into the afternoon, discussing all manner of topics. And, for a brief time, they forgot their troubles.

Edward stared at the protruding hump of one of Roberts' crewmen's backside as it swung in the hammock above him. He couldn't sleep in this unfamiliar place, with a mostly unfamiliar crew. Even the smell was different. The smell of sweet, slight Caribbean pine on the *Queen Anne's Revenge* was gone, and in its place that of red cedar. He could tell because the scent was almost foul in the sort of way that tickled your nose, and, as he wasn't used to it, it lingered in the space around him. The only blessing was that it was so powerful in the closed-off area of the ship that he had trouble smelling the normal odours emanating from men who had been working all day.

As if to repeal Edward's thought, the man above him expelled gas right on top of him. The hammock was poor protection from the flatulence, and Edward had to cover his face. He jumped from his hammock and walked away to escape the stench.

Edward donned his coat, boots, and a cap, and decided to visit the weather deck. As he poked his head out above the boards, a gust of cold wind hit him and nearly took his cap with it. He kept one hand on his cap as he stepped onto the deck proper.

The *Fortune* was a rare three-masted sloop-of-war with a solid gun deck and a small stern quarterdeck cabin, but no bow cabin. It was lighter and faster than Edward's frigate, and even had enough cannons to be a threat to ships like his. The superior speed was the key, and meant that it could do swooping arcs to fire broadside and right itself before it was left open to attack.

Something Edward only noticed now, being on board for one of the only times where the ship was moving, was that having no forecastle made it easier for the quartermaster to see their direction. It also offered a smaller profile to the wind, which no doubt contributed to *Fortune*'s speed.

I wonder if we'd be able to beat Roberts if we rid ourselves of the forecastle and aftcastle. It could certainly help in battle to have a bit of extra speed. Perhaps I should talk to Nassir about it.

Edward glanced around the ship, and noticed several crewmates walking about, checking the rigging and keeping watch, some enjoying the night air, and some playing cards.

Speak of the Devil.

He noticed Nassir conversing with one of Roberts' crewmates at the bow. He walked over to them, and waved as he approached. Nassir and the crewmate waved back, then Roberts' man finished talking and went back to his watch.

"Couldn't sleep either, Captain?" Nassir asked as Edward joined him at the bow railing.

He shook his head. "No. I've always been a light sleeper, but put me on an unfamiliar ship and it seems I'm even worse."

Nassir grinned. "It's the smell, no?"

Edward smirked and raised his brow. "You noticed it too? Is that keeping you up as well?"

"Cedar lingers. Much too strong for my tastes."

"Exactly my thoughts."

Edward faced the bow and leaned his elbows on the railing, letting the chill air of the night sea cool his face and body. The smell of the cedar washed away, and a more pleasant aroma replaced it. He closed his eyes.

Nassir chuckled. "Better?"

Edward nodded and opened his eyes. "Much," he said. "I was just thinking about something I should discuss with you."

"Oh?"

"I notice on this ship there is no forecastle, and the aftcastle is not as large as our own. Roberts' cabin is barely tall enough for him to stand upright in," he said with a grin. "So, would we be able to remove our forecastle and perhaps lower the aftcastle to give us more speed?"

Nassir stroked his chin in thought. "I'd need to see the ship to be certain, but I don't see a reason why we couldn't."

"Good, good. That could help us out in the future. Perhaps when this business is over we can look into it."

Edward went back to staring at the sea water as it crashed against the ship. The sails were low to avoid dangerous conditions should the weather change without warning and send the ship too far off course. There was little bounce in the *Fortune* as it crashed against the water, but he could still feel the slight dampness of spray against his pant leg. He knelt down and placed his hand on the bow, and the ocean's cold water splashed against his hand.

"Was there something else keeping you up, Edward? Something on your mind?"

Edward dried his hand on his chest and stood up again. "Anne, Roberts, and I were discussing whether someone is responsible for their own actions, or if another can influence them and is also responsible. Anne took the middle way in saying it's not wholly one side or the other, as both are correct, but Roberts believes that someone's choice is ever-present, and they cannot be influenced without their choice."

Nassir raised his brow. "How did you come upon such a topic as this?"

"I feel as though, because of my enabling Herbert in his madness for revenge, I am partially to blame for him taking the ship."

Nassir pondered the situation for a moment. "When our quartermaster first joined to run the helm, was it a choice, or did you force him to come aboard?"

"It was a choice."

"And I recall hearing he wanted revenge even then, no?"

"That's correct. He wanted me to promise that we would help him with his revenge."

"Then you are not to blame. There is no question in this."

"How can you be sure?"

"He had already desired revenge before boarding your ship. You did not create that desire. It would be the difference between him asking 'do you think I should get revenge for this?' and 'I'm going to get revenge for this, will you help me?' If it was the first question, then yes, you influenced him, but it was not. It was the second question, and you agreed to help him. If you hadn't agreed, he wouldn't have boarded, and might have sought help elsewhere."

"I suppose I had not thought of it that way. Thank you, Nassir."

"You are welcome," he said. "I believe I would have to side with your beloved on the topic. Perhaps thinking of it as a ship is best. Herbert has chosen the course, and he has asked you to adjust his sails. By helping him, he will reach his destination faster, and there is no doubt of that influence as he has no control over what you do, but he decides what his destination is."

"So, our friends are the crew of each of our ships," Edward said, a slight smile on his face. "I like that."

The wind seemed to have picked up since Edward and Nassir first started their conversation. It was chillier than before, and he was not dressed for the weather as he should be if he was to be working on deck.

One of Roberts' men approached them. "Could ye help us with the sails? The wind's changed, so we need to beam reach if we want to stay on course and keep our speed."

"Come, Nassir, let's show these men how it's done," Edward said with a grin.

Nassir smiled as well. "Yes, Captain."

"So, you're sure that this is where Herbert will have gone?" Edward asked.

"If he's not gone completely mad, then yes," Hank Abbot replied. "Porto Bello, and in fact the entirety of the Spanish Main, is a popular spot for pirates to raid, from what I hear, so it makes sense that Calico Jack would frequent the area."

Edward, Hank, Anne, and Roberts were on the quarterdeck. They watched the ever-expanding mass of land stretching across the horizon. They headed towards a small inlet with natural, grassy hills, and several ships either anchored in the water or leaving the inlet.

"Why would Calico Jack head here after Bodden Town? He already raided it, so why attack another immediately afterwards? Why not head to a familiar port to sell and spend their spoils?" Anne asked.

"I'm sorry, miss, I wish I had the answer. This is just what the people in town said they overheard during the attack."

"Could it be his base of operations?" Bartholomew pondered.

"I don't believe Calico Jack or his crew would let slip where his home port was located to their enemies," Edward said as he pulled out a spyglass.

"Then that begs the question of why his men would say where they were heading either."

"You think it could be a trap?"

"Perhaps, but not for us," Bartholomew said, then he pointed at Edward. "For you."

Edward gritted his teeth as he looked through the spyglass. *Damn it! Herbert, you'd better not have gotten into trouble.*

He scanned the approaching inlet with his magnifier, searching for his ship or signs of battle. They had a full view of the inlet, and he wasn't able to see any ships the size of the *Queen Anne's Revenge*. He could see several three-masted ships, and a few had a gun deck, but they were not as long as his.

Edward let out a sigh. "Well, unless it capsized, *Revenge* isn't here," he said.

"Let's hope it's because Herbert left, and not the alternative," Anne said.

Edward smashed his fist on the quarterdeck railing. The sound of the blow placed all eyes on him. "This wouldn't have happened had we been more active during the night." He let out a sigh, then glanced over at Roberts and the rest. "Sorry, this is all a bit frustrating."

"As long as you don't break my ship I do not mind the occasional outburst," Roberts said.

"Rather than acting a fool, why not pray that Herbert left a message for us at the very least?" Anne said.

After entering the inlet, Roberts and crew manoeuvred *Fortune* into an empty side of the harbour and dropped anchor. There were other larger ships stationed around the harbour, and they didn't want to attract any unwanted attention by allowing their ship and name to be examined.

Even should they have wanted to, there was no way Roberts' ship would be able to dock, as Porto Bello's pier was only meant for small fishing ships.

The tropical Porto Bello was covered in lush green trees on its tall rolling hills above and on the sides of the small town. Edward could see mixed palms and cedars and even some trees with blooming flowers on them which he couldn't recognise. They swayed and bowed in the wind, welcoming the newcomers to their home with gleeful dances.

Less welcoming were the many cannons lining the sides of the harbour, and the watchtowers dotting the landscape. The whitewashed stone battlements were well maintained, and he could see many men keeping a watchful eye on the ships in the harbour. No doubt those cannons were ready to fire at a moment's notice.

Edward recalled that Hank said Panama was a hunting ground for pirates, and it showed in the defences Porto Bello had installed.

"Let's head ashore and see what we can find out," Edward said.

Edward, Anne, and Roberts entered a longboat with a few other crewmates, and rowed to the dock. As they rowed, several men on the ships anchored in the harbour stared at them. They had wary looks in their eyes, and seemed to be trying to size up the new arrivals.

The Voyages of Queen Anne's Revenge

Though there was plenty of noise, birds off in the distance, wind rustling the trees, people chattering, and the oars beating the water, it felt silent in the middle of all those ships. Distrust was in the air, and soured the otherwise beautiful surroundings.

Anne chose to stare straight ahead, towards their destination, while Roberts was gazing at the scenery and didn't seem to notice those staring at them. Edward chose to return the glares in kind, despite being outnumbered.

They docked the boat at the harbour, and Edward helped his wife up to the pier. Roberts jumped over, dipping part of the boat into the water as he did so.

Edward looked at the other crewmates. "We shouldn't be long, so stay alert and be ready to leave soon." The crewmates nodded and continued mooring the long boat to the pier.

Edward did a quick scan of the harbour to find the harbour officials. There was a building just before heading into town which seemed to be what he was looking for, so Edward headed there with Anne and Roberts following behind.

Edward entered the building, and noticed an older, dark-complexioned gentleman at a desk. On his desk, which spanned most of the length of the small building, there were a multitude of papers of various shapes, sizes, and discolourations. The gentleman was busy scrawling on a piece of paper with a short quill.

The man said something in a foreign language, which Edward presumed to be Spanish, seeing as how this was a territory controlled by Spain.

"I am sorry, I do not speak the language. Do you speak English?"

The man peered at Edward, nodded and asked, "How may I help you, sir?" in near-perfect English, and then he went back to writing on his paper.

"I am looking for a ship that may have been here in the past few days," Edward said.

The gentleman looked up from the paper he was writing on. "You're the second Englishman in just so many days that has been asking for the same thing. You wouldn't happen to be from a ship called *Fortune*, would you?"

Edward glanced to his fellows. "By chance, we are," he replied.

The gentleman did a double-take, then cocked his brow. "Truly?" Edward nodded. "That is interesting," he said before opening one of his cabinets and pulling out a sealed letter. "Here, this was left for you. I presume you know who it's from? They did not give any names, only the ship name *Fortune*."

"Yes, I believe I know who wrote the letter. Thank you," Edward said. He tore off the seal and walked away from the desk as he read it.

"What does it say, Edward?" Anne asked.

"It's from Herbert... We're heading to Panama City."

9. HOW TO MEASURE A MAN

A few days ago

"You lied to me," Herbert said.

Christina and Herbert were in the quarterdeck cabin, a small war room with an ornate table and lavish chairs. Light from the stern windows poured in, and, coupled with the lanterns, illuminated the room. It also made the room hot and humid, despite some of the windows being open.

Christina had a distraught look on her face, and her wolf, Tala, was looking at her with concern. "I know, and I'm sorry. I thought the only way you would leave was if you thought Edward was going to stay behind and delay things."

Herbert cast his hot gaze on his sister, but he had a hard time being angry at her. After all, he had allowed himself to be deceived by not questioning her—or anyone else, for that matter—on Edward's supposed decision. He'd wanted to leave to pursue Rackham, and any excuse would have pushed him over the edge of reason.

Herbert sighed. "I heard gunshots," he said.

Christina raised her brow before glancing out the window and then back at him. "When?"

"As we were leaving Bodden Town," he said, his eyes on the floorboards. He was looking at the pinewood, but his focus wasn't there. He was days ago, reliving a memory he'd pushed away. "I know I heard them from the quarterdeck when we were heading out. God, Edward might have perished and we would not know it." Herbert held his hand over one side of his face, pressing on his temple.

Christina knelt down next to her brother and gripped the

side of his wheelchair and his other hand. "Hey, hey, you don't know that." She said the words, but her eyes spoke to a fear even she didn't want to admit. "Edward's been through worse than that. If what happened to him with Cache-Hand didn't kill him, then it's going to take a lot more than a silly riot to do it."

Herbert recalled the incident where one of Edward's former crewmates came back for revenge, and kidnapped him and John. Edward was the only one who came back, and it wasn't the story that Edward told that spoke to his resilience. Herbert remembered a day a few months back when the men were at a bathhouse, and Edward joined in. The memory of all the bullet wounds, knife wounds, and white scars ten inches long across his body still made him cringe.

"Yes, perhaps you're right."

There was a knock on the door to the war room, and Christina stood up before calling the person in. The crewmate poked his head around the corner. "We're dropping anchor in the harbour now, Herbert."

"Thank you, we'll be out in a moment," Herbert replied.

"If he is just a few days behind us, we must keep moving forward, so when he does join us we'll be able to show him something for our actions. If we're lucky we'll find Calico Jack somewhere here in Panama and we'll take him down together," Christina said with a smile.

Herbert wore no smile, his bravado and joy of chasing after a prey lost to the ether. He knew that Edward would see it as his crew abandoning him, and could only pray that Edward would forgive him.

Herbert and Christina left the stern cabin with Tala at Christina's side. Many who were not normally on duty were talking with each other while pointing towards the town beyond the docks, Porto Bello.

Herbert scanned the ships in the harbour, seeing a few that might have been the ships that attacked Bodden Town. None matched the description of Calico Jack's ship, and none flew black flags either, so there was no telling if they were pirates or common merchants. Their one advantage would be the distinct style of Calico Jack's ship. He rode a French-style man-of-war with three gun decks, and it was nearly as big as a galleon, though not quite as long.

As we've only been under the name Queen Anne's Revenge *for a few months now, it's doubtful that Calico Jack has heard of the change. I suppose we have more than one advantage in that case.*

Herbert wheeled himself over to the edge of the railing, and looked at some of the crew talking. "You there, prepare a longboat so we may dock," he said.

"Aye, Captain," one of the men replied.

Herbert opened his mouth to object, and managed to say "I'm…" before the crewmates were gone. In that moment, he felt unworthy of the title, because not only was he not truly the captain, but he felt he was a lousy one. Even so, deep down, some part of him liked being called by that title.

"I'll go and help them," Christina said, walking to the quarterdeck ladder. "*Rester*, Tala," she commanded the wolf, and it lay down to wait at Herbert's side.

As Christina went down the ladder, Alexandre was coming up them. "Quartermaster," Alexandre called. "Or, is it captain now? It is so hard to recall names and titles aboard this ship, as they seem to change so often," he said with a grin.

Herbert frowned. "Quartermaster is my title, and you may call me Herbert. What is it you need, Alexandre?"

"Victor and I wish to go ashore. Victor knows some from the area, and they may be able to *aider* us, if the harbour watch cannot."

Herbert nodded. "I wasn't aware Victor was from here. He doesn't seem to have the complexion."

Alexandre grinned and shook his finger as if speaking to a child. "*Non*, I did not say he is from here, I said he knows some from the area."

"True, I misheard you," Herbert said. "I apologise."

"You would do well to listen carefully, *mon ami*. People always tell more than they wish to. You need but to listen." Alexandre pointed to his ear before he made his way down the quarterdeck to where Victor was waiting.

Why did he say that? Herbert tried to make sense of what the French surgeon was trying to say as he scratched Tala's ears, but eventually he ceased and shook his head. *No wonder the crew dislikes him so.*

Christina walked back up to the quarterdeck. "Shall we go?"

Herbert nodded, hopped off of his wheelchair, and crawled to the longboat. Christina picked up the wooden chair and carried it down. With the help of a few other mates, they managed to get the chair aboard the longboat without issue. With the cargo secure, Christina, Alexandre, Victor, and a few others boarded, and then the crew lowered the longboat into the water.

Tala jumped up, placing her front paws on the railing near the boat. "*Rester*, Tala," Christina said once again, producing a whine from the red wolf.

The longboat fell into the water with a small splash, and bobbed up and down with the movement of the waves as it settled. After the bouncing subsided, the crew placed oars into the water and paddled towards shore.

As they passed by the multitude of ships anchored in the harbour, Herbert felt as though he was being watched. He looked at the ships they were passing, and could see the sailors casually glancing their way or even outright staring at them. Having such a large ship was a threat, even if they weren't here to fight. The sailors were no doubt studying them to measure their mettle in the off chance there was a battle.

Herbert decided to pay them no heed, and instead focussed on the task at hand. He scanned the dock and found a building which could be where the port authorities were stationed. He glanced over to see Christina staring at the various ships and men looking back at them.

"Christina!" he called in a harsh whisper.

Christina looked his way with one brow cocked. "What?"

"Don't antagonize them. We can't get into a fight here, not

with all these guns on us."

Christina sighed and turned her attention to the water at the side of the boat. She dipped her hand into the water and made lazy circles on the surface.

They moored the boat to the pier before departing from the vessel. The boat was close enough to the pier that Herbert could climb over, and then the crew helped him with his wheelchair.

Once he was sitting in his mobile seat, he told the men to come in close. They formed a wall of people around Herbert to contain the sound from their voices. "The air around here feels off. It's almost as if the ships in the harbour are expecting a fight," he said.

"Do you think they're Calico Jack's people?" Christina asked.

"It's hard to say, but I don't want to take any chances. We'll get the information we need and leave immediately. Christina and I will talk with the port authorities and see if they're aware of any ships matching Calico Jack's, and you two," Herbert said, pointing at Alexandre and Victor, "find out what you can from your friend and then head back to the ship. If you aren't back by the time we've raised anchor, head northeast to shore. I noticed some small islands off the coast which could hide our ship from those approaching from the sea. We'll stay there for the rest of our time here in Panama."

The men nodded, agreeing to the plan, and Alexandre and Victor headed straight for town. The other crewmates stayed with the longboat so they were ready for departure. Christina and Herbert went into the port authorities building.

Inside, there were a few sailors standing around who appeared to be swapping stories. They were all speaking Spanish though, so Herbert couldn't tell exactly what they were talking about.

He realised there was a problem. "Do you know Spanish, Christina?"

Christina gave him a look back that answered the question

before she even opened her mouth. "Maybe a few phrases."

"We're in the same boat then, it seems. Well, we'll see if we can manage, and if we need to we can come back."

At the back of the building, there was an older gentleman sitting behind a desk while working on some papers. Herbert and Christina approached the man and he greeted them in Spanish.

"Hola, la búsqueda de información," Herbert said in a broken accent.

The man behind the counter chuckled and said, "I know English, but that was a good attempt. You almost had it."

Herbert grinned sheepishly and glanced at Christina. "Thank you. We're looking for a ship that might have passed by here in the past few days, or possibly even today."

"What does the ship look like?" Herbert described Calico Jack's tallship to the man, but he shook his head. "No, no ship like that recently. Often, we do have galleons arriving, but no French ships. We do have the occasional French ship, but none of that size."

Herbert nodded. "Thank you for your time," he said before turning his wheelchair around and heading outside.

The disappointment hit Herbert immediately. This was one of the only developed towns in Panama on this side of the coast, so there weren't many places Calico Jack could have gone if this wasn't where he'd headed.

"So, if he wasn't here, where did he go?" Christina asked.

Herbert rubbed his chin. "I'm unsure. This was where he was headed, but he could have changed direction once out of Bodden Town's sight."

Christina sighed. "What do we do now?"

"Well, we have to hope that Victor comes through with some information we can use," he said. "Let's head back to the ship and have the crew raise the anchor. I don't want us in this harbour for any longer than we have to be."

Christina and Herbert both went back to the longboat, and they paddled back to the *Queen Anne's Revenge*. Back on the ship, Herbert let the crew know that they were still seeking information on Calico Jack's whereabouts. He had some crewmates return to shore with the longboat for Alexandre and Victor, and ordered the anchor raised so they could leave at a moment's notice.

Herbert noticed Jack on the bow of the ship, playing a tune on his fiddle. Herbert had tried to apologise for his harshness over the days of travel to Porto Bello, but hadn't been able to find the words. Now that he knew of Christina's deception, he had somewhere to start.

Herbert pulled on the rope to lift the platform so he could approach the bow. As soon as he reached the top, Jack was beginning to leave. "Hold, Jack, hold a moment!" he said.

Jack kept walking. "I do not wish to speak with you, Mr Blackwood. You said your piece days ago."

"Please, Jack, hear me out."

Jack stopped and placed his instrument at his side. "Yes?" he said, his mouth a line and his eyes full of daggers.

"I want to apologise. I'm sorry for what I said, and what I've done. I… was misinformed of the situation in Bodden Town, and if I had known the truth… well, we wouldn't be having this conversation."

"And yet you still pursue your quarry?" Jack said, glancing at the longboat and then back at Herbert.

"Yes, what's done is done and we are here now. What would you propose we do?"

Jack looked away and chuckled. "I would propose we return to our home and retrieve our captain. Though, I suppose we would have to determine his wellbeing first. Considering we left him for dead," Jack said loudly, "we don't quite know how he'll be when next we see him. From the look of things it doesn't seem as if you care." Jack motioned towards Herbert before moving towards the ladder again.

Herbert was struck by Jack's words, at first hurt, but soon angered. "I care deeply about our captain," Herbert said. "I've apologised for my actions… what more must I do to right this offence?"

Jack glared at Herbert, his brows furrowed. "There's the rub, isn't it? You may offer your sincerest apologies time and time again, and while the other party may accept it, it does not mean they will offer forgiveness. You may have been deceived into acting, and our situations have been similar in the past, but no one held your hand while you acted cruelly. I've always believed you can tell the measure of a man moreso by how he treats his allies than his enemies. To answer your question: to right this offence, and to receive my forgiveness, you will have to show me how you treat your allies, especially when faced with situations like this." Jack walked down the ladder. "I'll be watching," he said over his shoulder.

Herbert had no rebuttal. All Jack said was true. There had been no reason for him to be vicious when talking with Jack before, other than his anger. He would do better, but for now he needed to keep moving forward.

Edward is alive, and he will join us soon. I'll show him that this was the right thing to do.

The crew worked hard to bring the anchor back onto the ship for when they left. Raising the heavy iron piece was a laborious process, and in truth they probably should not have dropped it in the first place, but Herbert hadn't been sure how long they would have been on land.

Two hours into the middle of raising the anchor, Alexandre and Victor returned to the pier. They used the longboat to return to the ship.

Once they were on the weather deck, Herbert went up to them. "So, did you find any information?" he asked Victor.

Alexandre responded for him. "Victor's contact wants to meet with you, and discuss what we have to do for his *aide*."

Herbert glanced back and forth between Alexandre and Victor. "I thought this person was your friend? What kind of a friend will only help you with a favour?"

Alexandre wagged his finger. "I did not say he was Victor's friend, only that he knew them."

Herbert let out an angry sigh. "What does it matter?" he said, to which Alexandre shrugged with a smirk. "Does he truly know where Calico Jack is? What does he want us to do?"

"He will not say. He wants to speak with you first."

Herbert scoffed, and wheeled over to the side of the ship. "Let's get on with it then," he said before lifting himself from his wheelchair onto the railing.

As he entered the longboat, Alexandre, Victor, and Christina joined him. "Wait, Christina, I need you to stay behind to move the ship if we're not back by the time the anchor is secured."

Christina's jaw dropped for but a moment. "No, I'm coming with you." Herbert opened his mouth to object, but she held up her hand. "Would it be possible to not go through this dance right now? You know you'll just give in eventually, so let's save some time and move straight to that. Yes?"

Herbert's mouth slowly closed, and he motioned for her to join them. When he glanced at Alexandre and Victor, this time they both had grins on their faces.

They brought Herbert's wheelchair aboard, and then went back to the Porto Bello shore and onto the pier. Alexandre and Victor guided Christina and him through the town towards Victor's contact.

The town was lively enough, but seemed quite dull for having so many ships in the harbour. There were few food vendors out, despite it being early in the afternoon, and only one merchant selling general goods from what Herbert could see. Men and women with sun-tinged skin were talking with each other in the street, but the main bustle was coming from a small tavern near the harbour, and no doubt those were sailors, not locals.

As if somehow reading his mind, Alexandre said, "Most of the townspeople work in silver mines. It is... how do you say… lively, at night after the mine closes."

Herbert glanced around at the small town. Most of the buildings were one storey, drab, and made of poor quality wood and stone. There were also many beggars in the street, holding dirty caps out, listlessly asking for spare coin. "For having a silver mine, the town doesn't seem to have benefitted much."

"Spain strips much of its wealth. They send ships to collect the silver and bring it back to the homeland, leaving little for the townspeople."

Herbert shook his head. Spain and England were currently at war, so it made sense that they would want all the money they could have for the war effort, but to leave a town like this in shambles from it was a poor way to run a country. He supposed there were quite a few cities like this one, and no doubt on both sides.

Victor took them to a larger, more affluent home located next to a brothel. A fat Spaniard with a patchy beard mainly consisting of a mustache and chin whiskers guarded the front door. He was smoking and didn't move as Victor and the others entered.

Herbert looked down to see steps, which would be a problem for him. "Christina," he called.

Christina turned around and gasped. "Sorry, Herbert," she said as she ran behind him to push him over the stairs.

The fat guard didn't help her, and was content to watch the two of them trying to enter the building. He blew great puffs of pungent smoke into the air as he watched them from the corner of his eye. Herbert got the same feeling from him as those watching from the boats when they went ashore. He was being measured, weighed, and, as usual, found wanting.

I'll show them. Whatever task they want me to complete, I'll finish it.

Once Christina pushed Herbert inside, he was able to take over and wheeled himself forward to meet with Alexandre and Victor. Inside, there were other men waiting, watching, and smoking. They sat at tables or sprawled out on patterned blankets and rugs and pillows as they filled the air with smoke. Hebert could see many of them either had weapons directly on their person, or lying on the table in front of them.

"Where to now?" Herbert asked, ignoring the many eyes on him. Victor pointed up, and Herbert groaned. "You must be joking," he said with a sigh.

Victor walked to the right wall of the room, and pulled aside a blanket to reveal a set of stairs. Herbert wheeled himself into the small opening to examine his next struggle. Stone steps, two dozen of them, led to the second floor.

Christina leaned into the alcove and looked up the steps. "I can push you up," she offered.

"No, no," he said. "It's easier if I climb myself."

Herbert pulled himself from his wheelchair and flopped down on the stone floor below. He climbed up the steps, dragging his dead legs behind him as he did so. Though the day was hot, the stone was cold on his hands, as cold as his legs had been a few nights ago. His strong arms pulled him up each step with ease, and before long he was at the top.

Victor followed behind, carrying Herbert's wheelchair. At the top of the steps he set the contraption down, and Herbert was able to return to his seat.

Victor walked ahead of Herbert into the room on the second floor. Inside, directly in view of the stairs' opening, was a man sitting in a chair next to a table. He had been watching with a smirk on his face the entire time.

"This is who's looking for Calico Jack?" the man said, incredulous. He had a Spanish accent, but spoke English easily.

Herbert wheeled into the room to better see who was insulting him, and Christina and Alexandre followed right behind him. The man was a skinny Spaniard, who nonetheless looked lithe and agile. He was clean-shaven, and his hair was slicked back. He had a pistol on the table next to him, and beside that a plate of half-eaten food. On the other side of the table were two men, no doubt his personal guards. Their hands were hidden underneath the table, probably holding weapons at the ready. To the right side of the room, there was an open set of double doors, and two naked woman lying on a bed. Herbert did a double take upon seeing them, but once the shock of the sight was over, he stared at Victor's contact.

"Hello, sir. I am Herbert Blackwood, and this is my sister, Christina. I understand you have information on where Calico Jack is."

The man had a wide grin on his face. He glanced to the women in his bed, then back at Herbert. "You like 'em, do ya?" he said. "Give them a couple pieces of eight and I'm sure they'd have those legs of yours workin' in no time." The men at the table laughed.

Herbert ignored the comment. "It is customary to give one's name after receiving one."

"I was waitin' for this one to introduce me," he said, pointing to Victor. "But I suppose that's not possible at the moment, is it?"

The man and Victor exchanged glances, but Herbert was unable to decipher the significance of what he was saying.

"The name's Luis Delgado. So, you fancy yourself chasing down the King of the Caribbean, do you now?"

Herbert gritted his teeth. "Yes. I was told that you had information for us."

"Aye, I do, but not for you," he said.

Herbert's jaw dropped. "What is your meaning? Are you not a man of your word?"

"Oh, I am. I told… Victor here, that there would be a hefty price for the information I'm selling. I wanted to see who it was I was dealing with before then, because when you go against the King of the Caribbean you want assurances. You can't pay the price, boy, so piss off." The man turned around and went back to eating his food.

"What is it you want, exactly? Gold? We have that. Weapons? We have those too. Whatever price we have to pay, we'll pay it," Herbert said.

"It's nothing so simple as money or weapons, boy. You

would need to kill someone for me. That task is too much for a crippled boy to handle. Go home before my men here throw you on the street."

Herbert's blood boiled. He didn't come this far to leave empty-handed. "I've been a cripple since I was young, and I can handle a bit. Want me to show you how I handle a gun?" Herbert said.

Delgado looked at Herbert with a smirk on his face, and then got up and walked over to him. "Cheeky one, are you?" he said. "I like that." He backhanded Herbert hard in the face, knocking his wheelchair over and spilling him on the floor.

Christina and Victor started to draw weapons, but Herbert held up his hand. "Stop!" he commanded. The two stopped before things escalated, but both gritted their teeth and furrowed their brows in anger at Delgado.

Herbert turned himself over and crawled back to his wheelchair. Delgado stood in the exact spot where he had hit him, watching Herbert as he lifted the wheelchair back upright. Herbert carefully pulled himself halfway up the chair, and then punched Delgado in the nether regions. He doubled over, and then Herbert smashed his head into Delgado's. He was sent back and landed on his ass, clutching his head with one hand, and his groin with his other.

Herbert mounted his wheelchair, ready to protect himself or get out of the room, but Delgado's men were just sitting there at the table, laughing and pointing at their leader. They were saying things in Spanish that Herbert wasn't totally able to pick up. He was able to understand a few words, such as "knocked," "beaten" and "balls."

Delgado sat on the floor, in pain and rubbing both ends of himself for a bit. "Now, that's what I was looking for!" he yelled, but immediately he winced from the pain again. "Are you going to help me up or what?" he said, looking at Herbert.

Herbert extended his hand, and Delgado grabbed it and pulled himself up. "I need a drink after that one," he said in a lively tone.

Herbert's brow was now permanently cocked in confusion. He looked at Victor for an answer, but Victor just shrugged.

Delgado sat down at his seat and downed whatever was in his cup in one drink. Then he let out a great belch.

"I'm sorry, so now you're going to help us?"

Delgado nodded with a smile on his face. "You can always tell who a man is by how he reacts to an insult. If I needed a negotiator, and you had convinced me, I would have helped. If I needed a dog, and you left here with your tail between your legs, I would have helped. Today, I needed a fighter, and you didn't disappoint," he said while pouring himself another drink. "You didn't have to go for my manhood, though." Delgado once more rubbed himself as he took another long swig of his drink.

"So, you'll tell us where Calico Jack is?"

Delgado shook his head. "Not quite. Calico Jack never sailed here, and I've no idea where he is."

Herbert glanced at Christina. She had a disappointed look on her face, but it seemed to be more for him than her own sake. He wasn't going to be able to have his revenge as he'd wanted. In some way, deep beneath the surface, the news relieved him.

"But I know where one of his subordinates is going to be. From there, you should be able to do the rest."

Herbert's eyes lit up. Being able to find one of Calico Jack's men was good enough for now, and would go a long way towards repairing things with Edward when he arrived.

"So," Herbert said, "where is he?"

Delgado held up his finger. "Not so fast. The deal, if you'll recall, is that you'll need to kill someone for me. Only then will I give you the information."

Herbert glanced over at Christina, and she nodded. "Who is it?"

Delgado lost the smile he had been wearing since agreeing to help Herbert. "I need you to kill my brother," he said.

Herbert was shocked. "Your brother?" he blurted out.

"Why do you want your brother dead?"

"I prefer to keep such business in the family. Just know that he is heavily guarded, and it won't be easy. None can know it was me, or I stand to lose much. That's why I'm fortunate to have you all fall into my lap," he said while motioning to Herbert and the others.

"Where is your brother?"

Delgado got up, went over to a dresser on one side of the room, and pulled out a piece of paper along with a quill and ink. He began writing something. "My brother lives in Panama City. He is owner of a large brothel, and you will find him there surrounded by many armed men who work for him. Take care when you kill him. I wouldn't want you dying on me," he said with a smile over his shoulder.

Delgado handed the paper to Herbert, and it had the name of the brothel written on it: *Las Tetas*. Herbert didn't know exactly what it meant, but he could guess. Underneath that, the name 'Marco Delgado' was written.

Herbert blew on the ink to dry it, then folded the paper and placed it in his pocket. "We'll be back soon," he said, turning around and heading to the stairs.

"I cannot wait for your return," Delgado replied.

With the others' help, Herbert descended the stairs and left Luis Delgado's house. Herbert had a wide smile on his face. Though he wasn't going to get Calico Jack, he was closer than ever to one of his men, and it was only a matter of time before they found the rest.

Herbert turned around to face his comrades and his sister. "Let's head to Panama City."

10. PANAMA CITY

"Steady, now," Christina said while holding Herbert's wheel-chair place.

"I know." Herbert carefully gripped his chair and one end of the stagecoach they had been travelling on. After his grasp was secure, he moved from the coach to the wheelchair in one swift motion. Once seated, he wiped his brow of sweat and gazed at the sun, which was now lowering below the horizon. "There, that wasn't so bad," he said.

Christina smiled at her brother, then glanced around as the stagecoach sped off down the road. Surrounding Herbert and Christina were five crewmates who had also just left the stage-coach, and Tala. A short distance the road Alexandre, Victor, and five more crewmates emptied out of another stagecoach.

After hiding the *Queen Anne's Revenge* northeast of Porto Bello, Herbert and some crewmates had taken stagecoaches to Panama City the next morning. The trip had been slow and bumpy, the day was nearly spent, and they were all the more sore for it.

Herbert sighed and glanced down. *If not for these legs and that wheelchair, we could have ridden horses and been here hours ago.*

"Now, to find the brothel," Christina said as she absently scratched Tala's fur.

"First we should find an inn. We're not going to rush this," Herbert said. "We need to find the nearest inn from here, oth-erwise Edward won't know where to find us."

"That's assuming he even gets the letter you left," Christina said, eyeing her brother.

"He'll check for it, I'm sure," Herbert said, hoping his words would come true. He turned around to head down the road. "Come, let's move." Christina nodded, and they joined the other crewmates to enter the city.

Unlike Porto Bello, Panama City was bustling with activity. They'd had the coach leave them at the edge of the city where they could see the winding road leading to the centre of town. Dozens of people walked in all different directions, and another dozen stood around talking. The smell of fresh dirt, food, sweat, and the sea all found their way to the group as they took in the sights and sounds.

Travelling through the dirt road brought them through the heart of the city, and they were quick to find an inn in which they could stay.

Christina helped push Herbert up the stairs, and the crew all entered the establishment. Inside the inn there was a small area for receiving guests, a set of stairs to the right, and a large first floor for eating and drinking. The inn smelled of spilled ale, piss, and the collective odour of those in the room as well as those who had long since departed. It overpowered the smell coming from the food, but it was not unlike the smell in lower decks of the *Revenge*, so Herbert found it tolerable.

"Oh! Pets stay outside, miss," the innkeeper said, pointing to Tala.

Christina smiled and apologised as she pulled Tala outside and ordered her to stay.

They paid for some rooms, and sat at the tables to have something to eat other than the travel rations they'd had on the ride over. Herbert, Christina, Alexandre, and Victor sat with a few crewmates, while the rest of the men sat at another table nearby. They made sure to occupy the corner so that none could overhear them while they discussed their plans.

"Victor, you seem to have been in this area before," Herbert said. "Do you know anything of the brothel Luis mentioned, or of his brother?" Victor shook his head. "So we wouldn't be able to request an audience under the pretense of you catching up, would we?" Herbert's question was rhetorical, but Victor still shook his head once more. "I suppose the first step is finding it. After that, we can inspect it to see what we should do next."

"Why don't we just burn the whole thing down?" Christina suggested.

Herbert looked at her as if she were mad. "No! That's a horrifying thing to say. Why would you even think of that?"

Christina shrugged her shoulders. "Edward would do it," she said.

"No, he wouldn't."

"To have a second opinion," Alexandre began, "*la fille* has a point. It would be the safest... for us at least."

Herbert glared at Alexandre. "No fire." He took a drink from his cup. "I want this to be clean. We only have to kill Marco, so we should only kill Marco. There's no need to have anyone else involved unless we have to."

Alexandre bowed his head. "By your command, Captain," he said, producing some laughter from the other crewmates.

Herbert sighed. There was no point in telling the Frenchman to stop. He knew what he was saying and was just trying to get a rise out of Herbert. "We need to find out who Marco is before we can kill him, so I'll go to the brothel tonight and investigate. Perhaps I will bring some other crewmates with me as well, just in case." Herbert was looking at the men at his table and the one next to theirs.

"I'll go with you," Christina said.

Herbert gave her a similar look as before. "A brothel is no place for a young woman... well, not unless you're— no, absolutely not."

"What of it? I know what goes on there. You don't have to be afraid of me participating, if that's the problem."

Herbert was taken aback at first, but quickly regained his composure. "That's not the... The men might try to take advantage of you."

The anger was clear on Christina's face. "I can take care of myself, and besides, that's why the rest of the crew is there, is it not? We'll be watching out for each other."

Herbert stopped looking at his sister and instead stared straight ahead. "I've said all I'll say on the matter."

"You're treating me like a—"

"Enough!" Herbert yelled. His voice cut through the din of the inn, and caused a slight hush. All eyes were on their table, staring at him and his sister.

Christina's tan cheeks reddened a touch, and her mouth was stone. She didn't say another word as she left the table and headed for the second floor. On her way she pointed at the open doorway. "Venir," she commanded Tala, and the wolf raced to her side. She rushed up the steps before the innkeeper could say a word to her about the beast, and slammed the door to their room behind her.

Alexandre had a smirk on his face, and his dark, sullen eyes showed a hint of amusement. "That went well," he said.

Herbert looked at the crewmates sitting with them. "After we eat, we head out to the brothel. Choose five amongst yourselves to join me, and tell them to stay alert and find out any information they can on Marco. One way or the other, tomorrow Marco dies."

Herbert wheeled himself up to the front of the brothel names Las Tetas. It was late into the night, almost time for people to be sleeping, and yet lantern light poured from all the rooms inside the brothel. Judging from the noise alone one would think it were the middle of the day in a busy street.

The brothel was located in a secluded part of the city with few houses nearby, so they didn't have to worry as much about noise as others might. It was a large, three-storey house with many rooms, and many of them overlooking the sea.

Herbert looked at the shallow steps leading to a small patio and an open doorway. *I might be able to...* He pushed himself forward and leaned to one side, lifting the right side of the wheelchair up. He moved forward on the left wheel and dropped the right end down on the top step, then with another push over the side of the steps he was on the patio. The wooden machine creaked and groaned with the movement, but stayed together throughout the affair.

Someone nearby whistled and clapped. "Where'd you learn to do that?"

Herbert looked over to see a few men standing around, looking at him. The one who spoke was eating an apple. He was shirtless, and looked to be a local patron, with his tanned complexion and short, dark curls. He had several tattoos adorning his body in various patterns Herbert didn't recognise. Around his neck he also wore necklaces that clinked against each other as he moved.

Herbert chuckled. "You spend enough time in this contraption and you learn a few things," he replied. "Where did you learn how to speak English so well?"

"You spend enough time around you Brits and you learn a few things," the man said with a wink.

Herbert held out his hand. "Herbert Blackwood."

The man looked Herbert over for a moment as he took a bite of his apple. After a few chomps, he threw away the core and shook Herbert's hand. "Fernando." After shaking his hand, Fernando walked up to the door. "Care to join us inside?" he asked.

Herbert grinned. "I would enjoy some company, lads, but of a different persuasion. You flatter me with the offer."

Fernando laughed, and his friends joined in. "Cheeky. I like that."

"I'd be glad to join you for some ale," he said.

Fernando waved him in. "After you."

Hebert went into the brothel, followed by Fernando and his comrades. The first floor was filled with rooms, with a small area for dining and drinking. There were five tables strewn about, and Edward could see men and scantily clad women sitting at all of them. At one end was a stocked bar with what seemed to be one of the few men working at it.

The Voyages of Queen Anne's Revenge

He noticed and made eye contact with several of the patrons, all of whom were his crewmates. They nodded back to him subtly.

Some of the men cleared away from one of the tables, the women they were with leading them by the hand to different rooms. Herbert, Fernando, and his friends went to the now empty table.

A server came over to their table, a young woman and possibly the only one not working as a woman of the night. She was a local, and greeted them in Spanish, but when she noticed Herbert she spoke in English. "What can I get for you—?"

"Just fetch us some ale, dear," Fernando interrupted.

The girl's mouth went agape, and she glanced from Fernando to Herbert before she nodded and went to the bar to complete the order.

"So," Fernando said, "what brings you to Panama City?"

"I'm with a merchant ship, looking to make some deals between here and Porto Bello. We just arrived in the city after a day's travel, so I'm here to rest before business begins."

Fernando's eyes widened. "A day's travel?" he said. Herbert nodded. Fernando shook his head. "It must be hard with those legs of yours."

The server returned with the ale and passed a mug to each man. Herbert took his in hand and took a long sip from it.

"Yes, travel is rather difficult."

Fernando smirked. "What about your downstairs business? That work, or does it just hang low?" he said, pointing in Herbert's direction as he took a swig of his ale.

Herbert chuckled. "Oh, he works just fine." He didn't elaborate and hoped that the men would move on so he could try to find out more about this place. "This is quite the establishment," he said. "I don't think I've seen one quite so big."

"She's the biggest one in Panama City. All the men from the shore to the centre come here for a night with our girls."

"Must make a pretty pence." Herbert took another drink of his alcohol and peered over the edge of the cup at Fernando.

The ale tasted like the inn smelled, but he didn't let on about his thoughts, lest his guests not take kindly to the comment.

Fernando nodded. "That it does," he replied.

"I wonder if the owner would want some of what I sell? Do you know him?"

"I know him. What is it that you sell exactly?"

"This and that. My crew and I were seeing where the need was, and whether we could fill it," Herbert leaned forward in his wheelchair, "not unlike these girls," he finished with a forced grin.

Fernando laughed heartily at the joke. After a moment he pointed at Herbert, his cup of ale still in hand. "I like you," he said, and then he downed the rest of his drink. "Come, I'll introduce you to him." Fernando rose from his seat and walked away from the table.

Herbert's face lit up. "Ah, thank you, sir. You do me a kindness." He set down his cup and followed Fernando.

"Don't thank me yet. The owner is a fickle man."

Herbert glanced to the other tables, and noticed his crewmates were still there, but distracted by the women tempting them to their beds. He continued following Fernando into a room in the corner on the first floor.

Upon entering the room, Fernando's men followed in behind and closed the door. Fernando walked over to a desk at the back of the room, turned around, and half-sat on it.

"So, where's the owner?" Herbert asked, suddenly feeling nervous.

Fernando motioned to himself. "You're looking at him," he said.

Either he's lying, or I've been set up. "Oh, sneaky. Why didn't you say so to begin with?" *If I can just fire my pistol, the others will rush over here.* Herbert slowly moved his hands closer to his waist, where a pistol sat on his lap, covered by a blanket.

"I already know why you're here, Herbert, as do my men," he said.

His comrades grabbed his arms to stop him from grabbing

his weapon. "Hel—" he tried to yell, but the third man came up behind and placed his hand over Herbert's mouth while choking him with his large arm.

"I've always told my brother to watch the people he trusts, but he still couldn't see the spy right in front of him."

Herbert couldn't breathe with the muscle wrapped around his windpipe. His body struggled to pull air in, as did his arms to pull away from the men pinning him, but he couldn't win against their strength.

"You, though... I didn't expect him to send someone like you."

Herbert felt pain across his neck, face, and head, as each muscle strained to bring him life-giving air. He could feel the slow, methodical beating of his heart across the skin of his face. Thump, thump, thump, it went in his ears. It was slowing down as each second passed. Thump, thump, thump. Herbert's vision faded, black spilling into the corners of his eyes, and weakness sapping the strength from his arms. His eyelids sagged, and soon fell to a close.

"Goodnight, Herbert."

Those words from Fernando—or Marco, Herbert supposed—were the last thing he heard before he blacked out.

Christina awoke with a start. She was breathing heavily, and there was a cold sweat across her forehead. She didn't remember if it was a bad dream that had forced her out of her slumber, but if it was, the remnants of it took hold of her heart. A feeling a dread gripped her, and stayed with her even after she caught her breath and wiped her face with a wet cloth.

What is this feeling? Tala was beside Christina, fully awake as well, and whining. She kept glancing from her master to the door and back. "Do you feel it too, girl?" she asked while scratching behind Tala's ear. Tala responded with a loud bark.

Christina clothed herself, told Tala to stay in the room, and went down to the inn's dining area. The room was mostly empty at this hour, and much of the smell from earlier in the day was gone, but some still lingered in the air. The smell of the open cups of ale and the food still coming out of the kitchen was more prominent now.

As it was late at night, most of the crewmates were in their rooms already, but a few were sitting at one of the tables playing a game of cards. She went over to the men.

"Where is Herbert?" she asked.

The men glanced her way before continuing their game. "He's gone with some mates to the whorehouse. They gettin' the skivvy on how to go about it."

"Or gettin' their loins wet," another man said, causing the others to laugh. After a moment they stifled their laughter and glanced at Christina.

Christina ignored the comment and looked at the door to the inn, now closed, but with shutters open and showing the dark of the night. Lanterns lit the outside of the inn, but beyond that she couldn't see anything. A cold gust tried to penetrate the door, but instead made it bang and crash against the loose lock keeping it in place. The cold still seemed to hit her somehow, and a chill went up her spine.

"How long has he been gone?"

The same man who answered before peered at the ceiling in thought. "Hmm, before the sun fell, wouldn't you say mates?" The others at the table nodded. "Yea, near that time." The crewmate looked at Christina over his shoulder, and he had his brow cocked. From the look on his face, he could tell Christina was worried. "Nothing ta worry yerself over, Miss Blackwood. No one knows who we are."

The mate's words were little comfort to Christina. She absentmindedly touched and tugged at the wooden carved rose around a chain on her neck. She would never admit it to herself, but whenever she was afraid it would show in that nervous tic of playing with the memento around her neck—a constant reminder of one she lost, and could not let go of.

"We should check on him. Something doesn't feel right," she said, the fear she wanted to hide creeping out into her voice.

The men glanced her way again, but this time they stopped playing their game. "No need to trouble yourself. Everything is well, and your brother will be back before you know it." The other men nodded with the comment and joined in reassurances.

Their comfort did little to ease Christina's heart. "I can tell when my brother is in danger. I can always tell," she said, force behind her words this time.

The men looked at each other, some with slight smirks on their faces. The main crewmate who was talking with her walked over to her and began pulling her back to her room. "My dear, do not let your worries send you into hysterics. After a night's sleep you'll feel better."

Christina pulled away from the man, furious. "Enough!" she yelled. "I'm not in hysterics. Something is wrong, and you can either come with me and help my brother, or wait here and let a girl overshadow your valour."

The men were speechless at Christina's burst of anger. They stared at her, unsure of what to do. The room became silent, and even those who weren't in their crew were watching the scene.

"Hmph," Christina said, turning around and going back to her room.

She gathered a cutlass, a pistol, and a musket, and strapped them all to her person. Then she donned a cloak to help with the cold of the night and to cover the weapons up from prying eyes.

"*Venir*, Tala," she called to the wolf, who came running over to her.

She and the wolf went back down to the dining room, which was now empty of the crewmates. Their pride afforded them leave of the embarrassing situation, but did not spur them to prove her wrong, it seemed.

"I guess we're on our own, Tala." The wolf simply looked up at her, not understanding, but staying by her side regardless.

"*Pas nécessairement*," a voice said behind her.

She turned around to see Alexandre and Victor standing there, garbed for battle. They both looked as awake and fresh as always, and Alexandre looked as ready for physical activity as he ever would.

Christina smiled widely, and felt the twinge of tears forming in her eyes. She stifled them before they showed. "You heard what happened?" she asked.

Alexandre glanced at Victor and then grinned. "We rarely sleep much, if at all," he said. "I was itching for something exciting to happen, and this seems just the thing to save me from death by *ennui*."

Christina chuckled. She'd always liked Alexandre and his odd way of doing things. "Let's go then. Marco's not going to kill himself!"

The first thing Herbert noticed when he awoke was pain. Pain around his sore and dry neck, pain in his head, and pain around his arms.

As he blinked, and the focus returned to his eyes, he moved his head around to see where he was. His stupor faded, his memory returned, and he recalled being choked by one of Marco's men. He was lucky to still be alive, but he doubted he was any safer for having survived. He pulled on his arms and discovered they were tied behind his back.

"Finally awake, yes?" Marco asked from his chair in front of Herbert.

Herbert glanced around, still not fully aware of his surroundings. He hadn't been moved to a different location, it seemed, and Marco's allies were nearby.

Herbert tried to talk, but his throat felt raw and he coughed. He hacked several times until his throat seemed warmed up and he was able to talk. "So, your name isn't Fernando, is it?" Herbert asked, his voice hoarse from the punishment from earlier.

Marco laughed. "No, and you already know who I am now. At least I hope so. You look smart."

Herbert didn't see the need to hide his intentions any longer, but wouldn't mention the crew in case that was still a secret. "How did you know about me?"

"You don't remember?" Marco said, getting up from his seat. "Before you fell asleep I mentioned how I have a spy with my brother. He sent word of an English crippled assassin coming for my head." Marco went to the front of the desk and leaned his back against it. "Few of those in these parts, so here we are."

Herbert nodded. "No, I don't imagine there are," he said.

He was fortunate that they had left him in his wheelchair, because it afforded him an opportunity to escape. His hands were tied behind him, not around the back of the chair, so no one could see him fiddling with the knots. *If I can get my hands free, I can take out the knife hidden under my wheelchair.*

"Care to tell me why I'm still alive?"

Marco chuckled. "You do not sound happy."

"Simply confused. I can't think of a reason why you'd keep me alive."

"Well, I can tell you it's not because of your pretty face, or lack thereof." Marco had a smirk plastered on his face, and he took his time in replying to Herbert. "We know you didn't come alone, my friend."

Herbert cursed in his head, but stifled himself from blurting it out. The momentary shock caused him to halt his progress on the knot. "Is that so? This is new to me. I hope these phantoms didn't go spending my pocket money."

Marco poured himself a drink and took a swig of it. "You came here with four others, but there are more somewhere in town," he said. He pointed at Herbert. "The sooner you stop lying to me, the sooner we can finish this business."

Herbert swore again, and gritted his teeth. The momentary pause to stop himself from cursing before had tipped Marco to the lie, Herbert was sure of it. He continued trying to take the knots apart.

"If you tell me where your people are, I promise it will be quick. I can't promise painless, that I cannot do," Marco said with a wave of his hand.

Herbert wasn't going to let him take his life without a fight. If he'd learned anything on his time aboard the *Queen Anne's Revenge*, it was that no situation was without hope. He could feel the knots around his wrist loosening.

I need to keep him talking. "How about we just forget this whole thing happened and we can all leave here alive?"

Marco howled with laughter. "You think you still have a chance to barter with me?"

"Why not? If you don't, I can guarantee you won't make it through the night," Herbert said. "First off, I'll tell you I won't give up my crewmates, but let's say that I do. What then? You send some of your goons to take care of them? I'm not sure what your spy told you, but we're pirates. We're trained. You might be able to kill a few of us, but any one of my men are worth ten of yours."

Marco listened to Herbert without interrupting him, all the while taking sips of his pungent drink. It was just as Herbert wanted, and he was taking the opportunity to keep working on the tight knot on his wrists.

"Even if you kill me, my crew will still kill you. Trust me when I say we're focussed on revenge, and your brother has information we need. Either way, you're a dead man. But if you let us go, we can handle your brother ourselves and get the information from him by other means."

Marco shook his head back and forth, took another sip of his drink, and pointed at Herbert. "You see, you shouldn't have said that," he said.

Marco reared back and punched Herbert in the stomach, nearly sending him to the floor. The blow knocked the wind out of him, and a similar choking feeling overtook him. The sudden need for air arrested his thoughts. Between the pain of the blow and the dry gagging for air, Herbert couldn't keep untying the knots.

Marco punched Herbert again, this time in the face. His head snapped to the left and pulled his body over with it. His eye started swelling immediately. His cheek felt hot and aching, and he knew that there would be a bruise there later. After a moment he was able to regain his breath, but the pain lingered.

Marco pulled Herbert's face forward with one hand and the other gripped his wheelchair. "My brother may be a little shit, and he may have sent you to kill me, but he's still family," he seethed. "We'll have a talk after this, but no one lays a finger on my family. We'll take our chances with you pirates any day." Marco's men hooted in response. "Now, where is your crew staying?"

Herbert was dizzy from the punches, and his mouth was also swelling by now. He couldn't see straight, and it, as well as the pain in his stomach, was sending waves of nausea through him. He breathed in and out deeply, and soon he was able to see again.

"Fuck you," he spat.

Marco's grip on the wheelchair turned his knuckles white. He punched Herbert in the face again, and in the same spot as before. He kept punching him again and again until Herbert's cheek tore open.

Herbert's head felt like there was an anchor attached to it, pulling it down over the side of his wheelchair. The hot, throbbing, stabbing agony spread all across his face. Debilitating fatigue replaced his nausea. Herbert wanted nothing more than to sleep and be rid of the pain, but he forced himself awake. He needed to remove the knots, or he would die.

"What the hell is that noise?" Marco shouted, his accent coming back with his anger. He yelled something in Spanish to his comrades.

Herbert didn't hear any noise over the ringing in his ears.

He was able to hear the screaming Spaniard just fine, but hardly anything else.

He leaned forward and turned his head as best as he could to watch the door leading outside. One of Marco's men was approaching the entrance with a knife drawn. He slowly opened the door and peeked outside, only to have it slam open and hit him in the head.

Christina rushed in and halted just inside the room.

Christina!

The sight of his sister sent a wave of energy into Herbert's body. He needed to get out of the ropes, and he was so close. The energy he gained was just the thing he needed to finish the last bits of the knot.

Behind Christina, Alexandre, Victor and Tala were soon to follow. They each had weapons drawn, Christina with two daggers, Alexandre with a rapier, and Victor with a small sword and shield. And Tala, of course, had her fangs and claws.

Marco and his three comrades also had their weapons drawn. Before a battle could erupt, Marco flung Herbert's wheelchair around and placed a blade at his neck.

"Don't move, or I'll kill him," he growled.

For a moment, no one moved or said a word. It was a stalemate between the two sides. Christina began talking—or rather shouting—at Marco, telling him to let Herbert go. They argued back and forth, but Herbert stopped listening.

He focussed on the image of the knot around his wrists in his mind. He twisted and turned his shoulders, arms, and hands to release its hold on him. With all that was going on, he was able to move more freely without worry of being caught. Through his foggy mind, he could feel the ropes loosening. As the knots loosened, it gave him more room to move, and when he used his newfound space, the rope gave way even more. With one last tug, Herbert's hands were free.

Herbert slid open a secret compartment on the left armrest of his wheelchair, revealing a long dagger. He clutched the dagger tightly in his hand, and arched it over his shoulder. The blade hit Marco's hand, and he lost his grip on his weapon. Herbert pulled out the dagger as Marco staggered back, and then he leaned over to stab Marco in the stomach.

Herbert lost all sense of the others in the room, trusting in their ability to take care of themselves. They were fighters, all of them, and he knew that with their superior numbers and skills they would be fine.

Herbert stabbed Marco again and again in the chest. Blood gushed out with each piercing blow of the dagger, and before long Herbert's face and chest had turned red. He kept thrusting and thrusting, his teeth clenched and bared in anger. He stabbed and stabbed and stabbed until his arms could take no more, and they fell to his sides.

Herbert fell on top of Marco, heaving large, ragged breaths. It was only then that he noticed that Marco had fallen on top of his desk, and Herbert had climbed atop Marco while attacking him.

Marco's eyes reflected his last, painful moments of life. His face, chest, and legs were also covered in his own blood. Marco Delgado, Luis Delgado's brother, was dead, and their task was complete.

Herbert pushed himself off of Marco's dead body and flopped onto his back. As he struggled for air, he thought of the brothers' relationship, and just what had driven them so far apart that only death could reconcile the hate.

Herbert hoped that he and Edward wouldn't end up the same as the brothers, and that, with what they gained, Edward would forgive him for what he'd done.

11. STERLING PROMISE

For the second time upon waking, Herbert first felt pain. His body ached, but it felt especially concentrated around his face and stomach. Even though he had just awoken, he already felt tired.

He couldn't lift his upper body without sending spasms through his stomach, and when he lifted his shirt he noticed a grotesque welt forming. His left eye had swollen shut overnight, and he tried to touch the bruise, but even the slightest pressure was too much to bear.

He pulled himself up—forced himself, really—and every move was agony on his stomach. After a few minutes of struggling he was sitting up, propped on his hands as he arched his back to forestall the pain. He was already sweating from the exertion.

"Painful, is it?"

Herbert's gaze flashed to the source of the voice. "Edward!" he said, and then clutched his stomach.

Edward Thatch, his captain, was sitting in a chair not far from him. His eyes, his expression, and his demeanor were all as stone. He was leaning forward, his elbows resting on his knees, and his hands clasped in front of his face, obscuring his mouth and part of his great beard.

"When did you...?" Herbert paused for a moment and took a deep breath. "I'm sorry."

Edward stared at Herbert for a moment, his blazing gaze worse than the heat from Herbert's wounds. "You've given me a lot of time to think about what to do with you. The first thing I thought I would do was sock you in the face, but seeing as someone has already taken care of that I'll forgo physical punishment... for now," he said. "You and those who joined in your mutiny will be disciplined accordingly."

Herbert moved into his wheelchair, doing his best to avoid the painful areas. Once settled, he took a few deep breaths and wiped his brow. "They are not to blame," he said, taking in more air. "I am the one who told them to leave, and I am the one who should suffer the consequences."

"You and I both know that's not true. You put it to a vote. The crew had just as much a choice as you to leave Bodden Town, and they chose to join with you."

Herbert thought to tell Edward of the false premise which propped up the choice in his favour, but he refused to implicate Christina, so he stayed silent. Even so, it almost seemed as if Edward read his mind.

"Regardless of what influence you had on the men, their decision was still their own. They aren't children, so whatever sway you had on them, it was their choice to be swayed."

Herbert thought back on when Christina had told him the lie about Edward staying in Bodden Town. He wanted it to be true; he wanted it so badly that in his mind it *was* true. He pushed aside his misgivings so he could have the lie to make him feel better about what he did.

"I only ask that you do not punish Jack. He was against us leaving, and tried to convince me not to bring up a vote on the matter. He was more passenger than participant."

Edward nodded. "I'll keep that in mind," he said. "With that out of the way, did you find out any information on Calico Jack?"

Herbert's jaw dropped. "What?" he said.

"Calico Jack. Did you find out where he went?"

"Are—" Herbert stumbled over his words, still in shock. "Aren't you angry? How can you trust me after what I've done? From what it sounds like you aren't taking me off the crew. Why?" he asked, waving his arms with each question.

Edward stared at Herbert for a moment, and then looked off towards one of the open windows pouring light into the room. The sea air, and the scent of the town, flew in from the small frame.

"To be true, up until I entered this room, I was furious with you. At first I blamed myself for pushing you towards vengeance, but as I said before, you are grown and your decisions are your own. Seeing you here now, it's a painful reminder of my own madness, of which I have much. Freedom, revenge, family... I've fought for these, men have died by my side for these. I killed..." Edward paused and glanced at the floor, seeming to have one word in mind, but choosing another instead. "I've killed many people along the way, and almost died myself on many an occasion."

Edward looked at Herbert again. "When I saw you, lying there, bloody and beaten, I thought: What if I had gotten word about my father? Or what if someone had taken Anne away? I couldn't say how I would react in the moment, but more than likely I would have done the same as you, and probably not as cleanly. You had the decency to give the men a vote. Would I have? If our past is any indication, probably not."

Herbert grinned as best he could. "We're quite the pair, aren't we?"

Edward chuckled. "Yes, yes we are," he said. After a moment, he leaned back in his chair. "So, care to answer my question?"

"Right," Herbert said. "We came here to complete a favour for a friend of Victor's to get information he had."

Before Herbert could continue the story, Edward asked, "Victor?"

"Yes, Victor has a contact here in Porto Bello. That's who we were doing the killing for." Edward nodded, but remained silent. "Sorry, was that not what you were wondering?"

Edward waved his hand and shifted in his seat. "No, no. You reminded me that there's something else we'll need to discuss, but it can wait until later. Continue."

Herbert nodded. "I was going to mention that the only issue we have is that Victor's contact doesn't know where Calico

Jack is. He has information on where one of his subordinates will be, and that's what he was offering us."

Edward frowned. "I suppose that will have to do for now. Did he at least say who it was?"

Herbert shook his head. "No, he wouldn't tell us anything until I killed his brother for him."

Edward cocked his brow. "His brother?"

"They seemed to have some sort of ongoing feud. I was forced to be the end of it, and, well, you can see how that went," Herbert said, pointing at his eye.

Edward grinned. "The ladies won't be fawning over you anytime soon."

Herbert laughed, but stopped when pain lanced through him. "Not that they ever did before."

The two men were back in good spirits, and ready to move forward to find out about their quarry. They headed towards the exit of the inn room, but Herbert stopped just shy, as he was curious of something.

"What happened in Bodden Town? How did you escape?"

Edward lost his smile, and paused a moment. "I burned Bodden Town to the ground."

Herbert let out a nervous laugh, but when Edward didn't change his expression he stopped. "Wait, you're being true right now?" Edward nodded. "Oh, Father," Herbert said, his gaze hitting the floor.

He thought on the people he had come to know from there, some of whom were even part of the crew, and on how many people lost their homes or their lives. He felt it was especially tragic given how they had just survived a pirate attack days before, only to have it burn by the hands of another pirate. He wondered who had done more damage, Edward or Calico Jack.

"Was it… on purpose?"

Edward sighed. "I don't know anymore," he said.

It was a vague answer at best, but the look in Edward's eyes told Herbert of the conflict he was having within himself. If it had been an accident, he didn't seem to feel any remorse, and perhaps that was where his confusion lay.

"What of the Boddens?"

Edward furrowed his brows. "They are dead, and that was on purpose. They had one of their men kill some of the townsfolk as I was trying to talk them down, and then they tried to flee."

"Why would they do that?"

Edward shrugged his shoulders. "We will never know. It could be that Calico Jack or one of his men paid them to betray me and ensure we lost the town." Edward paused for a moment, and then shook his head. "Come, everyone is waiting outside."

Edward opened the door to the inn's first floor, and Herbert could see his crewmates and Bartholomew Roberts' crew sitting at tables and eating. When the two of them left the room, a slight hush fell over the dining area. Edward stood beside Herbert as he scanned the crowd.

"As you were," he said, and the crews went back to eating and talking amongst themselves.

Edward went to a table where most of the senior officers were. Roberts was sitting beside Hank, Anne and Christina were together with Nassir nearby, and Pukuh was sitting more or less on his own. They all had their eyes on Herbert and Edward as they joined the table. Edward sat beside Anne, and Herbert went between Christina and Nassir.

"Let's eat quickly now, so that we may make a swift return to Porto Bello," Edward said.

Christina leaned over and whispered to her brother. "How did it go?"

"We're still part of the crew, so I believe it went as well as can be expected."

Christina smiled. "That's good news, then."

"Yes, now we just have to talk with Luis and ensure he keeps his end of the bargain."

The inn's servers and cooks worked overtime to bring the

pirates their meals to break their fast. Before long they placed a plate of sausage, eggs, and local vegetables with exotic spices in front of Herbert.

The server didn't seem to pay his injuries any mind as she handed him his food. Herbert thought it was either to be polite, or she was too busy to notice, or perhaps she served many such customers on a regular basis.

Herbert tried to eat quickly, but the unfamiliar—but delicious—spices forced him to slow down and savour the food. He had never tasted anything quite like the sausage and the spices within, and it was the same for the entire meal. Out of all the random inns they had been in over the years, Herbert felt that this one had the best food. And, judging from the looks on the crew's faces and the time they were taking eating, the others agreed.

While Herbert was scanning the crowd, he noticed two people missing. "Where are Alexandre and Victor?" he asked.

"They are trying to work with the local authorities on obtaining proof of death," Christina replied. "We would have taken Marco's head, but the authorities were already on us so we couldn't very well be seen with a severed human head in our hands."

Herbert uttered a bark of laughter at the thought. "No, I suppose that wouldn't look good," he said. "What were Alexandre and Victor going to tell them to get proof of death?"

"When I asked, Alexandre replied with 'I have my ways.'"

Herbert shook his head. "Ever the ass," he said.

Christina smacked Herbert on the arm, but smirked. "It's not as if he were lying."

"I suppose not."

The crew continued their meal, and Alexandre and Victor returned as they finished and began packing up. In Alexandre's hands he held a sealed letter, and Herbert assumed it was from the authorities detailing how Marco had died. They had somehow managed to convince the authorities that they had the right to an official document, and the curiosity of how they accomplished such a feat maddened Herbert. It maddened him further because he knew if he asked, Alexandre would say "Oh, this and that," and would say it in French even though he knew the English words.

He may be an ass, but I cannot complain about his results.

Edward, upon noticing the duo enter, walked over to them and pulled them aside. He spoke with them about something for a moment, glancing Herbert's way a few times, and then they parted.

"Men, attention please!" Edward shouted to the crew as they were finishing preparations. "I'll be returning with the coaches presently. If anyone wants to take a horse, mine will be free as I will be travelling by coach. If you go by horse you will no doubt arrive sooner than us, so head to the *Queen Anne's Revenge* and we will meet you later tonight. Understood?" The crew responded with a holler. "Good. Now let's go get the bastard who burned Bodden Town!"

The crew responded with another resounding cheer, which echoed off the walls of the inn and surely woke any who were still asleep at this hour.

Edward's comments confused Herbert, so he wheeled himself over to Anne and bid her to come closer. Anne bent over and leaned close to Herbert. "I thought Edward was the one who burned Bodden Town?" he whispered.

Anne nodded. "It was an accident, but yes, that is true," she replied. Anne glanced to her left and right and leaned in closer. "Edward is telling the crew that it was one of Calico Jack's men who burned the town to further rally them together. If he told you the truth it means he trusts you with the knowledge, but you mustn't tell anyone else," Anne said, squeezing Herbert's arm. "Right now, we need the crew on Edward's side, and trying to explain the… muddied circumstances could cause those from Bodden Town to leave. You understand, yes?"

Herbert looked into Anne's eyes, the eyes of Edward's wife, the one who had the wit, strength, and charisma to protect her love at any cost. He knew Edward wasn't the one who had come up with the plan. His lack of remorse and loose tongue told Herbert that. Anne was the mastermind behind the cover-up, and it was all to protect Edward.

Herbert simply nodded, and Anne smiled. "Good. Once this is all over, we'll tell the crew the truth, don't worry. It's just for now."

"I understand," he said.

After Herbert and Anne had their talk, it was another while before Edward returned with the coaches. He had three for those who wanted to take them, which was enough so that all who wanted to return would be able to. Their caravan was forty strong, and from the looks of it, it was the biggest to travel the road from Panama City to Porto Bello.

Many of the townsfolk couldn't help but stare at the spectacle of so many people in one spot all mounting horses or entering wagons.

Edward approached Herbert. "Herbert, will you ride with me? I would have your sister join us as well."

"Yes, of course," he replied. He turned around and called to his sister, and the three of them went up to one of the stagecoaches.

Edward said a goodbye to Anne, who was going to travel in another coach, and they kissed before they parted. Afterwards, he called Alexandre and Victor over.

Why are they joining us? Could it be what they talked about earlier?

Herbert pushed aside his thoughts for the moment, as he would soon have an answer, and entered the coach. Edward was gracious enough to strap the wheelchair to the top of the coach, and soon they were on the road.

Once they were away from Panama City, Herbert spoke up. "Edward, care to tell us why we're riding as a group?"

Edward, instead of answering, looked over at Victor. Victor stared back at him for a moment, then let out a sigh and removed his cap. After the cap, Victor ran his fingers through his short black hair to let it down more.

Herbert wasn't sure of the purpose of the display, and first glanced at Christina to see if she understood something he didn't, but she shrugged her shoulders. He looked at Edward with his brow cocked. "I'm afraid this doesn't explain much."

Edward opened his mouth again, but paused for a moment and stared at Victor again. "It is better to show than explain first, as I know you wouldn't believe it if we just told you."

Victor glared at Edward as he unbuttoned the heavy coat he always wore, and then he opened it to reveal his white undershirt.

Herbert laughed at first, amused by the nonsensical display, but then he took in what he was seeing. His jaw dropped after a few seconds. "You're a—" he said, pointing at Victor, and then he looked at Edward. "He's a woman!"

"Herbert, this is Victoria. She's rather reserved, for good reason, but you two actually have some things in common."

"Victoria? Amazing," Herbert said. "Simply amazing. Who would have thought another woman was hiding aboard the ship?"

Christina was smiling. "I'm quite glad for another woman," she said. "Lord knows we must stick together."

Victoria smiled at Christina's comment, but it quickly faded.

"I've only known of her since Bodden Town, but Alexandre has known for quite some time now."

Herbert and Christina had trouble containing their excitement and astonishment. They wore wide grins. "Bodden Town? Oh, yes! I recall that you volunteered to breach the Boddens' gate to see if Edward was well."

"Yes, well, there was more to it than that," Edward said, then looked at Victoria.

Herbert's and his sister's smiles faded as they glanced from Edward to Victoria. Victoria had a stoic expression as she waited for Herbert and Christina to calm themselves. After a moment, she began speaking to them for the first time in her normal, undisguised voice.

"I, like you, once worked on Calico Jack's ship."

Herbert needed a moment to process the words. He shook

his head in disbelief. "I— In secret? Did he know you were a woman?"

"I don't know how long you were on his crew, but women were not allowed unless they were captives to later be thrown overboard when the crew lost interest in them."

Herbert shuffled in his seat, suddenly uncomfortable and unable to sit still. "So why did you leave his ship?" He clenched his hands into a fist. "Are you still working for him?" His voice rose. "Did he send you here to spy on us?" His lips curled into a snarl. "Captain, you cannot trust this woman. She should be left here, or killed."

Herbert felt his face grow hot, and this time not due to the wound near his eye. His anger nearly overpowered him, but in front of Edward and his sister he contained it.

"We are cut from the same cloth," Victoria said. It was clear from the look of her that the threat angered her, but her voice held a subtle, calm menace. She was slow to show anger, and seemed confident in her abilities should a fight erupt.

Edward nodded. "So, we kill her, and what do I do about the other former Calico Jack crewmate? You both joined my ship at the same time, served for all its years, and even came back when I was imprisoned to save me. The only difference is, one of you hid your identity as protection, and the other stole my ship. Judging by one's actions, I'd say the more likely spy would be you, Herbert." He cast a pointed glance in Herbert's direction.

Before Herbert could respond, Christina placed her hand on her brother's to stop him. "I want to hear what she has to say," she said. "Please, tell us your relationship with Calico Jack."

Herbert folded his arms and arched his back against the coach.

Victoria bowed her head a touch in Christina's direction. "I shall be brief, but it is best to start at the beginning." After a cursory glance to the other passengers, she started her story. "I joined Calico Jack's ship a few years ago in disguise as a man, as I had done in the past many times. Working with pirates was never an issue for me, and oftentimes a blessing as the money was better, and I was never found out. As you have seen, I do well in disguising myself, and pirates are idiots," she said with a smirk. Edward cleared his throat. Victoria grinned. "Most pirates are idiots," she revised. "After a few times sailing with Jack Rackham, I learned just how cruel a man he was. I decided to leave the crew at the next port, but it was long before port came, and Mad Jack found out about my identity. He kept the secret, but forced me to stay aboard. I will not tell you the horrid things he did to me, but please know that when I say I am no friend of his that I am not lying. Having said that, I was able to use my captivity well, as I learned about his operations and his contacts. I never wanted revenge, I just wanted to run, but being aboard this ship gave me hope that it could be done."

"So why reveal yourself now? Why not months or even years ago?" Herbert asked.

"Before now, it wasn't necessary to tell you my identity. And I didn't know how you or the crew would treat me after you knew the truth," she said, her lips pursed. "Now I don't have the luxury of standing by. If you want to kill Calico Jack, I can help."

Herbert nodded. "A believable story, I will give you that. However, you'll forgive me if I am still skeptical. If you aren't a spy, then why did you join this ship? Out of all the ships you had a chance of boarding, you approached this one out of what? Coincidence?" Herbert spat. "Pirates are idiots, are they? Spin some lies and they'll believe every—"

"Do you wish me to address your claim, or is this conversation pointless?" Victoria asked. Herbert sighed and waved his hand at her. Victoria looked at Edward. "I joined this ship because of your Anne," she said.

"Anne?" he replied, his brow raised. The others in the coach were also confused. "What does Anne have to do with any of this?"

The Voyages of Queen Anne's Revenge

"Anne was how I escaped Calico Jack," she said. "Before you ask, no, she doesn't know who I am. Anne is smart, and she would have recognised my face had she seen me before." Edward nodded at the comment. "She joined Calico Jack's crew some time after me, and, like me, she didn't know what she was getting into. She was quickly found out by the crew, and killed some of them and cut Calico Jack across the face before jumping overboard. Her distraction allowed me to escape as well, and luckily we were close to shore. I knew she would continue boarding ships for work, and resolved to protect her so she didn't fall into the same situation I did." Victoria looked at Christina. "Lord knows we must stick together," she said, echoing Christina.

"And that's how you ended up on my ship," Edward said at last. "I can't believe she's never mentioned that before."

"I can imagine it was not a pleasant experience, especially as she seemed so unused to killing at the time. I will also say that as you were catching onto Anne's identity, I came close to cutting you down. You should be grateful you are nothing like Calico Jack."

Edward chuckled, but it was a nervous chuckle rather than a humorous one. Victoria wasn't laughing; she looked all too serious.

"Any more questions?" she asked, staring at Herbert.

Herbert, his arms still folded, returned the stare for a moment as he thought, then glanced at the other passengers. "No, no more questions," he said.

Throughout the remainder of the coach-ride, Herbert remained silent. Victoria also didn't seem too talkative, despite revealing her true self to everyone. She hadn't been talkative as Victor, and Herbert guessed that it hadn't been just to hide her voice.

Christina continued asking Victoria questions like how she'd learned to disguise herself so well, where she came from, why she chose to try to work on ships instead of being a lady, and other menial queries. Herbert didn't listen to anything, and instead tried his best to sleep. All she said was probably full of lies, so why listen to her?

By nightfall, they arrived back in Porto Bello. Victoria donned her cap once more, and buttoned her baggy clothing to hide her identity once again.

"Why are you hiding yourself again?" Christina asked.

"We haven't told the crew yet, and it would be best to address them all together before they start asking questions and spreading falsehoods," Edward said.

"So we're going to spread the falsehood that she's an ally?" Herbert muttered under his breath.

"Something to say, Herbert?" Edward asked, the anger clear in his voice.

He arched his eyebrow and looked at his captain. "Hmm? No, no, nothing to add, sir."

Edward eyed him in the way he usually did to have men cower from him, but Herbert was unaffected. He stared back at Edward, and tried to mimic the same glare back at him. After a short time, they both looked away.

The cold air swept in from the sea and hit them as soon as they opened the door to the coach. It was unusually chilly for a place that had such harsh heat during the day, and the crew had to button their jackets and coats to stave off the sharpness of the wind.

After Edward, Alexandre, and Christina left, Herbert grabbed Victoria's arm and pulled her in close. "Just know that I don't trust you, and I'll be watching you from now on. If you are a spy, I'll know."

Victoria's face was rigid and unreadable. "Then you and I don't have anything to worry about," she said.

"Tch, yea, we'll see about that."

Edward retrieved Herbert's wheelchair from the roof of the coach and brought it down for him. Through some deft maneuvering, Herbert gripped the sides of the open doorway and swung from it to the door, and then into his wheelchair. His legs became twisted in the process, and he had to lift them up to get them aligned just right before he was comfortable.

"Ready?" Edward asked.

Herbert nodded. "Let's go see what I paid for with this eye," he said.

The coaches emptied, and soon Anne and Roberts joined Herbert's group. Herbert wheeled in the direction of Luis Delgado's place of business, leading the others there.

Once they arrived at the whorehouse, they were let inside. Thankfully, Luis was on the first floor this time.

When the group entered, they were met with bitter looks, and more than a few put hands on their weapons. Luis, for his part, grinned from ear to ear, and when he saw Herbert he spread his arms wide.

"My friend! You are back. With good news, I hope?"

"Yes," Herbert replied. "We managed to kill your brother for you."

Victoria stepped forward and handed Delgado the letter she and Alexandre had received from the Panama City authorities. He broke the seal and read through it. After a moment, he nodded his head, seemingly satisfied with its contents.

Delgado picked up a glass which seemed to be filled with rum. "To my brother, may he rot in hell," he said morbidly, and then seemed to repeat it in Spanish for those around him. With a cheer, he downed the drink in one gulp.

"There is something else," Herbert said. "There appears to be a spy in your midst. Your brother knew I was coming. I have that to thank for these injuries."

"Oh, is that so?" Delgado said.

Delgado started to walk around the room, staring into the eyes of each man while saying something to them in Spanish. As he paced the room, he pushed some of the men, and they answered his questioning. Given that none of them were killed on the spot, they all seemed to deny the accusation.

As time passed, and Delgado's questions became more incensed, the tension rose. Many of his men were sweating despite the cold of the night, and glanced warily at their neighbours.

One of the men darted towards an open window. He was ten feet away, and could jump out without fear of injury, as it was the first floor.

The crack of thunder from a pistol rang in the room, and the spy dropped to the floor. Edward held the weapon, the barrel of the pistol still smoking and releasing a hot metallic scent into the air.

The spy was still alive, bleeding from his back and desperately trying to pull himself closer to the window.

Delgado stalked over, and the wounded man noticed the footsteps. He turned over and pleaded with Delgado to spare his life. He put one of his hands in front of him, and the other held his wound. He continued glancing from Delgado to the window as he shouted and begged. Delgado ignored the pleas and didn't hesitate to execute the man with a swift stab through the neck.

Delgado watched the spy bleed out for a few seconds, and then spun around towards Herbert and the others with a wide grin on his face. "Sorry about that nasty business. Thank you for letting me know, and thank you," he said, pointing to Edward, "for the help. By the way, who are you? I see many new faces today."

"I am Edward Thatch, Herbert's captain."

Delgado furrowed his brows. "I thought *you* were the captain," he said, looking at Herbert. Herbert shook his head. "Well, no matter. So, let's conclude our business. You wanted information on Calico Jack's subordinate, correct?" Delgado walked over to the back of the room and rummaged through some of his drawers.

"Yes, that was what Herbert struck a deal for. Do you know this man's whereabouts?"

Delgado was still searching for something in stacks and stacks of papers lining the drawers of the shelves. "I do indeed. He needed help for his next assignment. He told me that he's doing an initiation of sorts, so he's not one of Calico Jack's subordinates just yet, but should he perform well he will be." Delgado pulled out a piece of paper and said, "Aha, here it is!"

Delgado brought the piece of paper over for Edward to examine. Edward took the paper and glanced over it. Herbert and the others leaned over to see that it was a map of the Caribbean Sea. Several ship routes, showing as dotted lines, crossed this way and that, and at the bottom of the map there was a list of dates, each spanning a week of time.

"What am I looking at?" Edward asked.

"That is the routes of various Spanish galleons, what some of you pirates are calling the Spanish Treasure Fleet. They make various trades to Spanish colonies in the new world, and bring back silver and gold mined from all over back to glorious Spain so that the colonies can rot with nothing but trinkets from the Old World."

Edward still had a confused look on his face, perhaps even disbelief. "So, if I'm to understand you correctly, the trial this man is taking to join Calico Jack's fleet is to steal from one of these galleons?"

Delgado nodded. "More or less. He has to make it a show, so the galleon has to be sunk and the treasure stolen, from what I was told." Delgado shrugged his shoulders. He went over to Edward and pointed on the map to an island northwest of where they were near one of the routes. "Providencia. That is where your man will be right now. He is getting ready to attack the galleon with some other ships."

"How much time do we have?" Edward asked.

"Not much," Delgado replied. "The galleon is due to be here in two days, and then it will stock up and take our silver before heading north. The restocking usually takes a day at most. Five days after that it will arrive there. I'm assuming your ships are smaller, so you can make the trip in three days, maybe four, which is just enough time to figure out a way to stop them."

Edward glanced at Herbert with a smile on his face. Herbert could tell that they were thinking the same thing. If Herbert hadn't left when he did, who knows whether this opportunity would have still been here for them?

"You said it's a fleet. Wouldn't that mean more than just the galleon is arriving?"

Delgado grinned and tapped his finger on his temple. "One would think that, and that's what our beloved motherland wants you to think." Delgado's grin widened. "This one does not have an escort, not for little Porto Bello. The Spanish try to keep it a secret, and most pirates are too busy trying to raid our shores to find that out. This is the one galleon with the least amount of treasure, but also the easiest to take," he said, balling his fist with the last few words.

Edward grinned, and Herbert thought that more than revenge was on his mind. "So, who is it we should be looking for in Providencia?" Edward asked.

"Strange fellow he is, you'll be able to find him with no issues, I imagine. For some reason he has this... treasure chest attached to his right arm," Delgado said, gesturing wildly as he did. "Calls himself some foolish name. What was it? Chest-Hand? No, that couldn't be it. Cask-Hand? No, that wasn't it either."

Edward's eyes were wide. "Cache-Hand."

12. DEBT OF JUSTICE

"Yea, that's the one. Cache-Hand. It's so… what's the word? Obvious. It'd be the same if you up and called yerself Blackbeard, or if Blackwood here called himself Weak Legs," Delgado said with a hearty laugh as he motioned towards Herbert.

"Excuse me for a moment," Edward said, and then he turned around to leave.

Delgado had a smirk on his face. "Don't tell me you're actually called Blackbeard? Sorry mate, I didn't know you were that plain."

"It's nothing you said, sir," Edward replied, then he looked at Roberts. "Roberts, take over for me, would you? Find out what we need to know." Roberts nodded, a look of concern in his eyes.

Edward left the whorehouse, walked a few houses down, and then stepped into an alley. He fell to his side against the wall of the home and was breathing heavily. He could feel the beads of sweat pouring from his forehead despite the cold of the night. His hands were shaking, and he felt nauseated.

Why does it have to be him? The picture of Cache-Hand, of William Locke's face, invaded Edward's mind like a sickness. The name repeated over and over in his head until Edward slammed his heavy fist against the wall. *Why that name? Why?*

The old, healed wounds across Edward's body began to ache again. The fresh pain was like a memory, his body's memory. His body was telling him of the danger, warning him to stay away from the one who did this to him.

Footsteps approached behind him, and he looked over his shoulder to see Anne standing there. Edward pushed himself off the wall and turned around. He wiped the sweat off his brow.

"It was hot," Edward said. "I needed some fresh air."

Anne did not say a word, and instead stepped over to him and embraced him. "My sweet Edward," she said, her gentle voice penetrating the pain.

For a moment he stood there, stock still, his heart beating in his ears, but then he reached his arms around and accepted his wife's love. Her warmth washed over him, as if she were sharing her calm to quell his storm.

"You are here, you are now, you are not then," she chanted.

With each breath they shared, Edward could feel his heartbeat returning to normal. He ignored the thoughts that plagued his mind, and focussed on the moment rather than the past. After a few minutes, he felt relaxed and fresh again.

Edward laughed. "You have a strange power over me," he said.

Anne grinned. "I should hope so, husband. After all, I am your better half."

"This is true," Edward said with a mirrored grin.

"Tell me what you want, and I would see it done," Anne said, a serious look in her eyes.

"You do not need to do anything. We, however, need to kill Cache-Hand. Only then will I be rid of this curse."

Anne looked at him, concern in her eyes. She placed her hand on his cheek. "There is no shame in fear."

Edward shook his head, pushing her hand away. "I'm not afraid," he said.

Before Anne could talk with him further, Edward turned around and left the alley. He head back to Delgado's whorehouse. Anne followed behind him at a distance.

Outside, the crewmates who had joined him, and Roberts, were waiting for Edward to return. They were talking with each other in hushed tones, and had concerned looks in their eyes. When he approached, they ceased talking.

Roberts waved to Edward. "Ho, Edward. Are you well?"

"I am well, friend. I felt close to hitting the floor with the heat in the room, so I had to step out."

Roberts scratched his face. "Yes, of course. It was rather stifling."

"So, was there any other information of use to us?"

Roberts shrugged his shoulders. "I'm afraid not," Roberts said, but then he grinned. "But we did learn that one of the other pirates helping Cache-Hand is Walter Kennedy."

Edward's mouth went agape. "Walter Kennedy? That's…"

Roberts nodded. "That's the man who stole my ship years ago. He's still with Kenneth Locke, it seems. It looks as if we both will have our justice soon enough, isn't that right old friend?"

After a moment, Edward smiled. "Yes, I suppose we will."

"Did you have any plan in mind for how to attack?" Herbert asked. "We only have two ships on our side, and they'll have three."

Edward stroked his beard. "I'll have to think on it some more. For now, we should head back to the ships and let the crew know the particulars of the day."

The crew were in agreement, and they headed back to the harbour to board the *Fortune*. They would need to head just northeast of Porto Bello to where Herbert had anchored the *Queen Anne's Revenge*.

Roberts rushed ahead to walk by Edward's side. He patted his friend on the back to get his attention. "Are you well, truly? You were quick to leave after learning whom we are attacking. I do not believe one among us is not aware of who that man is, and the trial you endured."

Edward gripped Roberts' shoulder and gave it a squeeze. "Trust my words when I tell you I am well. I only want to see this business concluded, and, as you always say, to see justice done."

Roberts nodded. "He also has one of your crewmates, does he not?"

Edward's eyes hit the floor. "Yes, Samuel Bellamy. He may still be hiding aboard their ship under a false name, if he wasn't found out. John, God rest his soul"—and here Roberts repeated the chant with Edward—"and I paid the price to see his cover maintained."

"You were told of the letter he left behind, were you not?"

"Aye," Edward said. "He swore revenge on Kenneth Locke."

"I don't think I have to tell you that, seeing as Kenneth Locke seems to be very much alive, Sam may have failed."

Edward glanced off to the *Fortune* floating in the water under the light of the moon. "I am aware of the significance."

"I shall pray for his safety, but you should prepare yourself and your crew for the worst," Roberts said. "Come, let's return you to your ship."

The crews boarded longboats and returned to the *Fortune*. After the long process of raising the anchor, which was faster with Edward's men helping, they dropped the sails to leave Porto Bello's harbour.

As they travelled north and east along the coast, the moon was approaching its zenith and giving a faint glow to the surrounding sea and trees of the mainland. It didn't take long for them to reach the small islands just off the shore hiding the *Queen Anne's Revenge*.

As they came into the waters between the islands, Edward's crew who were still awake were all watching and waving, hooting and hollering across to their partners. The *Fortune* furled the sails, dropped the anchor, and after half an hour they were able to secure the ships together with rope and lower a gangplank.

Edward held his back straight to keep himself at full height as he marched across the gangplank. He maintained a stern expression as he set his gaze upon his borderline mutinous crew.

Jack stepped forward, a smile on his face despite the look Edward was giving everyone. "Captain, you're back. We weren't expecting you for a few days more."

"The situation in Bodden Town turned dire, so we had to

leave," he said. "I must address the crew, please have any men sleeping woken up and bring them here."

Jack nodded. "Aye, Captain," he said before heading below deck.

"Herbert, Victor, join me on the quarterdeck."

Edward, Herbert, and Victoria all joined Edward on the quarterdeck, and waited for the crew to come to the weather deck. The tired men stumbled up to the deck, curious but exasperated. When they noticed the crewmates who'd returned, Roberts' ship, and then Edward on the quarterdeck, their tiredness faded away in an instant.

"Good evening, men," Edward said. "I have a few announcements to make regarding current affairs. Firstly, due to the scoundrel, Calico Jack, and his interference, the Boddens turned on us and caused the town to burn to the ground. Bodden Town… is no more."

Those words alone were enough to send a wave of disbelief through the weary crew, and Edward quickly lost control of the crowd. Most of the men causing a stir were those from the former town.

Edward raised his hands to try to calm the men. "I understand your doubt, but it is true. The only reason I am here today is thanks to the fire distracting the townsfolk. Our only home is now this ship."

The crew who had come from Bodden Town were overtaken by great melancholy in that moment, as well as concern over their family members still in Bodden Town. Many of them had their gazes downcast, and the other crewmates found them inconsolable.

"Do not despair, men," Edward shouted. "For those who hail from Bodden Town, I give you freedom to return there, and you will not have to follow the commandments to pay for your leave. However, for those of you who stay, I promise you we will be pursuing Calico Jack and will bring justice upon him. Calico Jack owes us for what he's done, and we owe it to the people of Bodden Town to return his violence back to him.

Do not let your grief take away from your vengeance, for we cannot let him escape a pirate's justice."

Edward was able to bring back most of those crewmates who had been lost in their own thoughts. They looked up at him, this time with a fierceness in their eyes.

"What do you say, then? Do you want to leave, or do you want to kill the bastard who attacked and burned your town?"

The crew hollered in agreement with Edward, the fire in their eyes inspiring those around them into a frenzy.

Edward nodded. "Good, because we have new information on where one of Calico Jack's subordinates will be. We will send a clear message to Calico Jack that he can't make us run and cower." The crew yelled a resounding "Hear, hear" back to Edward. "It is a man some of you may know well. Kenneth Locke, Cache-Hand, who killed our previous quartermaster, John, and who still has one of our crewmates, Sam, hiding in his crew. And he is working with someone you, crew of the *Fortune*, know as well," he said, motioning to the other ship's men. "Walter Kennedy, the man who stole your ship and left you for dead is with Kenneth Locke. These two owe us a debt of justice, and they need to pay for what they've done. We will seek them out and destroy them as repayment."

Both crews now cheered for Edward.

"We wouldn't have been able to get this information if not for the help of a specific crewmate. One who has been with us since the beginning, and helping behind the scenes. You all know this crewmate as Victor, but Victor has been holding onto a secret which we will reveal to you now."

Edward looked at Victoria, and she did the same thing for the crew as she did for Herbert and Christina. She removed her cap, and then unbuttoned her jacket to show off her figure.

"Men, welcome Victoria into the crew."

After a moment of confusion, the crew caught on. Each of them were once again in a state of disbelief, with many whispering to their neighbours or pointing.

"Victoria, like our quartermaster, Herbert, was a former

crewmate of Calico Jack's, and was a boon in finding his crew's whereabouts. I cannot say how she will dress aboard the ship any longer, but her clothes and her name should have no bearing on how you treat her."

Many in the crew nodded, but some showed visible signs of anger, though those were in the minority. Most seemed indifferent towards her being a woman, given that they had been working with two already.

"And, finally, the matter of you all voting to leave Bodden Town in its time of need, rather than staying to help," Edward said, his level tone taking on a hint of anger. "As I mentioned before, Bodden Town has burned to the ground due to what happened there. Had you all decided to stay, that could have been prevented. Lives and homes wouldn't have been destroyed, and we wouldn't have lost the safety that Bodden Town provided. You all are partially to blame for this happening, and owe a debt just as Calico Jack does."

Before Edward lost the crew again, and they began to object, he continued. "As such, all those who voted to leave Bodden Town in its hour of need will have their shares cut in half for the next haul. Afterwards, it will return to normal." Edward stared daggers at the crew, scanning the crowd and looking into each man's eyes.

The look seemed to quash any thoughts of going against the captain's decision. It might have also helped that the punishment, while severe for the moment, was light when compared to how many ships they raided.

Edward glanced at Herbert, who had been watching the speech, waiting to hear his fate. "Also," he said, looking at the crew again, "Herbert, as he was the one who instigated the vote," Edward paused and took in a silent breath, "will have half shares for the next three hauls. His rank and authority as quartermaster on this ship is hereby stripped. He will still man the helm, and you are to follow his orders as before, but only orders in relation to steering and navigation. He is not permitted to propose or take part in a vote, he will no longer be in charge of supplies and provisions, and any man found conspiring with him will be guilty of mutiny and punished by death or marooning."

Edward could not hold back the crew's objections any longer. They felt the punishment for Herbert was too harsh, and loudly voiced their opinion. Edward was silent as their voices grew louder and louder still. He looked over at Herbert, who was glancing between Edward and the crew shouting their support for the wheelchair-bound man.

Herbert raised his hand. "Please, everyone, stop," he yelled. After a moment, and another call from Herbert, the crew silenced themselves. "I thank you for your protection, but the captain is right and just in his decision. We have wronged, myself most of all, and this is the price I pay. I pay it gladly if I can only achieve forgiveness for my actions, and you too should feel the same... Forget Bodden Town, forget Calico Jack, forget revenge. We owe this man our freedom, and we abandoned him in his time of need. He could have died because of us. I accept my punishment, as should you," he said with a small smile.

Edward was looking at Herbert, and when Herbert glanced over to him, he nodded.

The crew's anger subsided after Herbert's admission and acceptance of the punishment, but one question still remained: Who would be in charge of supplies, and who would represent the crew's wishes as their new quartermaster?

"I elect Anne Bonney as our new quartermaster," Edward said, pointing to his wife. "And with your vote, the position shall be secured."

Anne looked at Edward with her brow raised, and then she glanced at the crew. The crew had been wanting her as the first mate for some time, but she had declined it, despite still serving in some capacity since. The crew watched her as she climbed the steps to the quarterdeck while glancing at Herbert and Edward.

On the quarterdeck, Anne placed her hands on the railing.

"I will accept the position of quartermaster, if you will have me. I promise to serve your interests, and if there are any decisions my husband makes which you do not agree with, I will knock some sense into him."

The crew chuckled at her comment, and many nodded and muttered words of agreement with the decision.

"All those in favour?" Edward asked the crowd.

All two hundred of the crew responded with a deafening "Aye."

"I welcome your new quartermaster," Edward said, lifting Anne's hand up in the air.

The crew, in the dead of night, shouted and cheered for their new electee, their morale high despite the lost shares and change. Anne, though at first reluctant, smiled happily to the crew who had just elected her, and soon appeared eager to take on a new experience on a pirate ship.

13. PARLEY PROPOSAL

William stepped up to the weather deck for the first time in the week and some days they had been travelling for. The cool, fresh sea air was a welcome respite from the stale, sweaty interior of the *Fortune*.

It was early morning, the sun just peeking out on the horizon, half-blocked by the island east of them providing them cover. The glow of the rising sun washed over the ship, casting great shadows from the masts over the deck.

The *Fortune* was lashed to *Queen Anne's Revenge*, and the two seemed to be caught in a dance with the waves. Each ship rose and fell independently, but in near synchronous movements. The slight difference caused the wood to creak and groan more than usual from the ropes tying the ships together.

Few men were up this early, but those that were wished William good day and praised his good health. He could see men from both ships mingling on the two decks, relaxing before the inevitable labours of the day began. Some were sitting on the steps leading to the upper decks, others leaned against the railings, and some sat with their backs against the masts.

William crossed the gangplank, holding steady to the railing as he did so. Every movement caused a slight but sharp pain to run through his chest. Though his fever had broken some days before, his ribs were still healing. It would be several weeks yet before he was fully recovered, and longer if he didn't give himself proper rest.

"Good day, William," Jack called on the deck of the *Queen Anne's Revenge*. "It is good to see you returned to your home. Are you well?"

William nodded. "As well as fortune allows me to be, under

the circumstances. Bones do not heal so easily, in my experience. How have you found it?"

Jack chuckled. "One time, in my tavern-hopping days, I was involved in a brawl of sorts, and my arm was broken. I was lucky the bone didn't pierce my skin, and I healed after two months, if I recall. It still aches during storms."

"I am not alone in my suffering for eternity then. That brings me small hope."

Jack waved his hand. "With a ripe young body such as yours, you'll be better in no time."

"Thank you, sir. I hope you are correct, as I hear whispers of a battle on the horizon."

Jack leaned against the port railing, his back to the *Fortune*. "Aye, that is true. We may head into a battle soon. I suppose you're not privy to all that has occurred here?"

William shook his head. "I have not had the luxury of my faculties of late."

Jack folded his arms. "Let me attempt to brief you. First, Herbert insulted me when I tried to dissuade him from voting to leave the captain. Then he stole the ship, managed to find out where one of Calico Jack's subordinates will be, and is no longer our quartermaster as punishment." Jack smiled at the last part.

"You seem happy over Herbert's misfortune," William said, more statement than question.

Jack raised his brow. "Misfortune? Misfortune is losing coin making a bad bet. Herbert deserved punishment for what he did. If not for Edward's mercy, and that the crew might riot, his action should have been considered mutiny." Jack's anger took hold of him for a moment, but he soon regained his composure, and glanced warily at the crew on deck. William supposed that there were still those who sided with Herbert, judging from Jack's expression.

William nodded and stroked his chin. "So you would have killed him for mutiny?"

Jack's eyes went wide. "No, no…" He let out a sigh. "I

163

don't know what I would have done differently in Edward's position."

"Perhaps you are simply agitated by Herbert's insults prior to taking the ship?"

"By rights I am agitated. I was trying to convince him not to propose the vote or leave Edward behind, but he didn't listen."

"And?" William said, his brow raised.

"And..." Jack paused for a moment, searching for the words. "He compared his actions to what I did against George Rooke years ago, and brought up my drinking habits when I've not touched a drop of drink in quite some time."

"So, he compared his actions to your pulling a gun on George Rooke and turning to alcohol in your time of need, and this angered you?" Jack nodded. "Then, and please do not take offence to this, sir, would it be more appropriate to say that the reason you are upset is because his words were true?"

Jack's eyes widened and his jaw dropped, but after a moment he seemed to reflect on what William said. His lips made a line, and his gaze lowered to the sole of the deck, staying there for some time.

"You may be correct," he said after a few moments.

"Do not trouble yourself over the past, friend. You are not the same person you were then. Only worry about who you are now, and work to ensure you do not repeat past mistakes."

Jack nodded. "I struggle with it every day," he said. "I do suppose I should let go of my anger. Herbert accepted his punishment with grace yesterday, and discouraged the crew from mutinying."

Before they could talk any further on the subject, Anne called to him.

William turned around and stepped to the side. "Princess, good day to you."

"And good day to you, but I'm not a princess any longer, as you'll recall."

William bowed his head a touch. "I will do my best to remember."

"A good day to you as well, Mr Christian," she said with a wave.

"How do you do, Mrs Thatch?" Jack asked.

"Better, now that we are home. If I may, sir, I wish to speak with William."

Jack waved his hand. "Certainly," he said as he lifted himself off the railing. He smacked William on the arm. "Good fortune to you, William, and thank you. You've given me a lot to think about."

Jack left Anne and William, and picked up one of his instruments nearby to play. After he left, Anne raised her brow. "What did you give him to think about?"

William shook his head. "A trifle, really. The man was angry with Herbert over some words he said regarding his past aboard the ship. I reminded him that only the present and one's current actions matter, not the past actions they regret."

Anne glanced over her shoulder at Jack, who was now playing a tune on his fiddle. "Sound advice from a friend," she said. "Perhaps you could assist me also?"

"Whatever could I help you with?" William asked.

"Did Jack mention to you about Herbert losing his position?" William nodded. "I was elected to replace him as quartermaster. Herbert will remain the ship's sailing master, but I will be in charge of the crew and supplies, and, of course, represent their wishes to the captain."

William couldn't help but flash a rare smile, as he felt overjoyed by her promotion. "That is excellent news, my la… Quartermaster," he said. "I suppose I answer to you now."

Anne smirked. "Yes, it strains credulity to believe you are up to the task of following my orders. The very thought of having to teach you proper chain of command causes my head to ache already."

"I shall do my best to learn quickly."

Anne and William chuckled together for a moment. William felt happy to see Anne smile, as her smile too seemed to be a rare display these days.

"I was wondering if you would assist me in creating a training regimen. I've already discussed with Alexandre a few considerations, and I should like your opinion as well."

"Certainly," he replied.

As the sun rose, the two discussed various activities and drills which could help improve their prowess in battle, including some manoeuvres which involved the use of more than one ship that they might be able to use in the near future.

Edward sat in the stern cabin's war room, staring at the map showing the Spanish treasure ship's routes. He had been staring at it off and on the night before and all this morning, but the various outlines of islands, land masses, and lines—both dotted and straight—began to blend together. He rubbed his eyes and tried to refocus on the details, but the map was beginning to lose all meaning to him. No matter how many times he looked, he could glean no information that could help him with his dilemma.

How are we to face a galleon and three other ships when we only have two?

After another moment, Edward threw the paper aside. The air of the room caught it, caused it to arc in the middle of its flight, and it swooped back onto the table amongst other miscellaneous papers.

The door to the war room opened, and Roberts stepped inside, closing the door behind him. "Good day, Edward," he said with a wave.

"Good day, Roberts. I trust you are well?"

"Very well, thank you. And you?" Roberts asked, and then he took a look at the table in front of Edward. "Judging from the mess you've made I would wager that a no?"

"You would be correct. I've been attempting to create a suitable battle plan, but the only one I have is too dangerous.

Thus why I've called this meeting." Edward glanced to the door. "Were you the only one on the way?"

Roberts nodded and adjusted his tall, bulky frame in the small seat. "Yes." He looked over his shoulder to the door. "I did not see any others approaching, though I am certain they are on the way."

Edward leaned back in his chair. The light from the cabin's windows and a few lanterns dotting the walls gave the room a soft glow. The dancing waves reflected the sun's light and made it dance on the ceiling. The day was warm, but not as blistering as the previous week had been. He still felt the need to pat himself off with a cloth, though, and the rag came back moist to the touch.

"It is a curious feeling, is it not?" Roberts asked.

Edward chuckled. "What?"

Roberts too was leaning back in his chair, his feet pushing against the oval table in the centre of the room. "We are closing in on vengeance years in the making for the two of us. The feeling is... surreal."

Edward mimicked Roberts and pushed his chair into a leaning position with his boots against the table. He gazed at the ceiling as he thought on Kenneth Locke's homely face, but he felt his heart beginning to race and his throat seize, so he shook it away.

"You've been waiting far longer than I," Edward said. He began squeezing his hand tight, the pressure and pain bringing him back to today. *You are here, you are now.* His wife's voice rang in his head.

"Yes, I've been waiting nearly... four years now. Travelled across the globe, and only now that we're upon the edge of this business am I beginning to think on the truth of it all."

Edward eyed his friend curiously. "What do you mean?"

"Well... I suppose over the years it's become quite removed. What I mean to say is..." Roberts pulled his boots away from the table and his chair landed back on the deck with a snap. "Walter Kennedy served as a destination moreso than a prize. As if I moved forward to find him, but I wasn't truly thinking of catching him. It felt as if I never would catch him, I suppose."

"And now he is at your door," Edward said. Roberts nodded and stared at the papers on the table, but he wasn't focussed on them. "What will you do when we catch him?"

Roberts looked at Edward, but his expression was unreadable. "I suppose... I don't know."

Edward also plopped his seat back on the sole. "You're not going to kill him?"

"My friend, not knowing means I could do any number of things. I simply have not chosen my course of action. I've never had to think on it until now."

"Very well, what have you been thinking until now of doing?"

Roberts laughed and sat up straight. "You ask a similar question expecting a different answer," he said, which made Edward chuckle as well.

"A reasonable objection."

"I have been saying since the beginning that I would bring God's justice upon him." Roberts appeared deep in thought for a moment, and then he looked at Edward again. "What will you do to Kenneth Locke?"

The name still had an arresting hold on Edward, but now he had a method to diminish the pain. He repeated his wife's chant over and over in his mind. Thankfully, his pause could pass for contemplation.

"I'm going to do the same thing you should do: Kill him, and remove the curse he's placed on me."

Roberts ran his fingers through his straight chestnut-brown hair. "I wonder if that is God's justice."

"Hmph," Edward scoffed. "No, of course not... It's pirate justice."

The sound of the door opening took their attention away from their conversation. One after the other, Anne, William, Alexandre, Victoria, Pukuh, and Herbert entered the stern cabin.

"Hold a moment, Herbert," Edward said, holding up his hand. I apologise if another summoned you here... but this meeting does not involve you."

Everyone in the room glanced from Edward to Herbert, and he to them. His jaw dropped for a second as his gaze shifted to Alexandre and Victoria, both of whom had no official rank aboard the ship, and one of whom he distrusted. The tension was visible by a slight redness on Herbert's cheeks, aside from the recent injury, which held a perpetual redness.

Edward felt no such tension or embarrassment.

"By your leave, Captain," he said with a modest bow before turning his wheelchair around.

"Wait, Herbert," Anne said. "I'm vetoing that order. You may stay."

"Veto, Quartermaster?" Herbert asked, his brow cocked.

Anne grinned. "It means I'm denying the captain's order, by my authority as quartermaster. If we are discussing battle plans, it is crucial you be privy to them so you may guide our crew when the time comes."

Herbert smiled. "I see," he said, turning around again. "Thank you."

As Herbert wheeled himself forward, the others in the room took their seats. Each person's mouth was a line, save Alexandre, who was smirking as usual.

Edward eyed his wife, and she stared straight back at him. "Now that everyone is present," he said, glancing at Herbert, "we may begin." Edward cleared his throat. "First, I was wondering if you are well, Victoria? Any of the crew troubling you?"

Victoria shook her head. "I believe from Anne and Christina they are accustomed to women being aboard. I had no issues."

"That pleases me," he said. "Now then, let's discuss why I summoned you all. From what we know, Kenneth Locke will attack a Spanish galleon on its route to Havana after it lands here in Porto Bello for a silver shipment." He picked up the sheet of paper with the shipping routes on it and handed it to Victoria to pass around. "He will be aided by Walter Kennedy, and another unknown pirate, totalling three ships of similar size to our own..." He looked each person in the eyes briefly. "We need to stop them... and not die in the process."

"The only plan I could come up with would be to attack them after their battle with the galleon. If luck aids our cause, they will lose against the galleon and give up, then we pursue them and finish them off."

"And if luck is not on our side?" Roberts asked.

"They defeat the galleon, take the treasure, and still have three ships to attack us with."

"How long until the galleon arrives at Kenneth's point of attack?" William asked, not having been privy to the conversation with Luis Delgado.

"A week or a fortnight at most," Edward replied. "The galleon will be here in a matter of days, then it restocks for another day, and then it takes four days to reach the island Providencia. If weather is not in their favour, or if a storm comes, it could delay them another few days."

"Then we should go to where they are, and attack them on land," William suggested. "On land they won't be as difficult to defeat, as we may have crews of similar size."

"We cannot rely on that," Victoria said. "We don't know the size of the ships or their crews, only that they are similar to ours. They could have the same number of crew as us for each ship."

William nodded. "That is a risk we may have to take."

"What about if we just attack one crew?" Anne suggested. The others in the room looked at her. "We can... say, land on Providencia, scout the pirates for their weak link, and attack them instead of all the ships."

"You might have the right idea, but we can't simply attack the crew. The others will rush to their aid." Edward stroked his beard.

"Simple, *mon ami*," Alexandre said. "Sabotage one ship, and they will be delayed. If you only damage it slightly… say, enough to warrant a few hours' repairs, the others may leave to their destination and wait for the damaged ship to catch up."

"I think that may be our best option yet," Edward said with a smirk.

Herbert chuckled. "There's a better way," he said.

Edward waved his hand. "Share it then. That is why you're here."

"The simplest way would be to recruit another ship to our cause," Herbert suggested.

"Where would we find someone to help us at this hour?" William asked.

"We could appeal to some of the ships in Porto Bello. I'm sure, at minimum, one of them would be willing to join our cause for the right price."

The talk of having another ship join them caused Edward to jump up from his seat. "I've got it! I know who we can recruit," he exclaimed.

Those in the room looked at him strangely, but they all wanted to know his idea. "What ship did you have in mind?"

"Not just any ship will do," Edward said. "We need *the* ship on our side if we want to win."

"And that ship would be…?" Anne asked.

"The Spanish galleon," Edward said with a wide grin. "We'll convince the Spanish to join forces with us against Kenneth Locke."

14. NEGOTIATIONS

"I believe you will need to explain this to us again, husband," Anne said with furrowed brows. "I'm afraid some of us may think you've gone mad."

"I've not gone mad," Edward replied. "If we have a galleon on our side, it won't matter how many ships they have on their side. We would be able to fight together and crush them, and then we won't have to fear picking at the scraps."

"He *has* gone mad," Roberts said with a raised brow.

Edward sighed. "I'm not mad. If we aren't able to convince the Spanish to join with us, we can simply focus on the other plan," he said with a wave of his hand. "Having the galleon is the safest way to achieve our plans."

"You are aware we're pirates, yes?" Anne said, incredulous.

"I am fully aware of what we are, and also aware of with whom we've been fighting. I don't believe we've had any encounters with Spanish forces, nor have we hit any of their harbours."

"Save Panama City," Anne said.

"Yes…" Edward said, glancing to Herbert, Alexandre, and Victoria. "Save for Panama City, we haven't attacked the Spanish, only the British. None in Panama City know who attacked the whorehouse, so we're safe there. Surely some of our exploits have reached Spanish ears."

Anne tapped her foot on the wooden floorboards of the cabin, and she had her arms crossed. Her mouth was a line, and she seemed to be searching her mind for some further objections, but she seemed unable to come up with more.

"It may work," she conceded.

Edward looked at Bartholomew Roberts. "You may be able

to assist in the negotiations as well, Roberts. If my name isn't common knowledge, yours should be well known."

Roberts raised his brow. "How so?"

Edward looked at Anne. "Portugal is in an alliance with England at the moment, is it not?"

Anne nodded. "Yes, it is, but I know not what this adds to the discussion."

"He aims to use my past exploits as proof of our camaraderie, Mrs Quartermaster."

"Your... past exploits?"

"You may recall a time I mentioned when I stole some rather valuable jewels? They were owned by the King of Portugal," he said, motioning with his hand.

"Ah..." Anne said. "And Spain is none too happy with Portugal at the moment, as it sides with the British. Especially so now, as not long ago there was a concentrated attack on Spain's borders from Portugal, from what I've heard."

"And we can use that to our advantage here," Edward said. "We'll hide the fact that we're pirates at first, but if we need to convince them we're on their side we can tell them everything."

"Are you sure this is wise?" Victoria asked. "Pirates have ravaged this country just as much as the British have ravaged Spain in this war. How do you know they will not kill you if and when they discover the truth?"

Edward thought the problem over for a moment. He ran his fingers through his wavy black hair, slicking back some of the sweat that had gathered on his forehead. "We will ask him to parley with us, at a location of our choosing, outside of Porto Bello... We can have men on guard to ensure nothing goes wrong while we discuss the alliance," he said. "We can be smart about this, and even if negotiations sour, we will leave with our heads."

"The next issue is," Anne said, "how do we secure the Spanish captain's attention?"

"I say we be direct and tell them about the attack and how we wish to help," Edward said. "Perhaps... you could draft a letter?" Edward looked at Anne as he said the words.

Anne's brows raised. "Me?"

Edward nodded. "You're far more formal than the lot of us. You would be the most persuasive and… respectful with your words."

Anne glanced to the others in the room. "You have a point, I suppose." She sighed. "My Spanish is a bit rusty, but I shall do my best."

"Thank you," Edward said. "In the meantime, Roberts, would you like to scout out a location with me?"

Roberts smiled. "Yes, that could be a bit of fun."

Edward rose from his chair and looked at all those in the room. "If no one else has anything to add…?"

Herbert shuffled in his seat for a moment, and then spoke up. "I have a question," he said.

Edward's mouth was a line. "Yes?"

"Should we not put this to a vote?"

"I believe I made it clear that you may no longer propose votes."

Herbert stared at Edward, his brows furrowed. "Yes, abundantly," he replied. "I believe the Commandments are clear in that every man shall have a vote on current affairs."

Edward looked down for a moment and clenched his teeth in frustration. "Shall we vote on when we decide to wake, or sleep, or shit, for that matter?"

"Edward!" Anne looked mortified.

Edward ignored his wife. "Votes are a provision only outside of battle. This is something that has always been in effect. This involves battle, and battle plans, so that means my decision on how we go about our attack is not a voting matter," he said, staring daggers at Herbert. "Understood?"

Herbert's face once more reddened around his cheeks. His injured eye still covered most of his embarrassment, but not all. His teeth and jaw locked in place for the briefest of moments as he and Edward stared at each other.

"Understood, Captain," he said eventually.

"Good," Edward replied with a nod. "Roberts? Care to join me?"

Roberts glanced from Edward to Herbert and back. "Uhh… yes, let's be on our way."

Edward walked around the oval table and left the room, with Roberts following behind. He called upon a few crewmates to arm themselves and join him on their expedition, and they gathered supplies for the short trip.

Edward didn't talk as they organized their supplies. His anger was plain to see, and plain to feel on his own face. He felt hot and flushed, and the sun beating down on him did not help.

Edward and company entered one of the *Queen Anne's Revenge*'s longboats and paddled to the shore nearby. The air was hot and humid, as expected this close to shore, and it didn't seem to get any better after they landed and entered the nearby forest.

The tall palms were side by side with thick cottonwood trees, hanging vines, chest-high bushes, and obtrusive roots. As the group moved through the forest, they had to keep an eye on their feet to keep from tripping.

"If we can find a clearing nearby, that should do," Edward said. "No need to stay so close, men. We won't be able to see everything all bunched together like bananas. Keep within sight of each other."

The crew shouted "Aye, Captain," and then split up into a few smaller groups.

Edward pulled out his cutlass and whacked at some low-hanging branches in his way. The closest branch shook with his strike, and the rustling of the leaves travelled up to the top, sending some local birds fluttering from their perches to escape the potential danger below.

Around him, he could hear the sounds of different birds and animals he wasn't familiar with. He thought he might have heard monkeys, but he couldn't be sure. The noise reminded him of the first time he had seen a monkey. It was his first time on a trip with his father. It jumped on the ship when they were docked and stole some food before someone could shoo it away.

"Edward, may I talk with you a moment?" Roberts said behind him.

"Of course you may," Edward replied as he moved aside some long leaves.

"I don't wish to inspire your rage, but… captain to captain, I feel you are being too harsh on the boy."

Edward glanced over his shoulder and took a breath. "Herbert?"

"Yes."

"Nonsense," Edward said. "I spoke my mind, as I always do."

"That may be, but your tone was cavalier. I have seen you act this way before, when you are angered with someone."

Edward stopped and turned around. "And what of it? By rights I should be angry. He stole my ship, Roberts!"

"Aye, and he's paid the price. You've doled out your punishment, and he accepted it with grace." Edward looked away from Roberts' gaze for a moment. "None are telling you to discard your anger—though that is sound advice—but I simply believe you would do well not to punish Mr Blackwood over and over."

Edward furrowed his brows in anger. "You presume too much, and reach too far, if you would think to tell me how to run my ship, Roberts."

Roberts didn't back down, and instead straightened his back and puffed out his massive chest to intensify his countenance. "You may soon find yourself losing your ship if you continue the way you're going."

"Are you with me, Roberts? Because from *your* cavalier tone it sounds like you aren't."

"Being your ally and agreeing with your every action are not one and the same," Roberts said. After a moment, the man took a step back and shook his head. "I do not wish for the same thing as happened to your former first mate, Henry, to happen to Herbert."

Thoughts of his departed best friend bombarded Edward. The sight of Henry falling to his knees with a gunshot at his back, and the smoking pistol in Edward's shaking hand took hold of him. He looked down to his hands now, holding a cutlass instead of a pistol.

Roberts didn't know about Edward's sin; he only knew that Henry decided to leave the crew, not what happened afterwards. Despite that, Edward's frustration and anger intensified.

Edward tightened his grip on his cutlass. "This conversation is over," he said. "Concern yourself with your crew, and leave mine out of it."

Roberts' mouth opened to say something, but Edward turned around and walked away. He went through the forest with leaden feet and a heavy heart. He couldn't tell if Roberts followed after him, and at that moment he didn't care.

What does it matter anyway? Edward thought as he hacked and slashed his way through the bush. *Either they're with me or against me. Why should I spare a second thought for my enemies?*

With no foil to Edward's thoughts, his self-rationalization continued unimpeded. He lost all awareness of his surroundings as he cut branch after branch, vine after vine, and bush after bush. He walked long enough that he forgot where he was going, but kept walking forward and cutting down everything in his path nonetheless.

When Edward noticed a lack of roots beneath his feet and obstructions in front of him, he finally looked up and took note of his surroundings. He had stumbled upon a wide field of grass surrounded by the forest. Somehow an acre of field was devoid of trees, and the local wildlife must have fed on the grass to keep it short.

Edward's chest heaved with each breath he took; the exertion of slashing his way to the field had taken its toll on him. His arm was tired, and sweat covered his face ear to ear.

As he gazed upon the empty field and rested, it was as if the forest had gone silent. He could hear nothing but the rustle of the leaves and grass swaying in the wind.

Edward sheathed his cutlass and searched for the tallest tree he could see. Once he found a suitable one, he climbed up its branches. He took care as he moved from one branch to the next, his feet and hands keeping him steady as he moved up to the peak. As he climbed, the branches became thinner and thinner, and the canopy over the forest receded before his eyes.

Just before reaching the top of the tree, he stopped and stood on the thinnest branch that could still hold his weight. He held onto the trunk and gazed around the forest from his new vantage point.

He was so high up now, he was able to see the ocean to his left, but he could only see a sea of trees on his right. He scanned the horizon out over the ocean until he found what he was looking for: the *Queen Anne's Revenge*.

He wasn't able to see the whole ship, but he could see the tip of the middle mast poking out from the forest canopy. While he wasn't able to see Porto Bello, judging by the location of the ocean in relation to the trees and the ship he could guess where it was. He had travelled far, and he was only ten or twenty minutes' walk to the town at most.

Edward looked below, and began climbing back down the tree. After a few minutes of careful descent, he noticed some of the other crewmates entering the clearing.

"Oi!" he yelled.

The crewmates followed the sound of his voice, and once they noticed him they grouped together at the base of the tree. By the time Edward had reached the bottom branches, they had all entered the field.

Edward jumped down to the ground and rolled before standing up and facing the men. "This is where we will have our meeting with the Spanish," he stated. "I want two of you to scout a path to Porto Bello; try to make it short but easy to walk. The rest of you, come with me. We're going to get this set up properly. We wouldn't want to disappoint our new allies," he added with a smirk.

Edward sat at a table under a fabric canopy in the middle of the clearing they had found the day before. Anne, Roberts, and William accompanied him at the table, and an assortment of men from both crews were scattered around the forest. Pukuh and Hank were leading the defence, and each of them kept a close watch on the proceedings.

Edward got up from his seat, reached over to take a piece of cheese from a plate in the centre, and threw it into his mouth. He barely even had to chew as it had been softened by the heat of the day.

"If you eat any more, there won't be any left for our guests," Anne warned.

Edward shrugged his shoulders. "All this waiting is taking its toll on my insides."

Anne gave him another look, and he promised her he wouldn't eat another piece.

The air around the table and in the field was hot and oppressive. It was nearing noon, and it was the most torrid it had been since they'd arrived in Porto Bello. The tension wasn't aiding the stifling heat either, as each man was on alert and ready to fire their weapons at a moment's notice. That alertness and nervous energy keeping them on edge was like a sickness that invaded their neighbours, and soon all the men were sweating and jumping at shadows.

The lot of them had already been waiting for three hours, and only ten minutes ago Pukuh had informed them that the guests were on their way. The captain of the Spanish galleon would arrive any minute, but they were later than they had all expected.

"Is everyone clear on our story?" William asked.

Edward grunted and leaned back in his chair. "I believe so,

as we recounted it not twenty minutes ago." William stared at him, his cold gaze saying all it needed to say. "I am a merchant by the name of Edward Teach, as is Roberts, who will go by the name of... Benjamin Kinney. We heard about the proposed attack and wish to lend our aid, as it involves pirates who wronged us in the past."

"And the terms?" William pressed.

"The terms..." Edward said, pausing for a moment. "We assist in the attack by ambushing the pirates, and take the fight to their deck while the galleon focusses on the biggest ship. When the battle is concluded, we take the pirates' cargo as payment."

William nodded. "Good," he said.

"I can't fathom why it matters when Anne will be translating," Edward said, gesturing to his wife.

Anne frowned. "We don't know if the captain speaks English as well, or if he has someone who can translate as well. We would do well to not say something regrettable."

The sound of branches crunching underfoot and the heavy rustling of leaves brought everyone's attention to the forest edge. The sounds grew louder, and before long a group of ten armed men broke through the forest and entered the small plain.

Two of the men stood in front of the others, taking in the surroundings and the people whom they were meeting. The other eight had a tight grip on their weapons, and also took in their surroundings, but in a more focussed and defensive way.

One of the two men in front wore a traditional Spanish naval uniform of gold colour with ornate decorative accents and a dozen wooden toggle buttons fastened at the centre. The man had several distinguishing medals on the breast of his uniform.

The other man wore a cloak covering his entire body, with a hood obscuring his face. Edward wasn't able to see inside the cloak, but from the two men's mannerisms, he could tell that it was a person of importance, even when compared to the Spanish captain.

Edward and the others rose from their seats and tried not to stare at their guests. He pulled at his coat and tried to straighten the creases that always seemed to form between his gut and his chest.

After a moment, the cloaked man whispered a few things to the captain, and the two approached the table.

"Thank you for joining us here, gentlemen," Edward said.

Anne translated the message, taking her time to ensure she said what she meant to say. Before she could finish, the captain held up his hand.

"I know your tongue. There is no need to strain yourself," he said.

"Ah, good. I daresay we were a bit worried over that," Edward said, and then he smiled and nodded to Anne.

"Then you may send the girl away now. I want no further delay—"

Edward held up his hand. "The *girl* is my wife and my quartermaster," he said, clenching his teeth afterwards to stop himself from saying something else.

The captain's eyes widened, and he and the other man stared at Anne. "A woman quartermaster?" The captain shook his head. "No matter. She can stay," he said. "Who are you, and how did you come to find out about this supposed attack on my vessel?"

Edward took a few seconds to breathe, and then began. "I am Edward Teach, and this is my associate, Benjamin Kinney. We are merchants who deal in this area, and we heard a rumour of the upcoming attack on your ship... Normally, we wouldn't act on such rumours, but we've had confrontations with the pirates in question, and wish to aid you."

The captain held a stern look on his face as he looked in the eyes of each person at the table, save Anne. The men behind him had their hands on their weapons, wary of the men surrounding them. The tension from before they arrived was only magnified by the arrival of the Spaniards.

Edward tried to mitigate the tension by continuing the conversation. "We have given you our names; it would be good to know how we should address you and your... companion."

"Hmph," the captain scoffed. "I am Miguel García, captain of the..." The man paused for a moment, glancing at those at the table, then shook his head. "I would tell you, but you would not understand the name, nor be able to repeat it," he said. "My companion does not need to give you his name." He seemed to hold much contempt for Edward and company, and Edward could not see why. "Where will the attack happen, how many ships, and of what size?"

"Our contact says it will happen off the coast of Providencia, and they have three ships of frigate class or lower."

"And your ships?"

"We have a frigate and a sloop-of-war. Over sixty guns between us."

Miguel nodded. "And why are they not in the harbour? Why choose to meet out here, and not in town?"

Edward breathed again. The tension was wearing on him, and he was sweating. It was lucky the day was hot, otherwise the sweat could be seen as a sign of duplicity. "They are not in harbour for the same reason we meet here: We don't know who we can trust."

The cloaked man leaned over to Miguel and whispered something in his ear. After a moment Miguel asked, "And what would you have in return for your *protection*?"

Edward nodded. "We wish to have the cargo the pirates have. A simple request, I should think, given the circumstances."

Miguel nodded. "Yes, that does seem reasonable," he said. "But tell me, how am I to trust a *liar*?"

Edward was taken aback, but he was speechless for but a moment. "I'm afraid I don't understand."

Miguel smirked. "We talked with the governor of Porto Bello after receiving your letter. The governor knew of your ship's names, but not their owners. You are pirates."

The Voyages of Queen Anne's Revenge

At the mention of the word, Edward and those spectating placed their hands on their weapons. Muscles were taut, ready to spring at the slightest movement. Eyes darted from one person to the next, waiting and watching for a surprise.

Edward's brows were furrowed, and he stared straight at Miguel. "That is quite the accusation you lay upon one who is trying to help you."

"I accuse you of the truth. Or do you wish to wait until the morrow when I see your ship's names first-hand? I know one of you is Bartholomew Roberts, captain of the *Fortune*. The other ship, *Queen Anne's Revenge*, I'm unfamiliar with, though I doubt a merchant would be working with pirates."

Edward glanced at Roberts and the others, and Roberts and Anne both nodded to him. "If you think us pirates, why come to meet us? Why did you not attack our messenger to draw us out and put us to the sword?"

"Bartholomew Roberts, though a pirate, stole from the traitorous Portugal. I felt we owed him a meeting at the very least."

Edward nodded and tapped his fingers on the table. "I believe re-introductions are in order. I am Edward Thatch, captain of the *Queen Anne's Revenge* and this," Edward said, motioning to Roberts, "is Bartholomew Roberts, captain of the *Fortune*."

"Edward Thatch?" Miguel questioned. "Where have I heard this name?"

Edward shook his head. "My ship was formerly called *Freedom*, if that aids your memory."

Miguel muttered the two names under his breath a few times until his eyes shot open and he looked at Edward in a new light. "You killed the queen's daughter!" he nearly shouted.

For the second time, Edward's jaw dropped. He glanced over to Anne, the living, breathing daughter of Queen Anne, sitting to his right. "I believe you are mistaken, sir. The reports stated that the pirates involved were unknown," Edward said,

183

referencing a newspaper they had come upon over six months before.

The paper said that Edward's Anne had been killed, as a symbolic way of disowning her after her repeated acts of delinquency. The last they had heard, the pirates in the false scandal were never named. News from the Old World was always rather scarce in the New, and unless it pertained to local events they rarely paid attention. Either that, or the Boddens never thought to mention it.

Did the Boddens know about Anne? I can't recall, Edward thought.

"That was revised months ago," Miguel said with a wide grin. "Come, come, no need to be shy of your exploits. You are both friends to Spain."

Edward glanced at his wife, and her gaze was stony as she stared in the direction of Miguel, but not directly at him. The subject was a sore spot with her; despite holding no love for her mother, the implication that one is dead to them does not inspire familial affection.

"I do not wish to brag, lest my ego grow too large. Let us discuss the attack," Edward said, trying to steer the conversation back. "I apologise for the ruse. We couldn't be sure of your trust in us. Pirates seem to have frequented this area."

Miguel waved his hand, then rose from his seat to take some of the cheese and meat off the plate on the table. "You haven't attacked any of Spain's ships or shores, so you have no reason to fear, my friends." Miguel took bites from the cheese. "Though, if you are not trying to deceive us, what do you stand to gain from attacking other pirates? Why not join them and attack us? If we had not of heard of this attack, I cannot say if we would have survived. If your two ships had joined the other pirates, it would have been assured."

Edward, too, took some of the food off the table and mimicked the Spanish captain. "The pirates involved in the attack wronged Roberts and myself. They stole his ship, and killed one of my crewmates. Another of my crewmates may still be in hiding with them as well, but the story of why is, frankly, too long and involved for today," he said.

Miguel shook his head. "Such treachery should not go unpunished. Why do you need our help with this?"

"We felt that if we could gain the help of a Spanish galleon, it would all but guarantee our success."

Miguel smirked and pointed at Edward. "Ah!" he said. "So, you plan to use me, do you?"

Edward chuckled. "Somewhat," he replied. "Consider this a partnership. One where we both benefit."

Miguel nodded. "I believe we can come to an agreement," he said. "We can work out the details on the way to Providencia. For now, let us say that we will sail together at dawn."

Miguel rose from his seat, and the cloaked man did the same. The Spaniard reached forward to shake Edward's hand, and with that their arrangement was sealed.

"On the morrow," Edward said.

After the handshake, Miguel and the rest of the Spaniards left to finish their trades for the day and prepare to sail. The cloaked man and Miguel whispered back and forth as they left.

When they were well and gone, the crews hooted and hollered their cheers. The tension that had permeated the area washed away, and a happy mood spread to each of them instead. Many of the men slapped Edward on the back, congratulating him and commenting on how well he did in the negotiations, despite the fact that everything went wrong. The fears of their covers being seen through and most of the negotiations hinging on their reputations were lost with the deal being struck.

After a few moments of revelry, Edward hushed them. "Back to the ship!" he ordered. "Tomorrow, we set sail."

15. TURNABOUT

Edward pulled in a deep breath as a yawn overtook him. The sun had yet to arise from the threshold of the horizon, and he had already been up for an hour to help prepare the ship. His jaw opened wide, cracking in the pre-dawn light. Other crewmates, a few of whom had been up even longer to secure the anchor, caught his yawn.

Before long, the crew secured the anchor, and they were ready to depart. Herbert was at the helm with Christina, the two of them working out their route. Anne was nearby issuing orders to the crew to get the *Queen Anne's Revenge* seaworthy. William was watching from the starboard railing, ordered by Anne not to work, given that he was still recovering. Pukuh, not just a warrior, was helping the crew with the sails, and despite his missing arm he was proving to be a match even for the seasoned sailors. Meanwhile, Jack was playing an instrument on the bow for all to hear to boost morale, and Nassir was there, talking with him.

To Edward's left, the *Fortune* bobbed up and down with the waves. He could see Roberts near the helm, and Hank, his first mate, shouting at the crew to get moving. They were slightly ahead of the *Queen Anne's Revenge*, and nearly ready to sail.

Anne walked over to Edward. "We can loose the sails on your order, husband."

"Let's let Roberts go on ahead. They'll need to match speed with the galleon moreso than we. We can give them the time they need and then do the same."

Anne nodded. "I am overwhelmed with disbelief over this situation. It's unthinkable that we were able to convince Captain García to side with us."

The Voyages of Queen Anne's Revenge

"Yes, it was surprising. I had expected more resistance, but according to him it's as if we're heroes to Spain."

"From pirate to patriot, it all depends on the country you're backing," Anne said. "Now we have an even number of ships, and possibly a greater number of guns in our arsenal. Any plans for the battle?"

Edward smirked. "I thought that was between my quartermaster and the helmsman?" he said.

Anne grinned. "Oh, but a captain should be intimately involved in all affairs aboard his ship. I wouldn't want to intrude."

"With your new responsibilities, I thought it might be best if the crew became accustomed to taking orders from you, so I'll let you take over for the battle this time."

Anne put up her hand. "No, no, I insist. It is a captain's duty to direct his crew in battle."

Edward couldn't help but chuckle with his wife. There had been precious few exchanges of that nature between them of late, and it warmed his heart.

He could only imagine how she were feeling at the present. He was so focussed on his own personal vengeance, he never stopped to think about how she might feel about the man who'd tortured her love and left him for dead. For a brief time, she'd even thought Edward dead, and the thought of how she had to have felt then sickened him. He never again wanted to see her face like the moment before she realised he was alive.

Edward grew serious, and pulled his wife into an embrace. "It will be over soon," he said softly.

After a few seconds, she pulled away from him and arched her eyebrow. "I know."

Edward leaned in and kissed Anne on the forehead, and she smiled. She stood on her toes and pecked him on the cheek in return.

"You know it's been four months now?" she asked.

Edward glanced away in thought, and scrunched his nose. "Four months... twelve days," he replied.

Anne's eyes widened, twinkling with amusement. "Oh, twelve days, is it? I believe I've forgotten, thank you for the reminder."

Edward pushed his wife playfully, and the two smiled and laughed together once more.

"Captain," Herbert called. "The *Fortune* has raised anchor."

Edward looked over to his companion's ship, and it was moving past them, slicing through the waves. Roberts was on the quarterdeck, and when he noticed Edward watching he tipped his hat to him. Edward returned the gesture.

"Let's get this underway, Herbert. Lay our course."

The helmsman grinned. "Aye, Captain," he said. Herbert leaned over in his chair and shouted, "Lay aloft and loose all sails!" as his first order.

The crew went up the rigging and unfurled the topsails so the wind could fill them, and then moved down to the other sails. The ship lurched forward, swaying back and forth, bobbing up and down, and all the while sounding off its usual groans and creaks.

Edward patted the wood of the railing. *You'll survive, girl. You've been through worse.*

The ship moved with the power of the wind between the two islands they had hid behind, and back into the open ocean. Roberts and the *Fortune* were already out and heading west, back towards Porto Bello to meet with the galleon.

Edward looked at the sails, filled to the brim with wind, trimmed appropriately, and yet something felt off. He turned to look at Herbert. "Herbert, do you find her a little slow today?"

Herbert glanced over at Edward, then at the sails, and then at the sides of the ship towards the churning water. "Perhaps the wind just isn't as strong as we think," he speculated. "I see no cause for concern, Captain."

Edward accepted Herbert's judgement on the matter. "It's not as if we'll need the extra speed regardless. We're escorting a galleon, after all."

Herbert chuckled. "True."

They followed the *Fortune* around the shore of Panama towards Porto Bello. After the near hour-long trip, most of which *Fortune* slowed down for, they neared the Porto Bello inlet. The sun had finally burst from its hiding spot on the horizon, and the glow afforded them better sight of the sea and surrounding area.

"Captain, I believe I see the Spanish galleon," Herbert said, pointing off the bow.

Sure enough, the Spanish vessel was there, sailing out of Porto Bello. It was a behemoth of a ship, with four masts and at least ninety cannons across two gun decks, and swivel cannons on the main deck. The sight of it was awe-inspiring and fearsome.

The two ships approached the galleon heading west as the Spaniards headed north. As they came closer to the massive ship, their own ships' sizes were brought into an inevitable comparison.

The *Fortune* and the *Queen Anne's Revenge* were alike in that they had a single gun deck, but the *Fortune* didn't hold as many cannons. It was shorter in both length and height, but swifter. In the presence of the galleon it looked as a dwarf standing next to a giant such as Roberts.

The *Queen Anne's Revenge* was longer and taller than the *Fortune*, had more guns, larger masts and sails, and was superior to most other pirate ships. Even with all that, Edward's ship—with masts removed—didn't look half as big as the galleon, so tall and wide was its berth.

Edward whistled as they drew closer. "If we had a ship as big as that, none would be able to touch us," he said.

"Don't be fooled by its size, Captain," William said, walking over to him. "True, a galleon's broadside could wreck a ship of smaller size than the *Fortune* with one, clean blast, but they are slow and troublesome vessels. Just as with most things of such a size, the larger they are, the easier they topple over."

Edward leaned against the quarterdeck railing. "Is that so?"

William nodded. "Notice the top half of the ship?" he said, pointing to the galleon as they approached. Edward pulled out his spyglass to get a better look. "It's bowed inward towards the top so the weather deck is more compact. This is to bring more weight to the centre of the ship in an attempt to keep it steady, but it still sways like no other in the water."

Edward scanned the ship with his spyglass, taking note of the shape it, as well as its movement. He chuckled. "It does sway like a bitch, doesn't it?"

Anne smacked Edward's chest. "Don't be so crude."

Edward looked away from his spyglass for a moment to grin at Anne. When he did, something to the south, towards Porto Bello, caught his eye.

Edward noticed two ships heading out of Porto Bello, itself nothing out of the ordinary. He looked through his spyglass to see two sloops of similar size to the *Fortune* a league behind the galleon.

Strange that they too are heading north.

Edward turned his spyglass back to the galleon, and looked at the crew on the weather deck. He could see them moving back and forth, maintaining the trim of the sails as the wind shifted. A new unease grew in his belly. He could see men running about with what looked to be boxes of something. As if that weren't enough, Edward also noticed fewer men than should be needed on the main deck. There were enough to man the sails, but that was all. There should have been more up top to relieve the others, should the need arise.

On their own, the ships, the movement on the top deck, and the lack of men manning the sails would be nothing. But together, it caused a stir in Edward, and he could not shake the anxious feeling overtaking him.

"Turn us to starboard, Herbert," Edward commanded.

Herbert turned in his seat and raised his brow. "Starboard? But we're almost beside the galleon."

Edward didn't repeat the order, and instead noted to himself that Roberts was just in front of them, and in thirty minutes would come within cannon range.

"Belay that. Get us next to Roberts on his port side. No, no, that won't work."

"Captain, could you please apprise me of the situation?" Herbert asked.

Edward must have had a strange look on his face, as Anne walked over to him. "Husband, is something the matter?"

"Please, everyone, cease your questions! I need to think," Edward shouted.

Those around Edward gave him strange looks, but no one asked him any further questions.

Even if we turn now, with the speed we're going and the speed of the galleon, we're still going to be in range of its cannons. If we don't turn now, we'll be dead in the water.

"The galleon is going to attack us, we need to move to starboard now and get out of its path," Edward announced. "Someone, get me a musket."

"What caused this change? Not moments ago you thought them our allies," Anne asked.

Edward pointed to the two ships approaching to their left. "I believe the Spanish hired those ships to aid them against Kenneth Locke, and to attack us. There's some strange movement on board the galleon as well," he said, handing his spyglass to Anne.

Someone brought Edward a musket, and he began loading it.

Anne looked at the approaching ships, and then to the galleon's deck. "There does appear to be some oddities, but why would they act our allies one day, and betray us the next?"

Edward frowned as he finished loading the musket. "I have neither the clairvoyance nor the patience to puzzle out whether I'm right or wrong. If I'm right, we'll escape with minor damage. If I'm wrong, we can laugh with the Spanish about it later," he said. Edward moved to the port side of the ship. "Turn this ship starboard, Herbert!" he shouted.

Herbert sank himself deep into his wheelchair and flung the

ship's wheel hard to port. The ship lurched with the sudden change in direction, and the men aboard were not prepared for the shift. Some fell to the deck, others grabbed onto the rigging or the fife rails, and some simply leaned to avoid tumbling.

Christina grabbed hold of Herbert's wheelchair, holding it close like a piece of driftwood in a storm. She also helped him from taking a tumble as well by planting her feet down to secure the both of them.

The ship cried out at the change in direction, the wooden planks stretching and straining against each other. The force from the wind pushed it in one direction, the rudder in another, and the sea a third, and the ship protested with its wooden voice, as it had many times before.

Edward held fast to the port railing in one hand and his musket in the other, and waited for the moment to pass.

Herbert eased the rudder back to have the ship turning in a looser arc. If they continued to turn at that pace it could rip the ship apart, and he knew that. At least now the worst of it was over.

Now that the ship was moving at ease and Edward had his legs firmly on the deck, he took aim and fired his musket at the stern of the *Fortune*.

The sound of the shot rang off across the sea, its echo bouncing off the water and wood. The men on the *Queen Anne's Revenge*, confused over the change in direction, became alert at the noise of battle, but when no other thunder met their ears they put away their weapons.

The crew on the *Fortune*, however, reacted as Edward had hoped. They first searched for the source of the noise on their ship, then turned to their companions. Roberts, on the quarterdeck, was quick to look Edward's way.

They were too far to shout, but Edward could tell Roberts had his brow cocked in confusion. He motioned towards the sloops approaching, and Roberts took out his spyglass and looked through it. Roberts then turned to the galleon, which was now turning starboard to match the course Edward's ship. Roberts understood immediately, and issued orders to follow the *Queen Anne's Revenge*.

The two ships were now turning as quickly as they could to the north, but they still had to go in a wide arc otherwise it could put too much strain on their hulls. Meanwhile, the three ships were closing in on them from the west and south.

While he waited for the *Fortune* to catch up to them, Edward walked back over to the helm. He tossed the musket back to the crewmate who brought it, and approached the railing.

"Men, I need your attention," Edward said. "If I am right, our Spanish allies set out to deceive us, and would have attacked us had we entered their cannon range."

The crewmates looked at each other, questions hot on their lips. Not a day before, Edward was telling them of the alliance they had with the Spanish galleon. They believed they were heading off to get revenge on Kenneth Locke and strike a blow to Calico Jack's crew, and this called everything into question.

Edward could sense their doubts, and sought to quash them before they grew any further. "We will still head north to pursue Kenneth Locke, however right now we're not out of the range of the galleon. I need you men to bring me more speed to this vessel. I'd say we have a good…" Edward turned to Herbert. "Would you say half hour?"

Herbert checked on the galleon's position and theirs. "That sounds about right."

"We have half an hour before the galleon is on us. We must broad reach the sails, so we're already at a slight disadvantage. William?"

William was promptly by Edward's side. "Yes, Captain?"

"I know you are still injured, but I need you to find us more speed. Can I count on you?"

Without hesitation, William saluted out of habit and shouted "Yes, Captain!" before turning around and yelling orders to the crew to change the positions of the sails. He went to each group of men responsible for each of the sails and attempted to tailor each one to the position of the wind.

"Christina, Anne, could you measure our speed for us?" Edward asked.

The women nodded and went to grab a chip log from the bow cabin. They rushed past the men working on the rigging and pulling the sails over to the bow's portside.

As they worked on the sails, the *Fortune* crept ever closer to their port side. Edward could see Roberts leaning out over the bow, holding onto the rigging to keep him aboard. Edward went to the stern and did the same, and soon the two were close enough to hear each other.

"They were to attack us?" Roberts yelled over the sounds of sails flapping and water pounding into a mist on the bow of his ship.

"I presume," Edward shouted back above the din. "Go on ahead, you can't take the broadside."

"And you can?"

Edward's mouth became a line. He took a breath and adjusted himself on the rope holding him to the ship. He wiped his face of sweat and salt water. "We must," he replied.

Roberts grinned, and then bowed to Edward, holding that sign of respect far longer than necessary. Whatever animosity he might have had from their disagreement seemed to be gone. After his bow, he turned to his crew and issued new orders.

The *Fortune*'s sails were trimmed and broad-reached, matching *Queen Anne's Revenge* in position, but vastly outmatching them in speed in the process. It wasn't long before the *Fortune* had already met and surpassed the position of Edward's ship, and they were in front of them once more.

"Eight and a half knots!" Edward heard Anne shout.

Eight and a half! Edward thought. He looked over at Herbert, who also looked astonished. "How in the Lord's name are we only eight and a half knots in a broad reach?"

"I don't know, Captain. Let me think it over. There must be some explanation." Herbert held his head in his hands as he mumbled over calculations in his head. Edward gave him a moment, but listened intently. "The *Fortune* can go sixteen to eighteen knots, fourteen to sixteen in a broad reach if not laden down with cargo. Our top speed in a broad reach is eleven to twelve knots if we're not…" Herbert's eyes shot open. "The cargo!" he shouted.

"What cargo?" Edward said, his brow raised in question.

"We weren't able to sell the cargo we took from the merchant ship. It's still in the hold," Herbert said.

Edward clenched his teeth together, anger washing over him. He cursed and ran down to the weather deck. "I want twenty men with me!" he yelled.

Volunteers jumped to and followed Edward to the crew cabin. Once in the belly of the ship, Edward woke their reserve crewmates still sleeping, some fifty or so men who would normally take over during the night. The men were groggy and irritated by the early wake-up, especially considering they had only just been relieved, not two hours before.

"Men, we need to jettison the cargo in the hold, as much as we can as quick as we can." The crew, still weary, looked confused. "There's no time to explain. Form a line from the hold to the top deck. We're going to dump it over the side of the ship."

The men started to form up and create a line extending from the hatchway to the hold all the way up to the weather deck.

As the crew formed the line, Edward opened the hatchway to the hold and descended a ladder with four other crewmates. He had to bend over to go inside the hold proper. In the hold there was an assortment of pungent barrels, boxes, and bags filled with spices and other miscellaneous cargo. The overpowering smell had permeated the hold. It made his nose sting and his eyes water the instant he sniffed, and he could not smell anything of the sea or the pine of the ship any longer.

Judging from the number of containers filling the hold, Edward estimated that it was several tonnes worth, and they had less than thirty minutes to clear it all.

"Let's get the barrels first, then we'll get the boxes and bags."

Edward went to work and grabbed the first barrel in his hands on his own, hefting the thing over his shoulder. His hands struggled for grip around the large, relatively smooth circumference. He took a few breaths and unbent his knees, then stepped back to the ladder and climbed up the first few rungs.

Once he was high enough, he dropped the barrel on its side, and the first crewmate rolled it over to the second, then on to the next in line until it got to the last mate before the ladder. The mates at the ladder passed it along to each other until it was on the next deck, and then the process continued.

The first few barrels were taxing, and Edward could feel the pressure across his shoulders, chest, hips and back as he worked. Once the rhythm of the work took over, the pain faded and he lost sense of everything else in the monotony.

Lift, walk, climb, drop; lift, walk, climb, drop.

Edward could hear nothing save the sound of his own hot breath, while all thoughts of the fight ahead fell to the ether. The feeling of the wood scraping his hands, the coarse grains grinding against his palm. The metal bilge hoops cool from the chilly hold pressed into his shoulder. His arms and legs stretched and strained with the exercise, growing into an almost stabbing pain as the time passed. Before he knew it, all the barrels were gone, and the raw stench of spices with it.

He glanced around at the other four men, who were carrying two barrels in pairs. His fatigue and pain hit him all at once, and he had to lean against the hull. He caught his breath in deep swells of his chest, panting tiredly. He arched his back and it cracked, sending a wave of relief through him, though it was only temporary. He brought a shaking, aching hand up to wipe the sweat from his forehead. His rough fingers scratched against his skin as the beads of water and salt were pulled together. He flung the sweat to the damp floorboards of the hold.

The Voyages of Queen Anne's Revenge

He pushed himself from the hull and went to the hold ladder. He climbed up it, following the last barrel on its track between the brigade of men. He went up to the gun deck, then back to the weather deck all the way up to see it tossed into the sea.

The sealed barrel fell into the water and floated, bobbing in the water as the *Queen Anne's Revenge* passed it by. Down the port stern, Edward could see a hundred barrels or so in a line extending so far back he wasn't able to see them all.

Off centre of the abandoned cargo, Edward could see the galleon, and he knew they were approaching the vessel's cannon range. The galleon was closing in on them, its presence even more overwhelming than before.

To the bow, on Edward's right, the *Fortune* was already heading north, and well out of the way of danger. He was glad for that fact at least.

"Speed?" he called.

Christina and Anne were on the bow still, and they looked to have been routinely checking the speed. Anne tossed the chip log into the water; the wooden piece fell in and pulled along the rope it was attached to. When it hit the sea, Christina turned over a small hourglass, watching intently as the sand fall through the small opening in the middle. After a half-minute, the last grains fell through.

"Time!" she called.

Anne grabbed the rope which the chip log had been pulling, taking note of each knot that had passed. "Ten knots!" she shouted.

Edward pounded his fist against the railing. *That's not enough!* He turned around to his crew. Many of them were still working, holding the rigging steady, making small adjustments here and there to try to improve their speed. Some looked at their captain, waiting to see what he was going to say.

"Men, secure the halyards. Brace for broadside," he said.

The crew dropping the cargo passed the order down the line so they could finish with what they had. The main sailors tied down the ropes holding the sails onto the fife rails at the masts, or along the sides of the ship to keep the sails in place.

Anne pulled in the chip log, and wrapped the rope up. She went over to Edward. "We did everything we could. If luck is on our side, she'll only be in position for half a broadside."

"And if luck is on their side, even half their broadside is enough to sink us, should it hit below the water-line," he said.

They shared a pensive, wary look. Though their lives were on the line, they had been through many similar situations in the past. They could see in each other the fear buried deep within, the fear that deadens with time and is mixed with anger and tenacity. Edward wasn't about to give up, and from that look in her eyes, Anne wasn't either.

The crew were piling bags filled with sand from the bow storage cabin across the starboard side of the weather deck. With the entire crew working, in a few short minutes they had stacked the bags high enough to crouch behind. They worked to stack more around the ladders leading to the quarterdeck and the stern, as the blast was most likely to hit there.

Edward and Anne checked the rigging to ensure the sails would hold in place while the crew were busy. They tugged and pulled on the lines, testing the knots and the location of the rope. Once satisfied, they moved behind the line of sandbags and knelt down.

Edward glanced around to the ship and the men huddled together behind the makeshift barrier. These men had the same, weathered fear in their eyes, preparing for the worst but ready to spit in God's eye for letting them die should it happen.

Edward tried to find a vantage point which would provide him sight of the galleon, but at their angle it was impossible. The quarterdeck and stern were blocking his view. Judging from where the ship last was, it was only a matter of minutes now.

He looked at his men once more, their tense bodies and light whispers so vastly different from their normal boisterous and easy-going nature. But there was more to it than this moment in time, and he could tell the mood aboard his ship was shifting. The betrayals, the battles, and the injuries were piling on top of one another, and it wasn't just Edward who'd paid the toll.

The sound of thunder rippled over the ship, shaking the wooden beams and planks in its wake. The tremor ran up Edward's feet, rattling his bones as it passed over him. He braced himself.

"Incoming!" he shouted.

The sound of the cannons was followed by a full two seconds of eerie silence, a moment of pure waiting. The cannonballs came and went in a flash, ripping through the wood and blowing holes through the hull of Edward's ship. The wooden beams and planks broke apart with violent snaps as the iron rained down on them.

As the iron crashed through the stern and the railings and the doors, it carried the pieces of its destruction with it. Wood, glass from the windows, and bits of metal flew in the wake of the cannonballs.

The deadly iron hit the sandbags, and the pieces of the ship followed immediately afterwards. Dozens of sandbags exploded from the impact of the cannonballs, flung away from the blast. Sand joined the other pieces of the *Queen Anne's Revenge* to pepper the crew, once a part of their home, now another weapon against them.

Edward felt sudden pain on his face, shoulder, and chest. As soon as he was able to feel the pain, and the warm blood seeping from his wounds, he noticed the attack was over. It had all happened so quickly he hadn't even had time to think.

He rose on unsteady feet, glancing at the horrors before him. Before he could take it in, movement caught his eye. He looked up to see one of the main mast's halyards loose, pulling away from its belaying pin on the fife rail.

Without thought, Edward jumped on top of the sandbags still intact and leapt into the air. He stretched out his hand to grab the rope, which was rapidly slipping from its confines.

Blackbeard's Justice

The sound of the scraping rope against the wood was the only thing Edward could hear at that moment. If that rope got loose, the mainsail would go loose, they would lose some speed, and it would mean another broadside would be able to reach them. The rope zipped passed the fife rail. Edward pushed his hand out farther, closing his fingers around the rope, and caught the end of it with the last inch to spare.

The force of the rope escaping the fife rail pulled Edward from his mid-jump up into the air. He swung forward on the rope over the port side of the ship. At the top of his arc, he looked over to see the galleon trying to turn back straight to pursue for another broadside. The next moment Edward swung back down towards the ship, but this time with the full tack pulled down from his weight. He slammed into the port side of the ship, and whatever was in his shoulder and chest sent a lancing pain through his body.

Edward took a few breaths, clenched his teeth, and climbed the rope back to the port side railing; he wrapped the rope around his arm, and pulled himself over the top. The pull of the heavy mainsail nearly toppled him as soon as his feet hit the sole, but he stuck his feet in and managed to get to the fife rail without incident. He fastened a halyard hitch around the fife rail and secured the mainsail once more.

He noticed the screams of the injured and the shouts of Herbert and the crew around him. Herbert was already back up to the quarterdeck, his face bloody but otherwise unharmed, and his wheelchair intact. Tala was beside him, barking to accompany his orders. He noticed Christina working the rigging with the other men to fix the sails and straighten their trajectory so they could outrun the three ships in time.

Anne and Pukuh were also uninjured, and helped with the foresails. Anne was shouting, but Edward couldn't hear what she was saying. He was just happy to see her safe.

Jack was diligently playing his music, trying to play above the din to inspire the crew to work faster with the beat he was playing. He could tell Jack had injured his hand, but the man played on regardless.

Edward looked at the destruction around him. Bits of his ship strewn about the deck, holes from the front of the quarterdeck out to the stern, broken railings, chips off the mast. Large iron balls, leftovers that couldn't make it through the whole ship, pitched and rolled with the movement of the *Queen Anne's Revenge*. Heavy, unwieldy things, far larger than could fit in any of their cannons, and a danger even without the speed behind them. This was worse than he had seen from several cannon broadsides in the past.

Crewmates had been struck in the legs, the arms, the chest, and the head. Legs had been torn off, arms split in twain, chests compacted, and heads…

Alexandre and Victoria, previously below deck, were now in the middle of the fray, tending to the injured and patching them up as best they could. Nassir was helping to carry the more severely wounded below for the tough surgery ahead. The three were already covered in the blood of their allies, and the deck around their feet was running red.

Edward ran down below deck, dodging past Nassir and one of the crewmates who had lost his leg, and down to the crew cabin. He checked the stern and noticed a few holes, but nothing low enough to worry about, and then jumped into the hold hatch. It was nearly empty, with half the original number of boxes left, and a few dozen bags.

He scanned the hold, and when he found no cannonball holes in the hull he moved on to the bilge. The stench of the bilge was an order of magnitude worse than the hold had been before they'd removed the spices. Edward had to cover his nose and mouth to stop it from overwhelming him. He lay down and lowered his head into the bilge, not wanting to enter the filth if it wasn't necessary. He couldn't see well, having just come from above deck, so he listened for the sound of gushing water. After a few seconds, and satisfied he could hear nothing resembling a breach, he closed the bilge hatch and took a few deep breaths.

Edward searched for the source of the pain in his shoulder and chest, and found it to be a splinter and a nail embedded in his skin. The splinter was in the side of his chest, but wasn't deep and rather easy to remove. The nail, on the other hand, took some doing. He had to pry at it with sweaty fingers, which soon became slick with blood. He took hold of the tip of the nail, and with a shaky hand yanked the metal piece out. He dropped the bloody metal to the sole of the hold, and it hit the wood with a clang.

His shoulder wound seeped blood, and he had to clamp down his hand over the hole in a weak attempt to stop it up. He could still feel the vestiges of the metal nail in the hole in him, as if something was missing. A piece of him lost for a time, but one that would come back later—yet it still pained him.

Edward pulled himself up and returned to the weather deck. By the time he was up top, the wounded had been given aid, and three dead men were now covered by a sheet and placed at the front of the entrance to the stern cabin.

He went up to the quarterdeck, glancing over the side at the back of the ship. It appeared that the galleon had stopped giving chase, and the two sloops had turned back as well. Normally Edward would have some sense of pride at having escaped, but he only felt anger at the betrayal by the Spanish.

Friends of the Spanish. Edward spat over the side.

Edward walked over to the helm, examining the destruction that had been wrought. Their masts and sails were miraculously unscathed for the most part, but the stern decks were riddled with holes and pieces of the ship lay underfoot at every turn.

He looked out over the bow to see the *Fortune* furling her sails to slow and join with *Queen Anne's Revenge*. Now that the threat was gone, they could talk about what to do next, but it was clear in Edward's mind what he wanted to do.

As Edward approached the helm, Herbert asked, "No breaches?" Edward shook his head. Herbert seemed to look twice at Edward, then asked, "What now, Captain?" as if he sensed Edward's mood.

"Now…" Edward said, looking Herbert in the eyes. "Now, we burn them all."

16. MEMENTOS OF WEAKNESS

"My boy, I tell you true, I am ever grateful for your insight and perceptiveness. You saved us once again," Roberts said with a boisterous laugh. He raised his cup in the air and then took a long drink from it.

Roberts and Edward were in the stern cabin of the *Queen Anne's Revenge*, talking about the recent events and what to do next. Most of the glass in the room had been shattered, the wood punctured with large holes, and the floor littered with their leftover splinters, but Edward had insisted on having the meeting there.

"If only I had noticed sooner, perhaps we would have escaped unscathed," Edward replied, and then he too took a drink from his cup.

"Nonsense. You acted as swiftly as any could be expected. Who would think we would have been betrayed? The Spanish seemed eager to work with us not a day before. None could spot the lie soon enough, so this was bound to happen."

Edward nodded. "I suppose you are right, but I don't believe he was lying the other day."

Roberts raised his brow. "Oh no?"

"You said yourself, none could spot his lie. Given our collective experience with liars, cheats, and tricksters, we certainly would have known."

"So, you believe Captain García was telling the truth?" Edward nodded. "Then what could have changed his position overnight?"

Edward shook his head. "I don't know," he replied. "But I believe it to have something to do with the hooded man with him."

The Voyages of Queen Anne's Revenge

Roberts leaned back in his chair. "Ah, yes, the mystery man. Strange fellow, to be sure, but you think him to be the mastermind of this deception?"

"It seems the most likely. He was whispering in the captain's ear the entire time, but stopped after we confirmed who we were. He probably thought it best to let the captain tell us what we wanted to hear, and then later told the captain what they would do, or at the least advised him to change his mind."

"You may be correct," Roberts replied, swirling the drink in his hands.

The sea air swept in from outside of the holes in the cabin, preventing the room from becoming stuffy, as it was prone to do. The splash of the waves as the ship crashed against them and the shouts of the men outside came in loud and clear as well.

"I want you to continue ahead of us," Edward said.

Roberts tilted his head, and his lips curled. "Continue on… to what end?"

"To the end of our enemies. I want you to head to Providencia and proceed with our initial plan of sabotaging one of the ships."

Roberts glanced around. "And what will you and your men be doing?"

"We need to repair our ship, so we'll be travelling rather slowly. Also, there are some… renovations I believe need to happen if we are to survive on the sea any longer," Edward took another drink from his cup. "I want you to take some of my crew with you as well. They can help you so you can continue at speed during the night." Edward placed his cup on the broken table in the middle of the room. "If all goes well, we should be able to arrive a day behind you."

Roberts' mouth was a line, and he stared at Edward for a moment before placing his cup on the mangled table as well. "You are sure of this?"

"Currently, this is the best way to proceed. If the two sloops that were with the galleon earlier today join her, it would be an even match for Kenneth Locke. We need to cripple one of his ships, perhaps take it for ourselves, and we may be able to destroy all of them. The galleon, the sloops, and the pirates."

Roberts rose from his seat and extended his hand. Edward got up and took Roberts' hand, and the two gripped hard, testing each other's strength. After a moment of equal back and forth, they laughed amicably, and Roberts slapped Edward's shoulder.

"Until next we meet, then," he said.

"Until next we meet."

Roberts turned around to leave, and Edward made to follow. "Oh!" Edward blurted out. "Before I forget, the cargo... Herbert didn't have a chance to sell it and—"

Roberts held up his hand. "I watched the scene firsthand, Edward. I know the toll you paid. You will find another means to repay me, I am sure of it. Don't let it trouble you."

Edward smiled and nodded. "Thank you, Roberts. As always, you are a true friend."

Roberts waved his hand. "Do not mention it. You loan us your crew to aid in our revenge. What more could I ask for?"

Edward folded his arms. "Well, you are already asking for coin..."

Roberts burst out laughing. "You have me there."

Edward also chuckled, and the two left the stern cabin. Repairs were already underway the weather deck, and the sounds of hammers hitting nails and wood met their ears. Roberts' crew were working with Nassir and Edward's crew in repairs to the railings and the stern.

Edward and Roberts went up to the quarterdeck of the *Queen Anne's Revenge* to address the crew. After a moment of calling for their attention they ceased repairs, and Edward could explain their plan.

"Firstly, I want to thank the crew of the *Fortune* for your help in repairing the damage we received. With your help, our ship is already beginning to look like its former self." At that,

The Voyages of Queen Anne's Revenge

Edward's crew hooted and hollered their agreement and thanks as well. "Roberts and I have conferred, and we think it best if you all move on to ensure our plans come to fruition. You'll be heading to Providencia ahead of us to sabotage one of the enemy ships, and when we meet with you again we will take the fight to Kenneth Locke and Walter Kennedy together!" Both crews shouted their enthusiasm to have this years-long story of revenge over and done with. "To ensure the *Fortune* arrives on time, I want twenty men to join them and help run their ship at night. Do I have any volunteers?"

Many of Edward's crew raised their hands, several of whom glanced at their neighbours and friends from the other ship, nodding and smiling at them.

"Choose amongst yourselves who to send, then pack your things and get on with it. You're to follow Roberts' orders as my own, you hear me?"

The crewmates who volunteered responded, "Aye, Captain!"

"Now, there is one other matter which requires a vote from you all," Edward said, bringing the crew's attention back once more. "In this battle, and those to come, lack of speed will be our disadvantage. We barely survived, and I have no doubts that a few extra knots would have saved us. I propose that we fix that. I propose we tear down the forecastle and the poop deck to give us more speed."

Thankfully, the crew seemed to like the plan, and nodded in approval before voting to pass the ship renovations without a debate. They appeared excited to see the ship in better fighting condition after being hurt by the galleon.

Edward took note of how the *Queen Anne's Revenge* looked in that moment. He tried to ignore the wounds and the battle scars, and instead to focus on how the ship used to look. He wanted to remember his home as it was, and tried to burn that image into his mind.

The three masts with the thick canvas, the decks of carved Caribbean pine, all the way up to the figurehead of Anne at the bow. Over the years, from planks being replaced, Nassir carving the figurehead, and changing sails, many things had changed aboard the ship. This was just one more change to make it their own.

It will still be our home. It will just be more our own that someone else's. More than Benjamin Hornigold's. Edward gritted his teeth. *More than Calico Jack's.*

It would be a fitting tribute to Calico Jack if he realised who Edward was, and that this used to be his ship. It no longer bore the name he gave it, and it would soon look nothing like it had. In both name and appearance it would soon be Edward's ship, his home, in full.

"By your vote, it shall be done," Edward said.

The crew cheered with the decision, excited to see the change and the added speed. Roberts said his goodbye to Edward and went back to the weather deck to instruct his crew and the new volunteers readying to help him.

After the cheers subsided, Edward waved down Nassir. "Nassir, could I speak with you?"

The tall carpenter nodded and climbed up to the quarterdeck. "What do you need, Captain?" he asked in his thick accent.

"I wanted to have your thoughts on the time situation. How long will we need to repair the holes and remove the decks?"

Nassir rubbed his clean-shaven face as he glanced at the damaged stern and then over to the bow. "It will save us some time with the poop deck if we do not repair it…" Nassir trailed off and mulled it over a bit more. "It won't be pretty, and I'll need many men working day and night, but two days and we should be finished."

Edward nodded with a grin. "She doesn't need to be pretty, she just needs to be fast. Mind the figurehead though; a talented carpenter carved that for me, and I think it goes rather nicely with our ship."

Nassir grinned as well, and thanked Edward before heading

off to brief the other men.

Edward then noticed Victoria bringing some planks of wood up from the storage to the stern, and walked over to greet her. "Victoria," he called. She nodded to him, saying nothing and continuing with her work. "Do you have a moment?" he continued.

"No," she replied before dropping the planks and walking back to the quarterdeck steps.

Edward stepped forward, trying to catch her. "I wanted to know if you've been having any issues aboard."

"None," she replied without turning around. She went down the steps, heading towards the ladder to the gun deck, her boots snapping against the wood as she moved.

Edward followed her. "I was also wondering if you could provide some insight on Calico Jack. What types of ships he commands, how many allies he has..."

Victoria turned around just before reaching the steps leading into the belly of the ship. "He commands a ship as any other. I know nothing of his other ships or allies, and I was more a prisoner aboard his ship than sailor, so I cannot tell you anything useful," she said curtly. "Any further questions, or may I return to work?"

Edward shook his head, and Victoria went down the steps to the gun deck. He was left speechless and stock still, as if he were lame of body and mind.

"That one spits fire, doesn't she?" Pukuh asked, coming up beside Edward.

"Yes, she does," Edward replied. "I suppose for a woman to have the courage to board a pirate ship, she would have to be of a certain calibre."

Pukuh nodded. "Far more than you or I, that is sure."

"I believe you are right." Edward stopped staring at the ladder and turned towards his friend. "She isn't fond of me, it seems."

Pukuh shook his head. "No, no, in her eyes there is deep respect for you. I know this. She simply doesn't enjoy chattering about nothing as birds do."

Edward raised his brow. "How do you know this?"

Pukuh chuckled. "She told me," he said. "I tried to see if she knew anything of Calico Jack's old moniker of 'Benjamin Hornigold.' She gave me a look that spoke to her confusion and gave a simple answer. As I pressed, she told me as I told you."

Edward joined Pukuh in laughing, a brief but welcome moment of levity. "Speaking of the pirate with two names, do you recall anything your father might have mentioned about why he turned out this way?"

Pukuh shook his head. "Nothing of note. I don't believe my father was with him throughout all his adventures, but all the stories he did tell were joyous and fantastic in nature. Although, those could have been exaggerated stories for a child, to put them to sleep."

Edward's mouth creased as he thought on it for a moment. "Perhaps we'll have to ask him about it when we see him next."

Pukuh's face was stone. "Perhaps we will... Of course, it would have to be after we inform him of how this happened first," he said, looking at where his right arm used to be.

Edward paused for a moment, thinking over whether he should ask what he wanted to ask. "I imagine it's not something you take joy in talking of, but how is your arm?"

Pukuh grinned as he looked at his right shoulder. "I believe you would call this a stump, no? Not much of an arm anymore."

Edward chuckled nervously. "I suppose not."

Pukuh's grin faded as he eyed the scarred and bumpy remnants of his right arm at the base of his shoulder. The skin had covered up the wound from so long ago, and some of the colour had come back to it, but scars from the hasty amputation remained white and jagged, streaking across his shoulder and over to his chest.

"I still feel it, you know," Pukuh said, glancing at Edward. "In the darkness of night, when I first wake, it itches, but when

I reach over to scratch it there's nothing there. The itch remains... Do you ever have an itch that you cannot scratch? It is frustrating, is it not?"

Edward shook his head. "The worst," he replied.

Pukuh nodded. "Imagine that, but never the ability to scratch."

"If only there were some way to help you," Edward said with a sigh.

"Do not mistake me," Pukuh said, shaking his finger. "The itch is a useful reminder. It reminds me of my weakness, and pushes me not to slack in my training."

Edward chuckled. "Only you would enjoy such a burden."

"Perhaps," Pukuh replied. "I should return to work, you said you wanted more speed for this ship, did you not?" He punched Edward in the arm, and then joined a group of men receiving instruction for the removal of the cabins.

Edward peered around the ship and noticed that his men were now boarding the *Fortune*, and they seemed to be making final preparations to leave. He walked over to see Roberts still on the *Queen Anne's Revenge*, greeting and thanking the men boarding to help them.

"Departing so soon?" Edward asked with a smirk.

Roberts grinned as well. "Yes, well, a certain captain wishes me to leave, and he's got a rather short fuse from what I've seen."

Edward folded his arms. "Oh, is that so?" After a moment of staring Roberts down, the two burst into laughter. After another moment they ceased laughing, but Edward still carried the smile. "Safe travels, friend. Find Walter Kennedy and give him hell," he said.

"I shall," Roberts said before tipping his hat. "We'll be watching the seas for your return in three days."

"We'll be there," Edward replied.

Roberts crossed the gangplank connecting their ships, and the crews released the bonds tying the vessels together. The two ships drifted apart for a few moments, and when there was enough room the *Fortune*'s sails were loosed and it took off north towards Providencia.

Both crews shouted and waved as they sent off their brethren. The sun shone bright that afternoon as they parted. Before long, the *Fortune* had become a dot on the horizon and soon the light reflecting off the water hid it from view.

Herbert gave the order to loose the sails and the *Queen Anne's Revenge* began crawling towards Providencia as well. Herbert made sure the sails were as full as could be, but not as much as when they had been trying to escape the galleon. Too much pressure on the masts over an extended period of time could wear them down.

After the *Fortune* was out of sight, Edward walked up to the quarterdeck. Some of the men were already working with Nassir on removing the planks from the poop deck. They started with the top planks and worked their way back. Nassir did his best to instruct them in the proper removal to save the wood, but more often than not they were too hasty. Edward hoped that by the time they reached the forecastle the men would have enough experience and patience.

Edward walked over to Herbert, who was at the helm. "Herbert, how much speed do you feel these modifications will gain us?"

Herbert turned to examine the men at work on the poop deck, and then glanced over at the forecastle. "It's tough to say... Perhaps one to two knots at most."

"That would put us only a few knots below Roberts' ship, no?"

Herbert nodded. "It would close the gap a bit, yes."

Edward smirked and stroked his beard. "Perhaps we should challenge them to a race when they're laden down with cargo? Then we may be an even match."

Herbert chuckled. "Perhaps."

There was a moment of silence between the two of them, and the sounds surrounding them filtered back in—the banging of hammers, the grunts and shouts of the men, the gust of wind and the splashes of sea water against the hull.

"We can't keep fighting each other as we have been," Edward said, peering at Herbert from the corner of his eye. "You know that... yes?"

Herbert raised his brow as he looked at Edward. "I know that. Do you?"

Edward stared at Herbert for a moment, the gaze lingering. In Herbert's eyes and tone, he detected a hint of annoyance. After taking his punishment, Herbert was rightfully upset at the way he had been treated. Edward had realised he'd wronged Herbert after Roberts berated him back in Panama, but his pride wouldn't allow him to apologise.

Edward removed his gaze and instead peered towards the bow at the water crashing against the figurehead and spraying onto the deck. "If what Calico Jack did in Bodden Town is any indication, he will try to split us apart more than ever before. We must stand together."

Herbert stopped staring at Edward and he too focussed on the sails and sea and ship in front of them. "I believe in the family you have created, and I believe in you. I know I may not have shown it very well over the past weeks, but I do. I know I have a weakness, but this family is my strength. You've reminded me of that. You conquered a town, you've gained us an ally beyond compare, and you've brought men together and made them better men by your example. Our family alone is what will help us weather the coming storm, and I will never take that for granted again."

Edward looked at Herbert, and there was no denying the resolve in his eyes. Edward nodded, and then smirked when he recalled something Pukuh had said to him in Bodden Town.

Herbert grinned and turned his head to the side. "What?"

"I trust in what you've said, and I will trust in you, but one of your statements is wrong."

Herbert cocked his brow. "Oh?"

"*We* are the storm."

17. A PERSONAL DECISION

Clouds covered the afternoon sun, blocking most of its light from reaching the sea. The wind became colder and more biting the longer the clouds lingered. Heat never seemed to last on the surface of the sea, and the splashing water only cooled the ship and crew further.

Even Edward, in his thick coat, layered on top of undershirts, and breeches and boots covering every inch of him, shuddered as the mist of the sea touched his face. "How can it never be that we are neither hot nor cold? Why must it be one extreme or the other?"

Christina chuckled daintily. "You would think after many years at sea you would be accustomed to the weather."

"One being accustomed to something and enjoying it are separate matters."

"Should I fetch you a blanket, oh Blackbeard the wicked?" Christina asked with a smirk.

"No, thank you," Edward replied, ignoring her jibe. "Tala will keep me warm, won't you girl?"

Tala's head was resting on her paws. When she heard her name, she glanced at Edward, but then ignored him.

Edward frowned, and Christina laughed. "Well, I suppose not," he said.

He peered out to the bow, towards their destination, Providencia, somewhere off on the northern horizon. Two hours prior, when the weather was fair, though hot, they had passed by the island of San Andrés. From Herbert's estimation they were one hour from seeing Providencia on the horizon, and two from landing.

The *Queen Anne's Revenge* now had no forecastle, and, aside from the masts and the sails, they were better able to see off the bow than ever before. The railing still needed some work, but Nassir had managed a crude implementation for the time being. The stern was another matter. The holes were repaired, and the ceiling for the stern cabin was in place, but there hadn't been enough time to cut or sand the edges. Some of the planks jutted out off the hull as if screaming out about the rushed nature in which they had been put together.

Nassir was still doing his best to fix the appearance, but planing wood by hand was tough work for an already exhausted man, and he was the only one capable. Edward had ordered him to rest for the day, as it could wait for another.

On a positive note, they had been testing their speed since the change, and there was a noticeable difference of a knot or two depending on the wind. Herbert's prediction had been on the nose, and the crew were thankful for it. Most of all, the men were excited to test their new speed in battle.

William had recovered even more over the course of the few days' travel, and had returned to full duty. He used his expertise to guide and instruct the men in maintaining the sails. The men were still getting used to the new speed and the way the wind travelled over the ship, and William helped speed that process up.

After adjustments necessary from the change in weather, William returned to the quarterdeck. "Captain, you'll be happy to note we're travelling close to fourteen knots."

Edward nodded. "I am pleased to hear that. Glad to have you running this crew, William."

William gave a slight bow. "The pleasure is all mine."

"How's your chest? Still giving you trouble?"

William shook his head. "There's still slight pain when exerting myself, but aside from that I cannot feel a thing."

Christina whistled. "You heal quickly. I recall it taking some time for me to heal after Plague attacked me. I was still feeling the pain for weeks after it happened."

Edward recalled the assassin called Plague sent after him

215

long ago, and what had happened to Christina. She had been lucky to survive a dagger to the stomach.

"Nonsense," William said. "You have a youthful, strong body. Had another been attacked in the same place they would not have fared as well as you had."

Christina was taken aback by the compliment at first, but then grew a devilish grin for a brief moment before switching to a shocked expression. "Youthful and strong? My dear William, I've never known you to flirt with a young woman's affections. And in front of my brother, no less." Christina fanned her face with her hand, feigning a swooning fit.

In a rare display, William's jaw went agape and he looked aghast. "I... That is..."

Herbert, nearby at the helm, shook his head. "Shameful, William. Simply shameful."

William stammered an attempt at a reply, but couldn't gather his wits to produce one.

Edward burst out laughing, which sent the other two into a fit as well. William glanced from person to person, and slowly closed his mouth and stood up straight.

William coughed. "That was not amusing."

The laughter of the three subsided into low snickering. Edward grabbed William's shoulder for support. "I'm afraid you'll have to forgive us, William, for we'll have to disagree with you. If only you could have seen your face," he said, grinning widely.

Before William could object any further, a mate shouted "Captain!" down from the crow's nest.

Edward and the rest looked up to the mate near the top of the main mast. "What do you see?"

"Two ships, north north-west. They're engaged in battle."

Edward looked off the bow, but couldn't see anything unaided. "Tell me when you're able to see what class the ships are."

The man in the crow's nest nodded. "Aye, Captain."

"Could it be Roberts?" Christina asked as she tugged at the

rose pendant around her neck.

"We can't be sure, but if it is him he may need our help. We can afford a slight detour if necessary. William, Herbert, send us straight in the path of those ships."

"Aye, Captain," the two of them replied in unison. Herbert turned the wheel a few degrees to port, while William instructed the crew in adjusting the sails to maintain their speed. In no time, they were heading north north-west, straight at the two fighting ships.

Anne came running up to the quarterdeck. "Why have we changed course?" she asked.

"There are two ships fighting ahead of us, and we're heading to intercept."

Anne raised her brow. "Roberts?"

Edward nodded. "Possibly. If it is him, he's fighting against someone from Kenneth Locke's group, no doubt."

"Unless he was caught by authorities in the area."

"Either way, we're going to help him out."

As the *Revenge* moved forward, the ships came into view. At first they were two dots, melded together on the horizon as small as a fly against the meeting of sea and sky. The minutes passed and the dots separated and became more distinct, eventually taking shape. Then, the shape took form, as a piece of clay, being molded before their eyes. They could see the separation of mast to sail, and sail to hull, each minute bringing new details into view.

"Captain, the two ships be sloops," the mate in the crow's nest yelled down.

Edward nodded to the man, and went back to watching from his post. He glanced at Anne. "It seems more and more likely to be Roberts. Prepare the men, Quartermaster. You're about to take control of your first battle."

Anne looked at Edward with a wide grin. "Aye, Captain," she said before stepping forward to the quarterdeck railing. "All hands, prepare for battle!"

The crew looked up at her, registered the order, many giving the briefest of smiles, and then shouted, "Aye, Aye!"

The men charged with manning the small cannons on the top decks prepared their armaments, while others gathered muskets and powder to use. William went below deck, presumably to tell the gunners of the coming battle, and soon returned with weapons of his own.

William stepped up to the quarterdeck and handed muskets to Anne and Edward, then went back to gather one for Christina and Herbert each before finally taking his own. The four held to their weapons, waiting for the ships to get closer.

Now that they were facing a sloop and had two ships instead of one, the mood was distinctly different from the galleon flight. It was no longer a desperate hope and fear, but an itch to destroy the lesser opponent and regain their pride. As if by magic, the mood carried itself to each of the crewmates, though none exchanged words. It manifested in excited laughter, crazed eyes, and jumps in their steps.

The faint sounds of battle sped across the ocean, and grew louder the closer they came—the loud roar of cannons, the sharp crack of guns, and the varied shouts of men's battle cries... or their death wails.

Smoke billowed out from the sides of each ship, lingering for a brief moment before the wind swept it away. No matter how the wind tried, the smoke was replenished with each roar and crack.

The ship closest to *Queen Anne's Revenge* straightened after their latest broadside and headed west south-west to try to flee.

The ship trying to flee had two masts, while the other had three. Provided this wasn't a random battle they'd happened upon, the one fleeing was not the *Fortune*.

"It's trying to escape," Edward commented.

"Intercepting," Herbert said. "Beam reach!" he shouted before he turned the wheel to port so the ship headed northwest.

"Beam reach!" William relayed.

The crew changed the direction of the sails as they were

now to be perpendicular to the wind blowing north north-east.

Edward looked at the approach the other ship was taking. Where it was headed, it had to have its sails in a close reach or close-hauled, which was not an ideal position for escape. The enemy ship would try to head north, as long as *Fortune* didn't cut them off. Failing that, if they outran the *Queen Anne's Revenge*, they could try to swoop around, but it would be risky as they would be tacking against the wind, and Edward and Roberts could still follow them.

We've got them, Edward thought.

Over the next thirty minutes, the ships stayed their courses, with the *Fortune* heading west to circumvent their enemy if they tried to head north. The wind stayed mostly true, with some minor trimming needed to maintain a beam reach.

The *Queen Anne's Revenge* was closing in on the enemy ship, on the side of which they could now see the name *Gallant* emblazoned. In a few minutes they would be in range to hit them.

"Fire a warning shot," Anne said. "Let them know we're here for them."

William nodded and shouted, "Chasers! Raking fire!"

A few men manning cannons at the bow, remnants from the forecastle, acknowledged the order, and prepared their cannons to fire. After a moment, the sound of three blasts rang out from the bow, and three puffs of smoke erupted along with cannonballs.

As expected, they landed well short of their mark, making three splashes into the sea far in front of them.

In a fearful response, the *Gallant* changed direction, trying to switch to a northward bearing. They were hard-pressed to switch their heading, however, and lost much speed in the process.

Herbert barely had to touch the wheel to switch them from going north-west to north. The change brought about the need to trim the sails further, putting them in a broad reach, the *Queen Anne's Revenge*'s fastest position.

The *Gallant* seemed to have forgotten about the *Fortune*,

which was coming up beside them, and would be in line for a broadside in short order.

After a ten-minute struggle, when they realised in full the situation they were in, the *Gallant* waved the white flag and furled their sails.

Cowards, Edward thought.

"Do not grow complacent, men," Anne shouted. "This could be some ruse."

As the *Gallant* slowed, the *Fortune* made to match its trajectory and speed to board. The *Queen Anne's Revenge* was still behind the two faster ships, and so Herbert didn't give the order to furl the sails right away.

Instead, as the *Fortune* was pulling up beside the *Gallant* on its starboard side, Herbert manoeuvred their ship over to the port side. Then he gave the order to furl the sails so they could slow to a stop beside the *Gallant*.

Now that they were up close, Edward could see damage from battle all around the hull. Holes from cannonballs were scattered here and there, but not much harm had been done before they had arrived.

Roberts wasted no time in having the two ships lashed together. Edward could see them dropping gangplanks and boarding, fully armed and taking the crewmates prisoner. They rounded up the crew to the waist of the ship, but Edward noticed Roberts was talking with the crew and searching for something or someone. After a moment, he called to his crewmates, and two answered by heading below deck.

The *Queen Anne's Revenge* approached and the crew began tying the ships together as the *Fortune* had done. All the while, the gunners had their hands tightly gripped to their linstocks, ready to drop them into their cannons at a moment's notice.

Edward pulled out a pistol from his belt and loaded it. He took his time pouring the black powder into the barrel, placing the cloth and the lead ball on top and ramming it into the shaft. As he finished, he headed over to the starboard side of the ship.

The Voyages of Queen Anne's Revenge

Edward jumped over the railing of the ship over to the weather deck of the *Gallant*. He walked over to Roberts, who was standing off to the side near the quarterdeck.

"Roberts, I'm glad we made it in time," Edward said.

Roberts shook Edward's hand. "Well met, Edward. I too am glad you arrived when you did. It could have been a long, arduous endeavour without your assistance." Roberts glanced at the *Queen Anne's Revenge*. "I see you've completed your modifications to the ship. It looks like a whole new vessel."

Edward glanced over his shoulder at his ship. "Aye, she's faster now as well. We might even be able to challenge you," he said.

Roberts flashed a slight grin, but said nothing. Before Edward could say anything else, Roberts' crewmates returned to the weather deck with someone in tow.

The man they were pushing and prodding along with their muskets was a lithe, average-looking man with light red hair and faded freckles across his cheeks.

Roberts' crewmates dropped the man, whom Edward knew was the Walter Kennedy he had heard so much about, to his knees in front of the captains. He fell on his hands, but quickly righted himself on his knees as he cowered in fear in front of Edward and Roberts.

Edward cocked and primed the pistol in his hands, then turned it over to Roberts. "Time for justice, Roberts."

Roberts looked at the pistol in his hands for a moment, and then pointed it at Kennedy. The look in Roberts' eyes was far more serious than Edward had ever seen before.

Kennedy's eyes, on the other hand, were filled with fear and despair. "Please, Roberts," he said with a trembling voice. "I—"

"Shut your mouth, Walter," Roberts seethed as he took a step forward and pressed the pistol against Kennedy's forehead.

Kennedy sobbed and closed his eyes, letting out a pathetic cry like a mewling babe. His whole body shook, and it looked as if at any moment he might soil himself. His hands clasped together in front of him, tightening in preparation for what was about to happen.

A moment in silence passed, with the three crews waiting for the foregone conclusion to this tale of betrayal. The clouds broke, and the sun of the afternoon shone on them. Even the wind seemed to have silenced itself in the face of this tale's climax.

And yet, the thunder of the pistol never roared into that silence. Instead, Roberts released the cock on the gun and lowered it to his side.

"Roberts," Edward said, a nervous chuckle following his call, "what are you doing?"

Roberts sighed, but then smiled. "You are correct. Now is the time for justice, Edward. My justice." He looked at Walter Kennedy with a strange look in his eyes. "I will grant you mercy this day, old friend. You will live to see another day."

Walter burst into miserable tears and fell to the deck, as if he were bowing before Roberts. "Thank you, Roberts. Thank you, thank you!" he kept repeating.

"Do not mistake my mercy for weakness," Roberts said. "If I see you after today, I won't hesitate to kill you. Live out the rest of your days as you will, but live them far away from here, someplace where we are sure never to meet."

Kennedy looked up at Roberts, tears still streaming down his face. He wiped his eyes. "I swear to you, I will do as you say."

Edward clenched his teeth and balled his fist. The sight filled him with inexplicable rage. He grabbed the pistol from Roberts' hand, cocked it, pointed it at Kennedy, and pulled the trigger.

Roberts grabbed Edward's hand and pushed it up towards the sky. The pistol fired, its thunder finally releasing, but the bullet flew up in the air, hitting nothing.

"What the hell do you think you're doing, Edward?" Roberts shouted as he pushed Edward back to the quarterdeck bulkhead. His anger turned his Welsh accent into a booming song.

For what Edward believed to be the first true time, he saw anger in Bartholomew Roberts' eyes. A great, deep well of rage billowed forth and pressed in on Edward, and he suddenly felt very small in the face of this giant of a man.

Edward tried to move his hands, but he wasn't able to. "I'm doing what you're not capable of, because you're weak. The only reason you're sparing him is because of a false sense of camaraderie which is long since removed," he said. "You leave him to roam the seas, and he will come back to kill you in the end, not the other way around."

Roberts kept his hands steady on Edward, not letting him go, and boring his gaze into him. "My reasons for sparing him are based solely on what he has done to me. If we are to serve as our own judge, jury, and executioner, we do not have the right to forgo the first two responsibilities." Roberts loosened his grip on Edward.

Edward pulled his hands away, dropped the gun on deck, and pointed a finger in Roberts' face. "I will tell you of mercy and what it brings. I spared the naval captain who falsely accused me of piracy, and he brought a fleet of warships to bear against me, resulting in my jailing. Kenneth Locke was marooned for killing one of my crewmates instead of being killed himself, and he came to torture me nigh to death. Had I done away with them when I had the chance, I would have been spared those atrocities. I do you a favour in attempting to save you future injury, but seeing as you don't desire my help, do yourself a favour and kill him while you have the chance," Edward said, pointing at Kennedy. "As for me, I will correct my mistakes, and kill anyone who crosses me or my crew." Edward pushed past Roberts and headed back to his ship. "You would do well to learn from my mistakes, Roberts."

Edward returned to his ship, leaving Roberts with the silence, and, he hoped, the weight of just what his decision meant.

18. PROVERBS 16:18

"That was not wise," Anne said.

Edward and Anne sat in the war room, now with a slightly lowered ceiling from the renovations, and fewer windows for light to enter. The repairs were complete, with minor, superficial improvements still outstanding.

Edward tapped his finger on the oval table in front of him as he eyed his wife. "As my wife, are you not to stand by my decisions?"

Anne's face was as stone. "You presume much to think I would stand by you as you push everyone away," she said, her words ice. "I choose when and where to stand by you, and when to tell you you're acting the fool."

Edward clenched his jaw and looked away, his tapping increasing in tempo. "What would you have me do? Stand idly by as my friend proceeds to sail into a storm of his own making?"

"As your wife, and your quartermaster, I would have you retract your earlier statements and offer apology to your ally and friend."

"Tch," Edward spat. "You would have me show weakness in the face of my crew?"

"If your pride won't allow you to apologise in public, then offer it in private. I care not how it is done, just have it done and over with."

Edward leaned back in his chair, reliving the event again and again in his head. He saw in Kennedy's eyes the same look as Kenneth Locke and Isaac Smith. He had known then that Roberts would soon find himself on the other end of that pistol if Kennedy were not executed, but Roberts had stopped him.

He stared his wife in the eyes. "If anyone should apologise, it's Roberts. I was saving his life, but he chose to throw it away."

Anne got up from her chair. "You're acting more a fool than I took you for. I take my leave of you before I say something I will regret. Just know that if you don't do the right thing you will lose more than my respect."

Anne walked towards the cabin door, her feet nearly stomping on the planks. Edward thought to say something about respect being for lords and ladies, not pirates, but he thought better.

After she left the room, another entered directly afterwards. Jack Christian walked into the war room and approached the oval table. "May I sit, Captain?"

"You're not attempting to lecture me as well, are you?"

Jack chuckled as he placed his hand on one of the chairs, but stopped short of sitting in it. "If you consider having a conversation a lecture, then I suppose I am."

Edward waved his hand, and Jack sat down across from him. "What did you wish to discuss?"

"I suppose the first order of business I should mention is that Roberts and crew are stripping the *Gallant* of valuables for themselves."

Edward nodded and scratched his chin through his thick beard. "As it should be. We owe them, and after dumping the cargo we have no way to repay that debt."

Jack frowned and leaned forward in his chair. "There is... something else you should know."

Edward raised his brow. "What?"

"The men returned from aboard Roberts' ship after what happened on the *Gallant*, and some overheard Roberts telling his first mate to prepare to leave."

"That doesn't seem odd. We head to battle soon."

Jack nodded. "Yes... but the men claimed they heard him wishing to head east."

"East? But that's..." Edward trailed off.

"He may be planning to leave us and not aid in the fight against Kenneth Locke and the galleon."

Edward gazed at the oval table in shock. He and Roberts had been through so much, and it was hard to think that this small squabble would set them apart. He began thinking on just what it was he had done and said, and whether Anne was correct and he should apologise. After a moment, he shook off the feeling.

"He was here before us; east must be where Kenneth Locke will attack us. That must be why."

Jack's jaw went slack for a few seconds, and he cocked his brow. He seemed at a loss for words. "That could be, Captain, but perhaps you would do well to ask him yourself."

"Would you send for him?" he asked.

Jack nodded, and rose from his chair. "I'll see it done," he said. "And, Captain, I wish to give you the advice I tried to impart upon Herbert before he went chasing after his enemy: Don't let anger cloud your mind. I may not be a shining example, but you can at least learn from my mistakes. Roberts is a friend and ally, and some due kindness may prevent a lasting rift."

Hearing the same thing over again wore on Edward's anger. That Roberts could be so troubled over what had happened that he would leave was a sobering thought. After some silent reflection, the stubbornness returned, and he thought it wasn't possible for Roberts to be so childish.

Edward simply nodded in Jack's direction, and Jack nodded back with a smile before he left the war room.

Roberts wouldn't leave over this. That would be foolish. Edward was more or less certain of that, but he stroked his beard and re-thought what he knew about the man.

After a few minutes, a knock came at the door. "Enter," Edward said. The door opened and Roberts walked in. Edward forced a smile. "Roberts, please, come in, sit," he said, motioning towards the seats at the table.

Roberts hesitated for a moment, and then stepped over to

the table and took a seat. "You wished to speak with me, Edward?"

"Yes… Did you follow my advice in handling your friend Walter Kennedy?"

Roberts grinned briefly, but it seemed more from surprise. "You still don't understand, do you?"

Edward sat up straight in his chair. "I believe it is you who misunderstands, friend."

Roberts' hand gripped the arm of his chair hard. "You undermined me, insulted me, and called into question my judgement in front of my crew." The normally sweet tones of his Welsh turned to a harsh melody. "You are lucky that my crew holds the both of us in high regard, or we would be having a very different conversation right now."

Edward could feel his legs and arms tense and itch. He took in a deep breath to calm himself. "I was trying to help you, that is all."

"Hmph," Roberts scoffed. "It is the height of pride when one thinks to offer help to someone who doesn't need it. A high mind comes before a fall," Roberts added.

"And who's to say you aren't the one with the high mind?" Edward spat with a wave of his hand. "You can't even see that you'll just be betrayed again." Edward held up his hand. "My apologies, you only seem to understand when quoting scripture. How does it go…? Ah, yes, you aren't able to see the beam in your own eye, or something along those lines."

"You distort the meaning of the passage, and it just shows your own lack of awareness," Roberts seethed, his eyes wide and full of anger.

Edward rubbed his face, frustrated with the talk. "Could we perhaps move on? We have a battle to sail to, if you'll recall."

Roberts sat up straight in his chair and folded his arms in front of him. He stared at Edward for a moment which seemed like an eternity. Edward felt as if he were being scrutinized, judged, and found wanting.

"So, you will offer no apology for what you've done?"

Edward clenched his teeth once again, then licked his chapped lips. "I tell you again: I was trying to help you. If you don't want that help, that's not my issue. I've done nothing wrong."

Roberts stared at Edward again, his hands still folded, and eventually Edward groaned. "Fine, you want an apology? I apologise for trying to help you do something you should be doing yourself," he said in a mocking tone.

Roberts sighed. "I asked Walter Kennedy where the others were headed, and he said they would wait twenty nautical miles northwest of Providencia for the Spanish galleon. That seems to fall in line with the map Luis provided. You may have the *Gallant* so you are still able to fight in the coming battle." Roberts rose to leave.

Edward bolted from his seat; his chest felt like it had been knocked around. "Hold, hold. You are leaving? Over this?"

Roberts shook his head. "No, not just for this. You've changed, Edward. Or... perhaps I've simply been able to see you for who you are now that we've had some time together," Roberts said, scratching his chin. "There is some sort of darkness within you, and while I do not claim to be a saint, I have lived by a code. It may seem as if I've changed my ways here today, but I have only tempered myself in that code to come out stronger. Walter Kennedy wronged me, yes, but he doesn't deserve death." Roberts placed his hand on the chair, and looked Edward in the eyes. "You seem to live by the whims and changes of the tide. Every person who wrongs you and situation in which you are wronged turns you into a more angry, bitter man... I suppose that is a tempering in its own way, but it is a tempering I want no part of."

Roberts turned around and headed towards the door of the war room, leaving Edward standing speechless. He was reminded of another time a friend of his left him, the scene nearly mimicked in his head with Henry's back flashing into his mind. The same feelings welled inside him as well—confusion, fear, anger, and an overwhelming sense of guilt over what he'd done to Henry.

"I thought we were brothers," Edward said, the words forming without thought.

Roberts turned around. "We were," he said, pulling Edward back to reality and making him realise he had said that out loud. "But, like Cain and Abel, we find our beliefs at a crossroads. Our beliefs in what a pirate is, and what one should do to those who've wronged us. And... before one of us kills the other, we should part ways."

Unwittingly, Roberts struck a dagger in Edward's heart. The guilt of killing his best friend Henry Morgan overwhelmed him in that moment. He was Cain to Henry's Abel, as he could soon be to Bartholomew's.

"Despite this, I wish you and your wife well, Edward. I will hold the memory of marrying you two as precious for all my days," Roberts said, taking a moment to breathe and compose his shaking voice. "I hope this world doesn't sink you into its depths."

Roberts left the war room of the *Queen Anne's Revenge* and closed the door behind him. Edward fell back into his seat, slumping down and pressing on his temples as an ache surfaced on the sides of his head.

I am Cain... am I? Edward thought. He gazed at the door, the lingering thought of Henry's and Roberts' backs in his mind's eye. *So be it.*

19. FORMATIONS

"With the *Gallant* in our possession we have a fighting chance against the Spanish galleon and Kenneth Locke. I want to discuss the battle plan I have in mind," Edward said to his senior crew once they had gathered in the stern cabin.

Edward had summoned Anne, William, Herbert, and Christina to the room after Roberts left and the *Fortune* sailed away. Edward listened from the room as quick and confused goodbyes were given, then had a crewmate gather them for the meeting.

All eyes were on him now, and they all had similar expressions of shock on their faces.

"Are we not to discuss what just happened, Edward?" Anne asked, not bothering to hide her annoyance.

Edward shrugged his shoulders. "What is there to discuss? What's done is done."

"What's done is—" Anne looked away, her jaw rigid from her clenching her teeth. "Our greatest allies simply sail away without so much as an explanation, on the eve of what is sure to be one of our toughest battles, and you think this is nothing to talk about?" she said, annoyance replaced with anger.

Edward looked straight into his wife's eyes, took a silent breath, and tried to maintain a level tone. "Roberts was with us only until we helped him capture Walter Kennedy, as I'm sure you'll recall. Our contract with him is completed, and he's left. He was gracious enough to leave us the *Gallant*, and with the size of our crew we should have no issues manning both ships."

"So..." Christina started, before glancing to those sitting at the oval table, "you're saying he just... left?" She chuckled.

"You'll have to do a bit better than that, Edward."

Edward stared daggers at Christina. "Watch your tongue, young lady," he said.

"Do not talk to my sister that way," Herbert warned.

"I will not tolerate disrespect," Edward said. "Tell her that."

"Am I not sitting in front of you?" Christina said. "You may tell me yourself if you have something to say."

The conversation continued to devolve into a slew of back-and-forth passive aggression between the three parties for a brief moment until—

"Enough!" Anne shouted. "As quartermaster I'll have you all thrown in the brig if you do not cease this inane bickering," she said, her arms folded in front of her chest. "Edward, we know Roberts' departure was due to your indiscretion. The crew demands answers, and they will not suffer your lies."

Edward looked at his wife, anger still coursing through him. His heart beat as quick as a storm whipping the waves, and he clenched his hands tighter than a rope knot. "They want answers, do they?" he said. "Fine, I'll give them answers."

Edward rose from his seat and stormed off to the stern cabin door. The four glanced warily at each other before quickly following behind him. They called to him, but he ignored them and opened the door to enter the weather deck.

The light of the sun shining down hurt Edward's eyes when he walked out of the stern cabin, but he didn't move to block the beams. "Men!" he called out. He walked to the quarterdeck ladder, and went up halfway. As he did, the crew gathered around him, whispering and watching. "Roberts has abandoned us," he declared.

The shock of the announcement was evident on all the crew's faces. Coming after the fight Roberts and he had had, they were reasonably sceptical, and angered that they were low on fighting power. Anne was right; he wouldn't be able to spin a lie this time.

"He was a coward who couldn't finish the job he was meant to do: get revenge. He abandoned us in our hour of need because of the creed you all swore to. This ship isn't called *Queen Anne's Forgiveness*, it's called *Queen Anne's Revenge*, and revenge is what we'll have." Edward paused for a moment to search the crowd. Even in that short speech he had said enough. The men no longer looked angered, and instead looked ready for a fight. "Who's with me?"

The crew shouted their answer, and stomped their feet to make the sole of the ship shake. Edward let it continue for a moment, the raucous nature spreading to each man as the noise and the shaking rose. He looked at Anne and the others, and raised his brow, asking in his head if this was what they had wanted. Anne gave a simple, curt bow of her head in response.

Edward raised his hand to cease the noise. "I need sixty men to man the *Gallant* for the coming battle. There also needs to be a helmsman, and a senior mate to lead the crew."

"I will be your helmsman," Christina blurted out before any other could speak up.

Edward looked at Christina, and then glanced at Herbert.

"Don't look at him!" she shouted as she stepped forward. "I am the most qualified to navigate a ship, and I'm not a child who needs her brother's permission to do something. Let me do this."

Edward looked Christina in the eyes, those wide, sky-blue eyes of hers. She had a twinge of a smile on her face, and she had her fists clenched. Edward nodded. "You'll be the helmsman for the *Gallant*," he said.

William took a few steps and held his hands behind his back. "If you'll permit it, Captain, I can lead the crew on the *Gallant*."

"This will be a difficult task with what I have in mind, and I know you're the best man for it. What say you, men? Do these two have what it takes to lead you?"

The crew shouted their agreement with a mix of laughter and pats on William's and Christina's backs. The two of them accepted the praise with grace, grinning and smiling at their crewmates and friends.

"Choose amongst yourselves who wishes to serve aboard the *Gallant* while we prepare a battle plan. We will not simply survive. We will *win* this fight."

"The *Gallant* is giving the signal," a mate from the crow's nest shouted. He was periodically focussing his gaze through a long spyglass.

"Good," Edward said aloud. He looked at the position of the sun, just coming down with several hours before it fell below the horizon. "Take us into position, Herbert," he said.

"Aye, Captain," Herbert replied. He turned the wheel of the ship slightly, then ordered a change in the sails to bring them circling around the faraway *Gallant*.

"You are certain your plan will work?" Edward asked Anne while looking through his own inferior spyglass. The muddied, scratched lens could only show him the position of the *Gallant*, but he wasn't able to make out anything other than its general shape. Beyond the *Gallant* he saw a blob barely the size of a speck nearby, which he wouldn't have been able to see if not for the signal from the other crew.

"From what the crew who helped Roberts mentioned, Kenneth Locke's spy arrived before us in the morning. If my counting is correct, and provided the galleon wasn't delayed, before the few hours of light we have are gone, the galleon should arrive. Locke will be too focussed on the coming battle to look closely at the *Gallant*'s crew, or in our direction."

"Let's hope that Locke doesn't enjoy gazing directly at the sun."

"From what I knew of the man, he was not the most attentive."

"Mmm," Edward mumbled. He put his spyglass away and rubbed his eye where it had been.

"What leads you to be certain the galleon will even come

this way still? We told them of the attack, it would be wiser to choose a different route."

"The captain of the galleon was a bold one. He challenged us when we met with him back in Panama, and I don't think he's one to back down from a fight. Also, if he was to take another route, why hire two sloops-of-war to assist as an escort?"

"It could have been a precaution," Anne said. "There's no guarantee that they will come, despite your assumptions."

Edward shrugged. "Well, if they don't, we still have the backup plan. We'll follow Locke back to land, and ambush them when we have the advantage."

Anne sighed. "I suppose that is an option," she said.

"Keep me informed of our situation, Quartermaster."

"Aye, Captain," she replied with a smile.

Edward went down the steps of the quarterdeck to the weather deck, which now stretched out all the way to the bow. He spoke with the crew, ensuring that the ship and their minds were prepared for the coming battle. There was a nervousness in the way the men spoke, and the perspiration dangling from their noses wasn't entirely from the heat of the day.

Edward noticed a noise coming from the bow, and when he looked over he could see Nassir there, half his body off the side as his knees held onto railings he had just fixed. He went over to see what the carpenter was working on.

When he approached and leaned over the side, he saw Nassir at it again with a hand plane, shaving off pieces of wood from the planks they had recently affixed. With each stroke of the large man's arms, bits of the Caribbean pine parted from the larger planks and fell into the ocean. Edward could see the pieces floating down the sea current with the waves like poor excuses for driftwood.

As Edward examined the bow, he noticed that Nassir was nearing the end of his work. "She looks good as new, Nassir!" Edward shouted over the sound of the waves.

Nassir jumped at Edward's voice, and almost dropped the hand plane into the sea. He gripped the tool close to his chest and then pulled himself back onto the deck. He was breathing heavily and looked startled. "Captain, you must watch what you are doing. My heart almost seized."

Edward chuckled. "Sorry, Nassir, I didn't mean to frighten you so."

Nassir took a few more breaths. "It is fine, Captain. Nothing was lost."

Edward reached down and offered his hand to help Nassir to his feet, which the carpenter accepted. "I only wanted to mention how the ship is looking well due to your skilled craftsmanship. You've done a fine job, and the ship is moving faster than she ever has because of it."

Nassir waved his hand. "You give me too much credit, sir," he said simply.

"Were there any troubles that I should be informed of?"

Nassir shook his head. "No, the work went smoothly. We were able to use the reclaimed wood, so there was little need for new pieces. The braces and the railings were simple enough, as the originals don't have nothing fancy to them. I made a new fife rail, with William's instruction," Nassir said, pointing to the fore mast. A rather large construction of wood went around the bottom of the mast with pegs at the top to hold the rigging. "They'll need some staining to match the look of the old wood though."

Edward looked at the new fife rail, and the bow railings, and there was a clear difference in the colour between the two. "Yes, I see that. The old girl is looking a bit weathered, it seems," he said, smacking the rails with a chuckle.

"She's been through much over the years," Nassir said, glancing around at the ship. He soon settled his gaze on the figurehead of Anne's likeness at the bow, an hourglass in one hand and a spear in the other.

Edward followed Nassir's gaze, looking at the flowing locks of hair and the robes covering the body of the figure. "Aye, she has," he said. "Hopefully, with your help, she'll have many more years ahead of her."

Nassir smirked. "Provided you stay out of trouble some of the time."

Edward chuckled. "I think we could manage some of the time."

Nassir returned to work, and Edward went over to starboard to gaze at the ocean. He was there only a moment before someone smacked him hard on the back. He had to take a step forward to steady himself before he could turn to see who it was. Pukuh was standing behind him, grinning.

"That bloody hurt, you bastard," Edward said as he rolled his shoulder, trying to remove the throbbing feeling.

"If the look on your face wasn't so sour I would not have to hit you. Come out of it, brother."

Edward folded his arms. "I'm doing just fine, and once this battle has concluded I'll be that much better," he replied. Edward looked over starboard, to where the *Gallant* was coming more into view. "What about you, brother? Are you well?"

"As well as ever," Pukuh said. "The phantoms of my right aches for a fight, while the left itches for it." Pukuh held up his left hand and clenched it into a fist. "It has been months since we had a proper battle."

Edward shook his head, but he had a grin on his face. "You pray for a battle? A strange thing indeed."

Pukuh wagged his finger at Edward. "Do not try to tell me you do not ask for the same. You've been wanting this for months as well."

Edward didn't want to think about it any more than he had to. He still felt a crippling dread when he thought of Kenneth Locke, and the only way to bring him out of it was the thought of crippling him. In one sense, he supposed he did want this, but in another sense he just wanted it to be over.

"Yes, it has been a long time coming," was all he could say.

Some crewmates called Pukuh over to help them with the trimming of the sails, and so Pukuh said a goodbye and headed over to work. Edward stayed behind, looking out over the ocean at the *Gallant*.

The Voyages of Queen Anne's Revenge

Somewhere, you're there, Edward thought. The pain gripped him again, and the throbbing wounds on his chest, his back, his legs, his arms, and his mind all cried out at once, but he silenced them. *Soon, I'm going to kill you.*

An hour after the *Queen Anne's Revenge* was in position in front of the setting sun, a call came from the crow's nest.

"Ship approaching south!" the man shouted.

Edward's ears perked and his eyes opened wide. He was on the quarterdeck with Anne and Herbert. He glanced off the starboard stern, but he couldn't see anything. "How many ships?"

The man in the crow's nest looked through his spyglass once more, moving side to side, but shook his head after a moment. "I can't tell."

Edward nodded. "Keep checking," he said. He glanced at Anne. "Do you think we should head over to the *Gallant* now, or wait?"

"I suppose the true question is, do we want to take the risk?"

Herbert looked off to port. "The sun's nearly gone now. We will have the same risk in waiting."

Edward stroked his beard as he thought over the options. "Take us in, Herbert. We need to be ready to take down one of those sloops as soon as they come into range."

Herbert gave the order to lower and trim the sails, then turned the wheel to starboard. The ship lurched forward, the wind only slightly in their favour. After a time, the speed built and the ship was under way.

As the *Queen Anne's Revenge* approached, Edward was able to see the other ships waiting for the galleon. From what he could tell at this distance, they both appeared larger than the *Gallant*, but, if he were to guess, not as large as Edward's ship.

"Three ships," the man in the crow's nest yelled. "One

large, two smaller."

"That's them," Edward commented. "We need to be ready to take on one of the sloops."

Anne nodded and stepped up to the edge of the quarter-deck. "Man cannons, to arms!" she shouted.

The gunners on the weather deck went to their stations and prepared the cannons to fire, while other men went down below to inform the crew on the main gun deck and gather weapons. Some men brought Anne, Herbert and Edward muskets, and the three loaded their weapons.

As seemed usual before battle, the feeling aboard and in the air changed. It became heavy, hard to breathe, and every task felt laborious and exhausting.

Edward could see one man hunched over, loading his musket with shaking hands. He dropped the ball and caught it before it rolled over the side of the ship, but then couldn't get the ramrod in the muzzle. He was swearing under his breath with each time his shaking moved the rod down the outside of the barrel.

Edward handed his loaded musket over to Anne and walked over to the man. When he got close, the ball fell off the top of the musket again. Edward stepped on the ball to stop it from rolling away as the crewmate reached forward. He looked up to see Edward towering over him, and immediately blanched.

"S-Sorry, sir," he said. "I'll get it next time, I promise."

Edward knelt down and retrieved the ball. "What's your name?"

"Clement, sir," he replied.

Edward placed the ball on top of the paper sitting on the muzzle. "That's a rare name for one so young in this age. Did your parents hate you?" he said with a smirk.

The young man chuckled. "Nah, it's after my grandpap." He picked up the rod, and this time he was able to get it into the musket.

Edward nodded as Clement pushed the ball into the barrel.

"No need to be nervous, Clement," he said. "All you have to do is look down the barrel and pull the trigger."

Clement grinned. "That's not the trouble..." He lost his grin, and looked away. "I don't want to get hit," he said.

"I'll tell you a secret that helps me, Clement," Edward said as he leaned forward and gripped the young man's shoulder. "Most people miss."

Clement grinned at Edward's words, and then nodded. Edward smiled back, shook the man's shoulder, and then went back to his place at the quarterdeck.

As the *Queen Anne's Revenge* drew closer to the *Gallant*, two things became clearer: the first was that the ships Kenneth Locke had were both three-masted sloops-of-war, one bigger than the others with a few more cannons from what they could tell. The second was that the galleon and its two sloops-of-war were slowing down. As they came closer, they were soon able to see that the three Spanish ships had furled their sails, and were drifting with the current.

"They mean to draw us in," Edward muttered.

The only moving ship at the moment was theirs, with three ships on either side waiting in somewhat calm seas. They each faced the other, a standoff on the high seas. Edward imagined that on the decks of the other ship it was deathly still and quiet. On his ship it was loud and frantic, with the sound of the ship crashing against the water, the wind whipping the sails, and the men shouting and grunting as they heaved to the rigging.

"Now, the question is... do we let them?" Herbert asked with a sidelong glance at Edward and Anne.

Edward and Anne looked at each other, both knowing what the other was thinking. "Take us in, Herbert," Anne said.

"Aye." Herbert relayed the order to the men, and twisted the wheel starboard once more.

The ship turned until it was almost heading back where they had come from. They headed south south-west in a beam reach, with the wind heading southeast. They wanted to keep their distance in the hopes they could draw out one of the sloops.

When they began heading towards the Spanish ships, the *Gallant* made to join them. They let loose their sails and were catching up to Edward and the rest.

After the *Gallant*, Kenneth Locke's ships followed suit, forced to join a forward attack. The bigger of the two was on the inside, next to the *Gallant*, but the both of them headed straight south towards the galleon.

Three sloops-of-war against a galleon... their plan was quite risky. Sloops may be faster, but one hit from a broadside could cripple them. Either Locke is desperate, or they had some sort of plan. What, though?

After ten minutes of sailing, the Spanish side finally began to move. The galleon stayed put, not dropping their sails an inch, but the two sloops opened theirs up. They headed west to intercept the *Queen Anne's Revenge* and the *Gallant*.

"I believe the sloops plan to hit us with a broadside, tack through the wind, and then head back to the galleon," Anne said.

"Why wouldn't they go south?" Edward asked.

"They're supposed to be protecting the galleon. If they head south, they would be hard-pressed to make it back up in time to stop all four of our ships from attacking the galleon. The wind would be against them every step of the way, and they would need to be close hauled to make any progress."

Herbert nodded. "That is sound reasoning," he said. "As far as they know, we could all be on the same side. They aren't close enough to see the name of our ship and know our allegiance. Those sloops will want to attack us and distract us from going after the galleon."

"And what should we do to counter them?"

Anne folded her arms and bit her thumb for a moment. "If they wanted to do the most damage, they would form up to hit us with both broadsides one after the other. To counter that, we need the *Gallant* to stay on their starboard so we can hit them from both ends."

Edward glanced off to port, where the *Gallant* was coming

up beside them. "How will we inform the *Gallant*?"

"Not necessary," Herbert said. "My sister will know what to do when the time comes. We'll have both ships on our broadsides, I guarantee it."

Herbert was smiling from ear to ear, confidence trickling through in his movements and his tone. Edward grinned and nodded back to him, infected by Herbert's optimistic mood.

The *Queen Anne's Revenge* headed east in an arc towards the other ships, with enough leeway to ensure they would end up on the port side of the farthest sloop. The *Gallant* followed suit, but kept its distance, seeming to understand what the plan of attack was. Soon, the four ships were heading straight at each other, two heading east, and two heading west.

As the minutes passed and the ships closed in, the mood and movements aboard began to change. The places the men went to were ones that were well guarded. Their hands gripped the ropes, the linstocks, the muskets, and the railings tighter. But most noticeable of all was the silence that crept in from the edges of the ship to the centre. Soon the breezing wind, the flap of the sails, the splash of the sea, the creaking of wood, and the smack of boots was all they could hear.

One of the enemy sloops changed direction, tacking into the wind as much as possible. They were trying to get outside of where the *Gallant* would be, and escape the double broadside. With Locke's ships still heading for the galleon, they wouldn't be able to turn in time to help and trap the enemy sloop.

Edward, Anne, and Herbert all peered over to their sister ship, waiting to see what she would do. What Christina would do. After a brief moment, the sails moved, and the *Gallant* changed course to match the other sloop and keep it in the pincer.

Edward, Anne, and Herbert all grinned widely at the sight. Anne gripped Herbert's shoulder, and he looked up at her, the two beaming with pride.

Edward smacked Herbert's back. "You taught her well," he

said.

"I wasn't the only one," Herbert replied, looking at Edward and Anne, the significance not lost on Edward.

The enemy sloop that tried to escape turned back and joined its brother again. The second sloop slowed itself down and closed the distance between them. The two ships matched in speed and went side to side.

"They've abandoned their initial plan," Anne commented. "Now they're trying to minimize the damage by protecting each other."

"We've caught them in a snare," Edward said with a devilish grin.

"Now all that's left is to tighten the noose!" Herbert gritted his teeth and repositioned himself before turning the wheel to port. "Moving to firing range," he shouted.

"Gunners at the ready!" Anne yelled in response.

The men manning the cannons loaded the powder into the pan. They made small adjustments here and there, using their eyes and their guts to estimate what the best angle would be to hit the oncoming ship.

Meanwhile, men in teams would be doing the same with the cannons below deck. Using their experience and expertise to aim the first volley and make it true could mean the difference between an easy victory or a protracted battle.

The *Gallant* followed with the *Queen Anne's Revenge*, coming in closer to the sloops on a broadside run. It didn't have the same number of guns the other sloops had, but with another ship aiding they could do some damage.

Mere minutes remained before the ships were all within firing range. Edward couldn't help but be stirred with excitement as the men were. It had been months since they'd had a real battle, and one where they would be the most likely victor. He had to hold himself back from smiling, despite knowing that once it started it could be far from exciting.

Anne intently watched the oncoming ships. Her eyes flitted between the enemy ships to the bow of the *Queen Anne's Re-*

venge and back every few seconds. After a moment she shouted "ready," and the crew tensed. Edward gripped the quarterdeck railing, waiting for the moment.

"Fire port!"

The gunners on the weather deck were first to drop the linstocks into the pan of the cannons. Some of the men turned away from the flare that erupted from the large beast they were in charge of, while others watched to ensure they hit their mark.

After the first volley, the gun deck was quick to follow suit, and fired their cannons as well. The two booms sounded distinct from one another, a smaller explosion followed by a larger blast.

Those sounds were as a dam breaking apart on the mouths of the crew. Silence died as the fight burst into life.

Before the cannonballs hit their mark, the enemy sloops fired their cannons off as well. The iron flew at them with unmatched speed, wreaking destruction on their path. The new planks and railings broke apart in the blast, sending wood everywhere.

Edward turned away from the assault, and when he looked up, what he saw made him laugh under his breath. The sloops were pitiful in comparison to the galleon they had faced not a few days before. The scene left behind was like night and day.

That was not to say that they went unscathed. Edward could hear the shouts of the injured amongst the yells of those still fighting. He looked over the side of the quarterdeck to see one man clutching a leg with an exposed bone, and another with a chunk of wood jammed in his eye, yet he was still alive. Many others were bleeding from various small wounds, but kept doing their duty.

Alexandre and Victoria were first on the scene, tending to the wounded. They were uninjured, but armed, in case they needed to switch from being healers to attackers.

As the crew reloaded their cannons, Herbert turned the ship to port. The sloop on their side could only go south if they wanted to turn back around, but the pirates could shoot another volley before then.

Herbert brought the *Queen Anne's Revenge* in close to the other ships. The men manning the sails changed the trim with each degree of movement as their brothers worked on reloading the cannons. Each man had his part to play, and because of their experience, both as individuals and together, they were playing it beautifully. This battle, compared to their first, was also as night and day.

"Form up, port-side muskets at the ready!" Anne shouted above the din.

Men holding muskets rushed to the port side of the ship and placed their weapons along the railing to keep their aim true. They pointed them at the other ship, searching down the barrel for anyone they could hit.

When the ships were close enough, Anne shouted "Fire!" once more. Blasts of powder not so loud as the cannons, and spouting lead rather than iron, shot at the enemy ship. The wave of lead shot cascaded upon the crew and felled many of them.

The sloop's crew returned fire, but they were sorely outmatched in numbers and in the size and power of their cannons. A few of Edward's men were hit, but not many, and none of them fatal shots.

Another wave of cannonballs from Edward's ship crashed into the sloop as they were passing the stern. One of its masts had snapped, and many of its crew were injured, but it was not wholly beaten.

As they came around, they were able to catch glimpse of the other sloop, and the *Gallant* coming about the stern as well. The second vessel wasn't damaged as much as the first, but Edward could see several crewmates lying bloody on the deck.

The *Gallant* was worse off, with several holes dotting the side. It was listing to the starboard side in the way that could only mean it was taking on water. Through Edward's spyglass he could see Christina and William at the helm, alive and well, though bloodied from battle. A few men were lying sprawled dead on the deck, but the damage to the crew was less than Edward had expected given the damage from the cannons.

"We can't go any farther than this, Captain," Herbert said. "Unless you wish to tack into the wind."

Edward assessed the situation, then shook his head. "No, we'll lose too much time chasing the sloops as we are. We should head back to the galleon before we lose the advantage against Locke."

"Aye, Captain," Herbert said.

The crew moved the ship east, back towards the galleon, and the *Gallant* followed behind. They soon heard the sounds of battle coming from the galleon, with much more cannon fire than in Edward's battle. He could see great plumes of smoke coming from each of the ships, most especially the galleon with its larger complement of cannons. All three ships still floated, and Edward had a mix of emotions over it.

"Slow us down, Herbert. The *Gallant* is taking on water. We need our men back onboard before the sloops come back around."

Herbert yelled to the crew to furl the sails, and the ship slowed. It took some time, and they drifted closer to the galleon as they slowed.

Edward expected to see the sloops turning about to renew their fight, but they continued heading west.

He couldn't help but burst out laughing at the sight. "They're sailing away, the cowards," he said.

Anne, who had been paying attention to where they were headed, glanced at him with a raised brow before looking back at the retreating ships. She too couldn't help but chuckle. "That's a boon for us," she said.

The sound of a powerful crash brought all eyes back to the galleon. They were still some ten minutes' sailing away from them, but it sounded as if it happened right beside them.

Edward pulled out his spyglass and peered through it towards the galleon. At first he saw nothing the matter, but as he looked more intently he saw what had happened. One of the ships under Locke's command had crashed into the galleon's stern. The crew had already abandoned ship, some swimming and others in longboats. The galleon's rudder had broken off, effectively crippling it.

"One of the ships crashed into the galleon," Edward said.

"Do you believe it by mistake or by design?" Anne asked.

"Hard to say, but the crews are heading over to climb up the side of the galleon." Edward relayed what he saw through the spectacle. "No matter," he said while putting away his spyglass. "That's one fewer ship we have to deal with."

The *Gallant* came up beside the *Queen Anne's Revenge*, and the crew helped their brothers return to the main ship. In no time the sixty crewmates who had volunteered, less their fallen mates, were back to their home.

Edward and Anne helped Christina and William back aboard. Christina was bleeding from her forehead and breathing heavily, one eye closed and covered in blood from the wound. William had grazes on his shoulder and leg from bullets, but wasn't the worse for wear.

"Good job, Christina, William," Edward said.

"Could have done better," Christina responded through ragged breaths. Tala ran over excitedly and licked Christina on the arms and cheek.

"Nonsense," Herbert protested, wheeling himself over to his sister. "You were excellent out there. I'll have to watch out if I don't want to be replaced," he said with a grin.

Christina smiled at the praise and the pride in her brother's eyes. "Thank you, brother," she said.

With the full crew aboard, Edward went to the edge of the quarterdeck. "Men, ready yourselves. The night is young, and this battle is far from over!"

20. DROWNING

"It looks as if they had a far larger crew than their ship demanded," Anne commented while looking through a spyglass towards the galleon. "They meant—at the very least—to board the galleon and take the fight to them."

Edward also looked through a spyglass at the carnage off the bow. Night had slipped in since their battle with the sloops, and it was getting darker as the minutes passed. The ship that had crashed into the galleon had slid off with the current and settled on the starboard side of the Spanish ship. It could be some time before it was moved as the crew was too occupied repelling boarders to do it themselves. It allowed Locke's other ship to attempt boarding from the starboard bow without fear of the cannons ripping them apart.

It was a desperate gamble if they had meant to do it, but Edward guessed it was half planning and half luck. *I suppose that's true of most battles,* he thought.

"Many of those men will perish on the climb," Anne said. "What are we to do? If we wait, the crew of the galleon could win, and not only would we have to face them next, but Locke will die."

"And we can't forget about Sam," Christina added, petting Tala as she rested near the helm.

"If Sam is there, he won't even know who this ship belongs to," Edward said. "Locke won't win against the galleon's crew with their numbers. We need to ensure both sides are left too wounded to continue fighting, and search for Sam."

"And how will we do that?" Herbert asked.

Edward thought on the problem for a moment. *From where we are, if we board we risk a three-fronted battle erupting if Locke sees us or his crew recognises who we are. We can't attack the galleon or we could end up at their broadside. Just because the rudder's mucked doesn't mean they're immobile. What can we do?*

"Captain," William said, interrupting Edward's thoughts. "The galleon is taking on water."

Edward looked through his spyglass and noticed what William was looking at. On the stern of the galleon, near where the other ship had hit it, there was a hole in the wood. Judging from the size and position it would be difficult to cover, and could sink the ship given enough time.

Edward grinned, an idea forming in his head. "That's how we'll win this fight," he said. He looked at the senior officers gathered around him. "We're going to enter the galleon from that breach, and fight our way to the top." Edward pointed at Anne. "At the same time, you'll attack Locke's ships with ours. All three ships will be in the drink when we're done with them."

Those around him looked at him as if he were mad, for a moment. In the silence of shock, they pondered the plan, and each person's face changed to reflect a sceptical acceptance.

"It may actually work," Anne said finally.

"Herbert," Edward called, "bring us in as close as you can to the galleon. We're going to need the crew who remain here to keep the men aboard the galleon from attacking us."

Herbert nodded and then focussed his attention on helming the ship. They were already on an approach, so there wasn't much to be done at the moment.

Edward stepped up to the quarterdeck railing and placed both his hands on it, leaning forward to speak with the crew. "Men, we have an opportunity ahead of us to bleed all our enemies dry. We're going inside the Spanish galleon from the stern, and I need fifty strong swimmers to join me."

Fifty volunteers formed up to join Edward in this expedition. Victoria was among them, but not Alexandre.

Christina stood up. "I wish to join," she said.

Edward shook his head. "I need you here, helping your

brother." Christina opened her mouth again, no doubt to object, but Edward cut her off. "That is an order," he said, his finger raised.

Christina pouted and sat back down on the sole of the deck.

William stepped forward. "I will be joining you, Captain. I believe the exercise would aid my constitution."

Edward chuckled. "Provided it doesn't kill you?"

William bowed his head a touch. "Yes, barring that," he said.

Pukuh was strangely silent during the volunteering process, though he was nearby and no doubt heard the plan. "Pukuh, will you not be joining us?"

The Mayan shook his head. "I will do better here. I am not as strong a swimmer as I was," he said, glancing at his missing arm.

Edward looked at it as well, and at the shattered pride in Pukuh's eyes. "Then you had better start practicing after this battle. I won't have you slowing the storm over something as trivial as losing one of your arms," he said with a smirk.

Pukuh looked at him, at first with light shock, and then he too grinned. "Soon I will swim better than you, and they will call me Pukuh, The Bringer of the Storm."

Edward chuckled, overjoyed by his friend's resilience in the face of every challenge.

As the *Queen Anne's Revenge* sailed closer, the men who would join Edward prepared for the journey. They would have to approach the galleon on longboats before entering the breach.

"As soon as we're away and inside the ship, give Locke's ships our broadside. We don't want them escaping if the battle doesn't turn in their favour."

"Aye, Captain," Anne said, a pensive look on her face. Edward turned around to enter a longboat, but Anne stopped him. "Don't die. Revenge isn't worth your life."

Edward smiled, trying to reassure his wife. "I don't plan on perishing anytime soon." He leaned in and gave her a kiss before entering the longboat.

The crew lowered the longboats into the sea, and they rowed towards the galleon. The moon's glow was the only source of light now that evening had set in. The flash of gunpowder from the ships in front of them was a poor substitute for a lantern, but they thought it best to hide their advance.

As they approached, the sounds of men screaming, cannons, muskets, and pistols firing, and steel clashing became louder. The sound of the wind was lost, but its bite was not. The cold of the night was just starting, and it would no doubt get worse before their battle was over.

Edward shuddered at the thought of entering the icy waters of the sea, his body preparing for the shock and suddenness of it.

The smell of burning gunpowder met Edward's nose, tingling with its acrid smell in the way that forces one to rub one's nose. The itch meant something else to Edward, and he imagined his crew felt the same—it meant a fight was on the horizon.

Twenty feet from the galleon's stern, a crossbow bolt hit one of Edward's men in the shoulder. Edward looked up to where the bolt had come from, and could see Spanish navymen on platforms halfway up the masts.

"On the masts!" he shouted before pulling his musket out and firing.

The crew joined Edward in firing upon the Spanish, while the rowers continued pulling the longboats in further. The Spanish fired bolts back at them in kind. A few fell into the sea, a few hit the boat with a thunk, and a few more hit Edward's men.

The crew aboard the *Queen Anne's Revenge* fired at the Spanish as well, providing cover for the boarders.

Edward's longboat made contact with the stern first. He pulled the boat along the behemoth to where the hole was. It had been covered over with planks now, but the outside was still open. The hole was half above and half below the water-line, and wide enough for one person to squeeze through if it was open.

Edward pulled out his golden cutlass, and jumped from the boat into the cold water. The sea stole his last shred of warmth, and he couldn't help but shiver. He focussed on the task at hand, pushed aside the thoughts of the frigid drink, and swam to the covered hole.

He jabbed his blade between the planks of wood and wiggled the blade up and down to pry apart the pieces. When that didn't seem to do any good, he pulled his blade out. It was covered in a thin film of tar used to seal the hole. He hit the wood vertically, poking holes in the planks above and below the water line to weaken the beams.

William appeared beside him, and the two kicked the planks with all their might. The water made their attacks weaker, but Edward's blade had done the priming work for them. With each kick, they could feel the nails holding them in place loosen. The two became more coordinated with each strike, and before long they were synchronized.

Two planks snapped in half with a loud crack at the end of Edward's and William's boots. Water once more flooded freely through the hole, and the pressure aided their cause. A few more kicks saw a whole plank dislodged, and more pieces of wood breaking off.

Edward could see men in the darkness beyond the breach. "Fire, fire!" he yelled while looking at his men and pointing to the new hole.

Edward and William moved aside and the men fired their muskets at the hole. Some of the shots missed entirely, but many made it through to the other side. When the firing subsided, the two in the water waded back over and looked inside. From what Edward could see in the void of the galleon's bilge, the shots had hit their marks.

Edward lifted up his legs and entered the small hole feet first, with the water guiding him in. He landed inside the bilge of the galleon and looked around, four dead men sprawled on the sole greeting him.

He went to the nearest plank and used his cutlass as a lever to pull it out. It was already loose from the kicking he and William had given it, and after a few mighty tugs it gave way and Edward was able to toss it to one side.

William entered the hole next, landing in a pool that reached halfway up his shins already. When he saw what Edward was doing, he pulled out a cutlass from his belt and did the same.

Edward was cold, wet, and his every movement laden down by the water soaked into his clothes. He couldn't even tell whether the beads dropping from his hair, forehead, and nose were salt water or sweat.

As Edward and William pulled out the planks, the crew filtered in through the hole one by one. Some of the men caught their trouser legs or arms on the exposed chips of wood from the new boards and the old breach. After Edward and William finished removing the wood, they sheathed their weapons and helped the other men through the breach.

With each new man, the water in the bilge rose another few inches. The sound of the rushing water, splashing in faster with the waves and pitch of the ship, overtook everything else in the small compartment.

Victoria jumped through the hole, landing next to Edward. Her short hair was matted to her forehead with the water, her cap lost in the sea. She held her usual buckler and short sword.

Edward grabbed her by the arm and pulled her in close. "How many more men are there?" he yelled over the din, spitting water in her direction.

"No more than ten," she yelled back.

Edward pointed towards the hatch leading to the next deck, where the crew had gathered, waiting. "Get them up there and start the fight. Stay alive and I shall join you presently."

Victoria nodded and then trudged through the chest-high—and rising—water over to the men, shouting something Edward couldn't hear. He went back over to William.

"Go join the others, I can handle the rest," Edward shouted.

William gave a quick salute, and then pulled one of the crewmates over with him towards the hatch.

Edward continued helping the others through the hole, which was now entirely covered by the sea. He counted each man down that came through until he reached eight, and then there were no more.

Edward grabbed hold of the man who had come through last, grasping through the shoulder-high water he could barely see in. "Are there any others?"

The man pointed as best he could towards the hole. "One more left, Captain."

Edward nodded and pushed the man along towards the bilge hatch. He went back to the breach, but still did not see another man come through.

Edward cursed, took a deep breath, and dove under. He moved through the murky mess towards the opening, and felt a body in front of him. He looked around but couldn't see much of anything. His hands became his eyes as he felt blindly in front of him. After a moment, another's hands grasped his own, and pulled them over towards a leg. Through his sense of touch, Edward could feel the fibers of pantaloons ripped and wrapped around the exposed wood.

Not wanting to risk losing his precious cutlass, nor accidentally cut the man he was trying to save, Edward pulled out a knife from his pocket. He traced the lines of his other arm to where the pants were caught, and sawed at the strings. The water made everything slick and the darkness didn't help Edward judge his progress. He just kept sawing as the crewmate kept pulling on his pant leg. After a moment, Edward lost all sense of resistance, and felt the strings of the pant leg slip through his fingers.

Edward planted his feet on the sole, but in the time he had been under the water it had risen above his head. He kicked his legs up, and his head poked through the water. He saw the other crewmate with him, catching his breath.

"The hatch is that way," Edward shouted over the noise. "We have to swim."

"I can't see a bloody thing," the crewmate responded, an undertone of fear in his shaky voice.

"Then die here," Edward said harshly. "Go. I'll be right at your tail."

The man nodded, took a breath, and dove into the water. Edward did the same, and he kicked his legs forward to the hatch.

The dark of the night could not hold a candle to the dark of the waters in the depths of the galleon's bilge. The moon gave some illumination to the night's activities, but the belly of a ship knew no light save by lantern, and there were no lanterns here.

Edward cleaved through the water, his muscular forearms and chest straining with each stroke. His legs paddled behind him, and the two worked together to push him in a direction he hoped was forward.

He moved up for a breath, but could no longer surface his head, and had to lean back to bring in another breath of air. He wasn't able to check for the mate he had tried to help, and even if he did it would be fruitless.

He sank down and continued moving in the direction he thought would take him to the hatch. His body was so cold it no longer felt cold to him. He felt a strange numbness in his hands and feet, not the same as when slept upon, but a strange void of feeling in his fingers and toes.

He wasn't sure how far he had gone, but if he was to take a guess he had to be getting close to the hatch. He went up for another breath of air. His fingers outstretched above him, he could feel the wood of the deck above him, but there was no gap in the water. He felt around for a few seconds, but could find nowhere to gather air.

Edward's heart beat faster as the urgency of escape hit him

all at once. He needed more air, and quick.

He pumped his legs and stroked with his arms against the cold sea water, pressing forward to the hatch. No matter where he looked, it was infinite darkness in front of him, with nothing to guide his way.

He felt pain in his chest, and his body called out for more air. His thoughts shrank to nothing, and all that drove him was the instinct to find the surface. As the seconds passed, small spots of light flashed across his vision, pulsing in with each heartbeat.

The beating slowed.

Am I to drown here? Edward thought, still pushing forward. He shook his head as best he could. *No! No! This isn't where I'll die. Not today!* Edward forced the spots away.

His fingers clawed at the wood above him, desperate for the edge of the hatch he knew should be near him. His legs beat against the water, ungracefully pushing it away like the killer it was.

The spots of light returned, taking over his vision one second at a time. Each pulse came slower, but with it the pain in his chest grew as well.

Edward's arms and legs became weaker and weaker with each stroke forward. They were heavier than solid lead, and as sluggish. His hands outstretched, Edward flailed and thrashed to gain each inch forward.

His finger grazed something unfamiliar, and it renewed his vigor, if by a small margin. He combed the area where he had felt it, and his hands soon gripped someone's forearm.

The owner of the forearm pulled, and Edward broke the surface of the water with a great splash and heave of a breath. His head whipped around, sending water flying off his slick hair as he tread water in the small opening to the bilge. William and Victoria were at the hatch, both as soaked as he.

"There—" Edward started, but had to catch his breath some more. He gulped down air as he treaded water. "There was another man ahead of me," he said, hoping the question was evident.

William and Victoria glanced at each other. "There were none before you," William answered.

Edward's eyes fell to the void below his chest, and the man whom he had tried to save. It would have been impossible for him to still be alive, and Edward couldn't even begin to think of the agony he must have felt in his last moments.

Edward pulled himself out of the bilge and onto the sole of the hold. The water was filling the ship in a rapid rise, and in a few minutes would snake its way through the cracks in the planks, up to the hold and beyond. The best part was that the Spanish galleon was a massive ship, and would take a fair amount of time to sink regardless of how quickly the water flooded it.

Around him, Edward could see the men who had volunteered to join him. They were either waiting and watching him, or keeping an eye on the open orlop deck from below. On all sides of him were barrels and boxes and bags filled to the brim with supplies of God-knows-what. The containers were stacked to fill every inch of the hold, save the bilge access port and a thin corridor to walk through.

Edward had the brief thought to search the containers for the silver, but there was no time to wait around. The water from below was already beginning to bubble up and spill out from the bilge hatch, and the sounds of battle raged above them as harsh as ever.

Edward pulled out his cutlass, the ring of the blade singing as it left its sheath. The tune it sang spoke of the promise of blood soon to be spilled on its edge, and filled each man with more courage than a dozen rousing speeches.

"Let's tear this ship apart, men!" Edward shouted.

Edward's crew had the sense to give their responses in brutish smiles rather than loud hollering, and all of them pulled out their weapons in kind if they hadn't already done so.

Edward motioned for the men to move, and they made their way up to the orlop deck carefully and quietly. As each man moved along, Edward could hear muffled screams and thunks of steel meeting flesh. After a few moments, he came to the steep steps up to the orlop deck, overlooking the ship's magazine of gunpowder.

He climbed up the steps to the orlop deck, holding fast to the sides as he did so. On the next deck, the dead bodies of two young men lay on the sole, bleeding out. They couldn't have been older than eleven.

Powder-monkeys, Edward thought. *They would have died anyway, had we not been here.* "Were there any others on this deck?" Edward whispered.

One of the men shook their head. "They all up top fighting."

Edward nodded. "Let's join them then, shall we?"

The men went up the next set of steps to the first gun deck, the one covered on the starboard side by one of Locke's sloops. When Edward emerged on the deck, he could see the Spanish running around, taking no notice of the new invaders coming up from below. They were dealing with Locke's crew who were shooting at them and entering the ship from the gun-ports.

Edward's men entered the battle, slashing at the Spanish running around the confined deck. Edward had to bend over to stop himself from hitting the top of the deck, so towering was he.

William led the charge against the dual enemies, and he was in top fighting form. He deftly dispatched half a dozen men in a row without stopping. They were powerless before his might as he manipulated them into making mistakes of which he then took ruthless advantage.

Edward turned from watching William and lunged at a man running over to the port side with a musket in hand. The man turned just before seeing the giant in front of him thrusting a blade towards his gut. Edward's blow took him off his feet, and he dropped the musket to grab the blade, but it was too late. A look of fear and confusion was plastered on his face, a permanent remnant of his last moments on earth.

When Edward and his men joined the fray, Locke's pirates initially thought them to be on their side, since they were also attacking the Spanish. With their guard lowered, Edward's men charged the other pirates, and in less than twenty minutes they had cleared the entire gun deck.

William advanced to the second gun deck, and Edward followed closely behind him. William dispatched the Spaniards with precision and wit, while taking in all his surroundings to ensure he wasn't caught unawares.

The gunpowder smoke was thick in the air on the second gun deck. With nowhere to release it, it billowed and piled up at the top. Edward's height, normally an advantage, was proving his downfall in more ways than one this day, as he couldn't breathe without taking a full whiff of smoke. After the near-drowning from before, the smoke was a welcome presence, but still not pleasant or easy on his lungs.

He fought his way to the stern of the ship, towards the captain's cabin. He could see three pirates at the door to a cabin, knocking against it with the butt of their muskets.

The deck was much more illuminated than the bilge and the sea water, and Edward was able to see everything with near-perfect clarity. He noticed a flash at his side, and he pulled his chest back, stepping on his heels as he did so. A blade stabbed in front of him, and Edward reached out to grab the arm holding it. He found purchase and pulled the arm forward, then elbowed the man in the face. He heard a snap as a nose broke. Edward moved to the side of the ship, reared back, and chopped at the man's chest, cleaving him halfway through. The man fell to the sole in an instant, dead before his body hit.

Edward was covered in the blood of his enemies, and still soaked with seawater. His hair and beard were dripping wet, and his blade coated in tar and blood. Every inch of him felt chilled to the bone, and exhausted from the effort he had had to exert until this point.

And yet, somewhere deep inside of him, he was revelling in

the chaos of it all.

An explosion erupted on the gun deck, the sound shaking Edward to his core. He noticed something dart past him towards the bow of the ship. He stepped forward and looked at the bow to see a cannonball lodged against the hull. The cannonball had taken out some of the Spanish as well as one of Edward's men, and two of Locke's pirates. He looked at the stern, and saw that the three pirates knocking at the captain's door had been eviscerated by the cannonball. What was left of them was splayed out from the door, their hands clutching at air as they breathed their last breaths.

What remained of the door swung open with a loud creak, and out stepped a woman and two men. The woman wore a cloak, but the hood was down, revealing her face. She had long black hair, a tanned, angular face, and a sour glare directed at the invaders. In her hands she carried a pistol and a short sword.

That cloak, Edward thought. *It's the same as the one worn by the figure who accompanied the galleon's captain when we tried to join them.*

The woman raised her pistol and fired it at Edward. Someone grabbed his arm and pulled him to the side, out of the way of the bullet. He looked at the person who'd grabbed him to see Victoria there.

Before he could thank her, she looked to the stern and gritted her teeth. She pushed Edward back in the other direction with all her might, and pulled up her buckler where he'd stood. The clang of metal on metal told Edward that someone had attacked, and looked to see the cloaked woman wielding her sword.

Edward stepped to the side to regain his footing, and two blades were thrust at him. He jumped backwards and swiped his cutlass at the blades, knocking them to the side. He bent down as he backed up and pointed his weapon at the two Spanish guards.

"Come now, gentlemen. Two on one is a mite unfair, is it not?" he said, not expecting an answer.

One of the men glanced at his companion. "*Este hombre es más tonto de lo que él parece si él cree que él nos puede llevar tanto.*"

The second man laughed. "*Cierto.*"

Did they just call me an idiot?

After the brief interlude, the two men stepped forward and attacked Edward at the same time. Their blades came one after the other, each meant to knock him off balance and unnerve him. Edward had experience with this type of fighter, but two of them was a challenge he hadn't faced before.

Edward kept stepping backwards out of the way of the attacks until he bumped into someone else. He glanced over his shoulder to see a man he was unfamiliar with, whom he was certain was on Locke's crew. Edward twisted around, pulled the pirate to the side, and tossed him into the Spanish guards.

The pirate toppled over the Spanish, and the three of them fell to the sole. Edward stepped up to them and slashed his cutlass in a wide arc. In one swift and powerful stroke he sliced all three necks open.

Edward rushed over to where Victoria and the Spanish woman were fighting. He circled the duo as their blades clashed, looking for an opening.

"I can handle this," Victoria said through gritted teeth. "Find your mark and finish this!"

Edward paused for a moment, but decided to trust her ability and moved to the stern. Before heading up top, he entered what he supposed was the captain's cabin. He searched the room, but there was no one there.

Captain Miguel must be on the weather deck, fighting with the rest.

Edward turned around and went to the nearest ladder. He climbed it up to the weather deck of the galleon.

The sounds of the battle hit Edward in full now that he was in the open air. The small pops of gunshots went off every second in erratic intervals, followed by the loud booming sound of a dozen cannons firing off nearby. The shouts of men fighting and the clash of metal rang out almost simultaneously, closely followed by death screams.

The Voyages of Queen Anne's Revenge

The air was filled with smoke from the constant igniting of gunpowder. The light musk of sweat and blood mixed with the smoke and the sea air and created a strange, unique aroma that spoke to Edward's animal instincts and made him grip his cutlass tighter.

Around him, Edward could see countless people fighting at every level and section of the ship. From the stern poop deck to the bow forecastle, pirates clashed with the Spanish defenders, and all the while their ships were sinking.

Edward turned around and rushed to the starboard side of the galleon, passing by men dueling and bleeding out. He looked over the side to see the two pirate sloops half-sunk into the ocean, and the *Queen Anne's Revenge* circling around. The crew on the weather deck fired at the pirates swimming their way.

The flash of the muskets and pistols and the flare of the cannons created beautiful bursts of light in the evening. The sparks flew from their containers, lighting their surroundings and reflecting off the sea for a moment as the flares dropped to the water or wood below.

The galleon had begun sinking as well, and from the look of the water, he could tell it was leaning towards starboard. With the size and instability of the galleon, Edward knew it wouldn't be long before it toppled over.

Edward scanned the galleon for the two people he was looking for. With the chaos aboard, the bullets flying, men running and dying, it was difficult to see anything with clarity.

How hard could it be to find a man with a chest attached to his arm?

Edward's eyes went from one person to the next in rapid succession, each one not the man he was looking for. *Wait a moment,* Edward thought. *Captain Miguel.*

On the bow of the ship, Captain Miguel was overseeing the battle, directing his men against the boarders and attacking them with his own musket.

Before Edward could make for the bow, a man with a feathered cap turned around after stabbing a man in the chest with a rapier. Edward recognised the man as one of Locke's trusted mates, Philip Culverson, and, judging from the up and down glance followed by widened eyes, Philip recognised Edward as well.

"You...!" Philip said, dumbfounded.

"Allow me to handle this one, Captain," William said, walking up beside Edward.

"Are you sure you'll manage?" Edward asked.

William replied with a curt nod of the head, and then positioned his blade in front of him to engage in a duel with the pirate. Edward stepped behind William and took a wide path around Philip, all the while pointing his own blade at him just in case. Philip kept one eye on Edward until he was far enough away not to be trouble.

Edward turned around and stalked over to the bow, avoiding the fights happening on all sides of him. He ran up the steps and cut down one of the Spanish along the way. The Captain's back was turned, and he was aiming down the barrel of a musket. Edward walked over to him, and one of his men rushed Edward, but he dispatched the man easily.

Edward pulled his blade back, and stabbed Captain Miguel in the back. Miguel's musket fired as the cutlass pierced his flesh.

He leaned up to Miguel's ear. "You should have joined us. You and your men would still be alive were that the case."

Edward pulled out the cutlass, and Miguel did a half-turn before his knees buckled and he fell backwards. He made a desperate attempt to hold himself up, but landed on the deck with one hand clinging to the forecastle railing and the other holding fast to the wound on his chest. His eyes were wide with shock and fear as he stared up at Edward.

"I didn't—" Miguel stopped short and coughed up blood, splattering dark red on his clothes as it seeped out his chin. "I didn't want this," he said, his words shaking like his body as his life left him. "It wasn't my say."

Edward looked down on him with all the rage he'd felt over

the betrayal. "I don't care," he said.

He stabbed Miguel through the throat, ending the man's life. His eyes retained the fear and shock it had in the seconds before his death, in part from the prospect of dying, and in part from the man who'd caused it.

When Edward pulled the blade out, he turned on his heel to see if any were about to do something about what he'd done to their captain, but all the men on the bow were too busy fighting for their lives. He turned back around to view the ship once more, and he spotted the man he was looking for on the weather deck.

Kenneth Locke, Cache-Hand, was there with his crew in the thick of battle against the Spanish. He looked just as Edward remembered him: unkempt, grotesque features, sweat and blood matting his hair to his forehead, and a wicked smile showing off his crooked yellow and black teeth.

His right arm, visibly more muscular than the left, ended not with a hand, but a chest full of gold pieces—the same chest that had been there when he was a part of Edward's crew years ago. His greed caused him to fall into a trap, locking the chest on his hand with no way to remove it. A strange thing that it was a trap laid by Benjamin Hornigold, and now Locke worked for him, though under the name Calico Jack.

Edward's stomach felt empty and hollow, and his heart beat faster at the sight of Locke. His breathing turned rapid, and his feet itched to move, but in the opposite direction. His wounds all over his body screamed pain once more, screaming not to his ears but to his senses. They called for him to run away and avoid that pain again.

Edward grabbed hold of the forecastle railing and gripped it until his knuckles were white. In his other hand, he held fast to his cutlass. He couldn't tear his eyes away from Locke, but it wasn't his face he saw in his mind. He couldn't stop seeing John, his former quartermaster, the tired old man. The memory of Locke running the blade against John's neck repeated in Edward's mind over and over, and with each flash his legs weakened more and more.

The feeling was so much more intense now than it had ever been. The feeling of losing not just John, but everyone he cared for. The possibility of that happening was there, and it gripped his heart like a vice and wouldn't let go.

You are here, you are now, you are not then, Anne's voice repeated in Edward's head.

His wife's voice took the place of the visions in his head, overlapping and taking them over until it was just her there. He relaxed his grip, took long and deep breaths until the feeling passed, and he replaced it with something different.

I will not lose anyone else to him. It ends today!

Edward ran down the forecastle, straight at Locke. He leapt into the air, his cutlass high, and as he landed he brought the cutlass down like a great pendulum.

Locke noticed Edward at the last moment, and he raised his chest-hand in the air as he turned around to face him. The blade bit into the chest, creating a large cleft between the wood and iron.

Edward pulled the chest down with his cutlass, placed his foot against it, and kicked the thing off his blade. He pushed Locke back with it, and Locke had to take a few steps back to keep his balance.

His eyes widened at the sight of Edward. He looked as if he saw an apparition. "You... You're dead," he said. "I killed you." His voice shook, a different kind of fear taking hold of him.

"Aye, and I've come back to kill you," Edward said. He slashed at Locke, but the other pirate deflected it. "Where is Sam?"

Locke's brow raised in confusion. "You've gone mad," he said as he backed away, his eyes still filled with fear. "Who're ya talkin' about? I don't know no Sam."

"Enough with the games, Locke. Tell me what you did with Sam, now."

Locke's eyes changed into a frustrated squint. "I told ya I

don't know who yer talkin' about."

Edward tightened his grip on his cutlass, his anger rising. He went on the offensive, slashing and jabbing at the other pirate. Locke stayed defensive, backing away and dodging or parrying the blows. With a large, powerful swing, Edward knocked Locke's cutlass out of his hand.

Edward continued pushing Locke back. He took advantage of the man's shock and tried to force Locke into a corner. When Locke stepped to his right, Edward moved with him and pushed him back to the left. He used light controlling jabs to keep Locke on his toes and stepping in the direction he wanted. After a moment, Locke's back hit the stern cabin bulkhead.

The smack on his back seemed to awaken Locke and knock him back into his senses, and he used the recoil to go on the offensive. He swung the chest on his arm in a wide arc, knocking Edward's cutlass out of the way.

Edward's hand stung from the blow, and he had to concentrate hard to keep his grip lest he too lose his blade, but it pulled his whole body to the side. His eyes followed his hand on instinct, and when he looked back at Locke it was too late to react.

Locke thrust the chest forward as if he were punching, and hit Edward in the chest. The force of the blow sent him reeling backwards. He tumbled over and fell to the sole. The pain from the blow was excruciating across his whole ribcage, and it felt like something had broken. The punch knocked the wind out of him, and he dropped his cutlass to his side. He reflexively curled up to cover his chest as he tried to recover his breath. It was a worse feeling than when he had been drowning earlier, as air was all around him, but his body couldn't take it in.

"No sorry sod of a ghost would be feeling that," Locke said as Edward writhed. "Yer so pathetic ya can't even die right."

Kenneth kicked Edward in the face, his head rearing back from the force. It also knocked Edward's body back to work, and he could heave air in. The pain in his chest and chin remained, and his vision blurred. He felt the taste of blood in his mouth, and possibly a loose tooth. He turned over onto his stomach and forced his weary head up to search for his foe.

Locke grabbed hold of Edward's hair and pulled him up to his knees. "I don't know where ya came from, but I'm going ta kill ya for sure this time," he said. "Remember what I did to that old fool? I'm going to find every last one of your crew and do the same to them." Locke pulled back the heavy wooden chest, the coins inside rattling, and aimed for Edward's head.

Edward grabbed hold of Locke's hand on his head and placed his other hand out against the chest. He stopped the punch mid-way with a loud thud before reaching around and gripping Locke's forearm. He then stood to his full height, forcing Locke to let go of his hair.

Edward stared down at Locke with all the malice he felt towards him in that moment. "Do you remember what I promised you that day?" he asked. "I promised you that I would live, and make sure the last thing you saw was my hands around your neck as I choked the life out of you."

The fear in Locke's eyes returned in full force.

Edward pulled Locke's arms down, forcing his upper body down as well. He kneed Locke in the face, smashing his nose.

Locke took a few steps back, clutching his broken and bloody nose. He gritted his teeth, glared at Edward, and went to uppercut him with his chest-hand.

Edward stepped to the side, dodging the blow. He levelled Locke with a punch straight to his jaw, and the man fell to the sole in a heap.

"You're too slow, Locke. My wife's punches are ten times as fast as yours." Edward backed up, keeping his eyes on Locke, until found his cutlass by the light of the moon and picked it up again.

Locke sputtered a hoarse laugh as he came to his knees. "Trouble with the missus, eh Thatch?"

Edward grinned. "Far from it," he said. "It wasn't an insult towards you, it was simply a fact. I train with her nearly every day. She could have killed you six times over by now, I'd wager."

"Captain," William called behind Edward.

Edward turned around to see William and Victoria, bloodied and soaked with sweat, on the weather deck along with his other crewmates. Victoria and the rest of the crew looked as if they had just come up from below.

"The ship's about to topple over," William said.

Before Edward could grasp the words William had said, the ship began angling down towards the sea. The shift was as sudden as it was drastic, and it didn't stop once it started tilting.

As the angle of the ship changed, Edward's legs had naturally adjusted to compensate, and only after the listing became more pronounced did he fully understand what was happening. He ran up to the port side of the ship as the deck changed to an incline, and jumped for the portside railing. He clung to the railing, wrapping his arm around the beams.

The loose equipment aboard the ship rolled and fell from one end to the other, cascading down and bouncing off the deck before being flung into the ocean below. Men lost their footing and tumbled backwards toward the starboard side. Edward could hear loud bangs and crashes within the ship as well. The large iron cannons, with nothing but their own weight to hold them in place, rolled to the other side of the ship, further speeding the ship's tilt. Just before the ship's side collided with the dark ocean below, Edward heard the sound of wood cracking open, and several small splashes preceding the larger one.

The ship hit the water with a thunderous crash. Seawater surged up the weather deck beneath Edward's feet and covered him in an icy chill all over again. The main mast and the fore sail both hit the pirate sloops, which were also sinking. The spars of the masts had broken through the decks of the sloops, joining the ships together in their destiny to sink to the bottom of the ocean. There was no possible saving the lot of them.

Edward looked down and could see his crew swimming in

the ocean, trying to avoid the sinking masts and rigging. He couldn't take a count, but with the rough look he estimated most of them had survived.

Edward looked to his right, and could see Locke dangling off the port railing just as he was. They locked eyes, and Locke scrambled to pull himself up. Edward moved to do the same, and climbed over the side of the railing to the port hull of the galleon.

In the dark waters off the side, Edward could see many men swimming their way, and others standing on the sinking side of the ship. Even then, some of the men still continued to fight, whether out of anger or blindness, he could not tell.

Locke came at Edward with everything he had, wildly swinging his one weapon at him. Edward knew his every move by heart. Locke moved the same as he had those months ago in Ireland. He hadn't grown, he hadn't gotten stronger, he hadn't improved himself as Edward had. Locke was no match for the Edward of today, the Edward he let live because he couldn't finish the job the right way.

There was one problem: the galleon was still sinking. In a few moments, the ship would be under water, and their fight wouldn't be able to continue.

No, no, I still need to question him about Sam. I have to get him to the Queen Anne's Revenge *before I kill him.* The words of Edward's wife filtered into his head once again. *If you want to knock a man off balance and get behind him, use his own attacks against him.*

Locke kept swinging his chest arm like a wild man, trying to hit Edward's head over and over. His right arm had grown strong over the years, and he had much more stamina than before, which meant he could keep fighting for some time.

Edward backed up a few steps, and baited Locke by leaning his head forward. Locke, too frustrated or foolish to care, swung at Edward all the same. Edward pulled back to avoid the blow, then placed his hands on the back of the heavy chest and pushed it with all his strength. Locke continued his arc further than expected and the weight of the chest turned him around. The man lost his balance and dropped to his knees. Edward pounced on Locke, wrapped his arms around the pirate's throat, and squeezed.

Locke tried to get up off his knees, but Edward pushed forward and placed his boot on top of the chest, effectively pinning Locke where he was. Locke pulled against Edward's arms as he pulled in stifled breaths. As the seconds passed and he began to lose himself, Locke clawed at Edward's arm, then elbowed him in the gut, but Edward never released his grip.

After a moment of the struggle, Locke's hand fell to his side, limp. Edward continued to hold the pressure for another few seconds, and then let go. Locke fell to the galleon's hull, his legs and body contorted unnaturally.

Edward stood up and caught his breath. The cold air filled his lungs, but it had never felt sweeter than in that moment. He had won the battle of three in the Caribbean Sea.

He didn't have time to celebrate, as the water touching his feet told him. He lifted Locke up and placed him over his shoulder. The man was a heavy load, but nothing Edward couldn't handle.

He searched for the *Queen Anne's Revenge* and saw it floating around where the bow of the galleon was pointing. It wasn't far, but between it and him were a few dozen people from all sides of the battle.

Edward looked behind him to see his crew there, swimming towards him, and not far towards the stern of the galleon he saw two longboats still intact. He walked over to the nearest one and tossed Locke inside.

He pointed to the second longboat and commanded his crew to fetch it. With the little surface left on the side of the galleon, he leapt from it into the longboat.

His crew swam to the boats and boarded them, while at the same time defending them from the Spanish and the pirates. For simple longboats, they were massive. The two were enough to fit the remainder of his crew inside with ease.

William and Victoria were in the longboat with Edward,

and they looked worse than he'd first thought, but not on the edge of death at least.

William was bleeding from a wound on his arm and breathing heavily, which was unusual. Edward figured it was his previous injuries and being bedridden for so long.

Victoria's face and chest were covered in blood, and she too was taking in deep breaths. She didn't appear to have any visible wounds, but her fatigue was evident.

"Are you both well?" Edward asked.

The two of them nodded, but didn't answer, which was good enough for him considering the circumstances.

The crew removed oars at the sides, and paddled their way towards their ship. As they moved, Edward looked down to the dim, murky waters of the sea, and the galleon which was being swallowed by its depths. All that wealth, treasure, and history was lost to Davey Jones, and it had all been done in a matter of hours.

The crew repelled those still alive trying to steal the boat from them, killing many in the process. None of the swimmers' guns would work, and the only choice was coming in close to attempt taking the longboats from their occupants. After a few lost fingers or their lives, the rest didn't dare attempt to board.

On the decks of the *Queen Anne's Revenge*, those same pirates and Spanish were trying to board. After having spent their proper weapons, they were no match for the crew still holding muskets and pistols and manning cannons.

Edward and company rowed the boats up next to their ship, and climbed aboard with ease. All the while, muskets still cracked with their burning explosions, and cannons still boomed with their bursts of iron death.

Edward slung Locke over his shoulder once more, and climbed up to his home. He dropped his enemy onto the weather deck, and jumped over the side to join his family.

As soon as he did, Anne rushed over to embrace him and kiss his forehead.

"I knew you would be safe," she said.

Edward chuckled. "You say that, but your voice sounded worried."

Anne smiled at him and embraced him again. The two stood there for a moment, warming each other with their love, until Edward stepped back.

"It's almost over," he said. "There's just one thing left to do." Edward stepped over to the port side and made sure that his crew were aboard, then turned back around to face the helm.

He saw a man not of his crew board at the stern, only to have Christina and Tala appear out of nowhere and attack him. Christina cut the man's chest open, and Tala tore his throat out.

Edward nodded with a devilish grin on his face at the sight. "Get us out of here, Herbert," he said.

Herbert smiled. "Aye, Captain."

"Someone bring me a pistol," Edward said.

After a moment, one of the crew brought Edward a loaded pistol. Edward thanked the man, then fired it at Locke's leg. The bullet pierced the man's thigh straight through.

Locke woke with a loud scream of pain, clutching his leg. Blood pooled beneath the wound and spilled over his pantaloons and hand. Locke's face contorted in pain, changing from clenched teeth to a rapid breathing and back again, all the while accompanied by another cry of agony.

Edward bent down to get to eye level with Locke. "Where… is… Sam?"

"I already bleedin' told ya, I don't know who yer talkin' about," he replied between his stifled cries.

Edward sighed and glanced over his shoulder. "Sam had taken a false name before joining Locke's crew. Does anyone remember what it was?"

Anne folded her arms. "James, I believe."

Edward nodded and turned back around to Locke. "He may have gone by the name James while he was with your crew. Black hair, foul mouth."

Locke's expression seemed to change as he glanced from Edward to Anne and to the others in his crew who were watching. "W-why would ya want to know about that sod?" He continued looking back and forth at the people gathered, and his expression changed again, this time into a sweat-soaked, uneasy smirk. "Ah, I gets it now. He was part of yer crew. No wonder he looked so familiar." Locke convulsed into a sickening fit of laughter.

Edward rose to his full towering height. "What happened to him?"

Locke was still laughing, but he stopped just long enough to say, "I killed the bastard," with a smug look in his eyes as he stared at Edward. "I killed him just like I killed that old fool Jo—"

Edward slammed his cutlass down on Locke's shoulder, severing the arm that had the chest attached to it. Locke's laughter turned into a sharp cry of anguish. He pulled his severed arm close to his chest as blood gushed from the wound. His body shook as he tried to close the wound with his good hand, but it was no use.

Edward dropped his cutlass to the sole with a loud clang, and then jumped on top of Locke, his massive body pinning the much smaller man down. He wrapped his hands around Locke's bloody throat and pushed down as hard as he could.

"You never got it, did you?" Edward shouted. "You never had the power between us. You should have bowed to me!"

Locke struggled with his stump and his fist and his legs, but nothing could stop Edward from choking the life out of him. His mouth opened in a pathetic attempt to draw air, and all he could do was croak as his throat tried to bring him life again. His eyes bulged and his face turned a garish shade of red.

"Not laughing now, are you?" Edward seethed, but of course Locke couldn't answer him. "Laugh," he screamed as he shook Locke by his neck. "Laugh, I said!"

But the man couldn't laugh even if he'd wanted to. After a moment, Locke's arms went limp once more, and he could no longer even try to resist the force on top of him. Edward squeezed tighter and tighter and tighter still, and there was a small pop.

Edward took a breath, released his grip on Locke's neck, then grabbed the man's severed arm and the chest which had been his companion for so many years. He lifted the chest above his head and smashed it down on Kenneth Locke's head. The heavy chest broke Locke's face, caving it in and sending a wave of blood out from it. Edward didn't stop there. He lifted the chest once again, the blood dripping from it on top of his head. He slammed it down on Locke's face again and again and again until there was nothing left of Locke but a red mess on the planks of the weather deck.

Edward dropped the chest in front of him, arms burning and chest heaving. He got up from his knees and to his feet once again. He was covered in blood from head to toe, and the whole business gave his own crew pause; they stared at him, wide-eyed and silent in their shock.

"This," Edward said, pointing to what was left of Locke, "is justice."

21. THE STORM

Unable to sleep, Edward leaned back in a chair in his captain's cabin and stared out the stern windows to the night sky and sea. The water below churned and spiralled away from the ship, waves dancing in its wake.

After a quick funeral for those that had died during the battle—thirteen, to be exact—the injured were patched up and the crew took some much-needed rest.

Edward held a glass of rum in his hands, watching it for a moment before he downed the contents in one great gulp. It burned as it went down, and the heat filled his cheeks and lingered for a long while.

The scenes of the battle repeated in his head over and over. The feeling of drowning, both in the bottom of the ship and when he saw Kenneth Locke, was as present as ever, and it made Edward furious. Locke's face was burned into his mind, and wouldn't go away.

Edward took another drink, and another, and another, and soon his head was light and Locke's face left his mind. The dark sky, full of bright stars, swirled like the water below, and mixed with the windows and the planks of the ship into a sea of dull colours. He had to close his eyes to stop the spinning.

Edward put down the glass and got up from his seat. His legs wobbled and his balance was precarious. He took a few steps, placed his hand on the windows, and used it to guide him around the cabin towards his bed. The rocking of the ship was no aid as he stepped forward, but he succeeded after a time.

He flopped into the bed, shaking it with his weight, and

his wife stirred at his side. "Can you not sleep, Edward?"

Edward shuffled and got underneath the covers. "I was celebrating," he said, a slight slur in his words.

There was a pause, then Anne said, "Try to sleep, your injuries need to heal."

Anne's words were lost on him in the haze of his mind. As the drink took over, he calmed and sleep soon washed over him. This time, a more welcome darkness enveloped him, and all thoughts of Locke dissipated into the ether.

Knocking at Edward's door woke him from his slumber. His eyes opened in an instant and he took in a sharp breath through his nose. Sweat covered his face, chest, and back, neither cold nor warm on his body. His head pounded with each movement, and the light of day hurt his eyes.

He looked at the bed, and Anne wasn't there. As his eyes adjusted, he turned to look at the room, but she wasn't there either.

The knocking came again. "A moment, if you please," he shouted, but he had to press on his temple afterwards.

He got up and clothed himself, making himself look a slight bit presentable, and then went to open the door. Herbert was in front of the door, and he had a wide smile on his face and a bottle of something in his lap.

"Good day to you, Captain," he said. "I thought we could share a drink to celebrate now that you've had some time to rest."

Edward's head still throbbed, and when he looked at the bottle in Herbert's lap it nearly made him sick, but he pushed aside the feeling. He stepped aside and held the door open. "Certainly. Please, enter."

Herbert wheeled himself into Edward's cabin and up to the table at the back of the room. He placed the bottle on the table in front of him as Edward acquired glasses for the both of them.

"So, what's this you have?" Edward asked, gesturing at the bottle.

Herbert grinned. "I bought this a few months back from the Bodden brothers," he said. "It's a highland scotch from their hometown. A rare vintage, from what they told me. For special occasions such as these, I believe it necessary."

Edward chuckled. "Better with us than where they are now," he said.

"Hear, hear." Herbert popped the cork and poured each of them a drink.

Edward took one of the glasses and sipped the scotch. He was pleasantly surprised by how smooth the drink was, nothing like the sharp and harsh rum he had had the night before. It had notes of toasted nuts and something almost sweet to it.

Hebert too had taken a sip of the scotch, and he smiled yet raised his brow at the same time. "Dad damn, that's good."

"You can say that again," Edward replied. "You made a good choice."

Herbert lifted his glass. "To your revenge."

Edward paused for a moment, his hand gripping the glass hard. He recovered a moment later and clinked his glass with Herbert's. "Revenge." He pulled back the glass and downed the drink in one gulp.

Herbert frowned, but smiled soon after. "Now, now, Captain. This drink is to be savoured."

Edward nodded, but didn't say anything. Herbert filled his cup once more, and Edward decided not to offend his generosity by trying to hold back.

"So, Captain… how do you feel?"

Edward stared at Herbert for a moment, not sure of what he was truly asking. "I'm well," he said.

Herbert frowned. "Come now, Captain, you must tell me more. You've just gotten revenge on Kenneth Locke. How does it feel?" There was a moment of silence as Edward contemplated the question. "You're... you're not still upset with me, are you?"

Edward shook his head. "No, no, of course not," he replied. "Truth be told, I thought you might have wanted to take Locke for yourself, given that he was one of Calico Jack's men."

Herbert looked surprised. "No, he was yours to kill. He wasn't one of Calico Jack's men when I was part of the crew."

Edward nodded and took a swig of the scotch. The smooth taste was still there, but a hint of smokiness bit the back of his tongue. "After you killed Gregory Dunn, you said you felt content. Does that still hold true?"

Herbert looked down at the glass in his hands, staring at the drink for a long while. "I don't know... It's been so long. I've grown cold to the memory. Calico Jack's officers no longer hold any appeal to me. I believe only the man himself could quell the burning inside me now."

"Then perhaps we should be more direct in our aspirations," Edward said. "We should sail straight for him... No more beating against the wind, as it were."

Herbert raised his brow and his jaw dropped. "You cannot believe that is the best course for us."

Edward set his cup down. "And why not? He wouldn't see us coming if we planned our actions right."

"The very notion is suicide, Captain," Herbert replied. "He has more men on his side than we do, more ships, more... everything. We have to do what he did to us: remove his support and then attack him head-on on even ground." Herbert took a drink and then placed his cup down as well. "This is especially the case now that we've... lost Roberts."

Edward leaned back in his chair. "You may be right."

After a moment of silence, there was a rap at the door. Edward called to enter, and a crewmate walked in.

"Captain, we was able to open Locke's chest."

Edward leaned forward, a slight twinge of a grin tugging at his cheeks. "And…?"

"The coins're fake, sir. Not real gold."

Edward shook his head as he chuckled. "Of course they are," he muttered. "You've checked all the coins?"

The crewmate nodded. "What should we do with them, Captain?"

Edward looked away in thought for a moment, and then touched the golden cutlass at his side. "Bring it here to my room. It will serve as a reminder of a battle well fought."

Herbert raised his glass as the crewmate left the room. Edward picked his up again and the two clinked them together again. Herbert drank the rest of his, and set the cup down again without refilling it.

"I should be heading back. I have to make sure Christina hasn't led us astray."

"I'm sure it's fine, but there's no harm in being diligent." Edward topped off his glass with a grin and then put the stopper back in the bottle before handing it back to Herbert.

Herbert began turning himself around, but stopped. "I suppose that reminds me. Where exactly should we be heading now?"

"Hmm," Edward said, stroking his beard. "That's a good question. The first order of business should be resupplying, so bring us to the nearest port. Perhaps you can send in Victoria on your way up? I'll ask her if she knows anyone who can tell us where our next target is."

"Aye, Captain."

As Herbert was heading towards the door of the cabin, it opened and Anne stepped inside. She held the door open for him, and the two exchanged greetings before Herbert left.

Anne walked over and sat down in front of the table across from Edward. Her long red curls bounced and swayed as she moved, but were stifled slightly by the cap she wore. She let out a sigh and removed the cap from her head.

"Difficult morning, Quartermaster?"

"Not so, husband, but without their captain present the crew are harder to control."

"You managed to bring them in line, I trust?"

Anne nodded. "After a time." She sat up and rested her arms on the chair. "So, are you feeling better after some sleep?"

"I am well now that Herbert brought me this," Edward replied with a smirk as he lifted his cup before taking another drink.

Anne frowned. "Can you talk with me, Edward?" she said, and then leaned forward and placed her hand on his. Her face shifted to a sad look of concern. "You were unable to sleep yesterday, and over-drank to the point of intoxication before returning to bed."

Edward put the glass down and held his wife's hand. "There is no need for concern. The battle was exciting, and I needed the drink to settle my nerves."

Anne squeezed his hand. "You know you can talk with me about anything, yes?"

Anne's concern bled into her voice, and it pained Edward to the core. She was calling out to him to open up, but he couldn't bear to dwell on the thoughts in his head even for a moment. He needed to move forward and forget about the man who haunted his dreams still.

Edward forced a smile. "I know," he replied and then kissed his wife's hand. "You are too good for me."

Anne grinned. "That's correct. Should you ever need a reminder, I will be here."

Edward chuckled, but before he could respond there was another knock at the door. "Enter," he said.

The door swung open and a crewmate walked in with the chest cradled between his hands as he leaned back for extra support. "Where do ya want it, Captain?"

Edward pointed to the side of the room, near the back

where he could see it from the table where he was sitting. "Over here should do," he said.

Anne was watching the crewmate over her shoulder as he brought the chest inside. "Why do you wish to keep that chest?"

"It may not have real gold coins, but it will serve as a nice trophy."

Anne nodded, still watching the crewmate as he set the chest down. "I should return to the weather deck before the ship falls apart. Will you be joining us sometime today, Captain?" she asked with a smirk.

Edward grinned along with her. "I'll join you shortly. I called for Herbert to send Victoria in so that we may set our course to find someone who may know where we can find the next of Calico Jack's men."

"Good. I know the men are eager to find their next quarry." Anne got up from her seat. "Don't be long, Captain. The men are also eager to congratulate you on your victory."

"I'll be sure not to disappoint."

Anne and the other crewmate left the cabin, and Edward was alone. With no other distractions, the noises from outside made their way into his cabin—the rush of water surging and slapping against the ship, the shouts and laughter of men working and enjoying themselves, and the subtle noise of sails moving and rope scraping against wood and iron.

Edward stared at the chest of false gold coins as the noise took over his thoughts. The chest was broken in several places, the bands of iron scraped and bent, the wood chipped and split, and had one large cut coming from the back halfway through the top. He recalled the fight, and how he had made that cut on the chest. Dried blood covered most of the chest in dark splotches, remnants of Edward's final ruining of its former master.

This is all that's left of you. You're dead and gone, and no one cares about you. You can't touch anyone where you are now. No one will remember your name or your legacy.

The Voyages of Queen Anne's Revenge

Edward took a deep breath in and held it for a moment before letting it out. For a moment, there was peace in his mind.

You'll remember, a voice called in Edward's head, shattering his peace.

He tightened his grip around the cup and drank the rest of its contents in one filling gulp. This time, the scotch stung as it went down his throat. The smokiness of the aged alcohol overpowered everything else and burned his insides.

The door to his cabin opened abruptly and Victoria walked in. Behind her, Alexandre followed. They both walked up to the table and sat down in the nearby chairs.

"What did you wish to speak to me about, Captain?"

"Welcome, and a good day to you as well, Victoria."

Victoria sighed, showing her distaste for Edward's jesting, and leaned her head on her hand. Alexandre carried his usual indifference in his sullen eyes, but a grin on his face.

Edward leaned back and let out a different kind of sigh. "I wanted to know if you had any more contacts who may aid us in our search Calico Jack's other allies."

Victoria sat up and looked away in thought for a moment. "There may be a man in Jamaica who could help us, although as with my acquaintance in Porto Bello, he will not provide information without something in return."

Edward waved his hand. "That shouldn't be an issue."

"Do you wish me to inform Herbert?" Victoria asked.

"No, no… Not necessary. I'll be heading up shortly. My thanks for the information."

Victoria nodded, then rose from her seat and headed to the door of the cabin. Alexandre stayed seated. Victoria seemed to have known Alexandre was going to stay, and she closed the door on her way out.

Edward raised his brow. "Something you wished to discuss with me, Alexandre?"

"*Oui.* I am concerned with your mental state. I wish to know how you are feeling now that you've killed Mr Locke."

Edward chuckled and scratched his brow. "Why does everyone insist on asking me how I'm feeling? I'm well, thank you for asking," he said, though he felt exasperated rather than appreciative.

Alexandre leaned forward in his chair, rested his elbows on his knees, and locked his fingers in front of his mouth. "Oh, is that so?" he said, long and drawn out.

Edward sat up straight at Alexandre's penetrating gaze. "Yes," he replied firmly.

"I've noticed you... what is the word... breaking down over the last year."

Edward's mouth was a line, and he clenched his jaw, annoyed by the Frenchman's oddness. "Oh, is that so?" he mimicked.

"Yes, ever since you shot your old friend, Henry."

Edward's heart skipped, and his stomach turned. His face felt hot, and a lump stuck to the back of his throat. His whole body tensed up, and his vision blurred around the edges.

"What are you talking about?" Edward forced out past the lump.

"There is no need to put on such airs. I care not what you've done, and would never tell another. That would ruin the game. I am, as I've said several times, an observer."

Edward gripped the edge of his chair's arm so hard it was in danger of breaking off. "How did you know? I've told no one."

Alexandre scoffed. "It is not so hard to know to one watching you. You leave to chase after Henry when he seeks to leave the crew, and when you return you are smelling of gunpowder and disappear into the stern cabin. The crew were too busy manning the ship in a storm to worry about you, and hours later you emerge, but without mention of why you shot your pistol... it is not *difficile* to make the connection, *mon Capitaine*."

Though there was no cause for it, Edward felt as though

his privacy had been violated. His anger overwhelmed him, and his blood boiled in his veins.

"You have continued to spiral since that time, and events have not aided in your *récupération*. I can—"

"Get out," Edward seethed.

Alexandre paused for a moment, and stared at Edward with a curious expression on his face, as if he was confused by Edward's anger.

"Get out before I rip your throat open with my bare hands."

Alexandre continued to stare at Edward for a moment, and then he rose from his seat. "By your leave, *mon Capitaine*," he murmured.

Edward sat stock still in his seat as waves of anger pulsed through him on lines across his forehead. The faces of all the crew and friends dead at his hands and others' flashed in his mind, and wouldn't stop. On some level, Edward felt good that those faces were haunting him. Like the chest they would serve as reminders, both good and bad.

One hour later

Edward stepped up to the weather deck, and the crew all around greeted him warmly. They congratulated him on yesterday's battle, and the ultimate fate of Kenneth Locke. He returned the compliments and congratulations in kind to the men who'd joined him and those who'd stayed behind and protected the ship.

He noticed William, Pukuh, and Victoria all working diligently with the other men on the rigging of the sails or cleaning the weather deck. Nassir was also off at the end of the bow, fixing planks which had been broken during the last battle. Alexandre was there as well, checking up on the injured.

He made his way up to the quarterdeck overseeing the rest of the ship. Hebert was at the helm, watching the skies and sea with his keen eyes. Anne and Christina were nearby, playing with Tala.

The day was half over, but there was plenty of sun left, and the wind was strong. The smell of the sea rejuvenated Edward and brought clarity to his thoughts.

"Captain," Herbert said, tipping his cap with one hand as he held to the wheel with the other. "Do you have our heading?"

"I will in a moment," he replied as he stepped up to the quarterdeck railing. "Men, hop to it. We must discuss where next to sail."

The crew stopped what they were doing and gathered close to the quarterdeck to listen to what Edward had to say. Once everyone on the main deck was present, Edward nodded.

"First off, I want to tell you how proud I am of all of you. It is thanks to your efforts that we made it through the last battle." The crew hooted their own thanks to him, and proudly patted each other on the backs. "We fought against five ships, and we won!" Another, louder shout from the crew. "We fought against a galleon, and won!" Again the crew yelled their approval.

"Our resident one-armed savage, Pukuh," Edward said, gesturing to his friend with a smirk on his face, "once said to me that I was the storm that other men feared." The men patted Pukuh on the back and he grinned. "But that was untrue... *You* are the storm," he said, now pointing in a wave across the crew. "You are the crew that other men fear, and will continue to fear. The crew of the *Queen Anne's Revenge* will soon be known across the Old World and the New."

The crew rallied and hollered and stomped their feet together, shaking the deck. Their faces beamed with pride as they looked at their captain.

"To make our names known, what say we continue our revenge against Calico Jack, the man who burned our town to the ground? The man who thinks we're weak. The man who thinks he can survive the storm."

The crew gave a resounding roar of approval to Edward.

"We will destroy all those who stand against us." The crew shouted another yes. "All those who think they're better than us." The crew yelled louder still. "All those who turn their backs on us," Edward said, looking at Alexandre as he did so. Edward was sure that the significance wasn't lost on him.

"We are the storm!" he roared with his fist raised. The crew repeated the saying, also raising their fists in the air. "Now get back to work, you ugly bastards."

The crew burst out laughing before they returned to their duties aboard the ship.

"Herbert," Edward called. "We're heading north-east, to Jamaica."

Herbert smiled widely. "Aye, Captain," he replied.

Anne came up beside Edward and looked up at him with a smile on her face. He returned the smile and gave her a kiss. The two of them gazed at the bow of the ship towards the bright horizon ahead of them, wondering where their next adventure would take them.

For a moment, Edward was at peace. His body and mind calmed by the sun, sea, ship, and woman he loved. But a certain red stain on the weather deck caught his eye, and, in a different way, he became the storm once again.

THE END

OTHER BOOKS
BY THE AUTHOR

The Voyages of Queen Anne's Revenge Series:

BLACKBEARD'S FREEDOM

BLACKBEARD'S REVENGE

BLACKBEARD'S JUSTICE

BLACKBEARD'S FAMILY

The Pirate Priest Series:

BARTHOLOMEW ROBERTS' FAITH

BARTHOLOMEW ROBERTS' JUSTICE

BARTHOLOMEW ROBERTS' MERCY

BARTHOLOMEW ROBERTS' SPIRIT

The Collection Series:

BLACKBEARD'S SHIP (Includes Books 1&2 of The Voyages of Queen Anne's Revenge & The Pirate Priest)

BLACKBEARD'S BLOOD (Includes Books 3&4 of The Voyages of Queen Anne's Revenge & The Pirate Priest)

ABOUT THE AUTHOR

JEREMY IS CURRENTLY LIVING IN NEW BRUNSWICK, CANADA WITH HIS WIFE HEATHER, AND THEIR TWO CATS, NAVI AND THOR.

Jeremy's first foray into the writing world was during a writing competition called NaNoWriMo, where the goal is to write a certain number of words in the month of November.

After completing the novel he started, and some extensive rewrites, he felt it was worthy of publishing and self-published his first novel, Blackbeard's Freedom in September, 2012.

After writing over ten books under two names, his passion for writing hasn't wavered over the years, and hopes to one day make it his primary career.

Let everyone know what you thought of his novels by leaving a review. He loves getting feedback on his books, and loves to hear from fans of his work.

Want to pirate one of Jeremy's novels? Visit http://www.mcleansnovels.com/free-book-link for a free copy of one of his books.

Lightning Source UK Ltd.
Milton Keynes UK
UKHW021819280223
417812UK00010B/300